"I'LL BET HE'S NEVER EVEN KISSED YOU ... HAS HE?"

"Mr. Maverick!—" Rachel snapped, only to have Slade cut her off rudely, a knowing grin splitting his face.

"Ah-a! You wouldn't catch me waiting for some balky woman to ask me to kiss her!"

"No doubt, since I can't think why any woman *would* ask you!"

"Now, *that,* Miss Wilder, was a most unwise remark—especially for a woman in your current position," Slade pointed out mockingly, his hooded eyes raking her captive body slowly, insolently.

"Why, you—you wouldn't dare!" Rachel stammered.

Then, his eyes darkening in a way that made Rachel's breath catch in her throat, he ground his mouth down on hers—hard. She had not guessed how brazenly and expertly his tongue would ravage her mouth. Slade kissed her more gently then, reveling in the involuntary whimpers that emanated from her throat as at last, to her horror and shame, she realized she was kissing him back. . . .

Other *Love Spell* books by Rebecca Brandewyne:
LOVE, CHERISH ME
AND GOLD WAS OURS

Rebecca Brandewyne

Heartland

LOVE SPELL BOOKS NEW YORK CITY

LOVE SPELL®

July 1999

Published by

Dorchester Publishing Co., Inc.
276 Fifth Avenue
New York, NY 10001

ISBN 0-505-52327-2

Printed in the United States of America.

For Mary,
dearest friend and special lady,
for always being there and understanding.
With love.

THE PLAYERS

On the Kansas Prairie
Fremont Haggerty, a farmer
His granddaughter, Rachel Wilder
Poke, a hired hand
Jonathan Beecham, a widower farmer
India Beecham (deceased), wife to Jonathan
Their children:
Eve
Gideon
Caleb
Susannah
Philip
Andrew
Naomi
Tobias
Gustave "Ox" Oxenberg, a farmer
Rye Crippen, a cattle rustler
Adam Keife, a young man
Seeks, a half-breed Indian

In Texas
Slade Maverick, a gunslinger

In Wichita
Livie Svenson, a farm girl
Preacher Proffitt, an evangelist
Digger Thibeaux, a gambler

CONTENTS

PROLOGUE
The Moon O'er the Prairie
1

BOOK ONE
The Drifter
17

BOOK TWO
A Spirit Brave and True
93

BOOK THREE
Ad Astra per Aspera
189

EPILOGUE
Heartland
357

HEARTLAND

It was a grey wintry day in eighteen seventy-five
When he rode into Wichita town,
A stranger, as anyone there could tell,
Despite his flat-brimmed hat pulled down
Low to shadow his handsome face,
To hide the glint in his eyes like blue steel.
His silver spurs jingled as he swung from his saddle,
Ground his cigar beneath one booted heel.

He wore a long black duster buttoned up to his throat
Against the raw prairie wind that blew.
A long-barreled Peacemaker was strapped on each thigh,
And well how to use them, he knew.
He was a loner, a drifter, a man hard as nails,
His heart encircled by a high stone wall.
He never once dreamed as he hitched his horse to a rail
That in Wichita lay his downfall.

She had hair yellow as corn silk and eyes green as mint,
A spirit brave and true as his aim;
And like the wild beauty of the prairie she loved,
She proved elusive, not easy to tame;
For she would have all of a man or nothing at all.
In his heart and soul, no dark door
Could remain locked against the pure, loving light of her,
Who would give him all of herself—and more.

The pearl moon, the diamond stars of an onyx night,
The silver mist drifting o'er a sapphire creek,
The ruby dawn breaking on the topaz horizon,
Such were the treasures she led him to seek.

Through her eyes, he saw as he'd never seen before,
Pewter clouds dripping with crystal rain,
An opal rainbow without beginning or end,
A garnet sunset igniting the plain.

The aquamarine sky, the emerald cottonwood tree
The gold of every shock of wheat,
The amethyst wild indigo, the jade buffalo grass,
Such were the riches she laid at his feet,
All the wealth of her world; and when she was done,
His past slipped away with her kiss.
Sweeter than sweet was the passion that welled inside him
As he claimed her for always as his.

Now, folks say, when the wind sweeps down from the north
On a night when the moon is high
O'er the prairie, one who looks closely can see
Two ghostly riders in the sky.
Ad astra per aspera . . . That was ever their creed.
Even death could not keep them apart.
For all truly worth having cannot be touched, only felt,
Forever cherished in the land of the heart.

PROLOGUE

The Moon O'er the Prairie

The Prairie, Kansas, 1880

There is nothing on earth quite like a clear night sky above the great midwestern plains known as the heartland. Upon the horizon, the firmament wraps itself so like a gunpowder-black duster about the imperceptibly rolling ground that sky and land appear as one, an immeasurable void. It is as though somewhere in the distance, if one walked far enough, one would reach the end of the world and step into nothingness. For only the stars dwell in this merging of darkness and darkness. Like countless silver spurs, they gleam, and hang so low that it is as though one has only to stretch out a hand to touch them. The eye can see forever—to the very gates of heaven, it seems, where the moon is a mote in the far vaster orb of God, who keeps His all-seeing vigil here as nowhere else, the heartland held securely in the infinite cradle of His palms.

So reflected the woman, Rachel, who, lost in quiet reverie, lay upon the sweetly scented wildflowers and mixed grasses that blanketed the prairie. It was a beautiful night . . . a perfect night. As she gazed up at the endless ebony expanse

3

overhead, she gave a silent prayer of thanks to God, for He had blessed her as surely as He had the stark but striking country that was her home. For every cloud in her life, there had been a rainbow, as well. Rachel could not have asked for more than that.

At the thought, emotion welled within her, a lump rose in her throat, and tears of joy trickled from the corners of her eyes, dampening the strands of hair at her temples. Surely, no one had a right to be this happy! But incredible as it seemed to her, she was. Closing her green eyes, she sighed deeply with contentment, her full breasts rising and falling for a moment, like a cresting wave, beneath the huge harvest moon beaming gold as a newly minted eagle in the sky. Her naked body, misted with the moist night air, glistened in the diffused half-light. Her long blond hair, unbound, rippled like shocks of ripe wheat with each gust of the cool, whispering wind.

She was one with the heartland, as surely as though she had been born and bred here. So, too, was the man, her husband, who held her fast in the circle of his sheltering embrace, the hard, muscular length of his dark bronze body still intimately entangled with her soft, pale golden one.

Both man and woman were momentarily sated. But earlier, their eagerness for each other had made their lovemaking swift, passionate, almost violent. Now, as Rachel basked in its afterglow, her mind drifting, she pondered how strange it was that, even now, after all these years, she still sometimes had difficulty grasping how utterly she and her husband belonged to each other. Their love was fiercer than the wild, savage plains they had claimed as their own. How much harder it must be, then, for him, who had always been so solitary and brooding, to deal with the intensity of their feelings for each other. Yet even so, there was no part of him she did not know, no plane or angle of his body she had not discovered, no nook or cranny of his mind into which she had not delved—though some memories, dark and painful, were best left undisturbed.

Because of those memories, the love they shared frightened

her sometimes, even as it warmed and thrilled her. For those who were one with the heartland knew that what it gave, it could also take back, cruelly and, more often than not, without warning. So, although her husband had finally, firmly, laid his past to rest, a small, superstitious part of Rachel was still afraid that, someday, his buried ghosts might rise once more to haunt them.

Yet she would have had no other love. Her husband was the only man for her, as she was the only woman for him; for she was certain that if he had it all to do again, he would choose her above all others. She alone had breached the high walls surrounding his heart and made a place for herself there, safe, secure. Yes, whatever their future, he was hers now, this man, forever. Only death would separate them now, and those who had survived the harsh lessons taught by the heartland no longer feared death. It was as much a part of them as the shadows they cast beneath the relentlessly scorching sun of a prairie summer. Determinedly, Rachel pushed from her mind the penumbra of her husband's past.

Somewhere in the night, a lonesome coyote bayed at the moon, an aching, haunting sound. *Ah-ooooo. Yip-yip-yip. Ah-ooooo.* A barn owl hooted, a red-tailed hawk screamed, and some tiny creature skittered through the brush. The breeze soughed like a breath primeval, stirring gently the myriad wildflowers and grasses that had bloomed brightly and greenly since spring but that now, with autumn's onslaught, were slowly fading to the softer golden color of straw.

In the distance, in a small window niche created for it in Rachel's farmhouse, the flame of the welcome candle burned brightly and danced erratically as a tendril of wind insinuated itself inside and caused a draft. Smoke wafting from one of the two tall fieldstone chimneys surmounting the roof suddenly billowed up to swirl away, ghostlike, into the sky.

Erected just that year, the house was a good one, two stories high and, though square and simple, reassuringly solid; for it was framed of stout, heavy timber and sided with clapboard, both still relatively uncommon on the Kansas prairie, where trees were scarce. Most wood, except that from cottonwoods, had to be brought by train or wagon to Wichita, the nearest town of any size, making lumber expensive. Thus the farmhouse was a luxury that Rachel, long accustomed to a dark, dank soddy, and then a crude cottonwood log cabin, still could not quite believe was actually hers. The house had been built with both love and pride by her husband, its walls whitewashed until they were the shade of fresh, clean cotton. In the moonlight, they fairly shone. At the front of the house, the wide, railed porch, where two painstakingly carved rocking chairs swayed and creaked slightly in the breeze, beckoned charmingly. Still, much as she loved her new home, Rachel was not ready to return to it just yet.

Though all its inhabitants were dearly cherished and more than welcome, the farmhouse, despite its size, was filled to bursting with her grandfather and children, so it afforded little privacy. Time spent alone with her husband was precious, and she did not intend to waste a single minute of it.

Snuggling closer, Rachel nestled her head comfortably on his shoulder. Her hand strayed to his broad chest matted with hair. How she enjoyed the feel of it, the skin smooth as finely tanned leather, the curls crisp as newly starched muslin beneath her long, slender fingers. Had there ever been another man such as he? She had never known one.

"I love you," she murmured.

Because of the kind of man he was, those words did not come as easily to her husband. But much to Rachel's pride and pleasure, he spoke them just the same, his low, husky voice still faintly accented, after all this time, by the native language of his long-dead mother.

"I love you, too, Rachel . . . my Rachel," he said. "God, how I love you!"

As though to show her how much, with one hand, he tilted her face up to his and brought his bold, carnal mouth down on hers. At first, he kissed her gently, very gently, as though she were a maid in the first blush of her youth, needing to be courted and coaxed. But after a while, encouraged by her receptiveness, he became more insistent. His tongue darted forth to trace lingeringly the outline of her parted lips, teasing their corners before finally easing inside to sample the sweetness within. Like wild honey, it melted, warm and sugary, on his tongue. The man relished the taste of her. Hungrily, his tongue began to twist and twine about hers, searching out every dark, moist crevice of her mouth to lick from it every dulcet drop.

The ember of Rachel's earlier desire for her husband began to smolder more hotly, fed by the rekindling of his own. She moaned low in her throat. Her hands crept up about his neck, pulling him nearer. Her fingers burrowed through the glossy hair that curled in thick, rich waves at his nape. Fervidly, she clung to him, wanting him, needing him, loving him. It was from the land that she drew her strength, but her husband was all her heart.

His hands cupped her face. His kiss deepened, grew harder, more demanding, bruising her tender lips. But she did not care. His passion only heightened hers. Avidly, Rachel explored him as he did her, her tongue swirling about his delectably, spurring his ardor on. Like that of a man starving, his mouth sucked hers, swallowing her breath; his teeth nibbled her lips. He tasted of fine cigars and good whiskey, a pleasantly masculine taste now as sweet and familiar to her as the man himself. It was difficult to imagine she had once chided him for such habits. How he had laughed at her then, before showing her what a mouth tasting of those habits could do. . . . Rachel's heartbeat quickened at the erotic memories. Her body trembled with yearning and anticipation.

Feeling her quiver like a startled doe poised for flight, her husband's fingers threaded in the shining tresses streaming like corn silk from her temples, then tightened, as though to hold her captive to his will and pleasure. His mouth burned across her cheek, searing her like a stamping iron before he buried his face in her cloud of hair, inhaling deeply her heady perfume. Lilacs. For as long as he could remember, Rachel had always smelled of lilacs. Together, this past spring, he and she had planted several of the fragrant bushes along the sides of the farmhouse porch. The clusters of pale purple flowers had bloomed until summer, scenting the air and the farmhouse, where blossoms had been strewn upon the kitchen table when Rachel had distilled their essence. Again, savoring it, he breathed in the bouquet of her perfume. The memories it evoked flooded his mind, images of Rachel, always Rachel, her countless faces in countless places. He knew them all now, her every expression, her every habitat, as well as he knew his own. At long last, he, once so alone, was now so close to another human being that they were like halves of a whole.

The man's eyes opened, drinking their fill of her. Some might have thought Rachel plain, but to him, she was the most beautiful woman alive. Her glorious mane of hair was like a sunburst about her arresting, heart-shaped face, each strand soft as a dandelion puffball against his callused hands. He caught one heavy tress and wrapped it around his throat as he whispered words of love and longing in her ear. His breath felt warm against her skin, making her shiver with delight, and more. Lightly, he kissed her eyelids and the crescent smudges her thick golden lashes made upon her high cheekbones, flecked with a smattering of freckles. He drew an index finger down her retroussé nose and generous lips, tugging at the lower one slightly before Rachel opened her eyes and bit the tip of his finger playfully, smiling up at him invitingly. At her look, the man laughed throatily, a laugh that dissolved into a low growl as, without warning, his eyes darkened and his mouth seized hers again, fiercely, his tongue shooting deep between her lips.

Eagerly, Rachel returned his kisses, her tongue wreathing his until both man and woman gasped for breath and she could feel the hard evidence of his desire for her pressed against her thigh, where his body half covered hers. Her hands tightened around his neck; then, fingers splayed, gradually slid down his broad back. She reveled in the feel of his flesh, slick and shiny with sweat, the way his muscles bunched and rippled beneath her palms as he clasped her, caressed her. His skin smelled of vetiver and musk, tasted of salt as her mouth slanted across his cheek. The coarse stubble that shadowed his face and grazed her lips and tongue was potent

testimony to his maleness, his virility, both of which intox-
icated her. She nipped his ear and nuzzled his neck, all the
while touching him everywhere she could reach. But this
time, her husband had no intention of permitting their lovemaking to end so quickly. Rachel's breath caught in her throat
as he suddenly grabbed a handful of her hair and forced her
head back, his eyes raking her lazily, appreciatively, from
beneath half-closed lids.

At his sensuous appraisal, a tingle of both vulnerability
and expectation chased down her spine. Her heart raced. He
was so strong. She, by comparison, was so fragile. How
easily he bent her to his will as, slowly, he pressed his mouth
to her throat, bared now as though in offering, blazing a trail
down its swanlike length to the pulse fluttering at its hollow.
With his tongue, he flicked the pulse, then sank his teeth
gently into her shoulder where it joined her nape, a particularly responsive spot. His bite turned into a kiss. Rachel
shuddered with rising excitement, intensified by her husband's hands roving over her body—knowledgeably, skillfully, wakening its every nerve until she felt so vibrantly
alive, so painfully sensitive that, increasingly, his every touch
was like an electric shock jolting her.

Sure, steely, supple hands, he had, this macho hombre of
hers, to claim her as his, and willingly was she branded. The
blood thrummed in her ears, an age-old song, as, covetously,
his palms cupped her ripe, round breasts, swollen and aching
with passion. Languorously, his thumbs followed the curve
of her roseate areolae, then fondled her nipples until they
flushed and grew rigid, begging to be tasted, taken. Heeding
their silent appeal, his lips enveloped first one, and then the
other, sucking greedily before his teeth imprisoned each in
turn to hold it in place for his taunting tongue. Rachel gasped
as a shower of sparks radiated through her body. She felt like
a shooting star in the melanotic night sky, burning, falling,
rushing headlong toward a fiery culmination. . . . Her head
reeled. Once more, a broken moan erupted from her throat.

"My love," she breathed, and gripped her husband even
more firmly, her nails digging into his back. "Oh, my love."

"Rachel," he rasped in reply. "Rachel . . . honey . . ."

Her breasts were like golden globes in his hands, the man thought, veined with delicate rivulets of blue through which her life's blood flowed. The cleft between them sloped like a fair valley down which his mouth traveled, his tongue lapping tantalizingly the perspiration beaded like dew upon her flesh. As they had just moments past, his palms glided over her nipples in a leisurely, circular motion before he squeezed her breasts, pushing them upward until they brimmed over his fingers. Again, his lips sought and found the spheres' enticing pink crests; his tongue darted forth to whirl about them deliciously.

Whimpering, Rachel writhed against him, wanting, needing more. Deep in the secret heart of her, the ignited tinder of her desire flared to spread like a prairie fire through her body, consuming her. Her husband knew well how to quench its blaze, but still, he made no move to do so. His lovemaking was unhurried, deliberately provocative, its incendiary effects only heightened by its prolonging.

"Sweet . . . sweet . . ." he muttered against her taut belly as his mouth wended lower, his tongue stabbing her with its heat.

He had already surveyed every part of her, and yet he wanted to map each anew: the sides he often tickled mischievously in the mornings, the waist so willowy that he could span it with his hands, and more. Again and again, his fingers snaked down her legs, then danced back up to dally along the insides of her thighs, tormenting her exquisitely by avoiding the one place she craved most for him to touch. Softly, she cried out her need, but her husband only ignored her.

"Patience, sugar," he chided, his voice dripping like molasses in her ear, a half smile curving his lips. "Patience . . . it has its own rewards, you know."

"Don't you mean virtue?"

"No"—his laugh was low, mocking—"for where's the joy in that?"

None, Rachel thought, remembering her lonely, spinsterish

life before he had come into it and made her his. *None at all*.

Acquiescing, she uttered no further protest, but allowed her husband to do as he wished with her. Once, she had feared him, had been terrified of the violent, wanton emotions he had unleashed inside her; for he was a dangerous man to cross, and she had dared to cross him. But that day was long past. Now, she loved him with all her heart, and she thrilled to the feel of his hands and mouth intimately upon her body, arousing her to a feverish pitch. She jubilated in the knowledge that she had gentled him, if but a little, as a green-broke horse was gentle—only outwardly, at heart still wild and free, potentially deadly. Still, Rachel would have had her husband no other way. He *knew* no other way, for he had journeyed the hard roads of life, never its easy ones. It was in the seamy brothels of the countless red-lamp districts of his past that he had learned the talents with which he enthralled her now, though he had touched no other woman since he had first taken her.

Now, he knelt before her and kissed her feet, then raised one dainty foot to his lips. His tongue flitted across her gracefully arched instep. One by one, he sucked her toes, which tasted sweetly of the wildflowers and prairie grass, the good, rich, dark earth upon which she had trodden earlier.

For a minute, his glance rested ardently, intrusively, upon Rachel's face. Her head was flung back in ecstasy. Her eyes were shut. From her parted lips, her breath came raggedly. For the barest instant, the man's heart stopped beating, then started to slam in his chest, like a blacksmith's hammer against a horseshoe. The sight of her countenance, naked in its passion for him, stirred his blood powerfully. His loins tightened agonizingly with desire. That look was for his eyes alone. No other man would ever see it. He would kill any man who even dared to try.

Rachel sensed his jealous, predatory stare. Her eyelids fluttered open. Her gaze met her husband's, locked with his. Time was caught, held suspended. Then, slowly, watching her all the while, he leaned forward, pulled her knees up, and spread her thighs wide. His hand found her, finally easing her scalding ache for him slightly as, rhythmically, he began to stroke the downy nest between her thighs, the velvety swells and folds of her no other man but he had ever known, or ever would.

She was hot and wet with wanting him, and the feel of her almost drove him beyond the limits of his control. Compelling himself to take a deep breath, the man steadied himself. Until Rachel, his life had been as bleak and barren as the plains in winter. She had filled it to overflowing, given him not only herself, but so much more; while he had had nothing to offer her in return but his name and protection. She might have had any man—any man at all, he thought, though he knew that she—shy, modest, oblivious of her sensual allure— would not have agreed. Still, she had chosen him. As long as they lived, he never wanted her to regret that choice. So, in this, as in all things, he intended to do whatever he could to please her.

Brazenly, he slipped one questing finger inside her, two, withdrew them, then inserted them again, repeating the motion over and over, further ensuring her readiness to receive him. And all the while, his thumb rotated upon the tiny, throbbing bud of her womanhood that strained against him desperately, frantic to unfurl. But despite her rapid intake of breath, the sinuous thrashing of her head, the arching of her body against his hand, still, he teased her.

Beneath him, Rachel sprawled shamelessly, exulting in the feelings he was wakening within her, helpless to stop his assault upon her, though she would not have if she could. It was as though all her bones had dissolved inside her, leaving her weak and pliant as a rag doll. Her body was a mass of unbridled sensation. She could feel the cool wind against her skin, in sharp contrast to her husband's warm breath. Beneath her, the grass, damp with the night air, was soft as a feather mattress, in counterpoint to his rough hands. The green redolence of the grass was tinged with the first bite of autumn and blended earthily with the perfume of the many wildflow-

ers sprinkled like gay confetti across the prairie, and with the
pungent, spicy fragrances that emanated from her husband's
flesh.

Rachel loved the masculine smell of him. Sometimes in
the mornings, after he had risen for the day, she would lie
abed a little while longer, her head upon his pillow, inhaling
the scent of him that lingered in the sheets and marveling
that he was actually her man, her husband. And once, during
his absence from the farmhouse, she had stepped from her
old metal bathtub and, on impulse, had robed her naked body
in one of his chambray shirts, feeling as though it were his
arms about her. He had seemed quite near then, not out in
the distant fields at all.

At the remembrance, a surge of tiny tremors shook her,
and then another, starting deep at her core and pulsing through
her body like ripples along a creek. Suddenly, within her,
the sense of hollowness that only her husband could fill grew
so unbearable that all thoughts save his filling that void were
driven from Rachel's mind. Blindly, she strove against him,
crying out her urgent need, her fervent surrender; and at long
last, abruptly, his mouth and body covered hers. His turgid
maleness probed between her legs, plunged swift and hard
and deep into her, taking away her breath and scattering her
senses to the wind.

Blacker than black, the night was then, abounding with
the magic of all things ancient and earthy, this ritual old as
mankind itself, nowhere more fitting than upon this primal
plain, beneath the elemental moon. Glorious, it was, and with
every atavistic fiber of her being, Rachel gloried in it. The
man's weight pressed her down heavily, but it was a burden
she bore readily. So close, they lay then, that they seemed as
one, each melded to the other, no space between, no room in
either's heart or mind for another—nor would there ever be.

His breath was like blistering smoke against her throat and
breasts as, suddenly, he wrenched his lips from hers, fused
them lustfully to her molten flesh, sucked her nipples, and
laved them with his tongue. Her hands tightened on his back.
Her nails furrowed his skin to his buttocks as, inexorably,

he began to move within her, and she rose to meet each welcome thrust. There was nothing for him then but her, and for her him.

Who rocked whom? Neither knew—nor cared. In perfect symmetry, they came together, beautifully, as is the way of lovers.

Like a hushed prairie wind that gradually builds to a roar, sweeping all before it from its path, so exhilaration swept through Rachel's body then, ruthlessly catching her up and bearing her aloft. Wild as a tempest, she was, exploding with lightning and thunder as she attained her shattering climax. In the end, even the man who carried her to rapture's peak was relegated to some dim corner of her mind. Only subconsciously was she aware of his hands clamping convulsively to her hips, lifting her, crushing her to him as she stiffened and shuddered and sobbed beneath him—a cry sweet and piercing as that of some lone animal on the plains. And he, her mate—now and always—answered, spiraling down with a twister's fury into the soft, all-encompassing liquid darkness of her, faster and faster, until, with a low, triumphant groan, he spilled himself within her.

A long, racking sigh shook the length of his body as he collapsed upon her. His heart drummed like rain against her own. Their gasps mingled to fill the night air as, slowly . . . very slowly, they relinquished their brief hold on the heavens, and the earth claimed them once more as its own.

After a time, smiling down at her, the man skimmed a damp strand of hair back from Rachel's face, his eyes drowsy and sated as they met her own. His mouth brushed hers, once, twice. Then, reluctantly, he withdrew from her, pulling her roughly, possessively, into his arms—as though he would never let her go—and pillowing her head upon his shoulder. Closing his eyes, he exhaled with satisfaction.

The man, lost in thought, did not speak. But Rachel, long accustomed to his moody silences, rested serenely in his embrace, listening to the sounds of his breathing grow gentle and rhythmic as, eventually, he drifted into sleep. The sight of him slumbering stirred her as much as his lovemaking had earlier, though differently. That he slept naked and unguarded, yet so peacefully at her side, told her far more eloquently than any words he might have spoken just how deeply he loved and trusted her. In her heart, she rejoiced at the profundity of his feelings for her.

Tenderly, Rachel kissed him. Then, quietly, so as not to disturb him, she stole from his arms to retrieve her garments strewn carelessly nearby upon the grass. As she dressed, her eyes roamed unabashedly over her husband's prone figure. How like a god he was, she mused, tall and muscular, his skin burnished by the sun and lustrous beneath the moon, hard as horn, smooth as hide, except where marked by scars grown pale with the years, testament to his strong will to survive. But it was in devil's guise that he had come to her, out of wind and rain and shadows, black-clothed, and insolent, smiting her with fear—and some other dark and wild emotion she had never felt before, but that, once unleashed inside her, could not be chained again. Like a hound of hell, the man had pursued her and claimed her for all time as his; and in the end, she had yielded to him gladly her virginal young body, her heart, and her soul. Never in her most fantastic dreams had she imagined it would be so.

Presently, she would wake him. Then, hand in hand, they would walk back to the farmhouse, feet treading the silver ribbon of moonlight that wound across the prairie. But now, for an instant, as the memories engulfed her, time turned back for Rachel.

Faintly, as from a distance, she seemed to hear the murmur of rolling thunder, the spatter of light rain, and the jingle of a bridle echoing on a faraway wind. And as she gazed at the horizon, there appeared, in her mind, a horseman, a flat-brimmed hat pulled down low to obscure his handsome face, a long black duster buttoned up to his throat. As though in slow motion, like a ghost rider, he galloped toward her, and the horse he rode was Fortune, and the man's name was Fate. . . .

BOOK ONE

The Drifter

Chapter One

The Prairie, Kansas, 1874

It was a harsh land, a savage land. A land where the sun burned too hotly in the boundless azure sky; where the rain burst with fury from the dark, roiling clouds that could mass of a sudden on the distant horizon; and where the wind blew wild and constantly, whipping unhindered across the vast, void plains that stretched for miles in every direction, their emptiness unbroken save for a few lone cottonwoods. It was a land that was the making of some—and the breaking of far too many others; and just as it had conquered countless men and women before her, it had, after a long, hard-fought struggle, vanquished India Beecham at last.

It was the grasshoppers that finished her. They had come in droves that August of 1874 (which would, as a result, be referred to ever after as the "Grasshopper Year"), like nothing she had ever before seen. In a massive, shining, whitish green cloud, they had come, millions upon millions of the hideous, chirring insects, to pelt from the sky like sleet during a blizzard. Thick as a four-inch layer of fallen snow, they had settled upon the land for days and, before finally, mercifully, moving on, had voraciously stripped it of all that grew there. What had once been fertile and thriving was afterward as barren and deteriorated as in winter.

Under the combined weight of the insects, the branches of trees brought west at such cost and trouble, and so carefully cultivated afterward, had broken; cornstalks had buckled, and the prairie grass had been smashed flat as a hoecake. The grasshoppers had swarmed upon watermelon patches, eaten even the tough, variegated rinds; devoured gardens row upon row, rejecting only the onions' papery outer shells; and gorged themselves on unripe fruit, leaving, in a terrible travesty, the pits hanging from the limbs of the orchards' trees. The locusts had munched through the quilts, blankets, sheets, coats, shawls, and burlap bags that people, in their desperation, had used in futile attempts to shield their rapidly disappearing crops.

Once the greedy grasshoppers had consumed every speck of green vegetation in sight, they had started on other types of food, and wood, leather, and cloth. They had attacked the soft cottonwood of log cabins and barns, the rough-hewn posts and rails of fences, and the smooth siding of shops and saloons. They had chewed the handles from tools. They had gluttonously gobbled bridles, harnesses, and saddles, finding the sweaty hide particularly appealing. After sunset, the insects had tunneled their way into homes, ravaging the meager contents of barrels, cabinets, and pantries; shredding painstakingly stitched and embellished curtains, and destroying furniture brought at great expense and hardship from back East.

India had watched helplessly as the acres of fruits, vegetables, and grains she and her husband, Jonathan, had planted that spring were ingested in scant hours, and she had thought with despair of the months of backbreaking work it had taken to clear the fields strewn with buffalo bones and stones, till the soil, and sow the seeds on which her family's livelihood and future had depended. Her mind fraught with worry, she had been unable to sleep at night, had stayed awake for hours, listening to the grasshoppers wreak their havoc upon the larder and the root cellar she had scrimped and scraped to stock, upon the precious contents of the bridal chest that had come all the way by riverboat and prairie schooner from Louisiana to Kansas with her, and even upon the very bed in which she had lain, sobbing soundlessly so Jonathan and the children would not hear. And from that moment on, India had given up her battle against the land, losing all hope and heart.

Now, on this late, Indian-summer afternoon, too thin, too pale, encumbered by pregnancy and looking far older than her thirty-four years, she stood outside her small sod house amid the devastation that had been wrought by the mindless horde of locusts. Though, in the weeks that had passed since the grasshoppers' invasion, she ought to have grown used to viewing her now blighted surroundings, India still felt shocked and dazed by the sight and extent of the damage done to the land. Somehow, she just could not quite seem to grasp the fact that the coarse stubble that littered the ground as far as the eye could see was all that remained of her world and dreams.

Although the insatiable insects had gone, the foul taste and stench of them lingered on. Wells, creeks, and ponds were so polluted with their excrement that water was unfit for drinking by either man or beast. Domestic chickens and hogs, and wildfowl, bloated from stuffing themselves on their unexpected grasshopper feast, tasted so vilely of the locusts as to be totally inedible. People everywhere were subsisting mostly on corn bread, gravy, and coffee sweetened with sorghum. Men who hankered for tobacco were reduced to smoking grape leaves instead.

A weary sigh escaped India's lips as she fished the last of the wet but now—thankfully—clean clothing from the rinse water in the old metal washtub balanced precariously upon a packing crate before her. Then she began the laborious process of wringing the garments out by hand. She took care to ensure that the excess water ran back into the washtub, for the commodity was scarce on the prairie and had to be hauled from the well, which lay several long yards from the soddy. Yet the dowser who had determined the well's location had told her and Jonathan they were lucky it was so near!

Her husband had thought the old half-breed Indian diviner they'd hired on the advice of their neighbors was an offensive crackpot. Certain that the dowser had really done nothing more than just put on a show with a forked stick to cheat them of their money, and that water was to be found anywhere beneath the land's surface, Jonathan had spent many fruitless days digging a well closer to the soddy. But the old half-breed had been right, and her husband had had an unreasoning hatred of both Indians and diviners ever since. It was a bone of contention between India and Jonathan that their nearest neighbor, Rachel Wilder, who had learned the art of dowsing from the old half-breed, should be India's best friend.

However, after their discouraging experience with the well, it had not taken India and Jonathan long to become aware that not a single drop of water must be wasted on the prairie. Even soiled water could be used to soak her vegetable patch.

At the thought, she looked at her ruined garden, and the pointlessness of her unconscious action struck her. A half whimper, half laugh that bordered on hysteria emanated from her throat, like the tortured wail of some mortally wounded animal. For a long, dreadful moment, she swayed on her feet, fearing she was going to faint. Closing her eyes tightly, she gripped the rim of the washtub to steady herself and waited for the sudden dizzy spell to pass.

Startled awake by its mother's distress, the baby nestled inside India's womb stirred abruptly, fretfully, and kicked her hard. Instinctively, she laid a soothing hand upon her burgeoning belly, breathing slowly until the agitated fluttering within stilled and she sensed that the child slept tranquilly once more. Then, squaring her shoulders, she forced herself to continue with her work; for life, despite all its afflictions, went on.

India's grey-streaked black hair, which she had so neatly coiled in a heavy mass at her nape that morning, now straggled from its pins. She pushed the loose strands from her face and mopped her dripping brow, gritty with dust, smoke, and traces of the strong lye soap still bubbling slightly in the big black cauldron of wash water hanging over the nearby, smoldering fire. Then she bent and struggled awkwardly to heave upon one hip the large wicker basket that sat to one side of the washtub and now brimmed with sodden laundry. The chore would have been difficult under any circumstances. Now, hampered by her coming child, as well as two sniveling youngsters who clutched fractiously at her skirts, it was almost impossible for India to manage. Moaning, she strained at the task, the underarms and bodice of her faded gingham dress running with sweat from the heat and her exertions. For a minute, it was all she could do to keep from sinking to her knees and crying in defeat.

"Here. Let me help you, Mama," Eve offered soberly as she hastened to her mother's side, her face grave with concern, her blue eyes shadowed with more painful knowledge than a thirteen-year-old should have had.

As she gazed at her oldest daughter, India smiled tremulously, blinking back with effort the sudden, hot tears that stung her eyes.

How young she is, India thought, stricken with remorse, *too young to be so wise. It just isn't right that a child should be forced to shoulder the burdens of an adult. Yet if not for Eve, I do not think I would have the strength to go on. Oh, Eve, I wanted so much for you. I never meant for things to turn out like this. I never meant for your life to be so hard, for you to have to grow up so fast. . . .*

Wistfully, India remembered her own childhood at her parents' magnificent plantation, Cypress Hill, along the banks of the Mississippi River in Louisiana, where a household of slaves had waited on her hand and foot, where the dining-room table had been laden with food, and where the only manual labor she'd ever done had been fancy embroidering, tatting lace, or quilting. How had she come to wind up like this?

Again disquieted by its mother's turbulent thoughts, the

baby inside her woke and began tossing and kicking once more. This was India's thirteenth pregnancy in sixteen years. She had delivered seven living children, two infants who had been stillborn and were buried in Louisiana, and she had suffered three miscarriages in between. It was enough to have taken its toll on any woman, and India was worn out. She was not looking forward to the birth of this latest child, for somehow, she felt sure in her heart that, this time, she would not survive the ordeal.

Anxiously, she glanced again at Eve as, together, they started to peg the clean laundry out on the line to dry. What would become of Eve and the other children if their mother died?

India knew that Jonathan couldn't manage on his own. He had never been very steady or practical. When she'd learned of her arranged marriage to the wealthy only son of the family whose land had adjoined theirs, she'd protested in vain to her despotic father that Jonathan Beecham was selfish and spoiled. Despite the objections, the match had been made. So, of necessity, she'd grown strong to compensate for Jonathan's weakness, knowing, even so, how he'd resented her for her strength—and, more, for his own need of it. Certainly, he had never been cut out for soldiering, for the War between the States. He had never been intended to languish in the Yankees' Rock Island prison—he, who had been used to having his every foolish whim indulged, his slightest craving satisfied.

India had expected that if he survived the horrible war, her husband would change. After all, she had reasoned, no man came unaffected through such combat. And it *had* altered him—though, unfortunately, not for the better. Instead, Jonathan had grown moody, morose, embittered, and, worst of all, just downright mean.

During the invasion of New Orleans, his parents had died of a fever that had swept the countryside, and the damned Yankees had so effectively shelled Beecham's Landing, Jonathan's inheritance, that the once-resplendent house was virtually uninhabitable. The fever had taken India's stepmother, too, and her father had been shot down while stubbornly resisting the hated carpetbaggers who had, after the war, swarmed like vultures down from the North, and greedily confiscated Cypress Hill because her father was unable to pay the high taxes they had levied upon it.

So, following the South's surrender, homeless, almost destitute, their families dead or scattered, Jonathan and India had headed west, where India, at least, had hoped they could make a fresh start in some peaceful paradise untainted by the scars of slavery and emancipation. But in Kansas, one wheel of their prairie schooner had hit an unnoticed rock and snapped an axle. For Jonathan, that was the straw that had broken the camel's back. Stubbornly, sullenly, he'd refused to budge another inch. And so it was that the stark, sweeping plains India had despised on sight, against which she had striven until they had finally crushed her, had become the unwelcome and unwelcoming place where she would live out the rest of her short, unhappy life.

Clumsily, never having previously been compelled to toil physically—he had been an officer, naturally, during the war—Jonathan had dug for them a cellar and erected for them a barn and a soddy. This last was an ugly, unclean house (though India would not have debased the word by labeling the squat turf dwelling as such). It had a hard-packed dirt floor; a single, tiny, rawhide-covered window; and a grassy earth roof on which tall weeds sprouted every spring and through which rain poured during every storm, bringing with it not only a drenching chill, but snakes and rodents, as well.

To India's amazement, Jonathan had actually brightened a little upon completion of their new abode, taking pride in all his strenuous work, the first he'd ever really done. But she, recalling the stately old plantations of their youth, had taken one look at the crude, inhospitable soddy and burst into tears. And Jonathan, not understanding she wept for all they had known and lost and would never have again, had believed her disappointed by and ashamed of his unskillful efforts; and he'd hated her for her tears.

It was then that he'd begun drinking in earnest. Even worse, however, was that he'd gradually grown more and more prone to abrupt fits of anger and violence that terrified India and the children. On several occasions, drunk and blaming them for his fears, his flaws, and his failures, he'd beaten them all. Each time, he'd wept like a baby afterward and begged India to forgive him. And since she was a woman alone in a man's world, with hungry mouths to feed, she'd swallowed her pride, her hurt, and her fright, and woodenly submitted to his inebriated mauling and quite often ruthless rape of her in bed.

Now, depressed, worn out, uncaring whether she lived or died, India knew she could not endure much more. Her friend Rachel would help her, she knew; but Rachel, though she seemed in many ways years older, was only eighteen, and had her own family and farm to look after, too. Besides, Jonathan loathed her, and India didn't want any woman, least of all Rachel, to feel obligated to endure his drunken tirades. India had few other friends—and no one to whom she could turn for assistance except her younger half brother.

She had not seen him for many long years—since shortly after the war, actually. But drawn together by their father's tyranny, they had been close in their childhood; and sometimes even now, after all this time, a letter would come, a few hastily scrawled lines enclosed with money that, deep down inside, India felt certain, much as she loved her half brother, was ill-gotten. He must still care about her, then.

She stared down at her increasing waistline, at little Andrew and Naomi, who tugged at her skirts; and then once more at Eve, so unnaturally solemn and adult. Beyond them, in the distant fields, her sons Gideon, Caleb, and Philip worked diligently to clear away the wreckage left by the grasshoppers. Nearer at hand, from the soddy, came the clatter of pots and pans and dishes as her daughter Susannah prepared the supper for cooking and laid the table. In the shade of the sod barn, Jonathan, bleary-eyed, nursed a bottle and, in fits and starts, warbled discordantly some ditty he had learned during the war—no doubt in a bordello, since, even from the very beginning, he had always been unfaithful to his wife. India's mouth tightened with disgust as she spied his sprawling figure and discerned the song's vulgar words.

No, she could not leave her children to her husband's mercy, she thought grimly. Surely, no matter what her half brother had done or become, he would look after the youngsters if anything should happen to her. She had an old address for him inside.

I'll write him today, she vowed silently to herself, *just in case something* does *go wrong when my time comes. I should have told him the truth years ago about the state of my marriage instead of letting him think everything was all right. Maybe then, things would have been different. Now, I can only hope I haven't left it too late—Oh, forgive me . . . forgive me, my dear children, for not doing any better by you. But I've done all I could, and now, I'm tired, so very tired. . . .*

Then, heaving an involuntary sigh, India slowly gathered up the empty wicker laundry basket and trudged toward the shabby soddy she called neither house nor home.

Chapter Two

Dry Gulch, Texas, 1874

A wild "blue norther" howled down from the high Tules bluffs and deep Palo Duro Canyon to sweep across the *Llano Estacado*—the Staked Plain—and beyond, where, like a stricken stray dog crouched before a runaway wagon, the small town of Dry Gulch huddled upon the land, cruelly exposed to the full blast of the wind's fury. Although no more than a tiny cluster of shoddy shacks, shops, and saloons apparently undeserving of any special notice, Dry Gulch was infamous far and wide. It was a pesthole of wantonness and wickedness, home to sodden drunks and soiled doves, violent crooks and vicious cutthroats. Many who lived there were wanted—dead or alive—in numerous states and territories.

Even so, no lawman who valued his neck would venture near the poisonous place. The last one brave enough to do so had been promptly and unceremoniously hanged from the lone tree that, tall and twisted, stood like a warning sign at the outskirts of town. Even the Texas Rangers were known to give Dry Gulch a wide berth. Strangers who, out of ignorance or daring, penetrated the town's limits (and did not sport a tin badge) might be shot on sight, with no resident lifting a voice of alarm or a finger of prevention. Indeed, harlots plastered their painted faces avidly to the filthy windows of the saloons where they plied their trade and tittered at the prospect of some poor and unsuspecting person shortly meeting his untimely demise.

Nor did anyone question the killer—or killers, as the case might be—as to his motives for cold-bloodedly gunning down those so unwary or unwise as to ride into Dry Gulch. The town's depraved inhabitants kept their mouths shut, and the villainous desperadoes who used it as a hideaway did likewise.

Usually, Dry Gulch shrieked with activity—revelry born of cheap liquor, cheaper women, and the frequent discharging of pistols wildly aimed by drunken brawlers. But now, although two hours of wintry grey daylight remained, the main street of town was deserted, and the sagging shutters of the tawdry buildings lining either side were barred tight against the bitter chill of the blustery wind. Snow flurries whipped and eddied along the desolate dirt road. Across it, a sole, scraggly tumbleweed was buffeted between the hitching rails until finally a strong gust lifted it onto the rotting boardwalk. The tumbleweed rolled down the cold, stiff planks and came to rest in the framed recess of two narrow, closed doors through whose long, grimy, frost-limned windows glowed the only light that shone along the street. Behind the doors, in sharp contrast to the stillness that blanketed the rest of the town, the dissonant music of a badly tuned and poorly played piano jangled, and raucous laughter rang out to be carried away by the wind.

Even a blue norther could not shut down the Red Garter.

Inside the saloon, motley men stood along the bar or sat upon creaking chairs drawn up to knife-scarred tables. Strumpets simpered salaciously and giggled as they called for the customers to buy them drinks. A few of the girls, their drunken patrons in tow, lurched up a rickety staircase that led to a seedy, dimly lighted hall lined with ill-furnished rooms.

In one corner of the saloon, the fat piano player thumped away, with no evident concern at the false notes that issued jarringly from the battered old instrument. Nor, with one exception, did the men hunched over a nearby card table pay the cacophonous music any heed. The single exception, Slade Maverick, winced inwardly as the piano player hit yet another off key, then, adding insult to injury, missed several notes of the song he was attempting to play. Outwardly, Slade's face remained impassive, his concentration riveted on the poker game that had begun early that morning and that had grown more and more tense and surly as the day had progressed. Now, the air was so thick with foreboding that Slade felt as though he could slice it with his bowie knife.

Nor was he the only one to suspect that a storm of trouble was brewing. Most in the saloon, realizing some time ago that the atmosphere hovering over the card table boded ill, had prudently vacated the vicinity of that particular corner. Only one of the local trollops, Lolly, had stayed behind— though this was due neither to any special bravery nor lack of common sense. It was simply that wild horses couldn't have dragged her away from Slade Maverick.

The soft lamplight of the Red Garter was kind to Lolly's hard face, so she appeared younger than she really was; and she was cleaner, too, than the rest of the sluts who could be had for five dollars, more or less, at any of the town's many bars. Lolly had been of good stock once, before a bad man had used and abused her, bringing her low, and then abandoning her; and some remnants of her decent upbringing still survived.

Her brunette hair was a mass of artfully arrayed curls, and she had tucked a single red plume just over her left ear. Her makeup was less garish than that of most, although she did have a black beauty mark carefully penciled high on one cheek and upon the generous swell of one breast, but the spots were small and enhanced her attempt at prettiness. A set of paste diamonds glittered at her ears, her throat, and her wrists, making her gaudy red satin dress trimmed with black lace seem more elegant than it truly was. In short, Lolly, despite being a whore, was a sight better than the trash that usually frequented Dry Gulch. No doubt, this was why she found Slade Maverick especially appealing, for he, too, was a cut above most of the town's riffraff.

Now, one slipper-shod foot planted squarely upon the seat of a chair, her skirts hiked up to display a shapely ankle and a red-gartered thigh, her elbow resting on her knee, hand upturned and chin laid in her palm, she watched as the men at the poker table examined the cards they had been dealt and placed their bets accordingly. More than once, Lolly's eyes strayed to Slade's tall, dark figure, and now and then, a wistful sigh escaped her lips as she looked at him.

He came only rarely to Dry Gulch, a fact that secretly grieved her, for she was half in love with him, although he had never encouraged her hopes and feelings for him. It was true he did not use her brutally, as many of the town's ruffians did, but use her, he did, all the same. In her heart, Lolly knew that she was nothing more to him than a convenient receptacle for his lust, that although he always chose her to share his bed whenever he passed through town, it was only because she made an effort to take care of herself and thus was not so dirty as most. For by Dry Gulch standards, Slade Maverick was considered "finicky," although those who prized their skins never openly remarked upon this. Fastidious, he might be, but he could also shoot the pip out of a playing card at fifty yards, and he was known to have a hot, nasty temper, besides.

A notorious gunslinger and bounty hunter, he was one of the few men in town who did not have a price on his head, who did not have his face smeared on any *Wanted, Dead or Alive* poster anywhere. But although he walked both sides of the law as he pleased (though more often the right than the wrong side), the fact that no lawmen or bounty hunters dogged his tracks was laid to his cleverness rather than to his morals. Certainly, if the need arose, he had no scruples about employing with deadly accuracy his two custom-made, ivory-handled, silver-plated, .45-caliber Colt Peacemaker revolvers, each of which had barrels fully seven and a half inches long and fired six potent shots.

Lolly felt safe as she hovered near him, but she was instantly alert when abruptly Slade made a surreptitious but sharp, commanding movement with his hand at her, his meaning all too plain. Frightened, and having learned from experience the folly of disobeying a man's order, she began to edge covertly away from the poker table as quickly as she could.

Slade had been playing cards for several long hours, certain all the while that he was being cheated. He had watched each man at the poker table carefully, and now, he knew for sure the identity of the culprit and that the man, known to all in Dry Gulch as "the Deacon," had been dealing from the bottom of the deck all along, and squirreling cards up his sleeves, too.

If there was one thing Slade Maverick couldn't abide, it was a card cheat. Even in Dry Gulch, men played honestly at the poker table—or they didn't play at all.

Now, as the Deacon's grasping fingers reached out to rake in the pot yet again, Slade's left hand shot out and slammed down over the money lying at the center of the card table. Like rice tossed at a wedding, dollar bills flew into the air. With an ominous clatter, a few silver coins rolled off onto the tobacco-splattered floor.

"Jest whaddaya think yore doin', Maverick?" the Deacon demanded, his beady black eyes suddenly wary and glinting hard as flint in the lamplight, his mouth clamping down meanly on the fat cigar he'd been puffing all day. "A full house beats three queens any day of the week—'n' ya know it!"

"Yeah," Slade drawled, "when the full house is dealt fair and square."

"I don't think I like yore tone, Maverick. It sounds ta me like yore callin' me a card cheat!"

"I am," Slade answered softly. "Yank up your sleeves, Deacon, so I and the rest of these boys"—he indicated the others at the poker table—"can see what you've got up 'em."

"Yore makin' a big mistake, Maverick. I've been killin' insultin' sons of bitches like ya since before ya was born! But I reckon I ain't so old that I cain't handle one more—"

At that, without warning, the Deacon jumped to his feet, simultaneously shoving over the card table in an attempt to send Slade sprawling. In the sudden silence that descended upon the saloon, gunfire split the air. The Deacon's pig eyes widened with shock as, in speedy succession, several bullets tore into his big, beefy body. Women screamed and scattered. Blood spurted and sprayed from the Deacon's gaping wounds, flecking the nearby surroundings with crimson. Arms flailing, he staggered back, pulling the trigger of his revolver reflexively as he did so, pumping slugs wildly into the walls and the overturned poker table. Then, groaning, he slowly dropped the pistol and doubled over, clutching his chest and belly as blood gushed between his fingers. He took two feeble steps, tilted heavily to one side, then crashed over a chair, shattering it. At last, with a thud, he hit the sawdust-littered floor of the Red Garter, his eyes glaring now at nothing, his stogie simply hanging from his stained yellow teeth.

Swiftly, Slade pivoted so his back was against the wall. He held two gleaming guns purposefully in his strong, sure hands, and one of the long silver barrels was still smoking. His midnight-blue eyes raked the bar rapidly, searching for signs of further conflict. There were none, but Slade was not so foolish as to relax his guard just yet. Birds of a feather flocked together, it was said, and he was a hawk in a nest of vultures—among whom the Deacon had been a buzzard of some account.

"Yank up his sleeves!" Slade barked to the men ringing the fallen poker table, motioning curtly toward the dead Deacon.

After a minute or two of deliberation, a couple of the men, muttering, stooped and jerked up the sleeves of the corpse. Three cards fluttered out onto the floor.

"Why, the sorry bastard!" one of the men spat, kicking the body in disgust. "He took a hunnert 'n' twinny-five dollars offa me—'n' he were a-cheatin' all the while! Looks like ya done us all a real favor, Maverick!"

"Does, doesn't it?" Slade observed dryly, dropping his Peacemakers into his holsters as he realized there would be no need to defend himself against the rabble in the Red Garter.

He retrieved the cash from the floor, carefully folding up the bills and stuffing them into his pocket—though he scorned the coins. Then he set his black sombrero firmly on his head, shrugged into his long black duster, and, grimacing, bent to hoist onto his broad shoulders the Deacon's sizable corpse. Regardless of the man's condition, he was worth $250 in Dodge City, and Slade intended to collect the reward. Without a backward glance—not even at Lolly—he sauntered wordlessly toward the Red Garter's closed doors, his silver spurs jingling loudly in the hush.

Outside the saloon, the wind pummeled Slade like a fist of ice. He pulled his hat down low and his coat collar up high against the gale before he started down the deserted main street of town.

"Mr. Maverick! Mr. Maverick!"

At the sound of the voice calling his name, Slade turned to see a boy racing toward him from the doorway of a dark, decrepit shanty across the road. It was young Timothy, the bastard son of one of Dry Gulch's prostitutes. He earned a bit of pocket change by running errands, sweeping up, and doing other odd jobs around town. One of his self-appointed duties was to go to the hanging tree every day and fetch the sack of mail left there, for not even the letter carriers of the United States Post Office would set foot in Dry Gulch.

"Mr. Maverick," Timothy puffed, red-faced and gasping for breath as he reached Slade's side. That the boy registered no surprise or horror at all at seeing the body slung across Slade's shoulders spoke volumes about the town's code of behavior. "This letter jest arrived fer ya," Timothy explained. "It's been some months a-catchin' up with ya—ya kin tell from the envelope, see?—so I thought ya'd best have it right away."

"Thanks," Slade said, dropped the heavy body to the ground, and flipped the boy a quarter, which he caught deftly, despite the wind.

After Timothy had gone, Slade ripped open the envelope to read the disjointed, tear-stained missive inside. When he had finished, he swore long and heatedly. His hand tightened into a ball, crumpling the envelope and two heavily crossed pages he held. Snarling, he jammed the wad of paper down deep into the pocket of his duster. Then he lifted and flung the corpse over the Deacon's huge gelding, untied his own horse from the hitching rail, and mounted up. Leading the gelding, Slade set his spurs to his stallion's sides and headed into the onrush of the wild blue norther.

From one of the small upstairs windows of the Red Garter, Lolly watched him gallop out of town, a droop in her shoulders and a pang in her heart. Then, slowly, she turned and started to undress for the slovenly brute who now lay upon her tarnished brass bed.

It was Christmas Eve, and such was the holiday cheer in Dry Gulch.

Chapter Three

The Prairie, Kansas, 1875

The day was dull and leaden, made even drearier by the dark, puffy clouds massed in the sky, and by steadily increasing snowfall. The whiteness of the swirling flakes contrasted sharply with the black garments of the handful of mourners gathered on the prairie to pay their last respects to India Beecham. Shivering, they huddled at the edge of her final resting place, eager to get her buried as soon as possible so they could return home to the warmth of their hearths.

It was so cold that the long, knitted-wool scarves of the mourners were frozen to their mouths, making breathing laborious, and the pallbearers' hands were like slabs of ice inside their gloves as they began to lower India's plain wooden coffin into the shallow grave gouged with considerable difficulty from the frigid earth earlier that morning. For a moment, it seemed as though their benumbed fingers would lose hold of the casket entirely. But at last, it was in the ground, and the reverend went on with the service, shouting to be heard above the wail of the wind.

Like a whip, each bitter gust lashed the mourners mercilessly, stinging their faces raw and scourging the women's backsides as it snaked up their skirts, revealing an inordinately indelicate amount of petticoats and stockings in the process. None of the men noticed, however, each being more intent upon shielding himself from the hostile elements than with peering up the women's immodestly billowing gowns.

"Unto Almighty God we commend the soul of our sister

departed, and we commit her body to the ground; earth to earth, ashes to ashes, dust to dust," the reverend yelled hoarsely through his rime-encrusted muffler.

Finally, the pallbearers turned their hands to their shovels, scooping up the snowy dirt heaped to one side of India's grave.

Thwack. Scrape. Thump. The sound of stout leather boots meeting shovels, steel shovels wresting their way into the unyielding mound of earth, and the gelid earth hitting the coffin rang loud as a bell in Rachel Wilder's ears, making her cringe. So this was how life ended, she thought sadly. It just didn't seem right, somehow. Poor India had deserved better.

Thwack. Scrape. Thump. As the solid clumps continued relentlessly to strike the humble casket, which, due to the season, was unadorned by so much as even a single flower, Rachel could no longer hold back her tears. They spilled from her eyes to freeze upon her cheeks, and a lump so big that she thought that it would choke her rose in her throat. She swallowed hard, forcing the knot down, trembling so with grief and rage that her grandfather, Fremont Haggerty, who stood at her side, put one arm about her to brace her, his hand patting her shoulder awkwardly in a kindly attempt at solace.

But his granddaughter refused to be consoled, and Fremont sighed heavily, shaking his head with worry as he watched her stubborn chin come up high and her teary eyes, narrowed against the wind and snow, fasten frostily, accusingly, on Jonathan Beecham's teetering, black-clothed form.

India Beecham had been Rachel's closest and just about only friend, and Fremont knew that his granddaughter blamed Jonathan sorely for her death. And—damn the man!—he *was* to blame. If he hadn't been off drinking and whoring in Delano, Wichita's red-lamp district, while his wife had been home, giving birth to their baby, with only their children— and the oldest, Eve, not yet fourteen—there to help her, India might still be alive. Instead, she was dead, and her sorry husband had dared to show up at her funeral, stinking of whiskey and reeling so, that Fremont thought that it was a wonder the man didn't topple into his wife's grave—or that, spurred by her anger and disgust, Rachel didn't shove him into it!

As Fremont glanced again at his granddaughter, he felt certain that had the notion occurred to her, she would surely have lost no time in acting upon it. If Rachel's look could kill, the diggers would be burying Jonathan right alongside India today. Fremont had seen that expression on his grand-daughter's face before, and he knew what it portended. He had no doubt the worthless Jonathan would feel the brunt of Rachel's tart tongue before the day was out—and it would serve him right if he did. Fremont certainly had no intention of trying to save Beecham's hide. A man ought to be able to hold his liquor, or he ought not drink—and that was a fact, pure and simple. Jonathan's continual whining about the War between the States and how it was to blame for all his inadequacies, particularly where strong spirits were con-cerned, was just out-and-out bunkum. Fremont had fought in the Mexican War back in '46, had even lost a leg in the campaign—and *he* wasn't a drunk. Beecham was weak, just downright weak. Why India, a fine, hardworking, and up-standing woman, had ever married the man, Fremont never had been able to figure.

Rachel knew, he guessed. But as, unlike most females, she was not one to chatter about another's confidences, he remained in ignorance of India's motives for wedding her husband. No matter. Whatever they'd been, she'd been too good for him. The entire countryside had known it. It sure was a pity, Fremont reflected, her up and dying the way she had, as though she had given her every last ounce of strength to her baby. For all that, the poor little mite didn't look any too healthy. In fact, it was just plumb puny, he decided, *tsk*ing, as he gazed at the infant cradled in Rachel's arms. It would be lucky to outlive its mother for very long, he reck-oned, and he secretly hoped his granddaughter would not become too attached to it.

As though sensing her grandfather's dismal thoughts,

Rachel hugged India's newborn closer to her breast, protecting it as best she could from the inclement weather. Despite being swaddled in several blankets and having her cloak wrapped about it, the baby, Tobias, continued to bawl as he had ever since the beginning of the funeral service. Now, as Rachel jiggled the infant and patted its back soothingly, her eyes snapped at the idea of the motherless tyke and his seven brothers and sisters being left to the mercy of Jonathan Beecham.

Although the man had fathered eight surviving children, he didn't know the first thing about them, and if young Eve hadn't had sense enough three days ago to send for Rachel, Tobias would have starved—or, more likely, choked—to death by now; for Rachel had arrived at the Beechams' soddy just in time to prevent the inebriated Jonathan from forcing a spoonful of cold, lumpy oatmeal down the throat of the hungrily howling newborn.

She burned anew with wrath at the recollection and pondered seriously whether the marshal of Wichita, the nearest town of any size, would actually hang her were she to take her shotgun and blow a hole through Jonathan. In the end, she reluctantly concluded that, regardless of the fact that she was a woman and Jonathan an unfit father, Marshal Mike Meagher would assuredly do his duty in the face of murder. Sorry that it should be so, Rachel then hoped uncharitably that Jonathan would, in an alcoholic stupor, fall down the stairs of some saloon and break his neck, so his beleaguered youngsters would no longer be subject to his authority. Then she reproached herself thoroughly for the wicked thought. Not only was it sinful (and Rachel was fashioned of good moral fiber, even if it was peculiarly her own), but over the years, she had observed that dreadful things most often befell those who wished them on others. Having a superstitious nature, she hastily spoke a silent prayer to God, telling Him she didn't *really* want Jonathan to come to any harm. Besides, she considered the possibility anxiously, if something were to happen to him now, what would become of the Beecham children?

Surely, Rachel thought, because of her close friendship with India, the youngsters would be placed in her care, as she believed that India would have wanted. Rachel knew that Jonathan had no living relatives and that India herself had had only a younger half brother. But from what India had told her, Rachel had concluded he was the family black sheep.

India's father had not been able to bend her half brother to his iron will, as he had her, and so, eventually, he had cast the son out of the house and cut him off without a cent for his ne'er-do-well ways. The son, however, had remained unchastened and unrepentant, and had continued his errant life. Thoroughly enraged at being thwarted, India's stern, unforgiving father had then struck the son's name from the family Bible, proclaimed him dead, and forbidden India ever to have any contact with him again. Although she had disobeyed her father's order, she had not seen her half brother in many long years; for shortly after her father had repudiated him, the son had joined the Confederate Army and left New Orleans. He had not returned until the end of the war. Later, word had reached India, by then in Kansas, that her half brother had been forced to flee from New Orleans to Texas, his flight precipitated by a scandalous duel. She had heard from him only sporadically ever since.

Because of this, Rachel was able to comfort herself with the notion that, if by some chance something *did* occur to Jonathan, India's half brother would not be located or, if he were, would be totally uninterested in claiming his half sister's children and thus would be only too happy to surrender them to Rachel's custody. After all, despite India's love for him (which had no doubt colored her romantic perception of him substantially, Rachel suspected), what else could one expect of a man who—in the face of his father's most stringent objections—had idled his youthful days away in saloons, brothels, and on Mississippi riverboats, drinking, whoring, and gambling for most of the war? A man who, following the South's ignominious surrender, had returned home to continue his wayward life, and who, as a result, had actually wound up shooting and killing another man over an octoroon courtesan in a French Quarter bordello? Doubtless, the scapegrace had already come to an evil end.

No, if something happened to Jonathan, she need not worry about India's half brother showing up to take charge of the Beecham youngsters. A man such as that could not possibly be capable of feeling any affection or obligation toward eight nieces and nephews he had never even laid eyes on. And if by some remote chance he did, well, Rachel would set him straight in a hurry, just as, for India's children's sake, she intended to straighten out Jonathan as soon as she could— even if she had to hog-tie the drunken bum and smash every last one of his whiskey bottles to do it!

Chapter Four

Men came to the confluence of the Big and the Little Arkansas rivers, and there, at the very heart of the heartland, that empty, endless prairie known as the Great Plains, they built a town.

That this was not their original intent did not prevent them from eagerly and astutely seizing the opportunity that knocked when, within the next few years, with the arrival of the pioneers, the temporary trading posts the men had erected evolved into a permanent settlement. For they were hard and shrewd, these trappers, traders, and entrepreneurs who first braved the Kansas frontier—farseeing enough to envision the future, enterprising enough to grasp a dream and make it a reality.

In their enthusiasm to make their mark upon history, to shape a small portion of destiny, and to leave to posterity a town where naught but prairie had once been, these founding fathers displaced from the land the very Wichita Indians with whom they had first trapped and traded, smoked calumets, and been friends. This dispossession, the men tried to carry out as honestly and humanely as possible, let it be said, with treaties and little bloodshed (though so many of the bewildered natives died of the pioneers' diseases, and of winterkill and famine, during their removal from the land that a stream along the Chisholm Trail was christened Skeleton Creek, after the bleached bones of the Indian corpses that strewed its banks). Ironically, the founding fathers also took from the Indians, the name for the town they conceived—Wichita, meaning "Scattered Lodges."

From its incorporation in 1870, it was a brash, upstart place, viewed askance by its older, more established rivals, such as nearby Park City. With this neighbor some fourteen miles to the northwest, the town vied vigorously for the Texas cattle trade—herds en route to northern slaughterhouses and needing a stopover midway through their journey. The founding fathers even went so far as to bribe leading drovers to steer their herds through Wichita rather than Park City, and paid the drovers fifteen dollars apiece for any cattle lost as a result of choosing the Wichita route over that of its competitor.

Nor was the town without internal strife. William "Dutch Bill" Greiffenstein's "Douglas Avenue" faction fought furiously with Darius Munger's bloc of "North Enders" over almost everything—from the plotting of Wichita, to the location of bridges across the Big Arkansas River, to street names—each clique determined that it should have the last word on all that counted. But it was this very type of heated confrontation that spurred the town's rapid expansion, as Wichita's businessmen strove mightily to surpass one another. Primitive in appearance, the town might be, with crude buildings, rough boardwalks, and dirt (often mud) streets. But lack amenities, it did not.

Soon, it boasted upward of 175 buildings, including three churches, two drugstores, six carpenter shops, two restaurants, three hotels, two billiard saloons, and four real estate offices, as well as a clothing store (the New York Store), and two stagecoach lines (the Southern Kansas, and the Kansas Stage Company). In addition, it planted numerous trees and shrubs, constructed an extensive stockyards, and organized its own railroad (the Wichita & Southwestern). It lured, from Burlingame, Kansas, editor Marshall Murdock to start publication of a daily newspaper, the *Wichita Eagle*, which presently faced an adversary in the form of the weekly *Wichita Beacon*.

The town had its share of doctors, lawyers, and teachers, too, although none of these enjoyed the same respect and status as that of Wichita's thriving businessmen. No doubt, this was understandable, however, since many of the physicians did not have medical degrees and were, in fact, quacks; attorneys were known to argue so fiercely during trials as to engage in fisticuffs in the courtroom; and schoolteachers too often had less book learning than their students.

Chaos was not tolerated for long, however. Ordinances aimed at instituting law and order were expeditiously enacted. Drunkenness, disorderly conduct or shooting a gun within the town's limits, and rudely assaulting someone brought ten-, twenty-five-, and fifty-dollar fines, respectively. The sale of liquor on Sundays was strictly prohibited, so wetting one's whistle on the Sabbath required a coyote's cunning.

But even Wichita, for all its foresight and good intentions, could not avoid every pitfall. For with progress comes not only benefits, but drawbacks, also; and Wichita was no exception to the rule. In many respects, the town grew according to well-laid plans—and in others, not at all as its founding fathers had envisaged.

Along the west bank of the Big Arkansas River stood the primary blot upon the burgeoning plat of the otherwise relatively decent and law-abiding town—the inevitable red-lamp district. It was this unsavory suburb that gave Wichita its—however undeserved—swiftly earned and widespread reputation of being a wild, lawless cow town, where all hell broke loose every hour upon the hour and fatal gunfights were an everyday occurrence. Sometimes referred to as "West Wichita," but more often called "Delano," this sector of violence and vice was the target of scathing criticism by every publicly high-principled politician (regardless of his private and frequent sampling of its wholly corrupt wares), and the object of outraged condemnation by every righteous, God-fearing female in town.

It was to this latter group that Rachel Wilder firmly belonged. So it was with a great deal of indignation and mortification that, mounted upon her mare, Sunflower, she sat fetlock deep in one of Delano's wide and presently miry streets, just out front of the Silver Slipper. She was so cold that her teeth chattered, for she was soaked to the bone from the wintry rain that showered upon her; and her voice was hoarse from hollering in a most unladylike fashion for Jonathan Beecham to come outside at once.

She knew he could hear her, for occasionally, he staggered to one of the upstairs windows of the saloon, flung it open wide, stuck out his head, and called drunkenly for her to go away. He was currently making his third such appearance.

"G'wan. G'wan, Missh High-'n'-Mighty Wilder, scat!" he yelled down at her, waving a half-empty whiskey bottle threateningly, as though he might hurl it at her. "G'wan home—hic—'n' lemme alone, why don'tcha? Damned—hic—fool, interferin' bitch! Who in the hell—hic—appointed you my keeper anyway? You aren't my wife!" He took a long, thirsty swig from the whiskey bottle. Then he wiped his drooling mouth off against his shoulder sleeve. "In fact, you aren't anybody's wife, you dried-up old prune! You hear me, you friggin' goody-goody? You got no right tellin' me what to do. So you jush g'wan now. Shoo! You're—hic—spoilin' all my fun with purty li'l—hic—Emmalou here"—he yanked into his arms the harlot he'd hired last evening, and started brazenly to kiss and fondle her—"'n' she's not takin' it a-tall kindly, are you, honey?" He leered at the strumpet knowingly, a sly, stupid grin on his face at the thought of his sexual prowess and how she would scream and moan and gasp with pleasure when he took her again (his $7.50 would get him his money's worth). Then, after a moment, he remembered Rachel, and frowning, he turned back to the window and bellowed down at her, "You hear me, Missh Prim-'n'-Proper Wilder? Get on down the road, like I—hic—told you! G'wan home to your cold, empty bed! Delano's got no ushe for hoity-toity prudes—'spesh'ly ones crazy as a heifer after chompin' locoweed—hic!"

Hot tears of hurt and humiliation stung Rachel's eyes at these insults, for they hit too close to home for comfort. She knew that, at eighteen, she was considered by many as headed for a permanent place on the proverbial spinsters' shelf, and, too, that there were those who muttered that she was "touched in the head." But knowing that she *was* unmarried, and likely to remain so, and that the other rumors whispered about her were wicked and untrue (and started mainly by Beecham himself, besides), didn't make the gossip any less painful.

Following his ungentlemanly tirade, Jonathan sniggered loudly, upturned the whiskey bottle to slurp some more of its contents, then lecherously buried his face between Emmalou's ample, near-naked breasts. She grabbed him and began to perform a lascivious act upon him, and with a smug smile curving her scarlet, bee-stung lips, she stared pointedly at Rachel to be certain the young woman was properly shocked. Then, with a howl of glee, the prostitute dragged Jonathan away from the window, reappearing briefly to make obscene gestures and scurrilous remarks at Rachel and to slam the window shut with a deafening bang. Unfortunately, however, one of its four square panes was broken; and some minutes later, through the jagged hole, raucous shrieks and boisterous groans of unmistakable delight reached Rachel's ears, causing her to blush crimson with embarrassment.

Had it not been for the thought of the poor, motherless Beecham children—left alone to fend for themselves as best they could at their run-down soddy—she would have turned her horse about and galloped home as fast as she could. But Rachel's resolve was strengthened by the heartbreaking memory of the youngsters' scared, sorrowful faces this morning, when she had ridden over to check on them and found they had spent the night alone, terrified by shapes and shadows that, come dark, had metamorphosed into Indians, coyotes, rattlesnakes, and other bogeys dreaded by all prairie children. Swallowing hard, she choked down her pride. She had never been one to accept defeat, and no matter how difficult it was proving, she somehow *would* make Jonathan Beecham honor his obligations! It was the least she could do for poor India's offspring.

At the thought of her dead friend, Rachel's stubborn chin came up high, and she squared her shoulders decisively, ignoring the passersby who gawked at her lewdly on the sordid street. She knew there were more than a few reprobates who, figuring any woman in Delano, even a lady, was fair game, would lay rough hands on her, and even rape her, given the opportunity. So she never, even for an instant, dismounted or relaxed her hold on the shotgun she gripped purposefully. Now, her fingers, numb despite her gloves, tightened convulsively on the stock and barrel.

"Jonathan Beecham!" she shouted again fiercely, trembling with fury and affront. "Jonathan Beecham! You sniveling scoundrel! Come outside at once! It's shameful, that's what, your carrying on like this—with poor India not yet a month in her grave, and your having eight grieving children at home, besides! Jonathan Beecham! Do you hear me?" There was no answer, and Rachel swore softly to herself. "Tarnation!" Then, raising her voice once more, she warned, "Jonathan, I swear that if you don't walk through those saloon doors within the next few minutes, I'll make you sorry you didn't, you contemptible varmint!"

The only reply to this was Emmalou's bawdy laughter and the vigorous (and therefore clearly audible) squeak of rusty bedsprings. Rachel flushed red again to the roots of her hair, and her lips clamped together in a thin, grim line. Then, a martial glint in her eye, she turned to the protectively watchful Negro mounted on an old mule beside her.

"Poke," she directed, clipping her words in her anger, "you get down from there and go inside that saloon and fetch Mr. Beecham."

Slowly straightening up in his saddle and gazing at her

mutinously from beneath the wide brim of his battered brown felt hat dripping with rain, the big hired hand shook his head.

"Lawd a-mercy, Miz Rachel," he groused, "Ah jes' knowed yo wuz gwine ter say dat! Has yo fergot' whut hap'ned de last time Ah went in der ter git dat man? Why, Ah wuz purt nigh kilt, Miz Rachel—an' yo knows it! Dey'um doan much cotton ter colored puhsons heah in Delano, an' Ah ain' 'bout ter have mah hide nailed ter no barn door on 'count o' dat shif'less Mistah Beecham! Naw'um, Ah sho'ly ain'—an' dat's mah final wud on de subjec'!" The Negro nodded his head tersely, then calmly hunched over his mule once more, paying no heed to Rachel's scowl.

"Poke," she said crossly, "I just don't know why I put up with you."

"'Cuz Ah'm jes' 'bout de onliest puhson in de whole o' Kansas—outside o' yore gran'daddy, o' course—whut ain' afeard o' yore sharp tongue, Miz Rachel," he replied matter-of-factly, unruffled.

"Sharp tongue?" she exclaimed. "Poke, hobble your lip! Just because I'm honest and dare to speak my mind, as everyone should— Why, if more people would do so instead of shilly-shallying around or lying outright, the world wouldn't be in such a sorry state!"

"Mebbe so, Miz Rachel," Poke agreed, "but nobuddy lahkes hearin' de truf 'bout hisseff—an' dat's a fac'! Hon'sty's got ter be measured out in small doses, an' den only ter dem whut woan tek offense. Ah knows dat yo mean well an' dat yo allus tries ter do de right thin', Miz Rachel, 'cuz deep down inside, yo is de kindheartedest puhson Ah eber did see. But in de eyes o' de world, yo gots a heap mo' gumption dan yo ought ter, an' dat's sumpin' dem whut lacks it jes' cain' fergive—'spesh'ly in a woman. Dat's why dey'um all thinks yo is a scold, Miz Rachel, pure an' simple; an' der ain' nothin' Ah kin do 'bout dat!"

"Hmph!" Rachel sniffed to show what she thought of this, but she could see that the Negro was unmoved and that he still did not intend to lend her a hand. She sighed, then spoke again. "Well, Poke, since you won't help me, it seems I have no other choice but to deal with Mr. Beecham myself!''

A bitter wind flogged the slushy plains, and from the bloated grey clouds rolling across the heavens, rain spattered steadily. Now and then, on the faraway horizon, a crooked fork of lightning stabbed the earth, and thunder rumbled an ominous warning. Fitfully illuminated, a horseman—a drifter—paused upon the snowy crest of a prairie hillock, a solitary silhouette against the sky. Beneath the wide, flat brim of his sombrero, his eyes narrowed as he gazed off into the distance at the roiling firmament. It was fixing to storm.

Absentmindedly chewing the tip of the cigarillo he was smoking, the man pulled the upturned collar of his travel-stained duster more closely about him, shivering slightly in the wind and wet. It had been a long, hard ride; and he would be glad of a shave, a bath, a hot meal, and a warm bed. Clucking to his horse, he set his spurs lightly to the animal's sides. If he hurried, he could make Wichita before twilight —and the storm—fell.

Presently, to his relief, for he was half beginning to think he had lost his way on the bleak, barren plains, the drifter spied the town rising darkly before him, like a lone ship on a vast sea. It was a welcome sight. He galloped toward it, slowing only when he had reached its outskirts. Coolly ignoring the prominent sign that strictly prohibited the carrying of firearms within the city limits, he partially unbuttoned his duster and folded its edges back so his revolvers would be readily available if needed.

As it always did when he approached some semblance of civilization, tension coiled tight as a spring within the man. His demeanor was wary. His eyes were watchful as he surveyed his dismal surroundings, taking in the number of squalid bars and brothels that lined the street, the sleazy miscreants and hussies who loitered on the boardwalk, despite the inclement weather. His upper lip curled in a sneer. So this was the infamous West Wichita . . . Delano. Well, it was no worse than many other places he had been—and better than some. Aware of the curious, surreptitious glances directed at him, the drifter trotted on down the road, his silver bridle and spurs jingling.

Instinctively, the town's residents gave him a wide berth, for they knew, without asking, what he was. Only three kinds of men wore two guns in the West: greenhorns, fools, and, more rarely, professionals. And this man—hard- and hungry-looking, lean of build, taut of muscle—was neither a greenhorn nor a fool. They had seen his ilk before, and even the worst of them wanted no truck with his dangerous, predatory breed: gunslingers, bounty hunters, men who walked both sides of the law. Those of the town's inhabitants who had criminal pasts carefully averted their faces as the drifter passed, each hoping it was not for him the man had come. None knew that it was not bounty hunting that had brought him to Wichita.

Observing those who hid their faces from him, the drifter lifted one corner of his mouth in a half smile. He might do some business here, after all, he thought. Then, recalling the reason for his being in Wichita, his amusement vanished. His gloved hands tightened on his reins, the only visible sign of his inner turmoil and wrath.

It was at that moment that he became aware of a disturbance ahead. Instantly, he pulled his horse to a walk, alert and poised for possible trouble. But his caution was unnecessary. As he proceeded down the street, he was able to see that the cause of all the ruckus was nothing more than an inordinately riled-up woman—somebody's wife or mistress, he was willing to wager. He would have won his bet, too, he decided; for she was mounted on a dainty brown mare and wielding a shotgun—as though she had ridden into town, hell-bent on collecting her man—and proprietarily screeching like an overwrought virago at some miserable drunk and a painted-up tart hanging out of an upper-story window of a saloon.

The drifter shook his head with disgust at the display. Thank God, he had never been so harebrained as to get himself hitched to any female. Oh, they were fine, mighty fine, on a long, lonely night, when a man was hungry for something soft and warm. But in the morning, it was time to move on—before they tied you up in knots so tight that you could never get loose. Yes, easy come, easy go . . . that was his motto. For only look what happened once one got her hooks into you: You couldn't even enjoy a drink—or anything else, for that matter—in peace!

Women! he snorted to himself. *Jesus!*

Changelings, they ought to call them, for once they got a wedding ring on their finger, they sure as hell changed! Even the shiest and sweetest of them turned overnight into the most unpleasant of termagants. If they weren't nagging you about drinking, it was smoking or gambling or whoring. He'd seen enough in his time to know that. And pity the imprudent husband who ignored his wife, for he would be made to pay, as this unfortunate fellow was obviously discovering.

Poor, dumb bastard, the drifter thought scornfully. *It's plain he's got no grit. If that high-strung filly were mine, I'd soon teach her some manners!*

He would have ridden on, but the unruly shrew's next words caused him to haul up short, his eyes riveted to her slender, incensed figure.

"I warned you, Jonathan Beecham!" she yelled. "I warned you repeatedly, fair and square—so don't say I didn't!"

Then, before even the quick-witted drifter grasped what she intended, Rachel Wilder pointed at the saloon window her 1869 Parker 12-gauge, breech-loading, "Damascus" double-barreled shotgun, cocked the hammers, and pulled the triggers.

Luckily for Jonathan, the harlot, Emmalou, had a strong sense of self-preservation, and she snatched him to the floor along with her just before the window and a goodly portion of its upper frame exploded into a million pieces, spraying glass and wood all over the room's interior and the road below. The shotgun's blast was horrendous, as was its kickback, but Rachel and her horse, Sunflower, were long accustomed to both. While Rachel steadied herself in the saddle and studied the effects of her aim (which, shortly, she would come deeply to regret), her placid mount did nothing more than toss its head and sidestep a little.

Lamentably, Poke's recalcitrant mule, Cider, was not so undisturbed. At the screams of several females and in the ensuing commotion, the mule began to kick and buck madly, nearly throwing the hired hand (who now clutched his saddle horn for all he was worth) and landing a solid, cutting blow to Sunflower's round rump.

In the face of this abuse, the mare lost its docility. Shocked and scared by the painful wallop, the horse whinnied shrilly, reared once, then, without warning, bolted. Caught off guard by her normally biddable mount's sudden, unexpected behavior, Rachel was slow to react. She scarcely had time to jam her shotgun into its leather scabbard fastened under the cinch of her single-rigged saddle, and then to duck to avoid hitting the Silver Slipper's overhanging roof, before Sunflower clattered wildly onto the boardwalk. The momentum of the mare was such that Rachel could not check its rash, headlong flight. Nor was there any space to maneuver in the confined area between the saloon and the hitching rails. Her heart now racing like a locomotive in her breast, Rachel could only flatten herself against the horse's neck as, unable to halt or turn aside, Sunflower crashed through the long, narrow, closed doors of the Silver Slipper, ripping one portal from its hinges and demolishing the other.

Had all her concentration not been focused on gaining control of the mare, Rachel would have laughed at the spectacle the bar's patrons presented as, dumbfounded at the sight of her, they hurriedly leaped to their feet, knocking over tables and chairs in their haste to escape to safety. But now, white-eyed and terrified, the horse had taken the bit between its teeth and was unmanageable. It was all Rachel could do to stay seated in the saddle. Her mind went blank, and sheer instinct for survival took over.

Like a deranged jackrabbit, Sunflower bounded around the saloon, hooves lashing out frenziedly, smashing furniture and denting tarnished brass spittoons, sending the cuspidors and their nasty contents flying. Rachel's stomach heaved from the jolting up-and-down motion and the stench of old chewing tobacco. Her head swam as the barroom spun around and around, and the floor surged up at her, then fell away, over and over, like some carnival ride gone hideously amok. Her bedraggled hat went sailing through the air. Some of her hairpins came loose, and strands of her long blond hair tumbled from the knot upon the top of her head, blinding her. At last, she lost her grip on the reins. Despite the cold wind and rain swirling in through the Silver Slipper's now wide-open entrance, sweat beaded her brow. Gritting her teeth, she grabbed the saddle horn and hung on for dear life.

To her utter mortification, several of the saloon's rowdy customers, who, having securely ensconced themselves on the scruffy bar that stood alongside one wall, the creaky steps that led upstairs, and the rickety balcony that looked down on the barroom, were now enjoying the impromptu entertainment, laughing uproariously and enthusiastically whooping their encouragement.

"Ride 'em, girlie!" they cheered drunkenly, and recklessly fired their pistols at the ceiling, increasing Sunflower's panic. "Bust that bronc! Yee-haw!"

Soon, the air eddied so with clouds of dust from the falling plaster and the floor's sawdust being churned up by the mare that, with Sunflower's every savage kick and buck, Rachel coughed and choked and gasped desperately for breath. By now, the horse had worked its way in a circle back to the front of the Silver Slipper, where, on either side of the doors, a single large window overlooked the street. To Rachel's horror, she recognized that Sunflower was about to plunge straight through one of the panes. Helpless to avert this fresh disaster, she buried her face in the mare's long, silky mane and, as she felt the horse's muscles bunch and quiver preparatorily beneath her, closed her eyes tight—and prayed. The next thing the young woman knew, the huge sheet of glass was riving and tinkling all around her as they hurtled through the window.

With a thud and a crunching of glass, Sunflower hit the

boardwalk, in the process bumping violently one of the square wooden posts that supported the overhanging roof of the Silver Slipper. The unstable pillar gave way at the powerful impact, snapping clean in two as its base skidded off the boardwalk. Then that portion of the roof previously upheld by the column collapsed with a shudder, just as, hooves flailing, the mare plummeted onto the road, slipping and sliding in the mud.

For a horrible moment, Rachel thought they were surely going to ram into an empty freight wagon parked across the street. But just in time to prevent the imminent collision, a strong, capable hand reached out, caught hold of Sunflower's bridle, and brutally jerked the horse to a standstill.

"Whoa," a low, masculine voice growled. "Whoa, there. Easy. Easy now."

At the authoritative command, the still-skittish mare pranced a little, then, finally, as though recognizing a master, obediently calmed itself, nostrils blowing, sides heaving. Rachel felt the horse come to a stop beneath her and realized that the nightmare had ended and that, astonishingly, she was still somehow in the saddle. It scarcely seemed possible.

Ashen, shaking all over now from the aftermath of her fearsome ride, her breath coming in quick, hard rasps, she slowly glanced up at her unknown rescuer.

So startled was she at the sight of him that her words of thanks died on her lips and she could do naught but stare at him. He was so handsome that in her dazed mind, Rachel thought irrationally that he was not real, but a ghost rider, one of those demonic apparitions the superstitious swore they sometimes glimpsed on a wild or misty prairie night. Upon her golden lashes, drizzle clung, so it was as though she viewed the man through a dark prism or a shadowy vignette as, mesmerized, her eyes swept the length of him.

Long and lithe as a panther, he was, and black and silver as a night sky lighted by the stars. Upon his head, he wore a black sombrero, its wide, flat brim pulled down low, obscuring his rugged, swarthy face. Thick and blue-black as his stallion's winter coat was the long, shaggy hair that curled at his nape. Beneath satanic black brows and hooded lids spiked with dense black lashes, his midnight-blue eyes glittered like those of some rapacious night creature. In their depths was a touch of mockery, and a hint of menace, too, Rachel thought with an unwitting shiver. His Roman nose was finely chiseled, set above a heavy black mustache and a sensual, dissolute mouth. Between his even white teeth, he clenched a thin black cigar. From its glowing tip, a wisp of smoke trailed away, specterlike, into the wind and rain. His cheekbones were well defined, the cheeks themselves spare, almost hawkish. The thrust of his stubbly jaw was proud, arrogant, as though he were accustomed to demanding, and getting, what he wanted.

Around his neck was wound a warm black wool muffler. His long black duster was buttoned up from his firm, flat belly to his throat and fitted his massive shoulders and broad chest snugly. At his waist was a black leather belt adorned by an engraved silver buckle and a knife sheath from which a silver blade gleamed barbarously. Slung low at his narrow hips was a black leather gun belt with two holsters, each of which sported a deadly, solid-frame, rod-ejecting Peacemaker revolver, its ivory stock ornately carved with the rearing horse with arrows that was Samuel Colt's trademark, its silver plating elaborately tooled. His tight black breeches hugged corded thighs and calves. Black leather boots, with shining silver spurs, encased his feet.

With fluid grace, he sat his stallion, obviously at home in a saddle, skilled upon a horse. His posture was vigilant but bold. This was a man who would not back away from danger, but was confident of himself and his ability to meet life head-on, regardless of what it held in store.

From his dress and his manner, Rachel recognized that her unknown rescuer was a professional, a gunslinger, a bounty hunter, the epitome of everything she had ever loathed and feared in a man: cool, sardonic, brutish, and animalistic. Sure of himself and his superiority, he was the kind of man who would take, without asking, what he desired, who would let no one and nothing stand in his way.

At the thought, gooseflesh pricked her skin as some strange, wild, indefinable emotion she had never before felt tingled without warning down her spine, frightening her, exciting her, bewildering her. She felt suddenly hot as a metal washtub in the summer sun. Her mouth tasted dry as an old buffalo bone. Her heart beat like the wings of a hummingbird. Abruptly, she became aware of how rudely she was staring at the man, of what a terrible mess she must appear after her ordeal, and of the devastating results of the awful scene he perhaps had witnessed in its entirety before coming to her assistance. Scarlet stained her cheeks. What a common, vulgar hoyden, he must think her, she thought with dismay, though she could not have said why his opinion of her mattered, for he was nothing to her, nor she to him.

Worst of all, however, was that, as the drifter glanced at the shambles of the Silver Slipper, and then back at her, one corner of his mouth began to twitch with humor; and to Rachel's everlasting shame, he drawled insolently, "Honey, if that's your idea of how to while away a rainy afternoon, I'd sure as hell hate to be your escort on a fine Saturday night!"

That was the crowning blow. She wanted to die of embarrassment right then and there. But Rachel had that backbone of steel that is inbred rather than acquired, and even now, it did not fail her. Proudly, she stiffened her spine and, determinedly, marshaled her wits. How dare this unkempt rogue presume to laugh at her, mock her, address her in such familiar terms, as though she were a loose woman? He was no gentleman; that much was certain. Rachel stoutly believed there was a place for everything—and this man definitely needed putting in his!

"Well, sir," she rejoined haughtily, "since I find such a prospect unlikely in the extreme, you need have no worry. I do, however, thank you for your swift intervention on this particular occasion. Now, if you will be so good as to release my mare, I'll trouble you no further. I have no doubt that, however questionable his character, Verne Lundy, the proprietor of the Silver Slipper, will—at least in this instance

—waste no time in summoning Marshal Meagher; and as I have no wish to be clapped in the calaboose, I must be on my way."

Despite her intention to rebuke him firmly, she was talking too fast, and rambling, Rachel knew. But she could not seem to help herself. Damn the man! Why did he have to have the darkest blue eyes she had ever seen? Like deep pools beneath a summer sky, they were. And the way he was looking at her! Why, it was as though—as though he were stripping her stark naked! It really was most insulting, and distinctly unnerving, besides!

The drifter, for his part, was thinking what a plain, unpalatable woman she was—too uppity by half, and with no good reason to be. Stiff as buckram, she sat upon her mare, making every effort to act the offended lady and put him smartly in his place, despite her looking the worse for wear, and regardless of the fact that the calamitous outcome of her earlier indecorous behavior was staring him in the face, proof of her wanton nature. Why, she was actually blushing as though he had made some improper advance toward her— the deceitful jade! Her high color made her freckles stand out most unbecomingly on her cheekbones, he decided, and caused her green eyes—really her only attractive feature, he mused derisively—to seem even greener. They, and her heart-shaped face, made her resemble an alley cat, which, despite her airs and graces, was without a doubt exactly what she was—the impertinent baggage! he reflected uncharitably. Remembering the words she had shouted at the inebriated dolt at the window just before firing upon him, the drifter's fingers itched to skin her alive.

"If you don't mind my saying so, aren't you forgetting something . . . ma'am?" he asked, his voice grown oddly hard and jeering now. "What about your . . . er . . . husband?" He indicated what was left of the saloon's upperstory window, where Jonathan Beecham was now standing unsteadily, cursing a blue streak.

"Fortunately," Rachel answered tartly, grimacing with disgust as she glanced up at Jonathan's angry figure and thinking, despite her relief at seeing him in one piece, that it really was too bad he had escaped injury, "that drunken wastrel is *not* my husband. I, sir, am unmarried, and after this episode today, I thank God that I have had the good sense to remain so!"

With that, finding that her rescuer had at last released her bridle, Rachel set her heels to Sunflower's sides and galloped out of town, Poke and the errant and thoroughly unrepentant Cider hard on her muddy tracks.

His midnight-blue eyes narrowed and cold as ice, the drifter watched her until she vanished from view, swallowed by the misty rain. Then, a muscle working tensely in his jaw, he headed purposefully toward what remained of the Silver Slipper.

Chapter Five

In a vain attempt to outrace the oncoming storm, Rachel fled across the prairie, pushing Sunflower hard as she dared and glancing occasionally over her shoulder to be certain Poke and Cider were keeping up. She headed not for home, as Poke had heartily hoped, but toward the Beechams' soddy. For she now recognized that despite all her concerted efforts since India's death, both to bully and to shame Jonathan into shouldering his responsibilities, he had no intention of even remotely reforming so he might care for his children. As it was inconceivable to her that they be left alone any longer to fend for themselves, Rachel saw no other choice but to load them up in the Beechams' wagon and take them home with her.

The strain of trying to work her own farm, and keep an

eye on the Beecham place, too, had already taken its toll on her, she knew, else she would not have lost her temper so badly as to have actually shot at Jonathan and that impudent drab of his. Now that it was all over, Rachel discovered she was so rattled that her hands were still trembling on her reins. She just couldn't imagine what had possessed her to do such a thing!

Worse was her gnawing dread that Verne Lundy would almost certainly send Marshal Meagher after her, and as she had no means at all of paying for the damage she had done, Rachel felt sure she would be put in jail. The notion was absolutely mortifying. Oh, why on earth had she ever taken it upon herself to ride into Delano after Jonathan? The Beecham youngsters weren't hers, after all. She ought to have followed the strictest code of the West and minded her own business!

Then she thought once more of India, poor India, her friend, and Rachel knew in her heart that if she had it all to do again, she would change nothing—nothing, that was, except her unknown rescuer, the wicked man!

Despite his handsome looks, he had had naught to recommend him but as beautiful a matched pair of Colt Peacemakers as she had ever seen. Custom-made, they had been, Rachel knew from their ivory handles and silver plating. The revolver was frequently preferred by professionals over the .44 rimfire Smith & Wesson American; for even though, once its chambers were exhausted, the American could be reloaded much faster, due to its simultaneous ejection of spent cases, the pistol had a European "feel" that those in the West, accustomed to the Colt's perfect balance, eschewed. Besides, a man who carried two guns, and knew how to use them, needn't particularly concern himself with the speed at which he was capable of reloading anyway, especially if he were adept at "border shifting," a technique in which the as-yet-unfired revolver was rapidly passed to the gun hand.

Rachel herself relied on her trusty old shotgun, which required no great skill to aim and was lethal at close quarters. More than once, it had come in handy at driving trespassers—especially a certain persistent, though most unwelcome, Rye Crippen—off her land. She also had an 1873 "Trapdoor" Springfield .45–70-caliber, single-shot rifle. But she used it only for killing game too large for the shotgun to bag.

By the time Rachel reached the Beechams' soddy, twilight was falling, and the heavens had at last split open wide to disgorge their contents. Rain was pouring, like tea through a sieve, through the roof of the barn, where she and Poke tethered their mounts alongside Jonathan's team of draft horses and single milch cow. The yard was like a swamp as, skirting the worst of the puddles, she and the Negro dashed across it toward the house. Hollering above the rain, her coat flapping wildly in the wind, Rachel pounded hard on the door.

"It's Rachel, Eve," she shouted, "and Poke. Open up, honey, and let us in!"

After what seemed an interminable wait, the latch was finally lifted and the door hesitantly cracked. Holding a kerosene lantern high, her eyes huge and anxious, Eve Beecham slowly peeked out into the darkness. Her eleven-year-old brother, Gideon, stood just behind her, an old Sharps carbine, now modified to accept metallic cartridges, held at the ready. Upon seeing that it really was Rachel and Poke who stood outside, the children exhaled audibly with relief and stepped aside to let the two welcome visitors in.

"Oh, Aunt Rachel, we're so glad you've come!" Eve cried, addressing Rachel by the honorary title the Beecham children had fondly bestowed upon her. Eve flung her arms around Rachel's neck and hugged her close for a moment. Then, at last, she stepped back and inquired quietly, though without much hope, "I don't suppose Pa is outside in the barn, tending to the stock?"

"No." Rachel shook her head, yearning to wring Jonathan's neck as she saw how the rain streamed through the roof of the soddy, drenching the muslin India had hung under the rafters some years back, in an effort to catch the dirt and grass that crumbled from the ceiling. The thin material was rotten now, hanging in tatters. As a result, snakes and rodents, washed through the roof by the deluge, slithered and scurried across the soaking floor. Rachel wanted to weep for India and her suffering. With effort, she blinked back her tears and went on. "I'm sorry, Eve. Your father's in town . . . on— on business . . . and not likely to make it back tonight. That's why Poke and I have come. We're going to take all of you home with us this evening. So get your things together— quick now! We haven't got time to waste!"

Even as Rachel spoke, she was swiftly and efficiently gathering what she knew that the youngsters, especially the baby, Tobias, would need—extra clothes and socks, nightgowns, diapers, combs, toothbrushes, and so forth—and tossing the things into the large wicker basket India had used for the laundry. Rachel wanted to be gone as soon as possible from the Beecham place, where memories of her dead friend haunted her and thoughts of Jonathan filled her anew with rage.

She knew, from the speaking glances the oldest children —Eve, Gideon, Caleb, Susannah, and even seven-year-old Philip—exchanged, that they had not believed her story of Jonathan's being in town on business, that they suspected that their father was in Delano, drinking and whoring instead. Still, they uttered not one word of censure or complaint as they began to bundle up their meager belongings.

Secretly, the youngsters were relieved their father wasn't coming home. They hoped he would never come home. They were scared to death of him. He was violent when he drank. He screamed at them and beat them, often for no apparent reason. They felt that, somehow, they were to blame for all his many problems, and they thought he would be happier and better off without them—just as, painful as it was for them to admit, they would be happier and better off without him. Sometimes, life just worked out like that, no matter how much you loved someone, or so their mother had told them.

While Rachel and the children finished packing and carefully extinguished the scant rushlights and the buffalo-chip fire in the hearth, Poke ran back to the barn to hitch Jonathan's team to the Beechams' wagon. The hired hand tied his mule, Rachel's mare, and the milch cow to the tailgate. Then he scrounged around in the barn until he found an old piece of canvas, which he threw in the wagon box. It would help protect the children from the rain.

He watched out the barn door for Rachel's signal, and once she appeared, lantern in hand, he climbed onto the wagon seat and drove up to the house. With Rachel holding the baby and Gideon toting the wicker basket, she and the youngsters piled in the wagon box and pulled the canvas over them. As soon as everyone was settled as comfortably as was possible, Poke cracked his bullwhip above the heads of the team. With a lurch, the draft horses leaped forward into the storm, foxfire occasionally glowing between their ears from the highly charged atmosphere, an eerie, bluish beacon in the night.

Upstairs inside the Silver Slipper, the drifter stood in the doorway of Emmalou's seedy room, his eyes surveying the yawning cavity blasted into the wall by Rachel's shotgun, the splintered glass and wood that littered the floor, and, more intently, the untidy man who now sprawled in an alcoholic stupor upon the soiled wrought-iron bed. After a moment's disdainful contemplation, the drifter strode to the washstand, poured from the porcelain pitcher into the matching basin a liberal amount of water, then deliberately threw it over the upper portion of the loudly snoring man.

Sputtering with anger and confusion, slinging water in every direction, Jonathan Beecham bolted from the bed, like a startled chicken flapping from a coop.

"What in the hell—" he spat, then broke off abruptly at finding himself suddenly yanked forward rudely by the front of his shirt until he was face-to-face with a decidedly threatening character.

"You Jonathan Beecham?" the drifter asked through gritted teeth, his smoking cigarillo all that separated his dark, stubbly visage from that of the other man.

"Who—who wants to know?" Jonathan stammered, becoming painfully aware, as some semblance of sobriety began to steal over him, that not only was he unarmed, but also minus his trousers—a most hapless state for someone confronted by what was obviously a very irate and professional gunslinger.

"Slade Maverick," the drifter growled. "That name mean anything to you?"

"N-N-No," Jonathan stuttered anxiously, for like most bullies, he was a coward at heart, and he was now thoroughly intimidated by the six feet, two inches of lean, hard muscle that gripped him ferociously. "Should—should it?"

"Yeah," Slade uttered menacingly, his blue eyes narrowing, "because aside from it belonging to one of the best hired guns in the West, it's also the name of your brother-in-law, you frigging bastard!" He gave Jonathan a savage shake that lifted the quavering man clean off the floor. "You don't remember me, do you? Well, maybe that's not so hard to believe at that. After all, I was just a fourteen-year-old kid when you and India got married. But I remember you." Slade paused, his eyes roaming contemptuously over Beecham's cringing, pasty-faced figure. Then he jeered, "Jesus! How my poor sister's put up with the likes of you all these years, I'll never know!"

"You're—you're India's half brother?" Jonathan managed to choke out, now absolutely terrified.

"Yeah, you son of a bitch! And I'm here to see that you answer for anything and everything she's ever suffered at your wretched hands!" Slade snarled, sending a horrible chill down Beecham's spine. Then, swearing, the gunslinger shoved the other man away. "Get dressed!" he ordered curtly. "You and I are going to take a little ride out to your place."

"Now? In this storm?" Jonathan whined, motioning toward the downpour blowing fiercely through the gaping hole in the wall, and wondering frantically how he might elude Slade and get out of town before the gunslinger learned India was dead.

"That's right," Slade replied grimly. "Now, get

moving—lessen you want me to speed you along." His hands dropped meaningfully to the butts of his Peacemakers.

"N-N-No." Jonathan shook his head vigorously, eyeing with horror the ivory-handled revolvers and quickly reaching for his pants.

Overhearing these last remarks as she entered the bedchamber, a broom in her hand and a disgusted frown on her face as she inspected the ruined room, Emmalou spoke sharply.

"He ain't goin' nowhere," she announced, scrutinizing Slade speculatively, her tongue darting out to moisten her crimson mouth. "He owes me seven dollars 'n' fifty cents that he ain't paid yet, 'n' he ain't leavin' till he do!"

Slade's eyes raked the blowsy strumpet insultingly, taking in her face heavily caked with paint, her body beginning to run to fat and crammed into a too-tight corset.

"*He* might not know any better," he sneered, indicating Jonathan, "but *I* do—and I'm willing to wager you're lucky to get three dollars on a good day. Take it or leave it," he stated flatly, peeling some bills from the wad of folded money in his pocket and flinging them at her.

Pouting at the gunslinger's high-handed attitude, as well as at his palpable lack of interest in her, Emmalou grabbed the cash and stuffed it down her bodice, between her heaving breasts.

"Lundy—what owns this dunghill—ain't gonna be so easy ta fob off," she declared, tossing her head and glaring at Slade. "He said that either Beecham here or that snooty Miz Wilder—it didn't make no dif'rence which—was gonna pay fer all the damage, else there was shore as hell gonna be trouble. He's already done sent fer the marshal—'n' I don't reckon ya'll talk so damned uppity ta *him*, mister, lessen he locks ya up in the hoosegow. 'N' ya know what? I hope he does, 'cuz in that case, I think I'll jest drop by 'n' have myself a real good laugh at your expense!"

"You do that," Slade grunted, unimpressed. He turned back to Beecham. "I take it that 'Miz Wilder' is the brazen hellcat who fired at you?"

"Yes," Jonathan responded, glowering at the remembrance of Rachel's deed and feeling slightly braver now that he had got his breeches on. "The meddling bitch! I shall certainly have some choice words for her when next I see her! I'd like to know who in the hell she thinks she is—shooting at me like that! Why, I might have been killed!"

"Yeah, you might at that," Slade remarked, grinning in a way that made Jonathan's skin crawl. Then, the gunslinger continued coldly. "I'd like to know who she thinks she is, too, Beecham—why she thinks you should heed her dictates."

Jonathan licked his lips nervously, but before he could dream up a satisfactorily evasive answer, Emmalou snapped, "She's the highfalutin Miss Priss what's been lookin' after his young 'uns since his wife died, that's who! But that don't give her no call ta tell *him* what ta do, do it? Nor ta treat me like I was dirt beneath her feet 'n' 'tempt ta cheat me of earnin' a livin'—'spesh'ly when all I done were ta try ta help the poor feller git over his mis'ry! Crazy old maid! If I ever see her agin, I'll plug her, that's what! She ain't the only female in town what knows how ta handle a gun!"

Emmalou raved on, but Slade no longer heard her, deafened as he was by the sudden shock and agony that assailed him, cruel and sharp as a knife. India dead? No, it just couldn't be true! Images of a young woman with flying black hair and merry blue eyes rose in his mind, haunting him. She was the only female who had ever loved him. Even his beautiful but distant mother had always been too busy to pay much attention to him, though she had laughed and been kind when she had. Slade recalled little of her but her smile and her perfume, her quick kiss and light step as she'd glided from his room, her mind already on other matters. His mother had never seemed quite real to him, but rather an angel he had worshiped from afar. In his father's majestic mansion along the banks of the Mississippi River—a house so huge that a forlorn little boy could hide in any number of places and not be found, had anybody bothered to look—India alone had truly cared. So many years, he had wasted, a stranger to his half sister, ignorant of her troubles; he would have helped had he only known. So many long, hard miles, he had ridden to make up for lost time. . . . No, it just wasn't possible she was dead.

With a rare show of naked emotion in his eyes, Slade stared at Jonathan's blanched face and knew the worst. In that moment, the blood rushed to his head, a red film hazed his eyes, and he went mad. With a tortured, enraged cry, he leaped for Beecham's throat, knocking him brutally to the floor.

Screeching with fear at the sudden turn of events, Emmalou dropped her broom and raced from the room, while Jonathan, arms flailing, did his best to defend himself. But he was like some small creature trapped between the paws of a cougar —helpless, panicked. His faced reddened, then began to turn blue, and his eyes bulged as Slade's viselike hands tightened around his throat, throttling him and pounding his head so viciously against the floor that those below in the barroom heard the sound. Beecham gurgled and gasped for breath, trying desperately to pry Slade's fingers free, to no avail. Then, finally, just when Jonathan thought he was surely doomed, the gunslinger released him. Like a man drowning, Beecham gulped air. But before he could wholly get his wind, Slade jerked him vehemently to his feet and punched him in the face, blackening one of his eyes.

After that, driven by anguish and wrath, Slade thrashed him mercilessly until Jonathan no longer resembled a man, but rather something trampled by a herd of stampeding cattle. Both his eyes were nearly swollen shut, blood spurted from his broken nose and trickled from his cut lip, and his chest and abdomen were a mass of bruises. At least three of his ribs were fractured. He was drenched with blood and sweat, as well as the rain that gushed in through what had been the window. Now, he swayed on his feet, held upright only by the merest vestige of male pride and the gunslinger's strong, pitiless hands. In some dim corner of his befuddled mind, Jonathan realized he could not take much more.

Then, suddenly, spurred on by Emmalou's shrieks and the thought of further mischief being done to his saloon, Verne

Lundy, the proprietor, was there, with Marshal Mike Meagher in tow. With an expertise born of years of intervening in barroom brawls, the two men deftly seized Slade and dragged him from Beecham's cowering figure just as the gunslinger delivered an especially powerful blow to the other man's jaw. His dazed eyes wide with incredulity and fright, Jonathan stumbled back, lost his balance, and tumbled through the large hole in the wall, somersaulting onto the partially collapsed roof, then sliding down its incline onto the street, where he came to rest facedown in the mud.

"Gawd a'mighty!" Emmalou bawled, scrambling to the orifice and gingerly peering out, "ya've kilt him!"

"Good riddance to bad rubbish," Slade rasped, cradling his right wrist ruefully as the prospect of a noose loomed ominously in his mind.

Briefly, he considered making a break for it. But even had his arms not been pinned so securely to his sides by his brawny captors (who were now in the process of disarming him), the thought of India's children, to say nothing of the disagreeable notion of having his face and description imprinted on the numerous wanted posters distributed throughout every state and territory in the United States, would have prevented Slade from running. Somehow, he must get this mess straightened out before it went much further. After all, it wasn't as though this were the first time he'd ever been arrested; nor, in all likelihood, would it be the last.

With Verne Lundy cursing mightily and dogging his tracks every step of the way, Marshal Meagher now handcuffed Slade and roughly hustled him downstairs to the outside. There, they discovered that the vanquished Jonathan was still alive and, except for his hurts sustained earlier in the fight and a sprained ankle suffered during his two-story fall, basically uninjured.

"It's a wonder he didn't break his fool neck. But then, I reckon he was just too drunk to know what hit him," the marshal observed acidly. "Lucky for you, stranger, else we'd be holdin' a necktie sociable in your honor real soon," he told Slade. "So, all things considered, I guess you won't mind payin' a fifty-dollar fine for assault and spendin' a few nights in the calaboose instead.''

"Not hardly," Slade intoned dryly.

"Good," the marshal said. Then he nodded to one of the town's policemen, who had arrived to assist him. "Earp, bring that 'un along, too." He motioned toward Beecham's crumpled form. "He's to be fined and locked up, as well—charged with drunkenness and disorderly conduct."

And so it was that on his first night in Wichita, Slade Maverick found himself ignominiously incarcerated in a seven-by-seven-foot cell, right next door to his despised brother-in-law, Jonathan Beecham. Not deigning to speak to the now stone-cold-sober and nauseatingly eager-to-please man, Slade dined on a tin plate of cold, mushy, and thoroughly unappetizing beans. Then he stretched out on a hard wooden bunk, atop an uncomfortably lumpy pallet. He hoped ardently that he would sleep. But instead, he lay awake for hours after supper, listening to the howl of the wind outside and the tattoo of the rain upon the jail's tin hip roof. Grieving deeply over India, he was silent in his pain, alone with his thoughts.

It was the longest night he had ever spent.

Chapter Six

Rachel did not understand why Marshal Meagher had not shown up at the farm to arrest her. She had felt certain he would come, as had her grandfather—even though upon hearing, last evening, Poke's animated recounting of Rachel's lively antics in town, Fremont Haggerty had laughed until tears had streamed down his cheeks, and slapped his knees and stomped his feet so hard upon the floor that he'd nearly cracked his wooden leg. Even the older Beecham children, overhearing the rousing tale, had forgotten their recent afflictions long enough to giggle uncontrollably, their eyes round with amazement and admiration at Rachel's haywire attempt to fetch their father home.

"Gee whillikers!" Gideon had cried, rising up from beneath his blankets spread upon the puncheon floor of the log cabin. "I'll bet Pa was fit to be tied!"

"Gideon," Poke had chuckled, wiping his own tears of merriment from his eyes, "yo daddy wuz hot 'nuff ter fry an egg on—sho' as shootin'! Ah ain' neber seed him so mad!"

It was only the expectation of Rachel's imminent arrest that had sobered them. But much to their surprise, neither the marshal nor his deputies nor even a lowly policeman had ridden out to the farm to cart Rachel off to jail. Of course, it was possible the storm had kept the lawmen away, but that still didn't explain why no one had arrived this morning; for now, the sky, though grey, was clear as it ever was in winter. The sun was even struggling to put in an appearance, making the half-melted snow sparkle like sugar.

Shaking her head in puzzlement as she gazed at the empty horizon, Rachel continued toward the barn. Perhaps the disreputable Verne Lundy had decided not to sic the law on her, after all, having any number of reasons, she felt sure, for avoiding it himself. She sighed, wishing she knew the truth one way or the other, so she could stop worrying.

Swinging her egg basket as she walked along, she inhaled the morning air deeply. It smelled fresh and clean, as it always did after a storm, as did the dark, muddy earth that squished beneath her boots. The brisk wind was cool; nevertheless, Rachel thought she detected a hint of spring in its bite. She hoped so, for she was tired of sullen skies, of snow and sleet, and of being so cold that she shook beneath her blankets at night, despite the fires in both stove and hearth. She longed for the blueing of the firmament, the greening of the prairie grasses, the blossoming of the wildflowers, and the gentling of the wind that blew always on the plains, soft as a lullaby in summer, loud as a symphony in winter, but ever present.

When Rachel opened one of the heavy doors of the barn and slipped inside, she was surprised to find that Gideon was already there, feeding and watering the animals, while ten-year-old Caleb milked the cows. The younger boy also obliged the litter of cats, who waited expectantly nearby, by giving each of them several squirts of the warm, foamy liquid as he worked.

"We talked it over—all of us—last night after you went to bed, Aunt Rachel; and if we're gonna be stayin' here, at least for a while anyway, we aim to earn our keep," Gideon explained at her inquiring glance. "We know it's been hard on you, lookin' after—after . . . Ma and us like you've done, and we don't expect no charity."

Rachel blinked back sudden tears at his words, for that was India coming out in the boy, she knew. She was touched by the unexpected announcement and saddened as she recalled her dead friend; for though Jonathan would have offered to lend a hand, he would have done so grudgingly and with every hope of refusal. But Gideon's young face was at once so fiercely proud and so heartrendingly set, as though he would burst into tears if Rachel rejected his proffered aid, that she knew she could not.

So, instead, she said crisply, "Why, of course, none of you wants a handout, Gideon. I never thought you did. There're plenty of chores here for all of us, and I expect you children to do your share, just as you always did at home. In fact, I'll be grateful for your assistance."

That much, at least, was true; for since the deaths of her parents during a tornado some years back, Rachel had had more than she could handle when it came to running the farm. Of course, Poke did most of the heavy work, and her grandfather helped out as much as his disability permitted. Still, it seemed as though there were never enough hours in the day.

"When you've finished here, Gideon, ask Poke what to do next. And you, Caleb, take those pails of milk up to the house and set them on the kitchen table for me when you're through," Rachel directed.

"Yes, ma'am," the boys chorused, beaming shyly.

At the sty, Rachel discovered Philip dutifully slopping the pigs. At the chicken coop, nine-year-old Susannah was scattering feed and gathering eggs, while the hardy dominique hens were busy pecking. Seeing there was little else for her to do, Rachel tossed her hunting dogs the scraps and bones she'd saved from supper last night, then returned to the log cabin. There, Eve had already tidied things up and laid the table for breakfast.

"Have you Beechams left me *anything* to do this morning, Eve?" Rachel asked ruefully.

"Cook the meal, Aunt Rachel," the girl replied, smiling. "I wasn't sure what Grandpa Haggerty and Poke would eat."

"Anything that isn't still kicking," Rachel joked, tying one of her muslin aprons around her waist and then selecting a few sacks and canisters from the small assortment on the kitchen shelves.

She reached for a clay bowl and a wooden spoon, mixed up dough, then rolled it out and, after dusting it lightly with flour, began cutting biscuits. Once she had these baking, she sliced rashers for the skillet, hoping the smoked bacon would not taste too foully of the grasshoppers that had struck last August. While the slabs of meat were sizzling on the cast-iron stove, she ground coffee beans and made coffee. Then she stirred up a pan of hominy and set it cooking. Lastly, she cracked and fried on the griddle the fresh eggs Susannah had collected. While Eve fed and changed the baby, Tobias, Susannah ladled into tin cups the milk Caleb had brought in, and put the sorghum on the table.

After that, everyone assembled for breakfast. Startling the more pious Beecham youngsters, Fremont spoke the blessing, thanking the Lord for the food on their table, but noting that it was their own hard work that had provided it, after all. That said, they all filled their plates and began eating hungrily, with little conversation. Despite the quietness of the meal, the children's presence cheered Rachel. It was as though they were family. She missed not having any brothers or sisters, any youngsters of her own. Somehow, the Beechams seemed to make up for her lack. She felt happier than she had in a long time.

Following the meal, Rachel noted that Eve and Susannah, and even two-year-old Naomi, were quite capable of clearing, scraping, and washing the dishes. So she donned her coat and, ruing the loss of her old felt winter hat yesterday at the Silver Slipper, tied a sunbonnet on her head in its stead. She informed her grandfather that she was riding into town to find out whether Verne Lundy had indeed set the law on her. Knowing that Rachel's mind, once made up, was seldom changed, Fremont muttered something about durned fools who couldn't seem to learn their lessons, then declared more loudly that she must please herself in the matter.

Her eyes sparkling with love for her gruff grandfather, Rachel replied impudently that in this respect at least, none could doubt she was surely his granddaughter. She planted a fond kiss on his whiskered cheek, earning several additional grumbled comments for her pains. Then she took up her trusty shotgun, loaded it, and stepped out into the wintry sunlight that streaked across the grey sky at last. She saddled Sunflower and set out at a lope toward Wichita.

Once in town, Rachel made her way down the wide, miry main street, Douglas Avenue, across one of the bridges that spanned the Big Arkansas River, and into Delano. Unlike Wichita, the suburb was almost deserted at this hour, its inhabitants still sleeping off the ill-effects of their overindulgence the night before. She dismounted warily all the same, tethering Sunflower firmly to the hitching rail out front of the Silver Slipper. As horse thieving was a hanging offense in Kansas, she had no worry that, even in Delano, any chance vagrant would steal the mare. It was her own safety that concerned her. Decency dictated that she refrain from entering the bar. But as it appeared highly unlikely that she would be observed, and she simply *had* to find out if she was now a wanted woman, Rachel finally dared to go inside.

Despite her nervousness, she could not prevent herself from gaping at her surroundings, her first clear view of the interior of a saloon. She was oddly disappointed to see nothing more than a badly marred bar, some broken-down tables and chairs (a state for which she felt she could not be entirely to blame), and a battered old piano. From the stories she had heard, Rachel had expected an abundance of crystal chandeliers, red velvet portieres, and paintings of nude women, at least. Plainly, the Silver Slipper was not at all on a par with the Syndicate, the Spirit Bank, or the Gold Rooms, some of Wichita's first-class establishments.

Verne Lundy was up and about despite the early hour. Rachel was not surprised that he was not in the least glad to see her. But to her astonishment, he greeted her politely enough, if sourly, before telling her to kindly state her business and then get out while a portion of his saloon was still standing.

"If ya've come 'bout anteing up fer all the mess—'n' rightly so, mind ya, 'spesh'ly after the way ya done hightailed it outta here yesterday, with nary a word of apology or a single red cent proffered fer same, I might add—it's already been taken care of, girlie," he told her. "'N' if it's worryin' 'bout yore hide what brung ya, ya kin set yoreseff at ease on that score, as well, 'cuz I ain't pressin' no charges agin ya —though I oughta—'n' the marshal ain't too keen 'bout lockin' ya up, neither. But ya'd better keep that friggin' Beecham outta here from now on, ya hear? Thanks ta him 'n' ya, I nearly lost my whole shittin' saloon, girlie—'n' my best goddamned whore ta boot! Why, it's a wonder pore Emmalou weren't blowed clear ta kingdom come! Thank God, there ain't a blessed female alive what kin shoot straight!"

"*Mr. Lundy!* Please remember to whom you are speaking, and temper your language accordingly." Rachel spoke primly but earned nothing but a sarcastic guffaw for her pains. Since she *had* wrecked his saloon, she felt uncomfortably that perhaps she deserved this, and so she hastily changed the subject.

"Did I correctly understand you, Mr. Lundy, to say that someone has already taken it upon himself to discharge the debt owing on my behalf?"

"If, by that, ya mean did somebody pay fer all the damage ya done? Yeah, somebody did."

"But . . . who?" Rachel asked, perplexed.

"Dunno, girlie—'n' don't care, neither. Last time I seed him, he was trussed up like a Thanksgivin' turkey 'n' on his way ta the hoosegow—along with yore friend Beecham. Go ask the marshal, why don'tcha? Or Officer Earp; he was here, too, when the both of them bastards was hauled off. Now, quit pesterin' me, girlie! I ain't got all day ta stand here jabberin' like a jaybird! I got work ta do!" At that, Lundy rudely turned his back on her, shouting, "Clem, where's them beer barrels I told ya ta brang up ta the bar? Ya'd better move yore ass, ya lazy son of a bitch, lessen ya wanna be fired!" Then, as an afterthought, he grabbed something from beneath the counter and tossed it at Rachel. "There's yore hat, girlie. Now, g'wan. Git!"

Relieved that she was not, after all, to be arrested, but confused as to why some unknown person should have compensated Verne Lundy for all the mischief she had caused, Rachel left the Silver Slipper. Then she mounted up and headed toward the marshal's office, bent on learning the identity of, and thanking, her benefactor.

She had not gone far when she chanced to notice Officer Earp strolling down the street. Thinking to save herself a trip to the grim, two-story brick jail, she pulled Sunflower to a stop and hailed the policeman. Because of his numerous, widely publicized escapades, to say nothing of the fact that two members of his family, Bessie and Sallie Earp, had been fined for prostitution since he had joined the Wichita police force, Officer Wyatt Earp was well known to the town's residents.

After Rachel had explained who she was and what she wanted, he obliged her by supplying the name she sought— Slade Maverick. But to her dismay, the policeman also informed her that as the prisoner was an infamous gunslinger who might well attempt to escape, he was not allowed to have any visitors. A visit to the jail would be a complete waste of her time.

Rachel was so shocked to realize that her unknown benefactor was the audacious man who had put a halt to Sunflower's rampage yesterday that she just mumbled her thanks to Officer Earp and rode on. She could not imagine why on earth the gunslinger should have paid for all the havoc she had wreaked upon the Silver Slipper, especially after all his insolent remarks to her in the road.

Not until the following day did Rachel learn to her horror that Slade Maverick was not only a notorious gunslinger, but India Beecham's black-sheep half brother—come to claim possession of his dead sister's offspring.

Chapter Seven

Taking a ring of keys from his desk, Marshal Meagher started down the jail hall, toward the row of cells where Slade Maverick and Jonathan Beecham were being held captive. The keys jangled as the marshal inserted first one, and then another, each into its proper lock, turned it, then motioned curtly for the men to step out.

"Your time's up, boys," he said. "If you plan to leave Wichita, you can pick up your shootin' irons out front. If you don't, the deputy'll give you a metal token so you can redeem 'em when you *do* decide to depart from our fair town. We don't hold with men goin' armed here—and you, at least, ought to know better, Beecham. At any rate, I don't want to see either one of you in my jail again, so stay out of trouble—especially you, Maverick! Despite what you may have heard to the contrary, I run a clean, decent town here, and I don't aim to have my record tarnished by any two-bit hired gun!''

"Yeah. Right, Marshal," Slade drawled. "Whatever you say."

The gunslinger shrugged into his duster, clapped on his hat, and hoisted his bedroll onto one shoulder. Then, spurs jingling, he swaggered from the cell, pausing, since he didn't intend to remain in Wichita, out front to collect his gun belt, revolvers, and other belongings that had been confiscated after his arrest. Squinting his eyes against the relative brightness of the noon sun after the dark jail cell, he stepped outside and strode around to the stable to claim his horse and saddle. Mechanically, he checked his saddlebags to be certain they were in order and inspected his leather scabbard to ensure that it still contained his 1873 Winchester .44-40-caliber rifle. Then he mounted up and set out after Jonathan, who was, Slade felt sure, skedaddling from town as fast as he was able.

A few miles east of Wichita, the gunslinger spied Beecham and swiftly overtook him. Much to Slade's amusement, he didn't even have to hint at drawing his pistols to persuade the thoroughly intimidated Jonathan to lead him to the Beechams' soddy.

The place was even worse than Slade had expected. India, he now realized, hadn't told him even the half of it. His heart ached for her as he surveyed the dismal soddy. How had she, who had come from one of the richest plantations along the Mississippi River, ever borne *this*? He didn't know. A muscle throbbed in his tense jaw. It was all he could do to refrain from once more laying violent hands upon Beecham.

"I'll just . . . ahem," Jonathan cleared his throat nervously, "I'll just . . . step inside and—and tell the—the children we're here."

"Do that," Slade growled, dismounting.

He made no move toward the house himself. For now, his sorrow and wrath mounting, he spied, lying some feet from its proper resting place, knocked askew by the ferocity of the storm two nights ago, the slipshod wooden cross that had marked India's grave. Slowly, he bent and picked it up, his mouth tightening as he saw there wasn't even an inscription. The nearby mound of earth beneath which India lay was still visible. Briefly, Slade passed the back of one hand across his stinging eyes. Then, with the butt of one of his Peacemakers, he hammered the pathetic cross back into place, vowing he would order a granite tombstone as soon as possible. The gunslinger's eyes were hard and glinting like blue steel when Beecham reappeared.

"There—there isn't anyone here," Jonathan announced with dread, flinching at Slade's harsh, condemnatory expression. "The place is—is deserted. Even the—the team and cow are—are gone."

"Well, now, where do you reckon everybody is?"

"I guess—I guess Rachel took 'em all over to her cabin —the interfering bitch! I told her to keep away from here, that I didn't want her around India and the kids. She's meaner than a rattlesnake—and twice as poisonous! What happened at the Silver Slipper's not the first time that frigging persimmon's tried to get rid of me, you know. She was always telling India that I was no good, that I ought to be sent packing—as if I didn't do my best under all the adverse conditions out here to try to make ends meet! Jesus! The jealous old maid! The *real* truth of the matter was that she just couldn't stand India having a husband when she didn't have one herself—not that anyone except Ox Oxenberg *would* have her, mind you. And he's so damned dumb that he doesn't have sense enough to come in out of the rain! Why else would he be interested in that crazy she-devil?"

"What do you mean . . . crazy she-devil?" Slade queried sharply, his eyes narrowing at the thought that perhaps India's offspring had been carried away by a dangerously deranged woman and that Beecham—the drunken fool!—had allowed it to happen. Still, despite her firing her shotgun at Jonathan that day in Delano, Rachel Wilder had not, at the time, struck Slade as being mentally imbalanced, merely powerfully provoked. And when he'd learned how she'd been caring for his nieces and nephews since his half sister's death, he'd gladly paid the cost of the damage to the Silver Slipper, thinking he'd misjudged her and treated her badly. Now, however, replaying in his mind the scene in Delano and viewing it in a wholly different light, Slade wondered anxiously what harm might have befallen the youngsters at her hands. "I asked you a question, Beecham!" he snapped. "What do you mean . . . crazy she-devil?"

"Just that . . . just what I said," Jonathan replied sourly, scowling. "Why, everybody hereabouts knows she's a lunatic! Don't let her fool you! She only *pretends* to be righteous and God-fearing. Deep down inside, she's got no morals at all. She's a she-devil, I tell you! She consorts with a heathenish old half-breed Indian, which no white woman in her right mind would do! Gives him beads and blankets and such—probably guns and liquor, too, I shouldn't be at all surprised to learn! Hell! She acts just like him, even! Grubs on the prairie for plants and roots and what have you, and boils all sorts of vile decoctions—heaven only knows for what purpose, though I have my suspicions about *that*!—and falls into a trance, and goes around with a forked stick, claiming she can find water underground—"

"Why, do you mean that she does nothing more outlandish than—than trade with what is probably just a harmless old medicine man, that she's just an—just an herbalist and a dowser?" Slade inquired, astonished and angered by his brother-in-law's ignorance and stupidity. "That hardly qualifies her as a 'crazy she-devil,' Beecham! You ought to get down on your knees and thank her for taking an interest in your kids, which is more than *you've* done, I might add, you goddamned bastard! There's no telling what might have happened to them otherwise, all alone out here. Now, get on your horse, you lousy excuse for a man and father. We're going to pay a visit to Miss Wilder—and I'm warning you: You'd better show her nothing but the utmost respect, or I swear I'm personally going to break your frigging neck!"

* * *

It struck Slade most forcibly upon their second—though no more amicable—meeting that Rachel Wilder's heart-shaped face was a lot more arresting than he had initially surmised. Indeed, he wondered if he had been blinded by trail dust to have ever considered her plain. Why, the way her blond hair shone like spun gold in the late-afternoon sunlight, her mint-green eyes shot sparks at him, her high cheekbones glowed the flaming color of a prairie sunset, and her soft, sweet rose mouth trembled with fear and fury as she stared at him, she was anything but homely. In fact, she was downright fetching, and despite his considerable sadness over India's death, more than a flicker of interest flared within Slade as he studied his half sister's best friend.

She was a good deal younger than India had been, so it surprised him that the two women had been so close—close enough, in fact, that Rachel's genuine grief at India's loss was evident, something that raised his estimation of her another notch in Slade's mind. But perhaps circumstance had drawn the two women together, he mused. Both their farms were isolated, miles from town or the nearest other neighbor.

Still, despite Rachel's attracting him physically, and her befriending his dearly cherished half sister, Slade found he could not like the young woman any better. No matter what his idiotic brother-in-law had claimed, it was not Rachel Wilder's bartering and concocting and divining that had kept her a spinster, the gunslinger concluded. It was her tart tongue—the brunt of which he had borne neither lightly nor willingly for the past quarter of an hour. She was a veritable shrew! *That* first impression of her, at least, had been right on target.

Slade was irate that upon learning his purpose in calling on her, she had not deigned to invite either him or Jonathan inside the log cabin, but had kept them standing—at gunpoint, no less!—in the muddy yard out front. Nor would she even agree to call the children out.

Now, her voice quivering with emotion, she continued the heated argument that had commenced shortly after his and Beecham's arrival.

"Mr. Maverick, while, indeed, I am not ungrateful to you, both for your timely rescue outside the Silver Slipper and your discharging my debt to Verne Lundy—which sum I shall certainly insist on repaying you just as soon as I can— I am *not* turning those poor youngsters over to either a gunslinger or a drunk!" Rachel declared, her green eyes flashing. "Uncle or not, you are *not* a proper person to care for them. Nor, unfortunately, is Jonathan a fit father, as his lamentable behavior these past few weeks has aptly demonstrated! I am absolutely sure in my mind that, under the circumstances, India"—here, Rachel faltered, fighting to hold her tears at bay, then went on determinedly—"India would have wished me to have custody of her children."

"Miss Wilder, I am not disputing the fact that neither I nor my miserable brother-in-law are ideal choices to rear eight suffering youngsters," Slade asserted, smoothly concealing his impatience at her stubbornness and pointedly ignoring her offer of repayment. "But with all due respect, ma'am, whether you like it or not, we *are* their blood kin; and close as you apparently were to my sister, you were not related to her and cannot have known her thoughts fully on this matter. If you will kindly put down that shotgun, Miss Wilder, I will show you the letter I received from India shortly before she died, in which she clearly states her earnest desire that I stand as guardian to her children should some ill befall her."

"I—I don't believe you," Rachel said, stunned and hurt that in India's time of need, she should have turned to her half brother instead of her dearest friend.

"Nevertheless, ma'am, I assure you I speak the truth," Slade responded gently, aware of Rachel's distress as he gingerly handed her the missive, making it plain he had no intention of trying to wrest her shotgun, which she had refused to relinquish, from her control.

She opened the envelope, scanned its contents, then slowly

refolded the two heavily crossed pages and put them back inside. She drew a deep breath.

"This changes nothing," she stated flatly, much to Slade's annoyance. "India—India simply cannot have been in her right mind when she wrote this. She was quite sick and depressed for many weeks before her death, and obviously, her judgment was affected."

"The only thing ever wrong with her judgment was choosing you as a friend, Miss Hoity-Toity Wilder!" Jonathan spat.

"Shut your mouth, Beecham," Slade snarled, rounding on him threateningly and causing both him and Rachel to jump, "before I shut it for you! If you had done your duty in the first place, none of us would be standing here now!" He turned back to Rachel, his tone so calm and even as he spoke to her that she found it difficult to reconcile the two sides she had seen of his personality. "The fact remains, Miss Wilder, that my sister *did* write the letter, and that you have no legal claim on her children. Now, I thank you kindly for looking after them in my absence. But you've no call to be troubled with them any longer, and I would appreciate your handing them over right now." He paused expectantly. Then, when Rachel made no move toward the house, he uttered softly, "Ma'am, I would surely hate to have to get the marshal out here to settle this."

Rachel's heart sank at that, and her shoulders slumped, for she knew that, gunslinger or not, the law would be firmly on Slade Maverick's side in this matter. He was right: She didn't have a leg to stand on legally when it came to the Beecham youngsters. She had nothing but the love she had borne their mother, and still bore them, to speak in her favor, and before the blind eyes of justice, it would not be enough. Further, though the gunslinger had, in a surprisingly gentlemanly manner, ignored her insistence on repaying the monies he had expended on her behalf at the Silver Slipper, he might, if she continued to oppose him, demand she honor her obligation to him immediately, and this, Rachel was well aware she lacked the financial means to do. To her despair, she realized she dared not continue to press him.

Oh, how she heartily wished Slade Maverick at the ends of the earth, in perdition, in fact—where he surely belonged, the devil! For if *he* had not come along to stick a burr under her saddle, Rachel felt sure she would eventually have arrived at some satisfactory arrangement with Jonathan. Now, all was lost. It just wasn't fair, she thought, incensed. It just wasn't fair at all!

She had not recognized, until these past few days, the extent of her deep loneliness since her parents, and now India, had died. She had not known until taking in the Beecham children just how much she would enjoy being part of a large, loving family. They had shown her a void in her life that would not easily be filled once they were gone.

There were her grandfather and Poke, of course. But they knew little about womanly concerns, about the simple, ordinary aspects of everyday life that Rachel had shared first with her mother, and then with India, and now with young Eve. Themselves loners, Grandpa and Poke could not possibly begin to know, Rachel had thought, what it had meant to her to hear the log cabin ring with talk and laughter, even with quarrels and the crying of the infant, Tobias. They could not possibly begin to understand the maternal longing that had stirred within her as she had rocked the baby to sleep at night and pretended he was her own.

Rachel had believed she had come to grips with her spinsterhood, had routed from her being those emotions unsuited to her station in life. Now, she knew she had only buried her yearnings deep inside her instead, unwilling to let go of her dreams, despite her realization that they would never become reality. For what hope was there of a husband for her?

Her father had been a schoolteacher, an abolitionist, a revolutionary, and a visionary—a man far ahead of his time. He had truly believed that all men—and women—were created equal, and he had steadfastly instilled these beliefs in his daughter, Rachel, his only child. In this, he had in many ways done her a great disservice, for as a result, she had grown into a woman out of step with the society in which she must live. She marched to the beat of a drummer different from that of other women, and all sensed it. Women knew instinctively that Rachel wasn't like them, that she "didn't belong." Men, less discerning, knew only that they were distinctly uncomfortable around her, that they felt somehow threatened by her. They were not used to having a respectable female boldly look them in the eye, politely interrupt their conversation, and resolutely put forth her own objectionable or contrary opinions, which, when examined and debated, sometimes proved superior to theirs.

Those few men who had come courting her had hardly shaken the dust from their boots before hitting the trail again, angered by the impression that they had been dispassionately stood against a yardstick and found not to measure up. It was the ultimate blow to the fragile male ego—and what was even worse was that Rachel was completely unconscious of having delivered it. Instead, having all her life been instructed otherwise by her father, she was profoundly confused and wounded that her innate intelligence and curiosity, her ingrained honesty and forthrightness should be deemed unappealing traits in a female.

It was not that she was wholly ignorant of the ways in which women beguiled men. It was just that she did not comprehend the reasoning behind the rules of the game and so saw no need to adhere to them. In her mind, they were foolish and deceitful, and why such characteristics should be praised and valued was beyond her. It was not what she wanted in a man; she could not believe that it was what a man wanted in her.

So it was that her only beau was Gustave Oxenberg—called "Ox" by all save Rachel. A big Swedish immigrant, he was as strong and stubborn as the animal for which he was nicknamed, and just as plodding. That he was also just as loyal, dependable, and stout-hearted was not generally observed. He found it difficult to address any subject that did not revolve around the weather or farming; and thus it was the considered opinion of the surrounding countryside that he persisted in his attentions to Rachel Wilder only because no other available female would long suffer his dogged but uninspired pursuit. In fact, it was widely held that Ox was so dull-witted that he was entirely unaware of Rachel's undesirability as a wife.

He was not, for he was not in the least as dense as people supposed. That he did not indignantly condemn Rachel Wilder as others did was due not only to his generous and equitable disposition, however, but also to the fact that, quite simply, he had loved her since the first time he had ever beheld her—quietly, earnestly, and with all his large heart. His love for her was as natural to Ox as the air he breathed or the food he ate, and he never once questioned why his eye should have settled upon someone whose nature was as alien to his as that of a deer to a buffalo's.

Rachel did not return his love, he knew. Because she did not, she would not marry him, he knew, too, and despaired over. He would have taken her on any terms, honored beyond words that she would consent to be his wife. But no matter how good and kind she thought him, how much she respected and cared about him as a friend, Rachel would not wed a man she did not love. Her young body did not ache with desire when Ox took her hand in his. Her heart did not beat like the wings of a captive bird against his heart. Her mind and soul did not cry out for his own, as though all her world would be dark and empty if bereft of him.

These were Rachel's dreams of love, born of the poetry and novels she had read as a child, and read still, the undeniable emotion that had leaped between her parents like foxfire between the horns of cattle when a storm swept across the plains. So strong had her parents' love been that when they had seen they could not outrun the tornado that had finally struck them down, they had died in each other's arms, each trying to shield the other from the twister's fury. Rachel had never felt such all-consuming emotion for any man, and she would give no less to her husband, nor accept any less as his wife. So, when love eluded her, she carefully folded her dreams and locked them away, and as kindly as possible tried in vain to discourage Gustave Oxenberg's suit.

This, then, was her life until India had died—India, who

had known Burns and Shakespeare, Byron and Tennyson by heart, and who had long ago turned the key on her own dreams and thrown it away. Now, with the advent of the motherless Beecham children in Rachel's life, the secret hope chest in her heart had been stealthily unlocked, the dust and cobwebs gently blown away, and the lavender sachets tucked among her dreams tenderly shaken loose. Against her sternest stricture, she had permitted herself to hope again for at least a part of all for which she had long ceased to hope at all.

And now, it was all to be snatched away by the gunslinger who stood before her, his midnight-blue eyes strangely unfathomable at his triumph, his pitiless crushing of this small, vulnerable piece of her heart. Rachel had never hated anybody as much as she did Slade Maverick in that moment. From the crown of his flat-brimmed sombrero to the soles of his black leather boots, she despised him utterly. What did he know about dreams, about love, this man hard as nails and tough as jerky? If he had a heart at all—which she doubted—Rachel suspected that it was made of flint. It was all she could do to refrain from giving him the full effects of a blast from her shotgun at close quarters.

Instead, squaring her shoulders and lowering her weapon, she politely but coolly invited, "Won't you step into the house, Mr. Maverick? Jonathan?"

"Said the spider to the fly," Beecham muttered, earning another sharp, warning glance from the gunslinger.

"*That* was the parlor, Jonathan," Rachel noted dryly, "and since I don't have one, I expect you're quite safe—from me, at any rate; though if I were you, I wouldn't press my luck with your brother-in-law. For some reason, he appears to have taken as inordinate a dislike to you as I have." She eyed Beecham distastefully.

He still bore the cuts and bruises from his fray at the Silver Slipper, and from these and his demeanor, she correctly deduced he had already tangled for the worse with his brother-in-law. At least she could give Slade Maverick credit for that, if nothing else, she thought. For she still could not believe that the Beecham youngsters would be any better off with him than with Jonathan. After all, what could a gunslinger possibly know about rearing children?

The men followed Rachel into the log cabin. There, Eve and Susannah were washing and drying the last of the dishes from the noon meal, and four-year-old Andrew and his younger sister, Naomi, were playing with a set of crude wooden soldiers on the floor. Tobias was asleep in the cradle Rachel had fashioned for him out of an old packing crate. As the four older children looked up and saw their father, it was as though they were suddenly turned into fence posts, so still and mute did they become. After an awkward moment, Eve, Susannah, and Andrew greeted Jonathan at last. But Slade was quick to note there was no enthusiasm in their voices, only a certain wariness and apprehension. Nor were the youngsters, after Rachel introduced the gunslinger, particularly thrilled at learning Slade was their uncle, come to fetch them home. Little Naomi, in fact, puckered up and shed tears at hearing the news, and ran to hide behind Rachel's skirts.

Slade supposed, quite correctly, that the sight of him was hardly very reassuring. He had had neither a shave nor a bath since his arrival in Wichita, and although he had changed his clothes, they were wrinkled and stank of horse sweat from being wrapped in his bedroll. His duster was badly stained from his travels, and his boots were caked with mud. Self-consciously, he rubbed his face, now sporting several days' growth of heavy beard, and glanced about lamely for somewhere to extinguish his cigarillo. He spied a spittoon in one corner and hastily ground out his thin black cigar, feeling Rachel's disapproving green eyes on him all the while. As the gunslinger was normally more fastidious about his appearance, he felt abruptly gauche and embarrassed beneath the young woman's steady scrutiny, and he was sorry he had not cleaned up a bit before calling for the children. He thought he and Beecham, who looked even worse and was shaking visibly from lack of liquor, must present a thoroughly disgusting picture. Slade could scarcely blame Rachel when, feeling his gaze upon her, she haughtily tossed her head and sniffed as though she smelled something rank.

Rachel, for her part, was thinking that Slade Maverick's presence was like having an unpredictable woolly buffalo loose in the log cabin. The two-room house had never seemed quite so small, its ceiling so low, its walls so close. In fact, *everything* appeared somehow to have shrunk before his dark, towering figure. The notion disturbed her. She wished her grandfather and Poke were here, but they had taken Gideon, Caleb, and Philip out riding with them to inspect the farm for damage from the storm.

This, Rachel explained to Slade and Jonathan as she began gathering the youngsters' few possessions and putting them into the wicker basket that had accompanied them from the Beechams' soddy. All the while, she was aware of the gunslinger's eyes upon her. Rachel wished he would stop staring at her. He was making her feel not only nervous, but oddly flushed and faint, as though she had run a long way and could not now catch her breath. The sensation was really most perturbing. She could not understand why he should have this effect upon her. It was true he was handsome, but he was also incredibly dirty. He had not shaved or bathed for over a week, she was willing to wager. He reeked of sweat, cigar smoke, whiskey, saddle leather, and his horse—earthy, masculine smells. Surprisingly, Rachel thought she also detected a hint of vetiver.

The more she dwelled on the scents issuing from his flesh, the faster she worked, until she was practically throwing the children's belongings into the basket. As she realized this, Rachel wondered if the recent strain under which she had been laboring had somehow affected her mind. These queer feelings and behavior were most unlike her. It was as though she were suffering from cabin fever or something, she thought, and seriously contemplated dosing herself with a tonic later.

Slade sensed Rachel's turmoil but mistook its cause. For a moment, he wanted to lay a hand upon her arm and reassure

her that the Beecham youngsters would come to no harm in
his care. But he knew she would not believe him, and after
all, why should she? He was a hard man who had lived a
hard life. It was not reasonable to assume that a drifter, a
gunslinger, could suddenly put down roots and hang up his
guns, with nary a backward glance. Though Slade definitely
intended to try, he did not know if he would succeed. He
could not blame Rachel for her doubts.

He glanced around the log cabin, noting the small things
here and there that revealed her touch: the myriad dried herbs
hanging from the rafters, the ruffled curtains at the windows,
the checkered tablecloth upon the table, and the braided rag
rugs on the floor. Everything, from the kitchen shelves to the
fieldstone hearth to the puncheon floor, was scrupulously
clean and orderly. He liked that; it spoke well of her. It
reminded him of his father's plantation in Louisiana, which
had always smelled pleasantly of soap and polish.

Slade had loved the stately old mansion, though not his
autocratic father, to whom it had belonged. They had never
seen eye to eye. His father had been the type of man who
would kill a horse—or a boy—trying to break its spirit, and
in the end, Slade had left rather than submit to his father's
iron will. The old man was dead now, as was Slade's mother,
a belle from the French Quarter of New Orleans. She had
been very beautiful, and many years younger than his father,
whose second wife she had been. She should have lived—
she had loved life—but a fever had carried her off. Now,
India, too, was gone. Slade was the last of the Mavericks.
The thought bothered him, somehow.

His eyes fastened once more upon Rachel—the proud carriage of her head, the straight backbone of her willowy figure.
She reminded him of a fierce, skittish filly. He wondered
what kind of life she led here, alone with an old man and a
Negro. It could not be easy for her. His gaze fell to her hands.
They were small and slender but red and roughened by hard
work. Perhaps she had just cause for her sharp tongue. Perhaps a woman who labored like a man deserved to speak her
mind like one, as well. He was slightly bemused by his

irritation at her doing so. He had always loathed pretense and deceit in a woman, and it was plain there was neither in Rachel Wilder.

With a start, Slade realized she now had the children and their possessions ready to go. He told Beecham to go out to the barn and hitch the team to the wagon. Jonathan grumbled under his breath but went. Perhaps Fremont or Poke would have a jug cached there. Beecham could use a drink. His nerves were frazzled at the lack of one, and at his brother-in-law's high-handed treatment of him, too. How dare the gunslinger just step in and take over as he had done, as though he had every right to do so? It made Jonathan mad—though not mad enough to do anything about it. During the War between the States, he had stayed well back from the front lines, as befitted an officer. He had not been so foolish as to risk his neck and leave his unit without a commander. It was just bad luck that he had been taken captive and confined in the Yankees' Rock Island prison. The guards there had been hard men, and Jonathan felt that his brother-in-law was cut from the same cloth. He was not eager to fight him again. Glad to escape from him, Beecham headed for the barn.

"I'll—I'll have Grandpa and Poke bring the boys over once they get back," Rachel told Slade, turning away so he would not see the tears that brimmed in her eyes at the loss of the youngsters.

"That'd be fine," he replied, feeling somehow uncomfortable now at his taking them away from her, despite his belief that it was the right thing to do. He touched the brim of his hat. "Good day, Miss Wilder."

The gunslinger stood so near to her now that Rachel knew for certain it *was* a trace of vetiver she had discerned earlier among the other masculine smells that emanated from his skin. She loved the grassy fragrance. It reminded her of the prairie in spring, when the mixed grasses began to turn green and the wildflowers to bloom. The plains were at their most beautiful then, before the hot summer sun baked them dry.

For the first time, as well, she noticed that Slade's voice was tinged with a slight accent—French, she believed, and recalled that India's stepmother had been born and reared in the French Quarter of New Orleans. It seemed incongruous to Rachel that the gunslinger should come from such a refined background, for there seemed to be little civilized about him now. It was as though he had deliberately cast off his past.

"Good-bye, Mr. Maverick," she said, and then, prompted by her own genteel upbringing, politely, if reluctantly, extended her hand.

The gesture both surprised and oddly touched Slade. Slowly, he drew off his black leather glove and took her palm in his. Their physical contact was brief, yet Rachel was startled to feel a tremor run through her body in response. His hand was warm, strong. Her own seemed lost in it. Yet his grip was curiously gentle, as though he feared he would break the bones in her hand if he clasped it too tightly. She had not expected that. When he released her, she quickly pulled her hand away.

The children had disappeared, but she could hear the sounds of Jonathan's loading them into the wagon. The log cabin itself was strangely still, as though it held its breath, waiting. But for what, Rachel did not know. Then, finally, Slade moved toward the door, and the jingle of his spurs broke the silence.

Outside, Rachel saw that Jonathan had tied his horse and the milch cow to the tailgate of the wagon. Eve, holding the baby, Tobias, sat on the wagon seat beside her father. Susannah, Andrew, and Naomi huddled in the wagon box, the canvas drawn up about them to protect them from the wind. No one spoke as Slade swung into his saddle and set his spurs to his horse's sides.

As the wagon pulled away, the youngsters stared back at Rachel, who stood forlornly on the stoop, observing their departure. Their eyes were sad and accusing. She forced a smile to her lips, and waved. But none of them smiled or waved in return. Rachel couldn't blame them. She felt like a traitor, as though she had failed them, somehow.

Through the blur of her tears, she watched until the small company was nothing more than a distant speck on the plains.

Then, sighing heavily, she went back into the log cabin. It was almost dusk, and she had chores to do.

Yet once inside, she did nothing more than sit in her rocking chair, not even rocking, just staring blankly at the old, empty packing crate that had served as Tobias's cradle. Unconsciously, she rubbed the hand she had offered to Slade Maverick. It was cold now; the peculiar tingle was gone. Rachel thought she should be glad of that.

After a long while, shivering, she rose, stoked up the fire in the hearth, and stretched out her fingers to the blaze. In some dim corner of her mind, it occurred to her that, somehow, the warmth of the flames was not at all the same as that of Slade Maverick's callused hand.

BOOK TWO

A Spirit Brave and True

Chapter Eight

The Prairie, Kansas, 1875

Rachel wished Gus, as she called Gustave Oxenberg, had not chosen that evening to come courting her, for she could not feel herself up to the trial it was to make polite conversation with him. Even worse was the fact that he brought with him a goat and its kid; he had heard that goat's milk was better for babies than cow's milk. He was shocked to learn the children, except for Gideon, Caleb, and Philip, were gone, taken away by their uncle, a gunslinger; and his loss at what to do now with the goat and its kid was plain. He had no use for the bleating creatures and had intended them as a gift to Rachel.

Despite her wishing the big Swede would stop calling on her, other than as a friend, she could not help but be touched by his thinking of the baby, Tobias. So, kindly, Rachel told Gus to put the two animals in the barn, that she would have Poke take them with him when he drove the boys home after supper. Then, seeing no other choice, she reluctantly invited her persistent suitor to stay for the evening meal.

It was a gloomy supper. Gus, for whom putting two words

together was difficult anyway, ate like a horse and saw no
point in talking at the table when there was food to be consumed, and the rest were so downcast at the prospect of the
Beecham boys returning home that they said little. The absence of the other children was keenly felt, besides, further
saddening everyone. Rachel could only be relieved when the
meal ended.

Immediately, the boys jumped up and started clearing the
dishes from the table, a chore their sisters normally undertook
and one the brothers dragged out as long as they could,
wanting to postpone the inevitable time when they must leave.
Rachel knew she shouldn't have permitted this, but somehow,
she just could not bring herself to discourage them. In fact,
despite her guilt, she worked even more slowly than the boys
did, moving as though her arms and legs were leaden. Fremont noticed that his granddaughter was unusually dilatory
this evening but, guessing the state of her mind, made no
comment. Lighting his pipe, he settled back into a chair to
read his Bible. Poke, sensing that Rachel was in no mood to
entertain, thoughtfully challenged Gus to a game of checkers,
earning her heartfelt gratitude.

But finally, there came the moment when the last crumbs
were wiped from the table and swept from the floor, the last
dish was dried and stacked upon the shelf, and the last flour-
sack towel was neatly folded and laid in its basket. At the
realization that there was no more work to be done, Rachel
and the boys looked at one another glumly, and a haunting
silence fell. Before anyone could speak, however, the stillness
was broken by the clip-clop of horses' hooves and the churning of wagon wheels in the yard out front.

"Why, who can that be?" Rachel wondered aloud, surprised.

Oil lamp in hand, she opened the door, startled and angered
now to see Slade Maverick standing upon the stoop, his hand
poised to knock. Why, he had such a low opinion of her that
he had not trusted her to have Poke deliver the boys, she
thought heatedly, insulted. Rachel started to tell him just
exactly what she thought of him, then closed her mouth

abruptly as she heard whoops and laughter, and, to her puzzlement, spied the rest of the Beecham youngsters waving at her excitedly from Jonathan's wagon as he guided his team of draft horses across the yard. Her heart jerking painfully in her breast, she glanced at Slade inquiringly, hoping but not daring to believe he had changed his mind about taking the children away from her. He cleared his throat, then spoke, obviously embarrassed.

"I . . . er . . . hate to impose on you like this, Miss Wilder," he began, "but as I . . . er . . . didn't go inside Beecham's soddy earlier, I . . . er . . . didn't realize how badly damaged it was by the storm. Half the roof's caved in, and it's knee-deep in water, besides. There're snakes and rats all over the place, and, well, plainly speaking, ma'am, it's not fit for human habitation. I wouldn't keep a pig in it, much less my nieces and nephews. I thought about taking them to a hotel, but it's so late, and, too, I figure they've already suffered enough upheaval in their lives as it is, and . . . well . . . I guess what I'm trying to say, Miss Wilder, is that I'd be much obliged if they could stay with you until I can get a log cabin built." Slade paused, reaching into his pocket to withdraw a wad of folded dollar bills. "I'll pay you for their room and board, of course."

Rachel's knees went weak at the sight of the cash. She had never seen so much of it at one time in her life, and the wheels of her mind turned furiously as she thought of all she could do with that money: hire more hands to work the farm so her grandfather could rest and enjoy his old age as he ought, increase the small herd of cattle she was slowly building from the poor calves heartlessly abandoned by the Texas drovers because the young animals could not keep up on the long trail drive north, buy herself a pretty new gown—how long had it been since she'd had one, and—for heaven's sake!—why should she think of that now? Still, Slade's offer of payment for keeping the Beecham youngsters, something she had done, and would gladly do again, out of love angered and humiliated her, for it made her feel as though the gunslinger were deliberately drawing a solid line between her and the Beechams, cruelly hammering home the fact that, no matter how much she loved them, he was family and she was not. And so her happiness at their return was marred.

"Naturally, I'll take the children!" Rachel snapped. "But I'm not some stranger running a boardinghouse, Mr. Maverick! Those youngsters are as dear to me as though they were my own, and I'll not take your money for caring for them!" She looked away and swallowed hard as she fought down the sickening temptation she felt to grab the dollar bills he held. "What kind of a woman do you think I am? Why, the very idea of your even offering, when India"—she drew a ragged breath and blinked back her tears—"when India was my best friend . . . close as a sister to me, even if we weren't blood kin—a fact you so kindly pointed out to me earlier. . . ." Her voice, quivering with heartache and sarcasm, trailed away.

"I apologize, Miss Wilder," Slade said, stricken. "I meant no offense, ma'am; truly, I did not. It's just that I know what an imposition this is and that you can't really afford . . . er . . . that you've just a small farm. . . . er . . . well, what I mean is, times are hard, Miss Wilder—" He broke off lamely, feeling like a callow fool at the sudden toss of her head, the dangerous flash of her eyes, and the squaring of her shoulders that told him he was only making matters worse by his indelicate references to her meager finances.

Farming, especially in Kansas, was a hard life, dependent upon such erratic and uncontrollable factors as the weather and the soil. The Great Plains' "sodbusters," as they were sometimes scornfully referred to, were more often than not long on hopes and prayers, and short on crops and cash. From India's letter, Slade knew that the grasshopper invasion last year had devastated small farms such as Rachel's, and despite her obviously genteel upbringing, he didn't think that it was likely she had a fortune stashed under her mattress. Behind her affronted demeanor, he sensed how her pride and love for the Beecham youngsters warred with her worry about how she would provide for them. He suspected, too, that she would rather have died than confess this, especially to him, a gunslinger, a man she could not consider respectable. Slade would have to help her somehow, he knew, but how, he hadn't figured out yet. Rachel Wilder was prickly as barbed wire. He had had little experience in dealing with such a female—a lady. The women he had known in the past had been only too willing to take his money.

"I manage as well as anyone these days, Mr. Maverick," Rachel stated icily, confirming his musings, "and will continue to do so. Further, much as I dislike the fact, I am already beholden to you for discharging my debt at the Silver Slipper, a sum I fully intend to repay you as soon as possible—"

"I thought I'd indicated to you that there's no need for that, Miss Wilder," Slade interrupted. Then, struck by sudden inspiration, he suggested hopefully, "However, if you insist, then how about your keeping the children and, in return, my calling your debt settled? After all, the unfortunate incident at the Silver Slipper arose from your trying to help my nieces and nephews in the first place, a circumstance for which I feel responsible anyway. Would that be agreeable to you, ma'am?"

"Why, yes . . . yes, it would," Rachel replied after a minute's consideration, for this arrangement was not painful to her, as the other had been. It was not the cold business proposition between strangers that the gunslinger had offered previously and that had shriveled her warm heart. Besides, he *was* right. If he had been here to handle Jonathan, the contretemps at the Silver Slipper would never have occurred. Her face suddenly lit up so, that Slade thought she looked like an angel standing there, her golden hair haloed by the flickering flame of the oil lamp. "Please, Mr. Maverick, won't you come inside?" she invited, with a smile that caused his loins abruptly to tighten.

Bemused by his reaction to this prim, proper female—not at all his type—Slade swept off his hat, holding it strategically before him as he ducked to avoid hitting the top of the log cabin's low door frame. Blissfully unaware of her effect upon him, Rachel stepped aside to allow him to enter. Then she was nearly knocked off her feet as she was assailed by the

Beecham children, who had now piled out of the wagon and could scarcely contain their joy as they crowded around to hug her, all talking at once. Rachel got them quieted down at last and introduced Slade to Fremont, Poke, and Gus. She was swift to observe that the gunslinger shook hands not only with her grandfather and the Swede, but also with the Negro. Her estimation of Slade Maverick rose a notch in her mind, for not many white men—especially southerners—would have done so. No matter how much she disliked him, Rachel was honest enough to admit to herself that it was to the gunslinger's credit that he had offered Poke his hand.

By the light of the oil lamp Rachel had set on a small, nearby table, Fremont's keen old eyes assessed Slade sharply from head to toe. Then, as though liking what he saw, the elderly man nodded briefly and told him to pull up a chair.

"Sit a spell, why don't you?" Fremont urged. "It's not often we have company, and I'd be interested in hearing what news you might have." He turned to his granddaughter. "Tell Beecham to stable his team, Rachel, and come on in. No need for him to sit out there in the wind and cold, like a durned fool, and work himself into one of his sulks."

"Yes, Grandpa," she responded obediently, though, privately, she didn't care if Jonathan froze to death.

Still, once Rachel got out to the wagon, she almost felt sorry for Beecham. He looked as though he'd been run over by a train, she thought. Then her heart hardened as she smelled strong spirits on his breath and realized he had been nipping from a bottle he must have had secreted somewhere at his place, though she thought she had found them all and got rid of them.

"Does Mr. Maverick know you've been drinking, Jonathan?" she asked.

"Don't know, and don't care," he growled. "He's not my keeper—and neither are you! Go away and leave me alone! Haven't the two of you done enough as it is—making my life hell and turning my own kids against me?"

Rachel's mouth tightened.

"*You* did that, Jonathan," she pointed out, "sucking up

to a bottle as you've done all these years. Liquor's been the ruin of many a man, including you. But it's not too late. Give it up, Jonathan, before it kills you.''

''Well, thank you, Miss Temperance, for your concern,'' he sneered. ''But, no thanks.'' Then he deliberately pulled his bottle from beneath his coat and swigged a long draft. ''Go on!'' he spat after wiping his mouth off with the back of his hand. ''I don't want or need any of your stupid sermons—or your damned hospitality, either, for that matter. I've had enough of you, and Maverick, too, to last me a lifetime. As far as I'm concerned, the both of you can go straight to hell!''

With that parting shot, Jonathan slapped the reins down hard on the backs of his draft horses. Rachel jumped out of the wagon's path just in time to avoid being run over as the vehicle lurched forward. Trembling at the thought that Jonathan hated her so vehemently that he hadn't cared if she were crushed beneath the wagon's wheels, she returned to the house. Closing her eyes, she leaned against the door briefly, struggling to compose herself before going inside. Then she lifted the latch and went in.

There, she saw that Eve was getting the rest of the children settled for the night. Fremont and Slade were seated before the fire, smoking companionably and exchanging occasional remarks, and Gus was losing to Poke at checkers even worse than he normally did. It was clear the Swede's attention was not on the game but on the gunslinger, and with a start, as she noted Gus's frown, Rachel realized he was sizing up Slade as a possible competitor for her hand. She blushed red as a beet, for until this moment, she had not thought about how her unwelcome relationship with Slade Maverick might be viewed by others. It had not occurred to her that anyone would cast him in the role of her suitor. The idea unnerved her, for she suspected that if the gunslinger ever came courting, he would not care if he measured up to her mental yardstick—as, indeed, he would not! she assured herself stoutly—and he would refuse to be bound by the rules of propriety. Rachel's breath came hard and fast at the notion.

She must take care never to be alone with him, she thought, flustered. For all of Slade Maverick's refined upbringing, he was no gentleman, but little better than Rye Crippen, one of the local ne'er-do-wells and a man she heartily suspected of rustling her cattle. She must not allow her love for the Beecham youngsters to blind her to the fact that their uncle had a notorious reputation and, for all she knew, perhaps even a price on his head, too.

Yet somehow, Rachel found it difficult to remember this when Slade's eyes met hers, for deep down inside, she was forced to admit he was, indeed, the most handsome man she had ever seen.

"Where's Beecham?" he asked, lifting one eyebrow as he saw she was alone.

"He left," Rachel announced, "I presume to drive into town."

Slade nodded, as though he had expected this.

"I'll take care of it in the morning," he stated, calmly enough.

But even so, a little shiver chased down her spine, and she knew she would not like to be in Jonathan's shoes when his brother-in-law found him. To hide her sudden anxiety, Rachel crossed the room, sat down in her rocking chair, and picked up her knitting. Recalling her manners, she attempted to engage Gus, who had declined another checker game, in conversation. But their words were few and stilted, with long silences in between, and to Rachel's chagrin, she spied an ill-concealed smile curving Slade's lips and knew he was amused by Gus's awkward wooing of her and her own lack-luster response. So she could only feel relieved when at last Gus glanced at his pocket watch and said he must be going. Hastily, she got to her feet to walk him outside, closing the door firmly behind her. But a few moments later, as she stood with her hand in Gus's, saying good night (for he had never, in all the time he'd called on her, worked up his courage to kiss her), she heard the lively sounds of a harmonica wafting through the chinks in the log cabin and was mortified to discern the strains of "Mr. Froggie Went A-Courting." Since neither her grandfather nor Poke played the instrument, and the children were now asleep, Rachel knew that it was Slade who dared to perform the wicked deed.

I'll kill him! she thought. *I'll blast him from here to kingdom come with my shotgun! How dare he?*

She was grateful that Gus, being from Sweden, was unfamiliar with the old Scottish folk song. Even so, she was incensed that his courting her should be mocked by the gunslinger. Once Gus had ridden away, she marched into the house, intent on letting Slade Maverick know just what she thought of him. To her dismay, her grandfather's eyes twinkled at her merrily, and a wide grin split Poke's face as, at her appearance, the gunslinger segued smoothly into a spirited rendition of "The Hart, He Loves the High Wood," seeming all the while not to notice her. The old English round made Rachel draw up short, mentally sputtering with outrage, for she knew its words well.

> *The hart, he loves the high wood,*
> *The hare, he loves the hill,*
> *The knight, he loves the bright sword,*
> *And the lady loves her will!*

Recognizing, in light of this, how foolish she would look if she delivered the lecture that hovered on her tongue, she merely sniffed and stamped off, her skirts swishing. Rudely ignoring the fact that Slade was company and she ought to have entertained him, Rachel busied herself in the kitchen until finally the gunslinger stood and slipped his harmonica into his shirt pocket. Gravely, he thanked her for a pleasant evening, but as she had the distinct impression he was laughing at her, it was all she could do to quell the strong urge she had to box his ears. Further increasing her annoyance was the fact that Fremont had so enjoyed their unexpected guest that he invited Slade to bunk in the barn, since the Beecham place had proved so inhospitable.

"Why, thank you kindly, sir," the gunslinger drawled. "I believe I'll take you up on that offer."

"Well, that's fine, then," Fremont answered, beaming, as Rachel groaned inwardly and longed to strangle her grandfather. "Poke'll show you where you can spread your bedroll, and we'll expect you for breakfast in the morning."

Not if I have anything to say about it! his granddaughter thought, fuming.

But then she was struck by malicious inspiration, and as she stifled her growing mirth, it occurred to her that she really ought to thank her grandfather for handing her a prime opportunity to even the score with Slade Maverick—the insolent scoundrel!

Chapter Nine

The following morning, Rachel rose even earlier than usual so none would observe her as she embarked upon her scheme of revenge. At first, she intended only a mild punishment for Slade's behavior the previous evening. But as the sky gradually lightened, so did her plan grow larger—until even she was slightly appalled by it. Nevertheless, the memory of his poorly repressed smirk and his impertinent harmonica playing spurred her on, and determinedly ignoring her scruples, she continued her preparations.

First, she mixed up biscuit dough, setting aside the small portion she meant for the gunslinger. This, she pounded and kneaded unmercifully, imagining she was pummeling the unabashed grin from Slade's handsome face. The more Rachel thought of him and dwelled on the refrain of "Mr. Froggie Went A-Courting," the harder she beat the dough, until at last it was the consistency of rubber, of glue. She fashioned a few biscuits as best she could out of it and popped them into the oven with the rest. Then she sliced bacon and laid it in the skillet to fry, and such was her agitation that she burned three of the rashers black on one side. It was at this point that Rachel's plot began truly to snowball. She decided that the charred strips would be good enough for Slade and that, while she was at it, she might as well make the remainder of his meal inedible, too. She cooked hominy and liberally salted several spoonfuls, which she was careful to keep to one side of the bowl. She scrambled eggs and added enough pepper to Slade's serving to throw a hound off a scent. She even went so far as to pour vinegar into some milk to sour it, just in case he didn't drink his coffee black, and she ground up extra coffee beans, also, so she could make certain of his having a gritty residue in his cup.

When Rachel was through, she stacked all the plates at her end of the table, so she could dish up the meal herself to ensure that only the gunslinger partook of the deliberately ruined food. Then she called everyone to the table.

She bade Slade good morning so sweetly that if he had known her better, he would have been warned something was amiss. But the female tactics to which he was accustomed consisted of pouting lips and clever paint and lacy garters and warm beds. He had no experience at all of the type of assault that could be waged with pots and pans and rolling pins and wooden spoons. In fact, such was his confidence where women were concerned that he assumed Rachel was as forgiving of his impudence as every other female he had ever known.

He did not know why he had teased her so last night; some devil had just got into him, he supposed. She had treated him in such a high-handed manner and made him feel like such a fool that the more he had thought about it, the more he had itched to take her down a peg or two. And Beecham had been right about one thing: Gustave Oxenberg *was* slow—too plodding to be yoked to blue-blooded stock like Rachel Wilder. For some strange reason, the notion that she might actually marry the Swede had irritated Slade no end, despite the fact that she had scarcely encouraged Gus's attentions. After all, one could hardly have expected her to expose her private feelings before a roomful of people. But even knowing she had a suitor, it had come as an inexplicable shock to Slade to meet Gus and to see him, obviously a frequent caller, so comfortably ensconced before Rachel's hearth last evening; and the gunslinger had been unable to resist thrusting a spoke into the Swede's wheel.

Even so, Slade remained bewildered by his own actions. After all, it was not as though he wanted Rachel Wilder himself. In his mind, neither her physical appeal nor her other fine qualities offset the fact that she was an ill-tempered filly sorely in need of a strong hand on her reins and a set of spurs at her sides. She would be nothing but a headache to her husband, and he could not imagine why anyone, even Gustave Oxenberg, would wish to wed her.

But Gus was a big man, taller even than Slade and several pounds heavier. Doubtless, the Swede required an inordinate amount of food to maintain his hefty frame, and from the smells wafting from the kitchen table, it appeared that being a poor cook was not one of Rachel's faults. Slade's mouth watered at the thought of, after weeks of travel, during which time he had subsisted mostly on tough jerky, eating a decent hot meal at last.

He sat down at the table, next to Rachel, smiling to himself at Fremont's rather irreverent blessing. Then he spread his napkin in his lap and waited politely but impatiently as Rachel dished up the steaming food and passed the plates around the table. With the exception of Rachel herself, Slade was the last to be served, and chafing at the bit, he eyed his plate longingly as she rose to pour the coffee, surreptitiously stirring into his cup a small heap of the ground beans she had saved for this purpose. He took his coffee black, so she poured the doctored milk into a glass and set it beside his plate.

"My goodness, you needn't wait for me," she exclaimed as she realized Slade and the Beecham children, having taken their uncle's measure and being bright enough to follow his lead, were looking at her expectantly, although her grandfather and Poke were already digging in. "Go on. Eat up, everybody."

Then, with studied innocence, she filled her own plate, covertly watching Slade from the corners of her eyes all the while. Everyone else's biscuits were so light that they fairly crumbled apart when opened to be spread with butter. Slade's were so hard that he finally had to saw them in half with a knife, and it was all Rachel could do to keep her shoulders from shaking with silent laughter at the puzzled grimace upon his face, for she knew he had yet to grasp what she had done. After he had finished buttering his biscuits, he picked up a strip of bacon and bit into it, unaware, until he began to chew, that it was burned to a crisp on its bottom side. It tasted absolutely foul, since by charring it, Rachel had exacerbated the fact that the hog from which it had come had feasted on grasshoppers before being slaughtered. Her eyes danced as Slade's face went white as, unable to spit out the bacon, he was forced to swallow it. She nearly giggled aloud when, following this, he poked his eggs suspiciously and, seeing nothing wrong with them, put a large forkful into his mouth. The pepper with which they were laced nearly choked him. All at the table stared at him, concerned—except for Rachel, who was doing her level best to stifle her merriment.

"Food . . . went—went . . . down the—the . . . wrong way," the gunslinger managed to get out between coughs and gasps and sneezes, his eyes smarting so badly that tears streamed from them.

Hastily, he reached for his coffee and drank it in two gulps, only to discover that it was gritty as sand. It was then that full comprehension of the wicked trick Rachel had played on him penetrated his mind, though he could not fathom how she had accomplished it, when she had served him from the same bowls and platters as she had everyone else and there was obviously nothing wrong with their breakfasts.

In fact, Slade reflected dismally, feeling slightly sick at the thought of the good meal he was missing—to say nothing of how his stomach was roiling—they were gobbling their food down with gusto. Who was it who had said, "Hell hath no fury like a woman . . ."? He was certainly learning the truth of that this morning. How he heartily wished, now, that he had never teased Rachel with his harmonica playing, for her revenge was likely to poison him.

Without warning, Beecham's accusations about her being a crazy she-devil and decocting all sorts of foul potions returned to haunt him. Good Lord! Slade thought. Was it possible she actually *had* poisoned him? After all, she'd nearly killed Beecham with her shotgun, hadn't she? He eyed her askance. No, surely not. His biscuits might be rock hard and his bacon burned to a cinder, but there had been nothing but an overabundance of plain old pepper in his eggs and grounds in his coffee. He saw, too, that despite her trying to hide it, her lips were twitching with humor. Why, she was laughing at him, Slade recognized, his eyes narrowing with anger and indignation.

Damn her! He'd show her! She wasn't going to get the best of him! Thus determined, he stood, wordlessly walked over to the basin on the counter, rinsed out his cup, and poured himself some more coffee—not trusting Rachel to do it. Then he resumed his place at the table and compelled himself to eat the vile meal before him. He gagged when he tasted the hominy, chock-full of salt, and almost broke a tooth on the leaden biscuits, the latter of which, he mused acidly, if used as ammunition, might have won the war for the South. But somehow, Slade got the food down, staying behind to finish it long after the others had all left the table. He even made himself drink the sour milk, and it was this that finally did him in. It fairly curdled his insides, and he knew, suddenly, that he was about to be violently ill. Cursing Rachel Wilder every step of the way, he leaped up from the table and rushed outside, where, bracing himself against one wall of the house, he heaved up the entire unpalatable breakfast.

To his utter outrage, while he was retching up his insides, Slade heard through the chinks in the log cabin the sound of Rachel humming blithely "Mr. Froggie Went A-Courting."

I'll murder her! he thought. *I'll throttle her with my bare hands! God help me . . . see if I don't!*

With this goal in mind, he marched to the well to wash off his face and rinse out his mouth. The water was freezing, and this further goaded his wrath. Dripping wet from his ablutions, a look on his face that had caused many a man to quail, Slade strode purposefully toward the log cabin, his fingers tightening with anticipation at the prospect of wringing Rachel Wilder's slender neck.

Chapter Ten

From a window of the house, Rachel saw him coming, and she had never been so frightened as she was then at the sight of the gunslinger charging like an enraged bull toward her. Her heart plummeted to her toes, and her hands felt cold as ice. Heavens! He looked mad enough to spit nails—and she knew without a doubt that *she* was the hapless target of his fury! She wondered frantically what he would do to her —and why she hadn't considered this before plotting her revenge. He would certainly rebuke her scathingly, likely shouting at her all the while. Perhaps he would even go so far as to beat her. After all, he was a gunslinger, no gentleman—and here she was alone, with no one but a handful of children to defend her, since her grandfather and Poke had already ridden out for the day. Oh, she must have been out of her mind to have fixed Slade Maverick such a breakfast!

Like a hunted animal, Rachel glanced about wildly for someplace to hide, but there was none. She was not normally a coward, but under the circumstances, she felt that caution, not confrontation, was the wisest course of action. She decided to run for the barn and try to get her mare and gallop away before the gunslinger caught her. Not bothering even to grab her coat, she ripped open the door and raced across the yard.

"Come back here, you spiteful woman!" she heard Slade yell as he spied her. "Come back here, damn you! I'll teach you to play your witch's tricks on me!"

Rachel paid him no heed. Indeed, the jingle of his spurs and the thud of his boots as he chased after her urged her to an even faster speed. In moments, she had slammed the barn door shut behind her. But before she could reach her mare, Slade was there, flinging the barn door open again so hard that it vibrated audibly as it hit the wall of the log structure. The morning was yellow with a sun that spoke of spring's coming, and silhouetted against its brightness, the gunslinger appeared to her like some avenging demon standing there in the door frame.

Dismayed, seeing she would now be unable to get Sunflower out of her stall in time to evade him, Rachel quick-wittedly scrambled up the ladder to the loft, her heart thrumming so loudly in her breast that she could hear the sound echo inside her head. Crouched on her hands and knees, she reached down to pull the ladder up behind her, but to her terror, Slade was already ascending its rungs, and he was so heavy that she could not shake him off. She even tried pushing the ladder away from the loft, but the gunslinger's weight was such that the ladder merely swayed precariously for a minute before falling back with a thud against the loft's edge.

Abandoning her futile attempts to dislodge him, Rachel snatched up a nearby bale of hay and, with all her strength, pushed it over the loft's edge. To her relief, the gunslinger was taken by surprise by her action and so was struck squarely in the head by the heavy bale. The impetus knocked him off the ladder, sending him sprawling. Not waiting to see if he was hurt, Rachel hastily caught hold of the ladder and began to haul it up. Swearing a blue streak, his head throbbing from the direct hit he had sustained from the woman who was, he was now thoroughly convinced, the she-devil Beecham had named her, Slade lurched angrily to his feet and lunged toward the rapidly disappearing ladder. His hands closed firmly around the bottom rung, and a very undignified tug-of-war for possession of the ladder ensued.

"Just wait until I get my hands on you!" he snarled up at Rachel through gritted teeth, his eyes narrowed and blazing like sapphires. "I'll make you sorry you ever even *thought* of poisoning me, you rancorous female!"

As this was exactly what Rachel feared, she blanched and yanked all the harder on the ladder. Still, despite her trepidation, the gunslinger's threats infuriated her, and she found herself unable to choke back the heated words that rose to her lips.

"I didn't *poison* you," she sneered, glowering down at him. "If I had, you can be sure you'd have keeled over dead at the table. All I did was ruin your old breakfast—and don't tell me you didn't deserve it after your harmonica playing last night, you ill-mannered rogue!"

"Well, pardon me, ma'am," Slade drawled sarcastically. "I was only trying to help you and old Ox along a mite. It looked to me as though your courtship could badly use some assistance, and although I don't care to brag, I've had considerable experience in that area. But I might have guessed that's all the thanks I'd get from you for providing a little serenading music to liven up what is surely one of the dreariest romances I've ever had the misfortune to witness!"

"O-O-Oh!" Rachel sputtered, fuming.

She was so mad that she inadvertently loosened her grip on the ladder and nearly plummeted off the loft's edge when Slade seized the opportunity to jerk the ladder to the ground. In a flash, he was hightailing it up the rungs. Once more, Rachel strove vigorously to dislodge him, but he wouldn't be budged, and panicked, she began to shove bale after bale of hay down on top of him. One arm held above his head in an attempt to shield himself from the barrage, Slade resolutely continued his ascent, cursing hotly as the bales clouted him one after another, the hay scratching his face, his neck, and his arms.

Rachel squeaked with alarm when, finally, despite her efforts to stop him, his head popped up over the loft's edge, and then he clambered into the loft. Turning, she took to her heels, but not rapidly enough to prevent Slade from hurling himself at her and grabbing one of her slender ankles.

"Gotcha!" he crowed triumphantly as her feet flew out from beneath her and she pitched facedown onto the hay-strewn floor.

"Let me go, durn you! Let me go!" Rachel cried, squirming and kicking violently as she tried to wrench herself free of his steely grasp. "Let me go, you brute!"

Her hands clawed for purchase, but there was none to be had as, ignoring her indignant, apprehensive shrieks, Slade ruthlessly dragged her toward him. As swiftly and expertly as any cowpuncher hog-tying a calf, he flipped her over and straddled her, pinning her body beneath his. Rachel fought him fiercely, arms flailing, fingers curled like talons as she struck out at him blindly, seeking to escape—to no avail. Her strength was no match for his. After a brief battle, the gunslinger caught her wrists tightly and pinioned them above her head.

"Now . . . Miss . . . Wilder," he panted, his low voice sending a shiver of fear mingled with some other indefinable emotion down her spine, "you and I . . . have a score . . . to settle."

Originally, Slade had intended to give her a good hiding. But now, as he looked down at her, his wrath slowly dissipated, to be replaced by another—stronger—emotion. He inhaled sharply, staring at Rachel as though he'd never really seen her before.

During their scuffle, her hairpins had come loose from the knot upon her head, and her hair had tumbled down about her. Now, for the first time, Slade saw how long and thick it was—like a mass of soft, shiny corn silk. It hung to her knees, engulfing her, framing her piquant, heart-shaped face as a gold-leafed oval frames a portrait. In that instant, in his mind, she *was* a portrait, still, silent, her mint-green eyes wide, startled, her hollow cheeks flushed, her moist mouth slightly parted, as though a photographer had taken her picture by surprise. Only her breasts moved, heaving with her every ragged breath, so it seemed as though he could actually see her heart beat, quick and light, beneath her bodice. Despite the nip in the morning air, a thin sheen of sweat born of their tussle glistened upon her face, and from her skin wafted the subtle scents of soap and lilacs that made Slade think of the coming spring. Unbidden, an image of Rachel running barefoot across the burgeoning prairie grasses and wildflowers, her hair billowing in the wind, her lips parted in laughter, filled his mind.

It occurred to him, strangely, that he would like to see her like that, wild and free as a deer, unburdened by her everyday troubles. The heartland demanded far too much of its women, he thought. It had been the death of India. Slade found the notion of Rachel succumbing, too, intensely disturbing as he felt her body, young and alive, tremble beneath his.

He murmured something—a curse, Rachel thought, though she did not know for sure, for the gunslinger had spoken in fluent French and she did not understand the language. She knew only that, for a moment, like a cloud the sun, a shadow darkened his handsome face as she watched him.

She felt transfixed by his eyes, like some small prey when its predator moves in for the kill. She could not seem to tear her gaze away. A tumult of emotion flooded her being at his nearness. She had never been so close to a man before. She could feel the length of his lean, hard body lying against hers, his weight pressing her down into the hay, and despite her fear and mortification at being trapped and helpless beneath him, she was forced to admit to herself that the sensation was not unpleasant. In fact, she tingled all over, for his body was warm, much warmer than hers. Heat seemed to emanate from him in waves, as from a slow-burning fire—a peculiarly masculine characteristic.

Without warning, a picture of herself huddled in her cold bed in the log cabin flashed into Rachel's mind, and in some dim corner of her brain, she thought how much less cold her bed would be if she had the gunslinger to share it. She blushed, for ladies were not supposed to think about such things—even if they did. Nevertheless, she could not dispel the perturbing image. She felt as though she were somehow drowning in the dark blue pools of Slade's eyes, that, presently, she would go down for the last time and that she would never be quite the same afterward.

Now, Rachel saw, too, things she had not noticed earlier, when she had been so intent upon spoiling his breakfast. Sometime either last night or this morning, he had shaved off his beard, leaving only his black mustache, soft and thick above his sensual mouth. He had bathed, also. He smelled of soap and vetiver, and of the hay that filled the loft—as silence filled it. Only the rasp of her uneven breathing, and of his, broke the stillness as they exhaled small white clouds of mist that met, like lovers' lips, in the frosty morning air.

Through the chinks in the roof, the morning light streamed in, illuminating them both, so they seemed cast in a halo of sunbeams and swirling dust motes, while all about them, the barn was shadowed, as though time had stopped, except where they lay, as though they were all alone in the world—one man, one woman. The air was fraught with an odd tension, as well, sharp and anticipatory, as though, at any instant, the highly charged atmosphere would explode, loosing something bold and wild and exhilarating, which would never again be contained. Rachel shuddered at the thought, wanting to run away and hide, but Slade refused to release her.

Instead, surprising them both, he demanded suddenly, harshly, "Are you going to marry Ox Oxenberg?"

"I don't think that's any of your business," she responded stiffly once she had recovered from being taken aback by his question.

"Miss Wilder, everything about you is my business if you're going to be looking after my nieces and nephews," he stated flatly, "and I don't suppose any plans you might have to wed that Swede would include building a room for eight motherless children onto his house."

"No, I don't suppose any plans I might have would—if I *had* any such plans, which I don't," she declared, her eyes still mesmerized by his, her heart still fluttering erratically at his proximity.

"What's the matter?" he asked tersely. "I thought Ox had been calling on you for months. Does he come here just to stuff himself at supper, or is he simply taking his own sweet time about asking for your hand? Jesus! If that's the case, I'll bet he's never even kissed you . . . has he?"

"Mr. Maverick—!" Rachel snapped, only to have Slade cut her off rudely, a knowing grin splitting his face.

"Aha! He hasn't, has he? Well, what's he waiting for? An engraved invitation? Lord, he's a bigger fool than I thought—a disgrace to the male species. Thank God, some of us are made of smarter stuff! You wouldn't catch me hemming and hawing around, waiting on some balky woman to ask me to kiss her!"

"No doubt, since I can't think why any woman—balky or otherwise—*would* ask you!" Rachel observed dryly, her ire at his needling momentarily overcoming her fear of him.

"Now, *that*, Miss Wilder, was a most unwise remark—especially for a woman in your current position," Slade pointed out mockingly, his hooded eyes raking her captive body slowly, insolently, before once more riveting on her face. "Previously, I *was* merely going to tan your pretty hide for your temerity in poisoning my breakfast. But that last gibe of yours was a direct slap at my masculine honor, and now, I'm afraid I'm going to have to insist on satisfaction accordingly—with or without an invitation."

"Why, you—you wouldn't dare!" Rachel stammered, her cheeks flaming as she realized he intended to kiss her.

"I wouldn't bet on that if I were you," he said, his eyes dancing wickedly as, despite her immediate cries of outrage and objection, her struggles to escape, he caught her jaw with his free hand and forcibly tilted her face up to his. "Pucker up, Miss Wilder," he commanded softly. "Willing or not, you're about to be kissed."

Then, his eyes darkening in a way that made Rachel's breath catch in her throat, he ground his mouth down on hers—hard. So hard that his teeth grazed the tender flesh of her lower lip and she tasted blood, coppery and bittersweet, upon her tongue as she tried desperately to resist his savage onslaught. She had never before been kissed by a man—at least, not like this—and she had never dreamed that it would prove so shattering an experience, wakening within her feelings she had not known existed, feelings that not only shocked and scared her, but, inexplicably, so excited her, too, that she could not seem even to think. Somehow, she had not expected Slade's mouth to be so hot and hungry, his tongue so sinuous and beguiling as he traced the outline of her lips, then roughly compelled them to part. She had not guessed how brazenly and expertly his tongue would ravage her mouth, searching out its innermost secret places, making her feel as though she were alternately burning with fever and shivering with chills.

Confused and terrified by her reaction to him, she continued her attempts to elude the gunslinger's encroaching lips and tongue, but her endeavors were useless. Despite her thrashing her head from side to side, his hold on her was secure and relentless, and he subdued her easily by tightening his fingers about her jaw and throat until she ceased her exertions and lay acquiescent in his arms, dazed and breathless from his determined assault upon her senses. Slade kissed her more gently then, reveling in the involuntary whimpers that emanated from her throat as at last, to her horror and shame, she realized she was kissing him back.

Lord, she tasted good! he thought. He hadn't known until this very moment just how good she *would* taste—or how much he had longed to claim possession of her mouth, to teach it a language sweeter than that which it usually spoke. Her lips were soft and quivered vulnerably beneath his, making his loins taut with sudden, sharp desire.

Slade knew then that he'd only been deceiving himself about his lack of interest in Rachel Wilder. He *did* want her. His fingers itched to strip away her cool veneer and find out what lay beneath it. He knew that he would take her right here and now in the loft, if he could. The thought further aroused him, so he deepened his kisses, growing once more insistent with the silent but provocative demands he made of her mouth. But this time, she did not try to pull away from him. Encouraged by her mute acceptance of his advances, Slade slowly slid his free hand down her throat to cup one of her breasts through the material of her bodice.

As his palm caressed her lingeringly, Rachel gasped against his lips, her fright renewed by this unexpected and extremely intimate contact. She wanted to die a thousand deaths, for despite her humiliation that he should dare to fondle her so, as no gentleman ought, something vital and electric stirred and sprang to life within her at his touch, some hitherto unknown thing coiled deep inside her. It reared its head, beautiful in its menace, like a diamondback rattler poised to strike, its poison, though of another sort, just as deadly, she knew somehow. Yet even so, some dark, treacherous part of her yearned to feel its fangs sink into her being, drawing blood, setting her ablaze. As the image formed in her mind, a low moan of passion echoed in the barn, and vaguely, she recognized that the animalistic sound came from her own throat.

Beneath Slade's skillful fingers, her nipple puckered and stiffened of its own volition, straining against the fabric of her bodice, waves of delight such as she had never before felt radiating from its center. The shock of it was such that Rachel writhed and bucked against him, afraid of what was happening inside her, afraid of where it would lead—or, worse, of where it would not lead. For somehow, she did not think that Slade Maverick was the type of man to marry her, even if he *did* succeed in claiming the prize that rightfully belonged to her husband.

That sobering thought drenched Rachel like icy water from a bucket, jolting her to her senses. Lord, what was she thinking of, to allow this man she had known only a few days to take such liberties with her? At this rate, he would soon have her skirts rucked up about her thighs—as though she were no better than a common harlot he might roll in the hay! What on earth was the matter with her? She must be a wanton, or mad, to have permitted him to kiss her, to touch her, and to have actually enjoyed it—because, God help her, she *had* enjoyed it! She was honest enough with herself to admit that, regardless of how disgraceful the admission.

Absolutely horrified by her behavior, Rachel started once more to struggle against him earnestly.

"Don't fight me, honey," Slade muttered against her mouth, his voice husky. "Don't fight me. I know you're a high-spirited filly, but I've a gentle hand on the reins when I choose. Let me show you. . . ."

His lips covered hers once more, stilling the pleas and protests that bubbled in her throat. At that, unable to think of any other way to stop him, Rachel bit down hard as she could on his lower lip, relishing the taste of the blood that spurted from the wound she inflicted upon him. Startled and in pain, Slade yelped and loosed her abruptly, sitting back on his haunches. One hand went to his lip, and he swore as he saw that his fingers came away smeared with blood.

"Vixen!" he spat softly, his eyes gleaming as they took in her disheveled hair tangled with hay; her pale, scared face; her wide green eyes; her mouth, bruised and swollen from his kisses; and her heaving breasts.

She didn't look at all the prim and proper Miss Wilder now, he thought with a great deal of satisfaction, but rather a woman of passion and promise. Indeed, the sight of her so stimulated him that it was all Slade could do to keep from brutally flinging himself on her and ravishing her then and there—as he might well have done, he realized sheepishly, had she not damned near bitten his lip clean in two! He must be out of his mind, trifling with her as he had! Virginal viragoes were definitely not his sort; nor had rape ever been his method of seduction.

"Miss Wilder—" Slade began, meaning to apologize as he stretched out one hand to help Rachel to her feet.

Before he could complete either his words or his action, however, she, mistaking his intent, hastily sat up and slapped him so hard that his ears rang like church bells on Sunday. Then, while he was still stunned from the blow, she shoved him away with all her might. Unprepared for the first, much less the second, attack, Slade toppled to one side, grabbing hold of Rachel in a vain attempt to regain his balance. Their combined weight was such that they rolled and skidded across the loft, and as, unfortunately, they were too close to its edge to halt their momentum, they both tumbled out onto the barn floor below.

Luckily, several of the bales of hay Rachel had hurled at Slade earlier had broken apart in the process and so cushioned their fall, so neither of them was badly hurt. Slade, who bore the brunt, pulled a muscle in his leg, while Rachel bruised her hind end hard enough that she felt certain she wouldn't be able to sit down for a week. Nursing their injuries, they shakily stood, groaning and scowling at each other.

"Damned fool woman!" Slade growled. "It's a wonder you didn't cause me to break my neck! Jesus! I can barely walk!"

"Well, what about my—my . . . posterior?" Rachel sputtered indignantly. "How do you think I can ride like this? I've got a farm to run, plus eight children to tend to—or have you forgotten that, Mr. Maverick?"

"Slade," he asserted firmly, one corner of his mouth starting to twitch with humor at her insistence on correctly observing etiquette, despite the fact that, just moments past, he had indecently pressed her down into the hay and made most improper advances toward her. "My name's Slade. After this morning, I reckon we can dispense with the formalities, don't you, Rachel?"

"Well . . . ah . . . y-y-yes, I—I suppose so," she agreed, flushing red as a chickasaw plum as her eyes were surreptitiously but irresistibly drawn to his mouth and she remembered the feel of it upon her own, the taste of his blood upon her tongue. "I'm—I'm sorry I—I bit you and hit you," she confessed contritely.

"And I'm sorry I placed you in a situation where it was necessary for you to do so," he replied. "I don't normally go around . . . er . . . forcing myself on unwilling women. I guess I . . . er . . . just lost my head." He paused for a moment, then continued. "Look here, Rachel. It seems we

got off on the wrong foot all the way around, and I think—
if for nothing more than the children's sake—that we ought
to try to make a fresh start and get along as best we can from
now on. What do you say? Friends?"

"All right," she said slowly, then added tartly, "provided,
however, that you don't—that you don't ever kiss me again!"

"That bad, huh?" Slade lifted one eyebrow devilishly, a
rueful, crooked smile curving his mouth.

"Your mustache tickled!" Rachel blurted without thinking.

Then, realizing with deep embarrassment that her words
had made it sound as though she had otherwise enjoyed his
kisses, she turned and fled from the barn, leaving Slade to
stare after her speculatively, stroking his mustache thoughtfully and grinning like a man who has just roped the finest
filly in the corral.

Chapter Eleven

Rachel returned to the log cabin to find eight pairs of wide,
round eyes gazing at her, seven of them filled with a mixture
of apprehension and awe.

Being youngsters whose intellect and adaptivity had been
honed to a keen edge by a hard life, the Beecham children
had straightaway taken their uncle Slade's measure and decided that the best means of safely surviving his guardianship
was simply not to cross him. So, although the reason for his
anger was unknown to them, the sight of him sprinting across
the yard after Rachel, shouting threats and insults at her, had
caused them to feel certain she would not emerge from the
barn intact—if at all.

After conferring among themselves as to what they should do, they had timidly decided that it would behoove them to wait and see what happened. Still, this had not lessened their anxiety on Rachel's behalf, and now, their relief at her appearance—in a state of disarray, but apparently unharmed, even so—was enormous. In their minds, that she had battled their uncle Slade and escaped virtually unscathed vested her with a hitherto unsuspected power, and they peered at her with new respect, wondering if she really was the she-devil their father often called her.

"Well, what are you all standing around staring at me for?" Rachel asked crossly to hide the fact that she feared they somehow knew of her shameful conduct in the barn. "Have I grown another head or something?"

"No, ma'am," the older youngsters chorused as one, gathering from her tone that it would be most unwise to inquire about what had occurred.

Only little Naomi, who was an exceptionally bright two-year-old and therefore both precocious and curious, dared to pipe up, popping the question that was uppermost in the children's minds.

"Did Uncle Slade spank you, Aunt Rachel?" she queried innocently. "Is that why you're so mad?"

"Certainly not! Why, the very idea—"

"Gee whillikers!" Naomi interrupted excitedly. "Do you mean *you* spanked *him*, Aunt Rachel?"

"Oh, for heaven's sake! Of course not!" Rachel answered, exasperated. "What a notion! However, I *am* going to spank a certain impertinent young lady if she doesn't stop asking such silly questions."

"Am I 'pert'nent, Aunt Rachel?" Naomi prodded, slightly crestfallen at being pronounced what was evidently a most undesirable thing.

"Yes, you are."

"Oh." Naomi paused for a minute, thinking hard. Then, artlessly, she declared, "I'll bet Uncle Slade's 'pert'nent, too, 'n' that's why you're so mad."

At that, Rachel took a very deep breath and silently counted to ten, all the while wondering what the penalty in Kansas was for throttling a two-year-old.

"Naomi—" she began.

"Yes, Aunt Rachel?"

"Not . . . another . . . word."

"Yes, ma'am."

"As for the rest of you"—Rachel glared sternly around the room—"wipe those smiles off your faces right now! You—Gideon, Caleb, and Philip—go outside and ask your uncle if he has any plans for you today. He might need your help over at the soddy. And you, Eve, find out if he and Jonathan will be wanting a dinner basket or if they'll be returning here to dine. Susannah, you and Naomi start clearing the table, and Andrew, you fetch a pail of water from the well and set it to boiling on the stove, so we can get the dishes washed."

As the children moved to carry out her instructions, Rachel climbed the ladder to the narrow, cramped loft that had used to be her parents' bedroom and that now served as her own retreat in the two-room log cabin. After pulling across the loft's width the curtain that gave her a measure of privacy when she required, she made her way to the bed, stooping to avoid hitting the low ceiling. Sitting down on the plump feather mattress covered by a cheerful patchwork quilt, she faced the dressing table that had once belonged to her mother and that was crammed in under the eaves. The stool was missing—it had not survived her parents' journey to Kansas from the Appalachian Mountains in Pennsylvania—and the mirror was smoky and cracked, but still, the dressing table was Rachel's most treasured possession.

Across its top, she had laid a pretty lace cloth she had painstakingly embroidered, and upon this were assembled her few real belongings: her mother's silver-backed hand mirror, brush, and comb; her own small silver jewelry box (which contained her hairpins, a pair of beautiful tortoiseshell combs, an engraved gold locket with a picture of her parents and a lock each of their hair inside, and a plain gold ring that had been her mother's wedding band); a green flacon of lilac scent, which essence Rachel had distilled herself; a carefully horded bar of fine-milled, store-bought soap that she used only on special occasions; and her father's three favorite books—the Bible, Plato's *Republic*, and a dictionary.

Solemnly, Rachel studied herself in the dressing-table mirror, one hand pressed to her mouth. Unwittingly, with her index finger, she traced the outline of her lips, as Slade had done with his tongue. Somehow, she had expected to find herself altered after his fierce kisses, but she was not. Except for her hair resembling a rat's nest and her mouth being unusually red and swollen, she looked no different from before. How could that be? she wondered. For she *was* changed, and somehow, she sensed she would never again be the same as she had been before the gunslinger had kissed her. Even now, there was a strange feeling deep inside her, an indescribable longing, a haunting ache she had never felt previously. What was it? She did not know. She knew only that she wanted something she had not wanted before.

Slowly, she trailed her hand down her throat, shadowed ever so faintly with bruises, to the breast Slade had touched. Unconsciously mimicking his caress, she slid her palm light as a feather over her nipple. Immediately, it quickened and hardened, the same waves of delight radiating from its center as had in the barn, so strongly that Rachel feared she might swoon. Her cheeks burning, she jerked her hand away, mortified by her action. Whatever had possessed her to do such a thing? It was that man, of course—that corrupt gunslinger! Hadn't she warned herself never to be caught alone with him?

Trembling, Rachel snatched up her brush and began to run it roughly through her hair, yanking so hard at its snarls that her scalp smarted and tears stung her eyes. Once the tresses were free of tangles and hay, she twisted the entire mass around and around down its length, then wound it up on top of her head. Holding the heavy knot securely in place with one hand, she opened her jewelry box, took out her hairpins, and began to jam them into her hair. She hoped she had enough of them. She would have to search for the others in the barn later. They cost money, and she couldn't afford to buy new ones. The loss of even a few of them amid the hay was another black mark on Slade Maverick's slate.

After Rachel had finished with her hair, she straightened the ruffled collar of her gown and smoothed her skirt to rid it of any wrinkles and stray wisps of hay. Then she pinched her pale cheeks to put some color in them. She surveyed herself critically again in the dressing-table mirror. There, now. She looked more like her usual, tidy self. Satisfied, she nodded curtly at her reflection. Then she went back downstairs to get on with her work, fully and firmly determined to put the incident in the barn behind her.

Slade, Rachel learned, had ridden into town to track down Jonathan and bring him home—at gunpoint, if necessary, she had no doubt. The three older boys, whose help would, indeed, be needed in building their new log cabin, had started out on foot for the Beecham place, hoping to catch a ride in their father's wagon if their uncle found him (and they did not doubt he would). Eve had gone out to the barn to tend the stock. Susannah was drying the last of the dishes, while Naomi, standing on a chair, did her best to put them away. Andrew, who had made a second trip to the well to draw another bucket of water—this, for baby Tobias's morning bath—was just setting the pail upon the stove to heat.

"Uncle Slade said to tell you he'd be pleased if you'd care to ride over to the soddy later with a dinner basket," Susannah announced, "but only if you weren't spittin' mad when you prepared it—whatever that meant."

Despite herself, Rachel couldn't repress the broad smile that sprang to her lips at hearing this. No doubt, after this morning, the gunslinger was afraid she really *would* poison him! And it would serve him right if she did, she thought— not that she would, of course. Seeks, the half-breed Wichita Indian from whom she had learned her knowledge of prairie herbs and wildflowers, as well as her skill at dowsing, had specifically cautioned her against practicing "bad medicine," explaining soberly that if one opened one's heart to "evil spirits," they would surely come in. Rachel respected Seeks immensely—he was as close to the land as a man could get, she thought—and she would feel terrible if she ever did anything to earn his disapproval. So, tempting as the idea was to slip Slade a little something extra with his dinner (though nothing fatal, naturally), she reluctantly abandoned the wayward impulse. Even so, she felt better having just imagined the gunslinger stricken with stomach cramps and stuck in the outhouse all afternoon.

Humming to herself, Rachel dumped the now tepid water on the stove into the basin on the counter, sponged Tobias off, dressed him in a fresh gown and diaper, then poured some warm goat's milk into the bottle she had fashioned out of an empty fruit jar and part of an old rubber glove. Sitting down gingerly in her rocking chair (which was not nearly as kind to her sore rump as her bed had been), she began to feed and rock him.

Toby, as she called him, was a handsome child, with a patch of downy black hair and dark blue eyes. He took after his mother, India, and his uncle Slade, too, Rachel realized as she gazed down at him. His disposition was sweet, also. Now that he was fed properly and changed regularly, he seldom fretted or cried. But to Rachel's secret worry, he was not a plump, healthy baby. His arms and legs were like matchsticks; his body was so thin that she could count his ribs, and he wasn't gaining weight as quickly as she believed he ought. Sometimes, he had trouble swallowing his milk, and then keeping it down afterward. Because of this, he nursed slowly, and it took a long time to feed him. Rachel didn't mind, though. She enjoyed cradling him in her arms, talking and crooning to him. Often, she wished wistfully that he were her own, and now, with India dead, she guessed he was, in a way. For she was, in essence, the only mother he had ever known—or probably ever would, poor little tyke.

Rachel blinked back tears at the thought, for it made her think of her own mother, dead and buried now these three years past. Even now, despite all her attempts to hold on to her mother's image, Victoria Wilder's face, in Rachel's memory, was blurred at the edges, as though viewed through a vignette. Yet, oddly enough, Rachel could recall many other things as sharp and clear as though she had seen and felt them only yesterday—her mother's hands, especially: their soothing touch upon her fevered brow, their deftness at separating the strands of her long blond hair and braiding it, their knack of turning hand-me-down dresses into a young girl's delight, their quickness in reaching out to help her lift a heavy basket of laundry, the graceful way they had pointed out the hidey-hole of a prairie dog or a meadowlark's nest. How Rachel missed those loving hands, red and roughened by hard work, but always there—until that terrible summer when they were gone too swiftly, too soon, and forever.

Now, India, too, was dead. Only her children remained, and of these, the last held a special place in Rachel's heart. Though she loved them all, she knew that, deep down inside, she loved Toby best. He was so tiny and frail, and his dark blue eyes often seemed to her so sad, almost as though he knew that his real mother had died, that Rachel ached to nurture and comfort him. Now, as she glanced down at him, she saw he had fallen asleep, his beautiful, rosebud mouth slightly parted, a trickle of milk at one corner, the thumb of the bottle's rubber glove resting gently against his lower lip. He breathed so quietly that, sometimes, her heart lurching to a halt, she had to press her head against his small body to be certain he breathed at all. But right now, thanks to his contentedly bulging tummy, she could readily discern the steady rise and fall of his chest beneath his gown. His feeding had gone much better this morning, she reflected hopefully, resolutely pushing her anxiety about him to the back of her mind.

Smiling at the picture Toby presented in repose, she carefully eased the half-empty bottle from between his delicate hands and set it down on the floor. Then, slowly, she stood, freezing momentarily as he stirred and sighed in his sleep. Finally, sure he was not going to awaken, she tiptoed over to the old packing crate that served as his cradle. For just a minute, she continued to hold him, his head against her breast.

Strangely, the yearning she had felt when Slade had touched her there rose once more within her, only different somehow, not so urgent and hot, but rather soft and warm. Briefly, Rachel wondered why it should be so. Then, because she had been reared on a farm, where she had, on occasion, witnessed animals mating and so was not ignorant of much she might have been otherwise, she realized, blushing, that, in a way, most babies started with a kiss. If you did the one and followed where it led, you just naturally sometimes got the other.

Unbidden, the thought that Slade's child would look a lot like Toby crept into her head. Unnerved, Rachel thrust the notion away. She already had one baby, even if he wasn't really her own, and she didn't intend to go rolling around in the hay again—especially with Slade Maverick!—just so she could get another one.

Lightly, she kissed Toby on the brow, inhaling deeply the sweet scents of milk and talcum that clung to his skin. How she loved the fresh, clean smell of him, like the earth after a spring rain, or clothes after they'd been washed and dried in the summer sun, or newly cut fields in autumn, or the first hard frost of winter. Of such things as these did Toby remind her. She was glad of his presence in her life. Reluctantly, Rachel laid him tenderly in the old packing crate and covered him with his blanket.

"Sleep tight, Toby darling," she whispered. "Sweet dreams."

Chapter Twelve

The days that followed after Slade's coming soon slipped into a pattern, much to Rachel's consternation, for despite their truce, she had hoped to avoid the gunslinger as much as possible. But at her grandfather's suggestion, he had taken up permanent residence in the barn until such time as the new log cabin could be constructed at the Beecham place, so Rachel saw him often.

Washed and combed, Slade appeared promptly at the kitchen table every morning for breakfast, greeting her pleasantly, although he remained wary enough to help himself from the steaming bowls and platters rather than waiting for her to serve him. During the meal, he conversed easily with Fremont, Poke, and the children, as though he had known them for years, and he livened up the table with his stories and jokes—the latter of which were more often than not at Rachel's expense, much to her discomfiture. Not wanting him to see he'd got the best of her, however, she bore his teasing stoically, now and then managing a few sly gibes of her own, which the gunslinger, grinning, tallied up on an imaginary slate. Fremont and Poke always hooted gleefully at this, egging him on with remarks about "scoring one for their side" and observations about Rachel's having "met her match at last."

After breakfast, Slade would send Gideon, Caleb, and Philip in the Beecham wagon, confiscated from their father, over to the soddy, while he himself went into town to round up Jonathan, who continued, despite all Slade's threats, to ride into Delano and drink himself into a disgusting stupor every evening. Rachel didn't know why the gunslinger even wasted his time bothering with Beecham. But when she asked him about it, he said that, worthless or not, Jonathan was still the children's father, and Slade felt he owed it to them and to India to try to sober him up and straighten him out— even though the effort was proving as futile as Rachel's own such endeavor had been.

"Well, you'd think he'd get tired of your dragging him out of some shoddy saloon and dunking him in the nearest water trough every day to bring him to his senses," she commented dryly.

"Yeah," Slade replied. "Frankly, I'm surprised he hasn't up and run off, but I reckon he just doesn't have the gumption.

One thing's for sure: He's the sorriest piece of sh . . . dung I've ever seen. Every time I even think about India being married to that bast . . . bum, I'd like to break his fool neck.''

"Save yourself the trouble. At the rate you're working him, he'll more than likely keel over dead from exhaustion. He looks dreadful, Slade. He shakes all the time—''

"That's from not getting any whiskey all day. I'm sorry —I know he's a sick man—but I don't pity him in the least, Rachel. He made my poor sister's life a hell, and Lord only knows what would have happened to the kids if you hadn't stepped in when you did. You know damned good and well that, for all practical purposes, he as much as abandoned them after India died.''

"I know. Still, you're a hard man, Slade.''

"Yeah, well, you're a hard woman, Rachel.''

"Why, I am not!''

"Sure, you are,'' he insisted, grinning. "How else could you have resisted old Ox's courtship for so long? Honestly, Rachel, if you don't intend to wed that Swede, you'd be doing the poor fellow a favor if you'd just shoot him and put him out of his misery.''

Frowning, Rachel tossed her head and sniffed.

"How do you know I *don't* intend to wed him?'' she needled. "Maybe I've changed my mind and decided to say yes, after all.''

At that, Slade's face went very still for a moment, and his smile vanished. Then he snorted derisively.

"Yeah,'' he drawled, his eyes shuttered so she couldn't read his thoughts, "when pigs fly and cows jump over the moon, maybe. You know as well as I do that you don't harness a high-stepping filly to a plodding ox, Rachel.''

"Gus is *not* plodding!'' she retorted. "He's as fine a man as they come—finer than you by a long shot! *Gus* is a gentleman!''

"Meaning that I'm not, I suppose. Well, and what's wrong with that, I'd like to know? After all, *I'm* the one who had the most . . . pleasurable experience of kissing you, aren't I? While he's still hanging around like a dejected stray dog, waiting for an invitation.'' Slade's eyes traveled the length of her body lazily, appreciatively, then returned to linger on her mouth. His lips curving in a devilish grin, he stroked his mustache pointedly. ''I'll bet old Ox sure does wish he knew what he was missing,'' he declared.

''O-O-Oh!'' Rachel exclaimed. ''How dare you remind me of that awful day—you—you scurrilous scoundrel! Lord, how I wish I were a man for just one minute! I'd box your ears good!''

''Well, if that's how you feel,'' Slade rejoined wryly, ''then would you mind not bringing the dinner basket today. Somehow, I get the impression I'll be a whole lot safer eating at the Douglas Avenue House instead!''

It had become Rachel's custom to ride over to the Beecham place every afternoon to deliver dinner to the two men and three boys. In this way, she not only received a small and, to her surprise, often enjoyable break in her day, but she was able to observe their progress, which was slow. This was due in part to the fact that with the advent of spring, the snow that had covered the prairie almost all winter melted more and more quickly with each passing day, leaving the ground sodden as a marsh. This made it difficult to dig the root cellar, which was not only vital to preserving food through the changing seasons, but was also necessary for protection during the dog days of summer, when tornadoes were most apt to come swirling down furiously out of the sky. In addition, the slab logs for the cabin, as well as the barn Slade had decided to build, had to be bought, cut, and hauled from one of the sawmills in Wichita, a time-consuming process. Heavy stones for the fireplace must be gleaned from distant fields and sometimes broken into more manageable sizes before being set into place, and a mixture of river sand and lime (which was produced by burning mussel shells and buffalo hair) was needed for mortar, both for filling chinks in the log walls and cementing the chimney.

Sensibly, Slade was erecting the cabin close to the well—which ought to have been done to begin with, he grumbled, instead of first putting up the soddy, and then digging the well.

"Well, I don't guess Jonathan thought of that," Rachel remarked. "Even before he took to drinking so much, he wasn't very practical. He had a hard time, at first, making a go of the farm at all. But then, I don't reckon he ever really had to fend for himself before coming to Kansas . . . what with growing up on a plantation and being waited on hand and foot by a household of slaves all his life."

"No, he didn't," Slade agreed. "The way I remember it, his daddy and mama always looked after him real good, spoiled him rotten, in fact. Nothing was too good for the one-and-only heir to Beecham's Landing—including my sister. But then the war came, the North won, and afterward, there wasn't much left in the South to inherit. A whole lot of boys died for a 'Glorious Cause' they didn't even understand, and half of those who survived . . . well, they wound up like Beecham—or worse. At least he's all in one piece."

"You—you fought in the war, didn't you, Slade?" Rachel asked hesitantly, curious but not wanting to pry.

"Yeah, in the C.S.A. I was still wet behind the ears, a nineteen-year-old lieutenant in the cavalry—mostly because the officers in my troop kept getting themselves killed until I was the only one left to promote."

"Is that where you learned to shoot?"

"No, that was back on my old man's plantation, Cypress Hill, before I left home and New Orleans both, in search of greener pastures."

"I thought—I thought that it was because you—you shot and killed a man. In a duel in New Orleans. I mean, that's what India told me, that you ran away from Cypress Hill because they might have—have hanged you for murder."

"India said that, did she?" Slade glanced at Rachel sharply, wondering what else she knew about his past.

Rachel nodded.

"Well, it's true. They sure as hell would have hanged

me—or at least I thought so at the time. Unfortunately, my aim wasn't as good back then as it is now, and I didn't know enough to make sure I'd actually accomplished what I'd set out to do. I was young, and I panicked and bolted—needlessly maybe, as it turned out, since I heard a few years later that I'd only wounded my opponent and that he eventually survived. I still don't know the truth one way or the other, because I never went back to New Orleans to find out. I figured I was safer that way, and by then, it didn't really matter anyhow. I had nobody and nothing to go back to, and I was already entered on the law's records as G.T.T.—Gone to Texas—anyway, so it just seemed better to let sleeping dogs lie.''

Slade paused for a long moment, remembering the night that had changed his life forever: *Moonlight streaming through the ancient elms. A woman running. Thérèse in a white gown. A cry. A shot. Which had come first? It didn't matter now. A spray of fragile gardenias flecked with blood. So much blood, spreading in a crimson stain. The recoil of the pistol in his hand. Death . . . cold, eternal death . . . and Digger smiling mockingly, his white teeth gleaming as he fell. . . .*

Abruptly, the gunslinger recalled himself to the present. Then, as though he resented Rachel's inquisitiveness, he spoke coolly.

''Well, I've got to get back to work. If I don't keep an eye on Beecham every minute, he hunts up one of those whiskey bottles he's got cached around here and winds up drunk before sundown. Thanks for the dinner, Rachel.''

He turned away, and for the first time, she was actually sorry to see him go. The glimpse of his past had intrigued her. The pain in his eyes at his memories had made her realize suddenly that he was not so hard inside as he pretended to be—and that he was very much alone with whatever grief he carried in his heart.

* * *

Every day toward sunset, Slade quit work at the Beecham place, and he and the boys returned to the log cabin—usually without Jonathan, who, sooner or later, somehow nearly always managed to slip away the minute the gunslinger's back was turned. It angered Slade no end, but short of tying Beecham up, he didn't know what he could do about it. He needed his brother-in-law's assistance with the heavy labor of digging the root cellar, hauling the logs and levering them into position, and fetching and setting the stones for the chimney. Bound hand and foot, Jonathan could scarcely be of any help—not that he was of much use anyway. But still, Slade reasoned, it *was* Beecham's house and barn they were building, and besides, the longer Jonathan was forced to go without a drink, the better Slade's chances for reforming him were —although the gunslinger had to admit he didn't hold out much hope for this.

Once finished for the day at the Beecham place, Slade returned to Rachel's house, and there, he busied himself doing whatever chores and odd jobs needed to be done. This was his unobtrusive way of repaying Fremont and Rachel for their hospitality, since otherwise, he would either have had to spread his bedroll in Jonathan's dank, dirty soddy or to check into a hotel. Slade wasn't too keen on either alternative— the first, for obvious reasons; the second, because he didn't relish the thought of spending much time in Wichita, with only a metal token in his gun hand.

After it got too dark to work anymore, he washed up and went inside the log cabin. There, he generally lingered after supper to wage several fierce battles against either Fremont or Poke over the checkerboard. Then he played his harmonica until the children drifted off to sleep, while Rachel sewed or sometimes sang softly, and Fremont and Poke, their eyes twinkling, did whatever they could to nudge matters along in what they firmly agreed was the right direction.

But Slade was not the only one to come and sit beside Rachel's hearth on a cool spring night. Often—*too* often, to the gunslinger's way of thinking—"old Ox," as he frequently referred to the Swede, arrived to call on her, and then a time was had by all. The air fairly crackled, as though charged by lightning, with Gus stubbornly attempting to ignore Slade—and Slade just as stubbornly refusing to be ignored. Like two dogs eyeing a meaty bone, they watched each other suspiciously, occasionally growling and snapping when one thought that the other was edging too close to the coveted prize.

Fremont and Poke were immensely entertained by all this. Rachel, who, had she been other than what she was, might have deemed it highly gratifying herself, could only find it terribly embarrassing instead. She knew that it was very upsetting to Gus and a source of great amusement to Slade, who, though he could not possibly be thought of (at least in her mind) as a serious rival for her hand, was apparently, nevertheless, thoroughly determined to prove to her that he could out-gentleman the Swede any day of the week. To this end, he set out wickedly to best Gus at every turn.

If, thinking to please her, Gus told her a piece of interesting news, Slade impudently topped it with one of his own. If Gus managed to bring himself to pay her a modest but sincere compliment, Slade flattered her outrageously, and at some length, about all her finer points. If, one evening, Gus shyly brought her a small bouquet of early blooming flowers, Slade conspicuously presented her with a bigger bouquet the next, grinning hugely and *tsk*ing over the fact that, while she had carefully arranged the Swede's offering in a vase, she callously dumped his in the trash.

Most humiliating of all, Rachel believed, was the manner in which the two men would simultaneously leap to their feet to pull out her chair for her at the supper table, neither giving an inch, so she was eventually maneuvered into place as regally as any queen in a litter borne by a pair of devoted slaves.

One especially tense night, each man actually tugged so strenuously on his side of her chair that the slender spokes snapped in half, causing the back to fall off, thereby reducing Rachel to sitting upon the stool that remained. For she was so angry at being made such a spectacle that she spurned each man's own chair, hastily offered in lieu of hers. Further goading her wrath was the fact that her grandfather slapped his knee and guffawed so hard at the incident that he rocked back too violently in *his* chair from the table, and before he could fully recover, he lost his balance and crashed to the floor. Then, as though all this weren't bad enough, Poke—blinding tears of mirth rolling down his cheeks—staggered up from his seat to help set Fremont and the fallen chair aright, accidentally mistook Fremont's wooden leg for the chair leg, and pulled it out from under him, sending him sprawling a second time.

At that, utterly incensed, Rachel jumped up from the table and stormed out of the house, heartily wishing every man above the age of twelve in perdition. A few minutes later, Gus appeared, looking so shamefaced and contrite that she didn't have the heart to scold him.

"I—I bring yoour shawl," he stammered, holding it out to her. "Is still chilly in the evenings, *ja*?"

"Yes, thank you, Gus," she answered quietly, wrapping herself in its soft folds, grateful for its warmth and his thoughtfulness.

For a moment, there was an awkward silence between them, neither knowing quite what to say. In the night sky, the silver crescent moon shone faintly, obscured by the thin veil of mist that sometimes drifted across the prairie during the transition from the dying winter to the new spring; and the stars twinkled sporadically. Somewhere in the distance, the hoot of a burrow owl reverberated on the evening wind. Gus shuffled his feet and cleared his throat gruffly.

"Vell, is early yet, but best I be on my way, even so, *ja*? I not mean to cause trouble with chair. I not realize my own strength sometimes, nor yoour . . . friend his, maybe. So, I will make better chair for yoou, bring next time I come."

Something in his tone caused Rachel to glance at him searchingly for an instant, torn. What was the matter with her? she wondered. He was a kind, decent, hardworking man, who loved her and wanted to marry her, even if he had never really come right out and said so in so many words. Surely, she thought, that should be enough to content any woman. Why, then, wasn't it enough for her? She did not know, but somehow, she intended to discover the answer. Speaking softly, she laid one hand upon the Swede's arm.

"Gus," she murmured, "before you go, aren't you going to kiss me good night?"

At her words, a mixture of disbelief and gladness and sudden confusion swept across his face, as though he didn't quite know what to think or do. Then he blurted, "*Ja, ja,*" and after a halting moment, he tentatively enfolded her in a clumsy, bearlike hug and kissed her.

Rachel did not know what she had expected—bells or fireworks or something very like them, perhaps—anything that would have convinced her she could love this man, could spend the rest of her life with him. But much to her bewilderment and disappointment, she felt none of the turbulent, white-hot emotion that had coursed wildly through her veins when Slade Maverick had pressed her down into the hay and savagely claimed possession of her mouth. Gus's lips were soft and warm and hesitant, as though he were unaccustomed to using them to kiss a woman; and all in all, his lack of skill and her own lack of response made it a very unsatisfactory experiment, Rachel thought. Not unpleasant, really, but missing something that Slade had seemed to know instinctively how to achieve, as though he had known her down to her very bones as well as he knew himself.

Gus kissed her only once, then quickly released her, as though fearing she might otherwise accuse him of trying to take advantage. But his clear blue eyes beamed shyly in the darkness, and a silly smile of happiness lighted his face.

"I tink maybe yoou are most vonderful voman in vorld, Rachel Wilder," he stated simply.

Then, as though embarrassed by his unexpected declaration, the Swede reddened and abruptly left her, retrieving his horse from the barn. After flinging himself into the saddle, he galloped away. Rachel watched him until he was out of sight, her lips quivering in a woebegone smile as, shortly thereafter, an elated bellow—like a Viking cry of victory— echoed across the plains to her ears.

Oh, Gus, she reflected sadly, gazing off into the distance from where the sound had come, *I'm not the most wonderful woman in the world. And, worse, I'm not even the right woman for you. I'm not the right woman for anybody, I reckon.*

As she stood there forlornly, lost in reverie, the door of the log cabin creaked open softly behind her, and Slade stepped outside, smoke wafting from the glowing tip of the cigarillo he had clenched between his teeth.

"We being attacked by Indians?" he inquired with feigned innocence. "I thought I heard a war whoop."

Angered at his interrupting her solitude, and not in the mood for his teasing, besides, Rachel opened her mouth, intending to tell him to ride west until his sombrero floated. Then, just as abruptly, she clamped her lips shut, determinedly refusing to rise to the bait. What was the point in sparring with him? she asked herself. He was an insolent rascal, and just like Jonathan, there was no hope of reforming him. She was better off simply avoiding him whenever possible. With that thought in mind, she attempted to brush past him into the house, but without warning, his hand shot out to close tightly about her wrist, restraining her.

Rachel eyed him scathingly, her silent insistence that he release her plain, but Slade paid it no heed.

"From that exhilarated roar we heard through the cabin walls, I take it that the Swede finally received his long-awaited invitation," he commented dryly.

"I don't think that's any of your business," Rachel replied stiffly. "Now, if you don't mind, it's chilly out here, and I'd like to go back inside."

"But I *do* mind," Slade asserted, his voice low, husky. "I mind very much, indeed. I mean—in the essence of all fairness, of course—I think I ought to receive an invitation, too. Don't you agree?"

"Certainly not!" Rachel snapped, her cheeks turning scarlet at the very idea, her heart beginning to pound far too hard and fast in her breast. "Gus is my—my suitor, and—and you're not!"

"Oh?" Slade raised one black eyebrow satanically, his midnight-blue eyes gleaming in the hazy moonlight. "And what makes you think that? Did I ever *say* I wasn't a candidate for your hand?" he questioned, his words and his touch sending a shiver down her spine as he gently but inexorably drew her to him. "Have I not called on you every evening, paid you compliments, and brought you flowers—even if you *did* spurn them for another's?"

"Well, y-y-yes," Rachel conceded. Then she added sourly, "But you've only done those things to annoy Gus—and you know it, Slade!"

"Do I? Are you a mind reader, then, as well as a witch? What would you do, then, I wonder, if I suddenly fell at your feet, swore my undying devotion to you, and begged for your hand in marriage?" he asked lightly, his lips curved in a peculiar half smile, his eyes hooded so she could not read his thoughts.

In the sudden, taut silence, Rachel stared at him as though hypnotized, scarcely daring even to breathe, her palms sweating, her pulse racing, her mouth dry. Her tongue flicked out nervously to moisten her lips. She swallowed hard. Surely, he was not serious. Surely, he was but making a cruel jest of her, she told herself stoutly—the hateful man! So, despite the fact that, strangely, unaccountably, some small part of her yearned to believe him, Rachel dared not suppose he was in earnest, lest he mock her for her foolishness. Taking a deep breath, she answered frostily.

"Why, I would find the sight of you upon your knees most gratifying, Slade, and then I would laugh at your thinking me so gullible as to fall for your lies."

"How do you know they would be lies?" he queried softly,

suddenly tossing away his thin black cigar, then clasping her without warning in his arms. He tilted her face up to his. "Hmmmh? How do you know they would be lies?"

"I—I just know," she insisted, trying to turn her head away, for his mouth was now very near to hers, too near, she thought. "Now, please, Slade, let me go. It's late, and I'm tired and—and cold."

But this last was not true, Rachel realized suddenly. She felt warm, very warm indeed, wrapped in his sheltering embrace. She felt somehow safe and secure, too, as though he were strong enough to lick the whole world, and carry without faltering the heavy weight of all her burdens, also. For a moment, the night was hushed. Only the hissing of Slade's discarded cigarillo as it soaked up the dampness of the earth, its orange ash sputtering, then finally dying out, broke the stillness that enveloped them.

Then Slade muttered thickly, "As far as I'm concerned, you can go inside anytime, Rachel. Anytime at all. All you have to do is issue my invitation first."

"And if I—if I don't?" she breathed, her eyes half closing, unable to meet his any longer, her mouth parting slowly, expectantly, of its own volition.

His response was to kiss her—as she had known it would be, as she had to admit she had inexplicably *wanted* it to be. Lingeringly, thoroughly, as though he intended to savor every honeyed moment of it, he kissed her, his tongue tantalizingly outlining her lips, then shooting deep between them, seeking the dark, moist recesses of her mouth.

At his tongue's invasion, Rachel moaned low in her throat, her hands, flattened against his chest, creeping up, as though they had a will of their own, to fasten around his neck and pull him closer. Her slender fingers splayed, burrowed instinctively through the thick, glossy black hair that curled at his nape as, deep within the secret core of her, the hot, wild thing she had felt before in the barn flickered and blazed into life with a fury, setting her afire.

Her heart beat against Slade's own, her head spun, and her

knees shook so, that, somehow, she knew she would have fallen had he not held her so tightly. She felt liquid as quicksilver, as though all her bones were dissolving inside her, leaving her so weak and pliable that, unwittingly, her lithe young body melted against Slade's. He was not so big and tall as Gus, but, rather, fitted her as though he were made for her, and she for him. She had felt small and lost in Gus's brawny arms, she recalled dimly, and he had held her as though she were far too fragile and dainty for him, a porcelain figurine he might accidentally break. But Slade had no such compunctions. He crushed her against his lean, whipcord body as though he *wanted* to break her, bending her back, supporting her with the strength of his arms.

His fingers tunneled through her upswept hair, itching to jerk the hairpins from it one by one so he could see it fall, each long, silky strand cascading down and wrapping about her like a golden thread, binding her to him. But Slade knew she could not return to the house, looking as though he had tumbled her in the hay. A kiss in the moonlight was one thing. Anything else, and he felt certain he would have to answer to the shotguns of the indulgent but no less protective Fremont and Poke. He did not wish to have to kill either one of them, but neither would he be meekly compelled to an altar.

He was a drifter, a gunslinger, no good for a woman like Rachel—and he knew it. She was not even his type. Yet with each passing day, bafflingly, maddeningly, Slade found himself increasingly drawn to her, like a moth to flame. When Gus had followed her outside, Slade had wanted to stride after him and knock him down violently—and this, despite the fact that he was grudgingly forced to admit he both liked and respected the Swede. And when Slade had grasped that Gus had actually kissed Rachel, he had wanted to murder him. Upon hearing the Swede's triumphant shout, the gunslinger's hackles had actually risen, and his hands had dropped to his revolvers and nearly slid them out of their holsters before he realized he could hardly ride after Gus and shoot him. Only once in his entire life had Slade ever before done such a rash thing over a woman—he, who was always so cool and collected.

But he had loved Thérèse—bold, beautiful Thérèse—and in the end, his love had killed her. She was sealed in a stone crypt now, forever—and his heart with her, he had believed. Yet he could not deny the feelings that stirred within him as his mouth devoured Rachel's, then slanted across her cheek to her temple, her hair. He nibbled her ear, making her tingle and shudder, and he whispered words to her that he knew she did not comprehend, for he had reverted instinctively to French, so much more lilting and beautiful than English, he thought, so much better suited to romancing a woman in the pale moonlight.

His words washed over Rachel like a river over sand, eroding what little resistance she offered as he kissed her again and again, his breath warm against her skin, his mustache tickling her, his lips like molten ore trickling down her throat to the pulse that throbbed jerkily at its hollow. She could feel the hard evidence of his desire for her pressed against her thighs through her gown, and inside her was a burning ache she had never felt before and did not understand. She knew only that she was like a feverish woman thirsting and that Slade's kisses, instead of soothing her, quenching her, were as blistering sun upon her flesh, salt in her mouth, increasing her fever, her thirst. In some dark corner of her mind, she realized she wanted more of him—much more.

She was shocked and frightened by the thought, and at last, she tore away from him so suddenly that she stumbled and nearly fell.

"No, don't touch me. Please," she gasped as Slade stretched out one hand to steady her. "Please."

Then, lifting her skirts, Rachel turned and ran toward the house, pausing at the door only to tidy her flustered appearance and catch her breath before going inside. Slade followed more slowly, giving her the time she needed to compose herself—and that he needed, also, he recognized ruefully as he became abruptly aware of how revealing his tight breeches were.

Lord, what was it about that woman that aroused him so? She was not beautiful in the classic sense, as more than a few he had bedded in the past had been. In fact, he suspected that there were many men who would not deem her more than passably pretty at best, and certainly, her temperament would not win any prizes. But still, there was some strange, arresting quality about her that intrigued him as no other woman since Thérèse had done.

Jesus, Slade, he thought, *from the way you're acting, one would think you were halfway in love with her, and you've hardly even known her a month! You'd better watch your step, lest you'll find yourself roped, hog-tied, and branded before you know it!*

And that was the last thing he wanted . . . wasn't it? For a moment, as he remembered the sweet taste of Rachel's mouth, Slade was no longer so sure anymore. Shaking his head, he wondered briefly what India would have said about it all. She surely hadn't written him to look after her children, with the hope of neatly marrying him off to their "aunt" Rachel in the process, had she? Or had she? Slade smiled wryly to himself in the darkness.

Lord, India, he mused, *now that I think about it, I think that's exactly what you* did *do! I guess you decided I'd rambled long enough, huh? Well, maybe you were right, and maybe I have. I don't know. I'll have to think on that one. God knows, Rachel sure as hell would be wasted on old Ox. Besides, as much as he eats, I reckon she'd finish him off right quick if he ever made her mad at mealtime. Lucky for us that she'd already cooked supper tonight before we busted her chair!*

Grinning widely at the thought, Slade returned to the house, devoutly praying Rachel didn't have any plans to even the score at breakfast again.

Rachel had slipped into the log cabin quietly, hoping fervently to go unnoticed. But her grandfather was not to be fooled. He glanced at her sharply, his keen old eyes taking in speculatively her flushed cheeks and the way a few tendrils of hair had escaped from the knot upon her head. Of course, both might have been due to the cool night wind, Fremont supposed, but somehow, he thought not. He shifted his penetrating gaze to the gunslinger, who had entered the house shortly after Rachel. Slade's face was like a mask, impassive, unreadable. Only his dark blue eyes glittered with emotion —but it was not that of a man who has just had his desire sated. After a moment, satisfied that nothing more improper than a moonlit kiss had taken place outside, Fremont leaned back in his chair, puffing contentedly on his pipe and secretly pleased as punch.

Lord knew, Rachel could do with a little kissing, he mused—she was fairly on her way to becoming an old maid, much to his despair—and somehow, he didn't think Gus had much gumption in that department. But Slade, now . . . *that* was another story. In fact, Fremont suspected that the gunslinger had virility to spare and, more often than not, succeeded in getting the milk for free instead of buying the cow—and that was not at all what Fremont had in mind. Over the passing days, he had had ample opportunity to observe Slade Maverick at close hand, and he had taken the man's measure and fully decided that, gunslinger or not, he was the husband for Rachel.

Not only did he not shrink from her tart tongue or quail before her wrath—which, alone, in Fremont's mind, would have qualified him for the job—but he was both intelligent and educated (because of his background, he had as much, if not more, book learning as Rachel), and he was gifted with a lively wit and a good sense of humor, besides. He was also strong and compassionate. He didn't shirk hard work, back down from a fight, or smoke, drink, or gamble more than he ought, and if he was given to whoring, Fremont had seen no evidence of it. From this, he had surmised that, while Slade had no doubt sown more than his fair share of wild oats, he was not the type of man who constantly needed a woman to bolster his ego. His disgust at Jonathan's endless carousing and ill treatment of India before she had died was plain, leading Fremont to conclude that if ever Slade Maverick decided to marry and settle down, he would be fiercely faithful to and protective of the woman he had chosen above all others. He was a loner and so would be a hard man to catch. But Rachel was up to the task, Fremont thought, and decided that if his granddaughter let the gunslinger get away, she was the world's biggest fool—and in that case, it would serve her right if she *did* wind up an old maid!

He looked over at the rocking chair, where she sat humming and rocking the baby, Tobias. It ought to be her child instead of India's she was holding, he reflected, though he didn't grudge her taking in her dead friend's youngsters. Still, as a result, the log cabin was now inordinately crowded. Fremont sighed at the thought, briefly missing the peace and quiet that had reigned previously. Nowadays, the air was always filled with talk and laughter and noise, and there was scarcely room to walk about once the children had spread their blankets on the floor and settled in for the night, as they had now, though Fremont noted that none of them was asleep yet. Doubtless, they were waiting for Slade's harmonica playing, and he was still locked in a fiercely contested game of checkers with Poke.

"Aha! Crown me!" the Negro crowed jubilantly, interrupting Fremont's reverie and attracting his interest to the checkerboard. "Yo'd bes' watch out! Ah've got yo on de run now, Slade!"

"Yeah, that's what you think, Poke. You aren't playing against old Ox now, remember?"

"Hmph!" the big Negro snorted, unimpressed. "Old Ox ain' as dumb as yo think, an' anyways, de bof o' yo'd have ter git up purty early in de mawnin' ter git de bes' o' me!"

Before Slade could inform Poke just what he thought of this remark, little Naomi piped up and, out of the blue, as youngsters sometimes do, asked curiously, "Aunt Rachel, are you gonna marry old Ox?"

"He's not 'old Ox' to you, Naomi," Rachel reprimanded her tartly, "and whether I aim to marry him is nobody's business but mine and his. Now, go to sleep."

"Yes, well, but . . . are you?" Naomi persisted.

"Not if he breaks another one of my chairs!" Rachel declared dryly, hoping to put an end to the child's questions before they really got started. "Now, hush, before you wake the baby. He's just now drifted off." She gazed tenderly at Toby, cradled at her breast.

For all of a minute, Naomi was silent, apparently thinking hard, for her face was screwed up in a thoroughly hideous grimace, Rachel saw by the lamplight, wondering what made children do such unattractive things. She astutely discerned from this, however, that the girl was not yet done pestering her, and indeed, this soon proved the case.

"Aunt Rachel?" came the small voice again.

"Yes, Naomi?"—this, in a half indulgent, half warning tone.

"If you're not gonna marry old . . . I mean . . . Gus, are you gonna marry Uncle Slade instead?"

Lord, India, why didn't you chloroform that child at birth? Rachel asked herself, mortified.

She wished the floor would somehow open and swallow her as she saw Slade's shoulders begin to shake with ill-suppressed laughter at her being put on such a spot, while her grandfather and Poke chortled outright. Now, she understood all too well why otherwise loving mothers often longed to pinch their children's heads clean off—something she had never quite grasped previously.

"Naomi, dear"—she spoke through gritted teeth, glowering at her grandfather and the hired hand, and not daring to look Slade in the face, lest she jump up and strangle him for snickering at her predicament—"the *only* man I'm going to marry is the one who brings me five hundred head of cattle for my south forty. Is that quite clear?"

"Yes, ma'am."

"Good. Then go . . . to . . . sleep!"

"Yes, ma'am." Naomi paused, then uttered contritely, "Aunt Rachel, I'm sorry if I was 'pert'nent again."

"Well, you were!" Rachel said crossly. "Now, for heaven's sake, hush!"

"Yes, ma'am. I won't make another peep, I promise."
Then, under her breath, she added irrepressibly, "But if I's
you, I'd pick Uncle Slade. I like him much better 'n old . . .
Gus. Uncle Slade's 'pert'nent—like me!"

Heedless of Rachel's speechless outrage, Slade, Fremont,
and Poke all guffawed hysterically at this. At that, deciding
she had had just about all she could take, Rachel rose stiffly
and carefully laid the baby in his packing crate, tucking the
blanket up around him securely. As far as she was concerned,
the only saving grace of the entire evening was the fact that
Poke had whipped Slade's hind end at checkers. Not waiting
for the gunslinger to take his leave, she bid all a terse good
night. Then she climbed up to her bedroom and yanked the
curtain across the loft's width as distinctly as though she had
slammed a door. After fumbling in the darkness for her box
of matches, she struck one and lit a single candle. Then she
set about preparing for bed.

From below, his laughter fading, Slade watched her silhouette against the curtain as, one by one, she removed the
hairpins from her long blond hair and let it fall. For a moment,
he wondered how it would feel to slide into bed with her and
wrap those tresses around his throat as he pressed her down
into the mattress and made love to her.

Then, slowly, he raised the harmonica in his cupped hands
to his mouth and began softly to play.

Chapter Thirteen

Some days later, Rachel awakened in the middle of the
night to the sound of cattle lowing fretfully in the distance.
At first, she paid little attention to the mooing, thinking, in

her somnolent state, that it was the wind. Then, suddenly sitting bolt upright in bed, she realized that it was because the noise was being *carried* by the wind that it had reached her ears. Cursing a blue streak, she jumped out of bed, not bothering even to dress, merely tugging on her stockings and boots beneath her nightgown.

After pulling aside her bedroom curtain, she scrambled down the ladder from the loft, stepping precariously over the slumbering children sprawled upon the floor as she made her way to the door of the log cabin. There, she threw on her coat and grabbed her shotgun. Then she headed outside toward the barn.

It was the creaking of the barn door as she swung it open wide that wakened Slade, who was bedded down in the loft. Due to years of sleeping with one ear cocked at all times, he came instantly wide-awake. Alert to the possibility of danger, he reached beneath his saddle, which served as his pillow, and eased out his gun belt. Quickly, he buckled it around his hips. Then he quietly snaked forward on his belly to descend the ladder to the barn below, intent on giving the intruder an extremely unpleasant surprise. He could see little in the semi-darkness, but over the sound of Poke's stentorian snoring in the lean-to, Slade heard the jingle of a bridle and Sunflower's nervous nicker.

Jesus! Some goddamned horse thief is trying to steal Rachel's mare! he thought angrily. *Well, we'll soon see about that!*

Stealthily, pistols now held at the ready, he crept on stockinged feet through the barn until he was level with Sunflower's stall. There, he pivoted rapidly so he stood squarely in the open frame of the stall door.

"Freeze—right where you stand," he hissed, "and reach for the sky before I blow you away!"

Rachel screamed and jumped a mile, nearly startled out of her skin. He had moved so noiselessly that she had not heard his approach, and for a moment, she feared she had been set upon by some stranger. Fast as she could, she leveled her shotgun, pointing it at the tall silhouette looming toward her from the shadows.

"Stand back, or I'll shoot!" she warned, edging behind Sunflower for cover.

Then, as Slade jammed his revolvers into his holster, cursing heatedly, she recognized his voice and, with relief, slowly lowered her own weapon.

"Jesus, Rachel!" he snapped as he strode into the stall, enraged and unnerved by the fact that, ignorant of her identity, he might accidentally have fired upon her. "What are you doing sneaking around out here like a goddamned horse thief? You little fool! Don't you ever pull a stunt like that again, you hear?" he snarled, grabbing her and giving her a rough shake. "Jesus! I might have killed you, for Christ's sake!"

"I—I didn't mean to wake you," she whispered, trembling with fright and the shocking realization, as he held her in his arms, that he was stark naked from the waist up. His dark skin was smooth and gleamed in the faint moonlight that filtered through the chinks in the roof. Here and there, an old scar shone white. His chest was matted with curly black hair that trailed down his firm, flat belly to disappear into his breeches. Embarrassed at how her eyes strayed over him, Rachel raised her gaze to his face, biting her lip. "I'm sorry. I—I just didn't think. I needed my mare—"

"At this hour! What for?" Slade demanded, his eyes narrowing as he became abruptly aware she was clothed in nothing more than a thin night rail and her coat. "Damn it, Rachel! You've scarcely anything on! Where did you think you were going dressed like that?" A sudden suspicion struck him. He inhaled sharply, then swore. "Jesus! You weren't riding out to meet Gus, were you?"

"Of course not!" she rejoined indignantly, mortified that he would even think such a thing. "It's my cattle. I heard them mooing, and it woke me up. Something's disturbed them, and I've got to go check on them. A durned cattle rustler is probably out there right now, making off with half my herd! It's that no-good skunk Rye Crippen, I just know it! The brand-blotting thief! I'm going to catch him in the act—and turn him over to the marshal for hanging!"

"Lord, you've got about as much sense as Naomi!" Slade declared, stricken and infuriated that she had even thought of doing such a thing. "Just what were you planning to do if you got out there and discovered four or five armed men instead? Shoot the whole gang of 'em by yourself? Hell! They'd have snatched you off your horse and probably slit your damned throat—*after* they'd all raped you first, of course, I'm sure. Did you ever think of that, you little fool? Cattle rustlers are the lowest of the low, right down there with horse thieves and killers. Now, get your tail back into the house before I tan your hide good! I'll handle this."

"You don't even know where the herd is," Rachel protested stubbornly, undeterred, her fear for her cattle overcoming her fear of him.

"I'll find it," Slade said curtly. "Now, get!"

He pushed her out of the stall, then made certain she was headed out the barn door before he clambered up the ladder to the loft to retrieve the rest of his garments. It was while he was yanking on his boots that he heard the unmistakable clatter of hooves in the barn below. He sprang to his feet just in time to see Sunflower vanishing through the barn door, Rachel clinging like a burr to the mare's bare back. Cursing under his breath and thinking how much he was going to enjoy wringing her neck when he caught her, Slade hastily tucked his shirttail into his pants, jammed his hat on his head, and shrugged into his duster. Then he scrambled down the ladder, bridled and saddled his big black stallion, and set out after her at breakneck speed.

Although Rachel was some distance ahead of him, she wasn't hard to spot in the moonlight—thanks to the white nightgown rucked up about her calves. Slade spied her atop a prairie hillock and galloped toward her, a muscle working tensely in his jaw. Yet even as he chased after her purposefully, he had to admire the way she rode, flying like an avenging angel across the plains, her unbound hair streaming out behind her wildly in the wind. In the end, he finally caught up with her only because his horse, Fortune, was much faster and had more stamina than her mare. As he came up alongside her, Slade leaned over in his saddle, grabbing her bridle and jerking Sunflower to a halt.

"By God, I ought to beat your pretty backside black and blue!" he growled. "I thought that I told you to go back to the house, that I'd handle this."

"You did," Rachel conceded coolly. "But they're *my* cattle—and you're not my keeper, Slade!"

"Damn it, Rachel! Why do you always have to be so stubborn? And more prickly than a cactus, to boot? You might at least have waited for me if you were so goddamned determined on carrying out this harebrained scheme!"

"I—I was afraid you wouldn't let me come with you, and if it *isn't* just Rye Crippen out there, if it *is* an armed gang, as you seemed to think it might be, you just might need my help, Slade. I'm a fair shot myself, and good as you may be—and so far, I've only your reputation to judge that—I don't know that you could handle four or five men alone, any more than I could."

"Well, I wouldn't like the odds, that's for sure," he confessed. "Still, I don't want you getting hurt, Rachel. But I guess I can't trust you to behave sensibly and return to the log cabin, can I?"

"No, you can't, because I won't—and that's final!"

"Well, at least you're honest. I'll say that for you. All right, then. You can come along with me. But you do exactly what I tell you, you hear? I'm not going to be responsible for your winding up with a bullet in you because you were too damned stubborn and stupid to follow my orders. Now, where's this herd of yours?"

"Just over that rise." Rachel pointed.

"Let's get going, then."

They rode on wordlessly, each conscious of the need for silence as they approached the crest. There, they dismounted, creeping forward in the tall plains grass until at last the cattle came into view.

"*That's* your herd!" Slade burst out softly, dumbfounded. Had he not been aware the sound would alert any possible cattle rustlers lurking around, he would have laughed out loud. "Why, if there's more 'n a dozen head there, I'll eat my hat!"

"Well, I never said it was a *big* herd," Rachel whispered, scowling at him furiously. "But it's mine, and I aim to defend it."

"But, Rachel honey, it's not even worth stealing," Slade pointed out logically, now somewhat exasperated that he had been forced to make a long ride in the middle of the night —and for no good reason. "Who in his right mind would want to risk his neck thieving a handful of what's got to be the sorriest, scrawniest cattle I ever did see?"

"Rye Crippen, that's who! The stinking varmint! And they're not sorry and scrawny, either! They're slick-eared calves—or they were until I branded them—cast off by the drovers because calves, especially leppies—the motherless ones—can't keep up with the herds on the trail north. Mostly, the drovers kill them, but sometimes, they give them to farmers along the way. I take all of them I can get, because they're free and I can't afford to buy them. I raise them on skim milk, then wean them and put them out to pasture. They're young yet. They just need beefing up some, that's all. One of these days, I'll have me a fine herd, and then I'll never have to worry again about the crops failing and there not being enough food on the table or hard cash in the tin box on the kitchen shelf."

Rachel's face looked so young and earnest in the moonlight that Slade found he didn't have the heart to tease her further. Sometimes, he forgot just how difficult her life really was, what with her parents dead and her having nobody in the world but her grandfather and Poke to care about her. No wonder she took in strays—stray children, stray animals, and one stray gunslinger, he thought. She knew so little love herself that she gave her own away by the cartload to make up for her lack. She hadn't allowed loneliness and grief to turn her in on herself, as she might have done—as Slade had done.

"Just who *is* this Rye Crippen, anyway?" he asked.

"A real ne'er-do-well from town. He hangs around Delano

mostly—drinking and gambling. I suspect he's a card cheat, a petty crook, and a sometime cattle rustler. I saw him one day on the range, sporting a running-iron in his boot, just as bold as you please. I said that his carrying one was a hanging offense, and he made several nasty threats to me, and then rode off. Naturally, I told Marshal Meagher about it, but of course, Rye wasn't so brazen as to go trotting into Wichita, with a stampless brand sticking out of his boot. My cattle have been disappearing one by one ever since. I reckon he just takes them for spite, since, as you so rudely informed me, my herd isn't big enough to be worth the risk or the bother.''

''Well, I call that pretty damned dirty—stealing a woman's cattle just for revenge. All the same, Rachel, if the bum *was* out there, he isn't there now. I don't see anything but cattle. But let's take a closer look, just to be sure, hmh?''

They mounted their horses and moved in among the cattle, who were now peacefully asleep or contentedly chewing their cuds. Rachel did a swift count and swore.

''I knew it!'' she burst out. ''I just knew it! Butterbean's gone!''

''*Butterbean?*'' Slade lifted one brow, his mouth twitching with amusement. ''Rachel, don't tell me you actually have names for all these sad-looking creatures.''

''Of course, I do.''

''And what, may I ask, is that quaint little brand I see upon each one's left hip? No, don't tell me. Lord, leave it to a woman! A Tumbling Heart, Rachel? What was the county clerk's reaction to that, I wonder, when he recorded it in his brand book? Honestly, couldn't you have settled for a Rocking R, say, or a Swinging W?''

''No,'' she replied shortly. ''This here's the heartland, and someday, the very land you're standing on right now is going to be known as the Heartland Ranch; and when that day comes, the Tumbling Heart brand is going to be famous far and wide. That's why I just *can't* let Rye Crippen make off with my cattle! They're my future—what I've dreamed of for ages—'' Rachel broke off abruptly, realizing suddenly that she was baring the innermost secrets of her heart and soul to the gunslinger, dreams she hadn't shared even with her grandfather or India. After a moment, she spoke again quietly. "I expect you think I'm just a foolish girl, wishing for all that when I might as well be wishing for the moon."

"No, I don't. I think you're a very brave and beautiful woman," he said, and for once, there was no laughter in his voice.

Rachel didn't know what to say to that. No one had ever told her she was brave or beautiful before, and she couldn't believe that the gunslinger had spoken seriously. He must be making fun of her, as usual, she thought—even if he *wasn't* grinning at her like a weasel who'd just made off with a plump chicken. She decided that it was best just to ignore his words.

After that, seeing that Rye Crippen was not to be caught that night, they rode silently back to the log cabin, each of them lost in thought.

At the barn door, Slade told Rachel he would see to her mare, so she could go on inside and get some sleep. She was tired, he thought. She worked too hard. Even so, he knew she would be up at the crack of dawn to get her morning chores done before she started breakfast. There wasn't a lazy bone in her body.

"Rachel," he queried curiously, "how long's it been since you've had a day off? And I don't mean Sundays. Driving eight kids to town to attend church isn't my idea of a day off."

"Well, I don't know, then. The day of India's funeral, I guess."

Slade could just picture it: Rachel doing the best she could to clean the inhospitable Beecham place from top to bottom so India wouldn't be shamed and gossiped about because her house was not only falling down, but filthy. Rachel cooking for all the mourners who would have traipsed back to the soddy after the funeral for a free meal. Rachel seeing that eight kids were washed, combed, and dressed, and shepherded to the graveside to bury their mother decently. Rachel shaking the reverend's hand and making sure he got paid his fee for coming, because Jonathan was too drunk to take care of it himself. Rachel scraping all the dirty dishes from the meal, and washing and drying them afterward. Rachel feeding the baby and getting the rest of the children tucked into bed. Rachel driving home in her wagon long after dark in the bitter winter wind.

That wasn't a day off—not in Slade's book, anyway. Suddenly making up his mind, he announced, "I've got to go into Wichita tomorrow for supplies. How would you like to go with me? Do some shopping or whatever it is that women do in town?"

Rachel gazed at him searchingly for a moment, wondering what had prompted his invitation. He had never offered to take her with him to Wichita previously, merely asked, before leaving, if there was anything she needed from town. So she did not know what to say, whether to accompany him or not.

It seemed, since his coming, that he had turned her quiet, ordered life upside down, made a mockery of her values, and, what was even worse, made her doubt them herself, confusing her, when she had always thought so clearly before. The unwelcome attentions he had most improperly pressed upon her had wakened strange feelings and longings within her, as though he had succeeded in opening some locked door deep inside her to unleash dark, primitive desires she had not even known she had harbored. Her violent, even wanton response to him had shamed and scared her.

Even now, Rachel found his very nearness, the sheer masculinity of him, highly disturbing. She was acutely aware of the thinness of her night rail, small defense against him, and she hugged her coat more closely about her, as though it might somehow protect her from him. But he made no move to take her in his arms, merely stood silently, awaiting her answer, and at last, she spoke.

"I'd—I'd be pleased to drive into town with you tomorrow, Slade," she said softly.

Then she blushed and bit her lip, for that was not what she had intended to say. She had meant to refuse him, and now, she did not know how to call her words back, felt, even, that it would be somehow rude and churlish of her to do so, especially when he had been so kind to her tonight, most unlike his usual self.

"Fine. I'll see you in the morning, then," Slade told her. "Good night, Rachel."

"Good night."

Slowly, as the gunslinger led the horses into the barn, Rachel walked back to the log cabin, wondering suddenly, wistfully, with a peculiar sense of disappointment, why he had not kissed her instead of simply bidding her good night. Perhaps he had tired of the game he had played with her. After all, he was a man of the world, and she but a Kansas farm girl, dreaming of castles in the air. It was silly to think she might have interested him, however briefly. She was nothing more to him than a passing amusement, plain as a speckled pup and ignorant of how to please a man. No doubt, he had secretly laughed at her inexperience when he'd kissed her, and pitied her when she'd unthinkingly poured out her heart and soul to him about her absurd hopes for the future. This last was, in all likelihood, what had prompted his kindness: He'd felt sorry for her.

Rachel was mortified and, what was even more painful, deeply bereft at the thought. How could she have been so foolish? She did not know. She could not seem to understand herself at all anymore.

It was a long time before she slept again that night.

Chapter Fourteen

Except in a few places shaded from the sun, the snow had melted at last, and now, the green shoots of spring burgeoned upon the dark, rich earth, undulating like waves upon a sea as the wild wind roared across the plains. There was an old saying in Kansas that March came in like a lion and went out like a lamb, and most years, the weather tended to support this adage. The Kansas wind had been known to drive those on the prairie, especially isolated women, both to madness and suicide. It was constant, ceaseless, and spoke as though alive, its moods many. It whispered, it moaned, it sang, and it howled. Sometimes, it blew so violently that it actually knocked a person down. But still, Rachel loved it passionately. It exhilarated her, made her feel as wild and alive as it was.

Her mint-green eyes sparkled. Her cheeks were flushed as she perched beside Slade on the wagon seat, hanging tightly on to her side, lest she be blown off. Before them, the long manes and tails of Jonathan's draft horses eddied and flowed; the buffalo-skin lap robe Rachel clutched against her with one hand to keep her skirts from flying up whipped and snapped; and sparks from the glowing tip of the cigarillo Slade clenched determinedly between his teeth streamed away in the wind.

Since one had to shout to be heard, conversation was nearly impossible, for which Rachel was grateful. After her impetuous verbosity last night, she was on guard against revealing anything else, intimate or otherwise, about herself to the gunslinger. The notion that she had, these past several weeks, appeared both ridiculous and pathetic in his eyes was too humiliating to risk further exposure, she thought. To protect herself, she had withdrawn into a shell of cool politeness, accompanying him this morning only because, much as she had wished, she had found no graceful means of extricating herself from the trip into town.

Slade was aware of the subtle change in her attitude and wondered at its cause. He did not like the prim, proper Miss Wilder. He wanted the Rachel of last night back, the one who had so bravely ridden out to face whatever danger might have threatened, and then had spoken so wistfully, so eloquently, of her dreams of the future, her freckled, heartshaped face piquant and beautiful in the moonlight. Her small herd of cattle had amused Slade, but her hopes for them and her future had not.

He had long realized he could not drift forever; nor was a gunslinger likely to live to a ripe old age. Unwilling to wind up pushing up daisies any sooner than he had to, he had for some time given much thought to his own future, though without actually coming to any solid conclusions.

Now, in many ways, India's letter had decided his future for him, forcing him to put down roots before he had intended; and though he had not planned on becoming a "sodbuster," still, Slade had to admit he had not found this new life unpleasant. In fact, he now recognized that the idea of someday owning a small place of his own had been in the back of his mind for some time. He had been reared on a plantation, so he knew about farming, and he had picked up a lot about ranching, too, from the robber barons of the West, who had occasionally hired him to fight their range wars.

There was something about Kansas, as well, that appealed to Slade. His years in Texas had given him a love of wide, open spaces. He liked being able to see for miles and miles. A man didn't feel trapped, fenced in, in such country, but free to roam wherever his footsteps led. That was important to a man like Slade, and so Kansas, with its endless, imperceptibly rolling plains, suited him just fine. Especially after her unexpected revelations last night, he was beginning to think maybe Rachel Wilder suited him just fine, too. There was something so . . . gallant—yes, that was it—about her; and despite the fact that she frequently annoyed him no end, he curiously found himself wanting more and more to cherish and protect her, even so.

Surreptitiously, he glanced at her sitting so still and silent beside him, loose tendrils of her golden hair billowing back in the wind from her arresting face, her eyes alive with some unknown emotion, a half smile, as though born of some secret, inner joy, curving her sweet lips.

Heartland Ranch. The gunslinger mulled the words over in his mind. They didn't have such a bad ring, after all, he decided.

Ahead, Wichita loomed upon the prairie, and as always, Rachel found herself fascinated at how quickly it had grown since its establishment. It now sprawled along the banks of the Big and the Little Arkansas rivers, spreading east, with Delano spreading west across the big river. Because the buildings interrupted its sweep, the wind was not quite so fierce within the city limits, and Rachel was able to relax her tight grip on the wagon as they at last pulled into town.

Slade drove the team through the city, down Douglas Avenue to the corner of Main Street, where he stopped directly across from the two-story brick Eagle Block, which housed the *Wichita Eagle* newspaper, various government offices, and a public assembly hall on the top floor, and the Wichita Savings Bank and several small shops below. Slowly, he maneuvered the wagon into place among the other vehicles crowded out front of the town's largest department store, Morris Kohn's New York Store, whose annual sales had already reached $60,000, thanks to Wichita's rapid growth. After carefully setting the brake, Slade hopped out of the wagon and assisted Rachel down from the seat, his strong hands encircling her waist briefly before releasing her. Taking her arm, he guided her up onto the boardwalk, which was littered with barrels and boxes of all shapes and sizes. They passed under the overhanging roof of the first floor of the two-story brick building, where he opened the door for her, then ushered her inside. There, he left her, saying he would return for her in an hour or so.

Rachel nodded absentmindedly, her attention already caught by the ready-made clothes on the dressmaker dummies, the bolts of material and yards of ribbon stacked on the shelves, the bonnets, scarves, and gloves displayed on the long counters, and the leather boots and button-down shoes arrayed along the floor. Grinning at her obvious delight, Slade departed, heading north down Main Street to Chris Kimmerle's Stone and Monument Works, which sold lime for mortaring and marble for tombstones. He needed to pick up both cement for the Beechams' new log cabin and barn, and the marker he had ordered a few weeks ago for India's grave. After that, he made his way down Fourth Street to the Planing and Mill Company, where he bought a wagonload of wooden posts. Then he went to one of the several local hardware stores, where he purchased various tools, staples and nails, and some rolls of Glidden barbed wire. Rye Crippen wasn't going to get any more of Rachel's cattle—not if the gunslinger could help it!

Meanwhile, at the New York Store, Rachel had, after goggling at just about everything, finally spied a length of fine, pale blue silk she knew would look very well with her fair coloring; and she had decided that, come hell or high water, she was going to have a pretty new gown. She could wear it on the Fourth of July holiday that summer at least. With the little time she had to spare, it would no doubt take her several weeks to complete the dress.

She opened her reticule, counted the money inside, and swiftly calculated she had enough for the necessary yards of fabric and spools of thread, and some matching ribbon for her hair. Stepping up to the counter, she had the clerk measure and cut the material for her. After he had rung up her purchases on the cash register, he wrapped them up in brown paper tied up with string. Then, package in hand, Rachel wandered back to the front of the store to watch out the window and wait for Slade.

At last, he arrived. To Rachel's surprise, for she had ex-

pected they would return home, he took her to the Empire
House hotel to eat dinner. Afterward, they strolled down to
the big river to watch the ducks that, glad of spring's arrival,
paddled in the water and sunned themselves upon the shore.
Overhead flew wild geese on their way to their summer hab-
itats in the north. Their haunting cries split the afternoon air,
mingling prettily with the rustling of the budding green
branches of the cottonwood trees that lined the riverbanks
and shook and swayed in the wind. It was a peaceful time,
spent in companionable silence.

Despite the fact that she had told herself that, from now
on, she must keep her distance from Slade, Rachel was oddly
sorry when the day ended and he reluctantly said they must
go back to the log cabin.

On Sunday, as was usual when the weather permitted,
Fremont drove Rachel and the children into town to attend
church. Rachel always felt somewhat guilty about this, for
she was a member of St. John's Episcopal congregation, and
India had been a Baptist. So Rachel thought perhaps she ought
to have taken the youngsters to the large, imposing brick
church at the corner of First and Market streets instead of her
own small, unassuming clapboard church on Lawrence Street.
But then, she reckoned India would have been pleased the
children had any religion at all, for Jonathan had strayed from
the fold years ago, as had Slade. Poke had not, but as Negroes
were not as yet welcome in any of the city's churches, he
remained behind, as well.

St. John's was the oldest church in Wichita, its first edifice
having been erected in 1869. Built of vertical slabs of lumber,
it had, despite the crosses at either end of the roof, actually
more closely resembled a rectangular stockade than a church.
After two years of use, as both a church and the town's first
school, the congregation had been forced to abandon the
building, not only because it was cold and damp, but also
because the weight of the heavy sod roof was causing the

walls to begin to buckle inward, and collapse of the entire church had appeared imminent.

The new church, while not very big, was a vast improvement over the old, beautiful and graceful in design, with a Gothic door and lovely stained-glass Gothic windows. It was set on a grassy lot planted with trees, and presented a charming picture from the street.

Rachel enjoyed the service. It was only afterward she wished she had not come, for it was then that both the reverend and one of the local schoolteachers accosted her and sternly reminded her yet again that the Beecham youngsters—with the exception of Andrew, Naomi, and Tobias, who were too young to attend—belonged in school. Although she worried frequently about the lapse in their education, Rachel did not want to send the children to school. The schools in Wichita were in a terrible state, dirty, poorly heated, and lacking even such essentials as proper books, blackboards, and maps. Some were actually housed in saloons and brothels! Appalled by the conditions under which they must labor, and for inordinately low pay, besides, schoolteachers came and went as often as the seasons. It was a disgrace, Rachel thought. Even so, Wichita's thrifty businessmen continued to vote down one school-bond issue after another, fearing that any excess taxation would drive away investors and stifle the city's growth.

Nor were the town's churches any more effective at improving the schools' adverse circumstances than they were at putting a halt to the vice and corruption in Delano. Tales of the lawless, unrepentant "Kansas sinners" had reached the ears of the church boards back east, and as a result, money to aid their brethren in the Midwest was not eagerly forthcoming.

Previously, Rachel had used the youngsters' grief and the winter weather as her excuse for not enrolling them in school. But now that nearly three months had passed since India's death, and the days were growing warmer, too, she did not know how to explain the children's continued absence.

"I'll speak to their uncle about the matter," she promised

the reverend and Miss Corbett, the schoolteacher, who, despite its being a daily struggle, was dedicated to her job and so was particularly persistent.

That night, true to her word, Rachel broached the subject with Slade and explained to him why she had not, before now, sent the youngsters into town to attend school.

"India taught them at home until she died," she elucidated. "I could, too—in the evenings, anyway. My father was a schoolteacher back in Pennsylvania, you know."

"Yes, I know," Slade replied. "But you have enough to do as it is, Rachel, especially now that it's planting time. Fremont and Poke have already told me how hard you work in the fields each spring. I'll do what I can to help you, of course. But even so, you'll be worn out at night." He gazed at her with some concern, thinking how exhausted she looked even now. Baby Tobias had had a fretful night, and as a result, she had not slept well. Mauve circles ringed her eyes, and her shoulders drooped. "You simply can't keep taking on so many burdens, Rachel," he chided gently.

She smiled wanly.

"Look who's talking," she pointed out. "I wasn't the one who spent the entire day stringing a barbed-wire fence. But I do thank you for it. You needn't have done it, you know."

"I know—and don't think I won't be collecting payment for it sooner or later, either," he teased, his eyes lingering on her mouth, making her blush and glance away. "I'll get it finished sometime this week. Then we'll see if this villainous Rye Crippen dares to make off with any more of your cattle!" Slade paused, then continued.

"As far as the children's schooling goes, I'll look into the matter the next time I'm in town. It may be that I can find at least one school that's halfway decent. Frankly, I've been wondering what I'll do with the kids once I've moved them into their new home. I've got to get Beecham's fields plowed and planted, too; and I don't mind telling you that the idea of trying to keep an eye on him, and eight rambunctious youngsters, besides—especially when one of 'em's a precocious two-year-old and one's a baby—has me kind of worried. Sometimes, I wonder how you manage, Rachel."

She laughed, really the first time he'd ever heard her do so, Slade thought, and he discovered he liked the sound.

"I guess I just have a knack," she said.

"I guess you do. Well"—he stood and stretched, his lean, muscular body reminding her of a cougar or some other predatory animal—"I'm tired. I think I'll turn in early. Good night, Rachel."

"Good night, Slade," she answered softly, her heart constricting at the thought that, soon, the Beechams' new home would be finished, and the gunslinger would take the children away from her at last. It was inevitable.

When that day came, Rachel's life would be very lonely and empty, she knew, and she hurried up to the loft so her grandfather and Poke would not see the sudden tears of anguish that blurred her eyes.

Chapter Fifteen

Several days later, at sundown, Gus came to call again, bringing with him the new chair he had fashioned for Rachel to replace the one he and Slade had inadvertently broken. The gunslinger was out in the yard, washing up at the well, when the Swede arrived in his mule-drawn wagon, the new chair carefully tied down in the wagon bed and covered with a blanket to protect it from harm.

"Hello, Maverick," Gus greeted Slade somewhat sourly after driving up, pulling his team to a halt, and spying the gunslinger.

"Ox." Slade nodded, drying himself off with a flour-sack towel, which he then tossed casually over his bare shoulder. He gazed with inquisitive interest at the blanket protruding from the Swede's wagon bed.

As he observed the gunslinger's scrutiny, Gus sighed, wishing heartily that Slade were not always hanging around Rachel's house. She was different, he thought, since the gunslinger's coming—most unlike herself, flustered and distracted, somehow; always blushing and hardly paying Gus any attention at all when he called on her. She was even quicker than usual to take offense, too. Gus would not have dreamed of offending her, although he *had* done so when he had snapped the spoke on her chair in half—something that never would have happened had it not been for the gunslinger. Really, it had all been Slade's fault! the Swede reflected angrily. If he had not kept yanking on the chair, that insolent, aggravating smirk on his face, as though he would best Gus come hell or high water, Gus would not have fought so hard to maintain his own hold on it, and it would never have fallen apart. The gunslinger was always butting in, Gus thought, trying to make a fool out of him in front of Rachel—and usually succeeding, too, he concluded miserably.

Why he not hurry up and get those Beechams' damned log cabin fixed? Gus wondered unhappily, his suspicions aroused. *Shooure is taking him long time. I voould have finished days ago, ja? I not fool he tinks. I tink maybe he take own sveet time so he can stay here with Rachel, try to cut me out like cowboy do steer in herd. He want to put own brand on her, maybe. But I not stooupid steer. I not be cut out. I tink maybe if he give me more trouble, I teach him goould lesson in manners, and din ve see, ja?*

So thinking, Gus set the wagon brake and jumped down from the vehicle. Pointedly ignoring Slade, he walked around back to the wagon bed and unchained and lowered the tailgate. Then he removed the blanket from the chair and began to untie the ropes that secured the chair to the wagon.

"What have you got there, Ox?" the gunslinger asked as

he casually strolled over toward the wagon to satisfy his curiosity about its contents.

"New chair I make for Rachel," Gus replied shortly, not glancing up.

"Kind of plain, isn't it?" Slade remarked as he studied the wooden chair, which, like most Scandinavian furniture, was purely functional, devoid of any ornamentation. "Plain ugly."

The gunslinger was vastly irritated by the Swede's present for Rachel. Something upon which Gus had obviously expended a great deal of time and care was not only sure to find favor in her eyes, but also to remind her unpleasantly that Slade had been primarily responsible for reducing her old chair to a mere stool. His fingers itched to smash the Swede's gift to smithereens before Rachel could see it.

"I make of oak," Gus explained, stubbornly refusing to be baited. "Chair is simple, *ja*, but strong."

"Just like you Swedes, huh?" Slade continued wickedly, grinning.

"I not so dumb as maybe yoou tink," the Swede averred stoutly, starting to grow incensed, despite his resolve to ignore the gunslinger.

"Oh, you're not, huh?" Slade needled mercilessly. "Then why do you keep hanging around here, where you're not wanted?"

"That for Rachel to decide, not yoou, *ja*? And I tink she pick me, not yoou. Gunman like yoou no goood for her, not willing to make honest voman of her like I want to do, and this, she know in her head, if not her heart, *ja*? I tink, in the end, it will be yoou who is not velcome here."

"Why, you dense-brained son of a bitch!" Slade swore softly. "What makes you so certain I'm *not* willing to marry her?"

"Vell, are yoou?"

"I might be." The gunslinger paused, waiting for this to sink in. Then he uttered mockingly, "I reckon that thrust a spoke into your wheel, now, didn't it, Ox?"

"I show yoou spoke in wheel!" Gus growled, thoroughly irate and frightened now at the idea that he might actually lose Rachel to this arrogant, insulting man. Rolling up his sleeves, he advanced on Slade threateningly. "I show yoou spoke in wheel! Yoou not make trouble for me one more time, yoou black-hearted snake! Throw down those guns and fight like man!" he bellowed. "I teach yoou to poke fun at Gustave Oxenberg, *ja*? Yoou not mess with me again! I mop floor with yoou! I make Svedish meatball out of yoou! I—"

"I get the general idea, Ox," Slade interrupted dryly, his eyes gleaming with anticipation at the prospect of giving the Swede a good thrashing and sending him packing once and for all. The gunslinger whipped the towel off his shoulder and flung it aside, then slowly unbuckled his gun belt and let it slide to the ground. His fists raised, he began to circle Gus warily, snorting derisively as the Swede seemed to hesitate. "Well, hell! What does it take?" Slade goaded, a taunting smile playing about the corners of his lips. "Come on, you galoot! What are you waiting for? An invitation? Jesus! I'll bet you even waited for one before kissing Rachel, didn't you? Me, now . . . I wasn't so polite."

At that, Gus let out an infuriated roar and, knuckles bared, head lowered, charged like a maddened bull straight toward Slade. He hit the gunslinger dead center in the stomach, the impact sending them both sprawling. His reflexes quicker than Gus's, Slade was the first to rebound, and as Gus started to his feet, Slade landed a powerful right to his jaw, knocking him back on his butt into the dirt. Shaking his head and rubbing his cheek gingerly, Gus sat up and began once more to wobble upright, only to drop a second time as Slade dealt a solid left hook to his chin. This time, after struggling to his hands and knees, Gus kept one eye locked on the gunslinger, and when he lightly danced in on booted feet to strike yet again, the Swede slammed into his legs, shoving him off balance and sending him reeling.

As Slade sprang unsteadily to his feet, Gus smashed him right in the face, blackening one of his eyes. Then he slugged him in the belly, causing Slade to stumble back so hard into the front wall of the log cabin that the rafters shook. At the sound of the gunslinger crashing against the house, Poke rose grumbling from his chair to open the door and find out what all the ruckus was about.

"Lawd a-mercy, Fremont!" he cried. "Yo'd bes' git out heah quick. Slade an' Ox are gwine at it hell-bent fo' leather in de front yahd—an' whoooeee! Dey sho' is havin' demseffs a time!"

"Are they really, Poke? I wanna see! I wanna see!" little Naomi exclaimed excitedly, jumping up from the table and skipping outside.

Soon, Fremont, Poke, and all eight children, including the baby, Tobias, whom Eve was holding, were gathered in the yard, cheering and hollering and egging the contenders on. Only Rachel, down in the root cellar, fetching some potatoes for supper, was unaware of the brawl.

By now, Slade had caught hold of Gus's shirtfront and was delivering several short, mean jabs to his face, bloodying his nose and mouth. To save himself, Gus grabbed Slade's rabbit-punching arm, then closed his fingers tightly around the gunslinger's other wrist and jerked his imprisoning hand loose from the shirt, popping several buttons and tearing it from collar to waist in the process. Then the Swede swung Slade around violently and pitched him headlong into the dirt so he slid along the ground, scraping his face and hands raw.

Just before Gus flung himself on top of the gunslinger, however, Slade recovered and rapidly flipped himself over, his feet coming up to kick Gus squarely in the groin. Doubled over and groaning, the Swede flew back, while, in a single motion, Slade stood and lunged forward to fall on him savagely. Sweating, bleeding, and cursing profusely, the two men rolled and tumbled and grappled their way across the yard, pummeling each other unmercifully.

"Get him, Uncle Slade!" Gideon, Caleb, and Philip shouted as one. "Get him! Get him, Uncle Slade! Get him good!"

Breaking apart, the opponents lurched to their feet, Slade inflicting another punishing blow to Gus's jaw as they did so. His arms spread wide, Gus toppled back against the open tailgate of the wagon. Instantly, the gunslinger was at the Swede's throat, choking him and pounding his head against the floor of the wagon bed.

Swearing through gritted teeth, Gus stretched out one spatulalike hand, fingers splayed, and mashed it against Slade's face, trying to force him away, and at last, Slade was compelled to release him. Gus gave him a mighty push, and the gunslinger staggered back. As he did so, the Swede, his blood rushing suddenly and painfully to his head, a red film hazing his eyes, seized without thinking the stout oak chair in the wagon and ferociously bashed it over Slade's skull, shattering the chair and nearly killing Slade in the process.

The gunslinger keeled over like a poleaxed steer.

"I guess . . . that chair . . . wasn't—wasn't as . . . strong as—as you . . . thought . . . huh, Ox?" he rasped, smiling crookedly, before his eyes slowly closed and he collapsed in a crumpled heap upon the ground.

"Slade!" Rachel screamed in the sudden, horrified silence at the sight that greeted her eyes as she came around the side of the log cabin from the root cellar. "Oh, my God! Slade! Slade!"

Dropping her basket of potatoes where she stood, she ran to kneel at his side, her face ashen as she bent over him and quickly pressed her ear to his chest to see if he was still breathing.

"Oh, my God," she said again, her voice something between a shriek and a moan as she sat up, her gaze taking in with horror and disbelief his cracked and bleeding skull, his black eye, his split lip, and the other assorted cuts and bruises that marred his body from the waist up.

Her eyes turned accusingly to those who surrounded her.

"Who did this?" she demanded harshly, her voice rising. *"Who did this?"*

Her glance fell upon Gus, who was almost as badly battered as Slade.

"You, Gus?" she shrilled incredulously. *"You?* Why, Gus? *Why?"*

Too embarrassed and ashamed to tell Rachel they had quarreled over who would wind up getting her, the Swede mumbled something about the argument's having arisen because of the chair he had made for her.

"What chair?" Rachel queried sharply, looking about wildly. "What chair?" She spied the splintered pieces of wood lying scattered about the unconscious Slade, and realizing then what had been used to strike him down, she snatched up one of the broken-off chair legs. Slowly, she advanced toward Gus, holding it before her and thrusting it at him menacingly. "Do you mean *this* chair, Gus?" she asked. "*This* chair? The one you made for me? The one with which you durned near *murdered* Slade?"

"*J-J-Ja*," he stammered nervously, eyeing her warily, for she looked half crazed with anger and pain, and he was half afraid she might actually do him some injury.

Even as the thought crossed his mind, Rachel started screaming and crying, and she flew at him like a wild thing, beating him frenziedly with the chair leg about the head and shoulders, as though she intended to kill him. While everyone else stared at her speechlessly, shocked and petrified, Gus warded her blows off as best he could with his upraised arms until finally her grandfather, abruptly jarred to action, reached out and grabbed hold of her, shaking her roughly.

"Rachel. Rachel!" Fremont snapped sternly. "Stop it. Stop it! Slade's not dead, is he?"

"No, no, not yet—but like to be," she whimpered as she came to her senses at last. Sobbing, her breasts heaving from her ragged gasps for breath, she slowly cast the chair leg aside, studying it dully for a moment, as though she could not believe she had actually used it against Gus. Then, biting her lip in shame at her unexpected, hysterical outburst, she turned back to Slade. "Help me get him into the house," she said. "*No!* Not *you*, Gus! You, Grandpa—and Poke."

Together, the three of them lifted the gunslinger's insensible body and carried him into the log cabin. Once there, however, they found themselves faced with an unanticipated predicament. There was no place to put Slade except in Rachel's bed. He would not be comfortable on the floor, where the youngsters were crowded together at night. Nor would Fremont, who might have relinquished his bed to the gunslinger, be comfortable there. For although Rachel would willingly have given her bed to her grandfather and slept on the floor herself, Fremont could not, because of his disability, climb the ladder to the loft.

"Ah'll try ter carry Slade up der, Miz Rachel," Poke offered.

"No, Poke." She shook her head firmly at the hired hand, fearing that the strain might be too much for him. He was not, after all, a young man. "I'm afraid he's too heavy even for you to manage. You might slip and fall and hurt your back, or even break your neck, and then where would we be? No, you'll have to go outside and ask Gus to do it," she declared reluctantly. "He's the only one among us strong enough to carry Slade up there."

The Negro returned a few minutes later with the Swede, who wordlessly hoisted the gunslinger over his shoulder and carried him up to the loft, where, at the direction of Rachel, who had followed him up, he laid Slade gingerly on the bed.

"Thank you, Gus," she murmured, ashamed of her earlier behavior toward him. She knew that the Swede would not have deliberately wounded the gunslinger in such a manner, that he had done so in a fit of unreasoning rage, which he now genuinely regretted. "I appreciate your helping me, especially after what I did to you out in the yard. It was very wrong of me, and I apologize."

"Is I who should be sorry, *ja*? I not mean to cause trouble again. I not mean to hit Slade so hard, hurt him so bad. He make me mad, and I lose temper, forget own strength again. Break new chair for yoou, too," Gus noted, his voice filled with remorse. He paused. Then he asked, "Do yoou tink he will—will be all right?"

"I hope so," Rachel answered quietly as she sat down on the side of the bed and placed on the night table the bottle of carbolic acid and the washbasin of warm, soapy water she had brought up to the loft with her.

She dipped a cloth into the washbasin, then wrung it out and began gently to cleanse Slade's wounds, pushing aside his thick, glossy hair to see how bad the injuries to his head were.

"I hope so, too," Gus said. "He put up goooud fight, fought fair. I tink maybe he goooud man, after all—else yoou vooould not . . . care for him. I tink maybe yoou fall in—in love with Slade, Rachel, *ja*? I am . . . very sad here, in heart, that yoou not . . . love me, but I . . . care for yoou and not want to cause yoou unhappiness. If—if the gunslinger make yoou happy, I try to be happy, too, for yoour sake. So. I— I tink maybe next time I come, I come only as—as friend. But . . . maybe yoou not—not want me even as—as friend now—"

"Oh, of course, I do!" Rachel cried softly, tears stinging her eyes, for she was deeply touched by what had obviously been a very difficult speech for the Swede. She stood and laid her hand on his arm. "I hope you'll always be my friend, Gus," she told him earnestly.

He gazed down at her silently for a moment, pain etching his face. Then he smiled sadly and spoke.

"Yoou only person ever to always call me Gus," he said.

Then, abruptly, as though overcome with emotion, he left her. Rachel watched him go, a lump in her throat. Then she slowly turned back to Slade to finish washing away the blood that encrusted his scalp, which was cut in several places. One of the gashes was quite deep, and it was this, she surmised, that had rendered him unconscious.

Rachel knew she would never forget the sight of Slade lying so still on the ground. For a dreadful eternity, she had believed he was dead, and her heart had stopped; her mind had emptied of all but one thought: *Please, God, let him be alive. I'll do anything if you'll only just let him be alive.* When she'd discovered that the gunslinger still breathed, her relief had been overwhelming. Joy such as she'd never before felt had flooded her being, followed by that terrible, hysterical wrath that someone had struck him down, and which she had vented on Gus, the culprit. At the remembrance, she thought of the Swede's words to her: *I tink maybe yoou fall in love with Slade. . . .*

Was it true? Rachel wondered, her heart lurching a little in her breast at the notion. *Was* she falling in love with Slade Maverick?

She could think of nothing more disastrous, for he would surely not return her love—and, worse, might even find it not only amusing, but pitiable, as well. That, Rachel knew, she could not bear. No, she did not love him. The very idea was preposterous. Gus had simply reached a mistaken conclusion.

But still, Rachel's slender hands trembled slightly as she unstoppered the bottle of carbolic acid, poured it onto a fresh cloth, and carefully treated Slade's wounds to ensure that infection did not set in. Then, from her dressing table, she took a pair of embroidery scissors, a needle, and a spool of strong thread; and after snipping away a few locks of his black hair, she sewed shut the deep gash in his head, glad he was still insensible and so did not feel the pain she must otherwise have caused him.

After that, she rose, and as she did so, the stray locks she had snipped from his hair floated from her lap to the loft's floor. Impulsively, she bent and retrieved them, tucking them into the pocket of her apron. Then, picking up the soiled cloths and the washbasin, she descended the ladder to the kitchen, where Eve and Susannah, who, in Rachel's absence, had finished cooking the supper, were now setting the meal upon the table.

"Well, Rachel, how is Slade?" Fremont inquired from his chair before the hearth, laying aside his pipe, which he had been cleaning.

"Except for a deep gash in his scalp, which required stitching, his cuts and bruises are not serious," she replied. "But he is badly concussed, I fear, and still unconscious. There is nothing much I can do for him now but try to keep him warm and comfortable until he regains consciousness, and hope that fever does not set in.''

She opened the door to throw out the bloody water in the washbasin, then went back inside to rinse and wipe the porcelain bowl clean. Climbing her small stepladder in the kitchen, she took down a few bundles of the dried herbs that hung from the rafters. With mortar and pestle, she crushed the leaves to a fine powder and stirred them into the hot water she poured from the kettle on the stove into the washbasin. Then, gathering up the bowl and fresh cloths from the shelf, she returned to the loft.

Rachel divested Slade of his boots and socks, and eased him under the blankets, then checked his forehead again. It still felt cool to her touch, for which she was grateful. Nevertheless, she dunked a cloth into the warm herbal mixture, then wrung it out and pressed it to his forehead and temples, knowing that it would soothe him.

Long after everyone else in the house had retired, Rachel kept her vigil at the gunslinger's side, going downstairs only to eat, finally, the supper Eve had thoughtfully saved for her, and to freshen the herbal mixture. At last, after several long hours, Slade's eyes fluttered open and, in the soft glow of the lamplight, focused slowly on her face as she bent over him to replace the cloth on his forehead.

"Rachel?" he whispered tentatively after a moment of dazed confusion.

"Yes," she said, relieved he knew her. "How do you feel, Slade?"

"Like I . . . died and went to . . . heaven. I thought . . . for a minute there . . . that you were . . . an angel." He managed a crooked smile, then groaned as his hand went to his head, fingers probing gingerly the deep gash Rachel had sewn shut and that had since swelled to the size of a goose egg. "Jesus. That was . . . sure some crack . . . Gus gave me. Guess I . . . oughtn't to have . . . made him so mad."

"No, you oughtn't," she chided gently. Then she urged, "Don't try to talk anymore now, Slade. You need to rest. Can I get you anything?"

"Just a . . . drink of water."

Filling a glass from the pitcher on the dressing table, Rachel helped him drink a few sips of water. Then he lay back and almost immediately slept. But it was a natural slumber; and as she checked his forehead again, glad to find that it remained cool to her touch, she knew then that his concussion was not as bad as she had feared, that he would probably be all right after a day or so of rest.

Rachel was exhausted. Still, afraid Slade might awaken once more—thirsty again or even disoriented, despite the fact that he had seemed in full possession of his faculties—and would need her, she did not go downstairs. Instead, as was the practice on the prairie when there were not enough beds to go around, she fixed the bolster so it ran firmly down the middle of the bed, separating her from the gunslinger. Then, fully clothed, she lay down on her side, stoutly assuring herself, as she did so, that there was, after all, really nothing improper about bundling, as the old custom was known.

Nevertheless, it felt strange to be sharing a bed with Slade, Rachel mused, as though they were married, and for a moment, she could not help wondering what it would be like if they were. She blushed at the notion, knowing that there would be more done in their bed than just sleeping, that Slade was a man who would surely demand his rights whenever he pleased. For a man who would not wait for an invitation to kiss a young woman to whom he was not even engaged would certainly not be deterred by the lack of one from his own wife! Her heart beat fast at the realization. Involuntarily, she wondered what it would feel like to have the gunslinger do more to her than just kiss her. At the thought, the strange, violent feelings he had aroused in her previously rose, unbidden, to the surface of her being, making her ache and tingle with longing.

In her mind, Rachel was suddenly beset by the wild image of Slade awakening in the night and, discovering she shared the bed, flinging aside the bolster to press her down into the mattress and, despite her protests, make passionate love to her. She was mortified by the unwitting picture she conjured. There must be something terribly wrong with her, she decided, distressed, to imagine such a thing, to wish such a thing would actually happen; for to her horror and humiliation, Rachel realized some treacherous part of her actually *did* wish for such a thing to occur!

Her entire body flushed hot with shame—and some darker, more primitive emotion she did not care to face. Her breath came quickly and shallowly, and she held herself very still, afraid the sleeping Slade might somehow be able to read her mind and would awaken right then and there to make her disgraceful wish come true.

But though if he had known of her desire, the gunslinger would have been more than willing to gratify it, he continued to slumber deeply, ignorant of Rachel's presence in the bed. It was only toward sunrise, when his eyes slowly opened and he gradually became aware of his surroundings, that Slade learned she lay beside him. Ignoring the throbbing in his skull, and smiling with amusement at the sight of the bolster she had wedged snugly between them—as though it might actually protect her from him!—he rose up on one elbow to study her silently.

She was fast asleep, her countenance looking very young and innocent in the grey predawn light. Loose tendrils of the hair she had not bothered to unpin last night curled about her face, framing it softly, and her lips were parted slightly. Her chest rose and fell gently with each slow, even breath she took.

This is what it would be like to awake to her each morning. The thought crept, unbidden, into his mind. *You could do a lot worse, Slade.*

He glanced at the open curtain of the loft, then down at the log cabin below. Fremont was nowhere in sight, but Slade could hear him snoring in the small bedroom beneath the loft, and all the children were asleep on the floor of the log cabin's main room, unlikely to stir for a while yet. Carefully, the gunslinger eased his way under the bolster, moving cautiously so as not to wake Rachel or cause the bedsprings to squeak. Then he leaned over her still figure and, unable to resist, kissed her full on her sweet, oblivious mouth.

Chapter Sixteen

Rachel was dreaming. She knew she was. She must be, for Slade was kissing her, and she was kissing him back, eagerly opening her lips to him, her arms to him, wanting all that he offered—and more.

In her dream, he bent over her, one corded leg covering her thighs, his tongue darting forth to trace lingeringly the outline of her vulnerable mouth before parting her lips to explore the yielding softness within. Down into the deep, dark, honeyed pool of her mouth, his tongue plunged, wreathing and licking and savoring her sweetness, probing hungrily every crevice he found, as though he feared to miss some dulcet drop.

As his lips devoured hers again and again, a sultry bud of desire burst wildly to life within Rachel, as though he were the spring sun, warm and wakening her with his heat, and she were a blossoming flower straining desperately to unfurl, a yearning that only grew stronger and more fervent with each passing moment, each searing kiss. Savagely, he kissed her, his breath swallowing hers, his mouth and tongue scorching her like a hot brand, marking her as his; and despite herself, somewhere deep down inside, Rachel knew she wanted this, wanted him. . . .

Her tongue melted irresistibly against his, twisted and twined about his own, matching it swirl for swirl. Her teeth nibbled his lips, as his did hers, making her feel dizzy and faint. The intensity of the experience was only heightened as, without warning, his teeth sank into her lower lip, drawing blood that tasted of salt and copper upon her tongue, bittersweet. Pain and pleasure both erupted within her, sharp and poignant, increasing her torrid longing for him as, more gently, he kissed away the droplet beaded like scarlet dew upon her mouth.

"That was for the barn," Slade murmured against her lips. "And this . . . this is for me, because I want you. . . . God, how I want you!"

It's only a dream, Rachel thought languidly in some dim corner of her mind, only half awake as his mouth closed over hers once more. *It's only a dream, a bold, beautiful dream born of the peculiar feelings that have beset me ever since his coming. I wished for it so hard earlier that, now, I'm dreaming it's really happening. But it isn't, not really. It's only a dream, nothing more.*

Reassured then that she need not worry about the impropriety of her action, she clutched him to her fiercely, like a wild thing, reveling in the feel of his sleek, naked back beneath her palms, the way his powerful muscles bunched and rippled under her fingers as he clasped her, caressed her. For once, she need not hold her emotions in check, she told herself, need not restrain herself from kissing and touching him, as, deep down inside, she had wanted to do since the very first moment he had ever taken her in his arms, she admitted to herself now.

Brazenly, his tongue ravaged her mouth, sending a rapturous shiver down her spine, for it seemed as though he meant to go on kissing her forever, draining her very soul from her body, and then pouring it back in. His lips slashed like a whip across her cheek to her temple, her hair. His breath was warm against her skin, making her shudder with delight, and the thrill that shot through her as his teeth nipped her earlobe was exquisite. In her ear, he muttered words of passion and wanting, words she only half heard, only vaguely comprehended, such was her drowsy state, the tide of tempestuous emotion sweeping through her, ruthlessly catching her up and bearing her aloft, strong and churning as a cyclone.

His fingers intertwined themselves in her hair, tearing at her hairpins, scattering them, as he scattered her senses. Her long blond hair tumbled free, cascading down about the two of them, enveloping them in a silken veil that shone like spun gold in the early light streaking through the cracks of the shutters that covered the loft's tiny window. Inhaling deeply the lilac scent that wafted from her skin, Slade buried his face in her cloud of hair, drew a single, soft strand across his lips and throat.

"Rachel, Rachel honey . . ." he breathed.

His mouth blazed a trail of fire down her throat, making her quiver with excitement, and a little fear, too, as his hand closed about the swanlike column, tightening briefly, possessively, before he began to undo, one by one, the tiny buttons of her gown. Such was his expertise that Rachel was scarcely aware of his manipulations. She knew only that no man had ever made her feel as Slade did, wild and wanton as the wind, as though he alone could tame her, could quell the torturous ache that started deep at the secret heart of her and spiraled like a turbulent dust devil through her body, brutally ripping the lid off her long-suppressed desires and setting them free.

It was not until the gunslinger pushed aside the now open edges of her bodice and began to yank impatiently at the ribbons of her camisole that Rachel came suddenly and fully wide-awake, realizing at last that this was no dream, but real. Shocked and startled, she gasped and would have cried out had not Slade, sensing the abrupt change in her, swiftly clapped his hand over her mouth, his eyes gleaming like india ink as they met her own.

"Shhhhh," he whispered warningly. "You don't want to wake the whole house up and have them find us up here in bed together, do you?"

Frightened by even the thought of that happening, Rachel shook her head, her heart pounding, her body burning with the tumultuous feelings he had ignited within her when she had believed that it was nothing more than a dream.

"Then be still," the gunslinger hissed, before taking away his hand and silencing with his mouth any protest she might have made.

Rachel tried to turn her head away, to push him off her, but he was too strong for her. He wrapped his fingers roughly in her unbound hair, compelling her trembling lips to acquiesce to his own demanding ones, his body pinning her to the bed, pressing her down into the soft feather mattress so there was no escape for her.

"Don't fight me, sweetheart," he muttered against her mouth as his free hand slid down her throat to her chest to finish untying the ribbons of her camisole. "You know you want me as much as I want you."

"No, I don't," Rachel moaned quietly. "I don't."

But she knew that her words were not true—and so did he.

"Then why is your heart racing like a locomotive?" he taunted softly before he ground his lips down hard on hers once more, cutting off her reply.

As he kissed her deeply, Slade slipped his hand slowly beneath one edge of her camisole, inhaling sharply as he covetously cupped her round, bare breast, swollen and aching with passion. Despite herself, Rachel's breath caught in her throat as he touched her there, his palm gliding lightly but inexorably over the soft, ripe mound, heightening unbearably the fiery longing that had seized her in its grasp. Leisurely, his thumb traced a circular pattern about her dusky-rose areola, then flicked her nipple, causing it to pucker and stiffen, as though it had a will of its own. Waves of ecstasy surged in all directions through her body, like a shower of sparks, jolting her, making even her toes curl, it seemed.

Without Rachel's even recognizing that they did so, her fingers crept up to entwine themselves in his rich black hair. Her arms tightened around his neck to draw him even nearer as his lips left her mouth to travel once more down her throat, flung back now in undeniable exultation. He rained quick, ardent kisses upon the slender pillar and the pulse that throbbed erratically at its base, then nipped the sensitive place where her nape joined her shoulder, causing a bolt of lightninglike pleasure to shoot through her, electrifying her. Lingeringly, sensuously, his tongue licked away the sweat that beaded the hollow between her breasts before, slowly, his lips enveloped the flushed, rigid nipple he had teased just moments past.

Rachel gasped as, greedily, he sucked the tiny, hard button, causing a warm, fluttering sensation in her belly that was soon overshadowed by the ever-growing and deepening ache between her thighs. It was agonizing now, terrible in its potency, an insufferable void that shrieked silently to be filled and that was only worsened by the tantalizing feeling of Slade's masculinity pressing, hard and virile, against her thighs through her skirts. She yearned to cry out, to beg him to ease her torment, but she dared not, could only thrash her head wordlessly from side to side and bite her lip to stifle her whimpers as his teeth closed about her nipple and his tongue stabbed her with its heat.

Within moments, she would have given herself to the gunslinger, Rachel knew, willingly, gladly, driven to surrender by his relentless, inflammatory kisses and caresses. It was only the fretful, hungry wails of the baby, Tobias, breaking the stillness of the morning air that brought her at last to her senses.

"Oh," she gave a small sob of disappointment at the sound. And then louder, more sharply, her eyes flying open wide, she gasped, "*Oh!*"

As his gaze met hers and reality dawned on him, Slade swore softly, stormily, then slowly, reluctantly, released her. Still cursing, he rolled back to his side of the bed, slamming the displaced bolster back down between them as, after a breathless, flustered moment, Rachel began hurriedly to tie the ribbons of her camisole and do up the tiny buttons of her gown, wanting to scream at her unusual fumbling. Leaping from the bed, she snatched up her brush and hastily ran it through her disheveled hair, then, with shaking fingers, braided it haphazardly into a single plait. After that, not daring to look at Slade, she scrambled down the ladder from the loft to pick up the miserable child from the packing crate.

"Hush," she crooned. "Hush. We'll soon have your tummy full."

Scurrying outside, she cranked up the bucket of the well, in which she had stored a bottle of goat's milk last evening to keep it cool and ready for this morning. Retrieving it, she went back inside and, after stoking up the embers in the stove, shoved in several dried buffalo chips from the nearby chip box and set a pot of water to boiling, in which she heated the bottle. Presently, Toby was sucking contentedly, while Rachel rocked him.

As she did so, the rest of the youngsters, wakened by his earlier bawling, began to stretch and yawn, and from her grandfather's small bedroom came the sounds of his stirring.

What a narrow escape! Rachel thought, still breathless and distracted, her cheeks flaming, her heart thrumming horridly in her breast at the mortifying knowledge of what would have happened in the loft had not Toby demanded his breakfast.

What a damned inconvenient interruption! Slade mused heatedly upstairs, with a great deal of annoyance.

Then he smiled ruefully to himself. Perhaps it was just as well the most unwelcome intrusion had occurred when it had, he thought. Otherwise, it might have come at a much more awkward and embarrassing moment, for a few minutes more, he knew, and he would have been rucking Rachel's skirts up about her thighs to take her right there in the loft. The blow on his head last evening must have addled him more than he'd realized, he thought. If they'd been caught . . . well, he'd be on his way to a shotgun wedding now—his own! Not that he would have complained too loudly, Slade decided as he glanced down at Rachel below.

How beautiful she was, he reflected, soft and sweet as a kitten, really—despite her sharp little teeth and claws—with a wealth of untapped desire lying beneath her cool surface, just waiting to be released. Slowly but surely, she was thawing toward him, he knew, else she would not have permitted him the liberties he had taken this morning. It was just a matter of time before she would be his.

And what then? Slade asked himself slowly. *She's not the kind to give herself lightly. She'll expect marriage, a home, and kids—and she deserves them, too. If I ruin her for any other man and don't wed her, I'll have ruined her life, as well. I'm not that heartless, not that cruel. Thérèse is dead and buried. She'll never be mine again. But I'm alive, and so is Rachel.* . . .

Despite her tongue and temper, Rachel would make him a good wife, the gunslinger knew from his weeks of being around her day in and day out. She was arresting and intelligent, with a clever wit and a lively sense of humor to match his own, hardworking and caring, taking on more than her fair share of life's burdens. There was something fey and wild about her, too, he thought. She had a closeness, a oneness with the land that intrigued him, as though she listened to the elements, and they spoke to her. In many ways, she was like the wind that swept across the prairie, he reflected, gentle one moment, tempestuous the next, and always elusive. Sensuality and passion lurked deep within her, also, Slade sensed instinctively, despite her attempts to restrain it. She was, he felt, a tempting mixture of innocence and knowledge, as though she were half child, half woman, waiting breathlessly, expectantly, to be wakened to the full measure of her potential—as he longed to waken her. She interested him, challenged him. Ever since he had first come to her farm, he had lusted for her, had itched to strip away ruthlessly both her modest clothes and her genteel veneer to expose the voluptuous body and the willful wanton he suspected lay beneath, suppressed, pent-up, because she did not know what it was to have a man. In fact, all things considered, she was everything he could have wished for in a wife, like no other female he had ever known. Indeed, the idea of wedding her must have been at the back of his mind all along, else he would not have teased her about it the other night, would not have deliberately set out to best Gus at every turn, with the

Thrill to the most sensual, adventure-filled Romances on the market today...

FROM  LOVE SPELL BOOKS

As a home subscriber to the Love Spell Romance Book Club, you'll enjoy the best in today's BRAND-NEW Time Travel, Futuristic, Legendary Lovers, Perfect Heroes and other genre romance fiction. For five years, Love Spell has brought you the award-winning, high-quality authors you know and love to read. Each Love Spell romance will sweep you away to a world of high adventure...and intimate romance. Discover for yourself all the passion and excitement millions of readers thrill to each and every month.

Save $5.00 Each Time You Buy!

Every other month, the Love Spell Romance Book Club brings you four brand-new titles from Love Spell Books. EACH PACKAGE WILL SAVE YOU AT LEAST $5.00 FROM THE BOOK-STORE PRICE! And you'll never miss a new title with our convenient home delivery service.

Here's how we do it: Each package will carry a FREE 10-DAY EXAMINATION privilege. At the end of that time, if you decide to keep your books, simply pay the low invoice price of $17.96, no shipping or handling charges added. HOME DELIVERY IS ALWAYS FREE. With today's top romance novels selling for $5.99 and higher, our price SAVES YOU AT LEAST $5.00 with each shipment.

AND YOUR FIRST TWO-BOOK SHIP-MENT IS TOTALLY FREE!

IT'S A BARGAIN YOU CAN'T BEAT! A SUPER $11.48 Value!

Love Spell ✦ A Division of Dorchester Publishing Co., Inc.

Get Two Books Totally
F R E E —
An $11.48 Value!

▼ Tear Here and Mail Your FREE Book Card Today! ▼

PLEASE RUSH
MY TWO FREE
BOOKS TO ME
RIGHT AWAY!

Love Spell Romance Book Club
P.O. Box 6613
Edison, NJ 08818-6613

hope of getting rid of him once and for all. So the prospect of marrying Rachel should have pleased Slade.

Instead, as the gunslinger contemplated it, he was filled with dismay, for he realized suddenly, humiliated, that, unlike Gus, he had nothing to offer her but himself. He owned nothing of value in the world but his horse, his saddle, and his Colt Peacemaker revolvers. Cypress Hill, which might have been his (if his father had not cut him out of his inheritance), had been confiscated for failure to pay the exorbitant taxes intentionally assessed on it by carpetbaggers.

And though Slade had labored for many long, hard weeks now on the Beecham place, as though it were his own, it actually belonged legally to Jonathan, drunken Jonathan, who now whiled away almost all his days and nights in Delano. Since Slade had finally completed most of the heavy work on the new log cabin and barn, he had given up in disgust the vain attempt to reform his brother-in-law. For all the gunslinger knew, Beecham might have gambled the place away by now, or mortgaged it, or sold it—though Slade did not think even Jonathan was so unfeeling as to leave his eight children homeless. Even when he had virtually abandoned them after India's death, he had known that Rachel would take care of them, no matter how much he disliked her, or she him.

Still, the fact remained that the Beecham place was not Slade's.

How, then, could he ask Rachel to make love with him, to marry him, when he could give her nothing in return? When she, in fact, had more than he? A farm and livestock—and little need, with her grandfather and Poke about, for his help with either, though Slade knew she was glad of it.

Why, Gus had ten times more than he to offer her, he thought, and still, she would not wed the Swede. How, then, could a mere gunslinger hope to prevail? As matters stood now, he knew he could not.

The only man I'm going to marry is the one who brings me five hundred head of cattle for my south forty.

How well Slade remembered Rachel's words. He recalled, also, her remarks to him the night they had ridden out to try to catch the villainous Rye Crippen in the act of rustling her cattle, the hopes and dreams she had confided to him for her small herd and future. Perhaps she had not been joking, after all, the evening when she had so mockingly stated her requirements for a husband. Maybe, despite her obvious sarcasm, she had been, in her heart, in deadly earnest.

He would have to take action now, Slade recognized, if he wanted Rachel Wilder for himself—before Gus or some other man cut him out of the running. And he *did* want her, the gunslinger admitted to himself. He was tired of whores, who cared nothing for him, nor he for them. Now, instead, he wanted Rachel lying golden-haired and naked beneath him in his bed, warm and willing as she opened herself to him, took him deep inside her. If she were his wife, he could take her anytime he pleased. The idea appealed to Slade. Yes, he thought, marriage was the solution to both their problems.

So, despite Rachel's most stringent objections, the gunslinger insisted on getting out of bed that morning and riding into town. He had nothing worse than a mild headache, he declared—indeed, one not even as splitting as some caused by the hangovers he had frequently suffered in his wilder days of youth.

Although Rachel was still extraordinarily upset by what had passed between them in the loft during the hour just before dawn and was therefore glad he would not be lying in her bed all day, expecting her to wait on him hand and foot, still, she could not help but worry about Slade. Though the swelling had gone down some, he still had a knot the size of a hen egg on his head. His left eye was black and blue, his lip was split, and he had various other cuts and bruises from the waist up, besides. He looked, she thought, much worse for wear, and she could not, in good conscience, truly believe he was well enough to be up and about.

Short of tying him to the bed, however, she had no means of preventing his leaving. So, in the end, she was forced to resign herself to the inevitable and hope that if he grew groggy and fell off his saddle on the way into Wichita, some kind-hearted person would find him and bring him home.

After breakfast was finished and the gunslinger had departed, Rachel went upstairs to her bedroom to wash herself and change the garments she had slept in. It was while she was untying the apron she had worn all last night and this morning that she remembered the locks of Slade's hair in her pocket. Slowly, she removed them, and then, on impulse, pressed them to her lips. The locks were soft and black as jet and smelled faintly of the grassy scent of vetiver that clung always to the gunslinger's skin. Involuntarily, Rachel glanced at the bed, which he had made neatly after rising, and where, just a few hours ago, he had lain atop her, kissed her passionately, and pressed his mouth hotly to her breast.

Her cheeks stained with crimson at the memory. Her whole body flushed as though feverish. Sitting down on the edge of the bed, she buried her face in her hands, smothering the sobs that rose in her throat. What was happening to her? she asked herself, bewildered. She had never felt so mixed up in her life, torn as she was between her hitherto unswerving morals and the shocking desires she had not known she possessed.

Rachel knew, after this morning, that she ought to order the gunslinger off her property and never see him again. But how could she explain her reasons for doing so to her grandfather and Poke, who both liked and respected him as a man of "gumption," and who thoroughly enjoyed his company in the evenings. Slade fit in so well at the log cabin—as Gus never had—that it seemed as though he had always been there and belonged. Both her grandfather and Poke would be deeply hurt and horrified if they ever learned how she had lain beneath the gunslinger in her bed and he had pressed his attentions on her to such an extent. They might feel honor bound to try to force him to wed her, and then he might kill them.

Even worse, Rachel was reluctantly forced to admit to herself, was the horrible, sinking sensation she herself felt at the pit of her stomach at just the thought of him riding out of her life, never to return. In that moment, she looked deep

down inside herself, and she knew suddenly that Gus had
indeed guessed the innermost secret of her heart, the knowledge she had somehow sensed all along but had refused to
face until now: She was falling in love with Slade Maverick.

*And this . . . this is for me, because I want you. . . . God,
how I want you!*

With an ache of wistful longing, Rachel recalled the gunslinger's words to her as he had wrapped her in his strong
embrace that morning. He wanted her, yes. She knew that.
He was a virile man with carnal appetites, and he had been
without a woman for some time now, she suspected—at least
since his arrival in Wichita several weeks past, so far as she
was aware. But was it that alone or, what seemed somehow
even worse, mere amusement or pity that drove him to take
her in his arms? For he had not spoken of loving her, or of
marriage.

Her heart heavy with sadness at the realization, Rachel
stood and, from the jewelry box on her dressing table, slowly
drew forth her gold locket. Springing its tiny clasp, she
opened it and, tears blurring her eyes, tenderly laid the locks
of Slade's black hair inside, next to those of her beloved
parents. If she never had anything more of the gunslinger
than this, if the hopes and dreams that now burgeoned in her
heart remained forever unfulfilled, she would still always have
a small part of him here, in her locket, and pressed like a
flower into the pages of her memory.

If she had to, she could live on that for the rest of her life,
Rachel thought valiantly, a solitary tear trickling down her
cheek at the poignant knowledge that she might well have
to.

BOOK THREE

Ad Astra per Aspera

Chapter Seventeen

Wichita, Kansas, 1875

Once in town, Slade spent most of the morning tracking down Miss Corbett, the schoolteacher, speaking with her at some length, and then diligently examining, at the rear of the local boardinghouse in which she lived, the small shed where she held classes. The wooden building was in disrepair, but it was not in nearly as bad shape as some of the places that served as the town's schools, she hastened to assure him, and naturally, she insisted stoutly, she had done her best with what limited funds she had managed to coax from the school board to make the single classroom as hospitable as was humanly possible.

"I'm sure you have, Miss Corbett," Slade conceded, liking her, though she was homely and graceless, for he sensed that beneath her unattractive exterior beat a compassionate and dedicated heart. "And this is where the children would come every day for lessons?"

"Yes, sir. And of course, at dinner, when we have a short recess, they would have the use of the backyard here. Mrs. McGinty, the widow who owns the boardinghouse, has even kindly consented to the hanging of a swing, as you can see, and there is space for the youngsters to jump rope and play ball. We are fortunate in this, as many of the classrooms around the city do not have any sort of playground at all.''

Miss Corbett, he learned, had been teaching in Wichita since its founding. Currently, she had a contract with the city that ran for one school term, which was four months, and for which she was paid twenty-five dollars per month. Her contract would be up at the end of April, after which time she expected that it would be renewed without difficulty, due to the scarcity of good and available schoolteachers in Wichita. Because the number of schools in town was small compared to the number of children who were eligible to enroll, she explained, classrooms were crowded, and all youngsters under the age of six were prohibited by law from attending classes. Nor was attendance of all the students who *were* enrolled regular, especially during the planting and harvesting seasons. Naturally, she quite understood the reasons for this, Miss Corbett said, and so she did not expect to see at school children who were desperately needed at home to work in the fields.

"But *any* education at all, no matter how erratic, is better than *none*, Mr. Maverick,'' she asserted staunchly.

"Yes, I'm sure you're right,'' Slade agreed. "How soon could you enroll my nieces and nephews, then, Miss Corbett?''

"The sooner, the better, Mr. Maverick. Our sad little quarters may be cramped, but I can always make room for students who are eager to learn!''

"Then I shall have my nieces and nephews here at precisely eight o'clock tomorrow morning. Good day, ma'am.'' The gunslinger tipped his hat politely.

"Good day to you, Mr. Maverick, and thank you.'' Miss Corbett, obviously from the same genteel background as Rachel, Slade thought, extended her hand and shook his own firmly. "I shall look forward to teaching the Beecham youngsters.''

This matter thus disposed of, Slade proceeded to the Southern Hotel for dinner. Then he rode out to Gustave Oxenberg's farm, where, after an awkward, sheepish moment, he and Gus heartily made up their quarrel and arranged to help each other with their spring plowing and planting, as well as to lend Rachel a hand with her own. After they had got their amenities and business out of the way, the Swede spoke proudly.

"I get letter this morning, from Old Country," he confided somewhat bashfully but beamishly to Slade. "Gooud friends of my family come to Wichita, arrive soon, three or four months, maybe. Name Svenson. I know them since I was little boy in Sveden. They have three fine, strapping sons, Erik, Peder, and Harald, and daughter, Livie." He paused, recalling his friends. Then he continued. "Livie was just freckle-faced girl when I leave home to come to America. She will be all grown up now. I vonder if she is married yet? I vonder if she will remember me?" he mused aloud, then reddened with embarrassment at his apparent disloyalty to Rachel. Defensively, he said, "Rachel and me, we decide is better to be just friends."

Hearing this, the gunslinger smiled slowly. "I think that's for the best, Gus," he declared, affably clapping the Swede on the back. "And who knows? Maybe your Livie won't turn out to be the type of woman to insist on five hundred head of cattle for her south forty before wedding a man!"

"I don't believe it!" Gus exclaimed. "Is that why Rachel not want to marry me, because I not have five hundred cows in pasture?"

"No," Slade said, grinning, "but I'm fairly sure it's why she won't agree to marry me, even if I *do* go down on bended knee to ask her!"

"*Are* yoou going to ask her?" the Swede inquired suspiciously, wanting to make certain the gunslinger's intentions toward Rachel were, in fact, honorable.

"All in good time, Gus," Slade answered. "All in good time. I've got some things I need to settle first, and then, I promise, you can be the best man at my wedding."

"I will hold yoou to that, Slade Maverick," Gus vowed,

smiling, though the gunslinger did not mistake his steady gaze or the sincerity of his tone. "Rachel is gooud voman, deserve gooud man. Yoou be gooud man to her, or maybe next time, I crack yoour skull clean open wide, *ja*?"

"No, thanks. Once was enough for me, believe me," Slade averred, rubbing the lump on his head ruefully. "I'll treat her right, Gus, I swear. And if I don't, well, you know where to find me."

"*Ja*, and don't yoou forget it!"

"After that wallop you gave me, I'm not likely to do that. Just do me a favor, Gus," Slade drawled wryly, as he swung into his saddle. "Don't give us any chairs as a wedding present!" Before the Swede could reply, the gunslinger cantered off, pausing only to call back over his shoulder, "Best of luck with your Livie!" before he disappeared over the horizon.

The visit to Gus had reminded Slade that Rachel was still without a proper chair to sit on at her table. So he rode back to Wichita, where, at a local furniture store, he spent part of what remained of his hard cash after his buying the many supplies needed for the Beecham place to purchase a brand-new chair for her. He arranged to have it delivered to her farm late that afternoon. Then he made his way to the offices of Atwood and Little, attorneys at law, exiting well over an hour later, with two legal documents in hand. After that, Slade headed purposefully across the big river into Delano, in search of Jonathan.

The red-lamp district was even dirtier than the actual city itself, which, despite its growth and progress, was neither clean nor well maintained, as though it had burgeoned too fast for its founding fathers to keep pace with it. In both Delano and Wichita, the streets were a mess, a wide maze of dangerous wagon ruts and deep potholes, a sea of mud when it rained and flooded knee-deep after a downpour. Piles of trash littered the boardwalks, blowing, along with clouds of dust, into stores and houses alike with every strong gust of wind. The boardwalks themselves, due to the lack of any city regulation, were of varying grades of lumber that at best were riddled with splinters, knotholes, and nails, and at worst were missing planks entirely. All along the boardwalks and false storefronts, so many signs and shingles were posted at such numerous heights and angles that they not only constituted an eyesore, but a real hazard to the inattentive who might accidentally run into them. Dogs, and their excrement, were such a nuisance that a three- to five-dollar fee was charged for keeping even a cur in town, and local policemen chased after as many stray mutts as they did criminals. Along the banks of the little river were so many cattle pens and pig sties that the city's water supply was foully polluted (and was, as a result, often referred to by drovers as "buffalo tea"); and dead livestock was sometimes to be found floating on the river's shallow waves.

But just as with the school-bond issues, the thrifty Wichita businessmen feared driving away investors with excess taxation aimed at cleaning up the city, and so did no more about the filth than they did about the vice and corruption in Delano and elsewhere within the city limits proper.

After sunset, saloons, gaming hells, and dance halls on both sides of the Big and Little Arkansas rivers flung their doors open wide, and drinking, gambling, whoring, and violence took over. There were more than fifteen saloons in town (not counting those in Delano), each of which paid a licensing fee of twenty-five dollars per month to stay in business. The beer served in local brewer Emil Werner's saloon alone was rumored to be so potent that a policeman who sampled a mug there staggered out afterward wearing an inkwell instead of his hat.

Nor was gambling deemed any more disgraceful than drinking. Indeed, Officer Wyatt Earp had for a time supplemented his salary as a policemen by working as a keno dealer, as well. In addition to keno, the most popular games played were faro (also known as "bucking the tiger," because of the tiger painted on the faro box), poker, roulette, and chuck-a-luck. Prostitution was illegal, but as local policemen routinely collected fines for harlotry from all the known trollops in town (and, ironically, charged those lacking a steady stream of clients with loitering instead), it could be argued that the practice of whoring was, in essence, not only licensed by the city, but also condoned by it. In fact, when several of the Delano drabs had begun running nude races from the dance halls down to the Big Arkansas, the Wichita City Council had merely outlawed daylight bathing in the river, suggesting that the activity be conducted at a more discreet hour so as not to offend any of the city's more righteous folk. So long as the cattle and buffalo trade thrived, and skylarking cowhands and hunters continued to fritter away, often in the space of just a few days or even hours, months of wages on the city's less desirable attractions, Wichita was not about to clean up her act.

In 1872 alone, almost 80,000 head of cattle had passed through the city's sprawling stockyards, and deposits at the various local banks had totaled $5.5 million, far in excess of towns three times Wichita's size in Kansas. The two years subsequent, while not as prosperous, due to a national financial panic in 1873 and the grasshopper plague of 1874, had still proved profitable enough that Wichita had remained the queen of the cow towns, "the Peerless Princess of the Plains," as she was so often fondly called.

As far as the buffalo went, in the first three months of 1875 alone, Hayes and Brothers, a local buyer of animal skins, had purchased thousands of hides and robes at a cost of $50,000, making it the largest dealer in furs in Kansas. Even buffalo bones were worth five to ten dollars a ton in Wichita, which shipped them mostly to Philadelphia, where they were pulverized for use as fertilizer. Buffalo horns were especially valuable, as the price paid for them was thirty dollars a pair. They, too, were sent by train from the city to various factories back east, which turned them into ladies' fans, gentlemen's pipes, umbrellas, and so forth. Bits of hide scraped from the bones went to manufacture glue.

At the horrendous rate the massive herds of buffalo were being slaughtered, they would soon be gone from the prairie. But cattle and farming were Wichita's future, and Rachel was astute enough to grasp this, as Slade now realized. But cattle and farming on the scale Rachel envisioned required land, lots of land, and she did not have nearly enough. It was Slade's intention to start acquiring the additional acreage she would need to make her hopes and dreams come true. It was the least he could do, he thought, if he wished her to marry him, since he had so little else to offer her.

It was not until after dark, however, that he found his worthless brother-in-law, for Jonathan was not in Delano, as the gunslinger had supposed, but in Wichita. This, Slade deemed a real pity. Though local policemen *would* come to the town's red-lamp district if summoned, they did not claim jurisdiction across the big and little rivers and so tended to look the other way as far as violence there was concerned, a circumstance the gunslinger had been counting on. For as the carrying of firearms was not prohibited in Delano, either, as it was in the city limits proper, Slade had intended on backing up, with his Peacemakers, any threats he might have to make to his brother-in-law to accomplish his goals. Now, he would have to hope his threats alone would suffice, else he knew he would undoubtedly have to risk thrashing Beecham and being fined and jailed again.

Jonathan was ensconced at Emil Werner's saloon, the Summer Garden, a place so noisy and rough that even its owner had carelessly confessed that it ought to have a policeman present and on duty around the clock. Its orchestra was so loud that, in August of that year, the *Wichita Eagle* would be moved to publish an article complaining about its ruckus, and lewd behavior and drunken brawls occurred frequently on the premises.

Alone at a table in one corner, Jonathan sat, his bloodshot eyes rimmed with red, a half-empty whiskey bottle before him. From this, he occasionally took a slobbering swig, not even bothering to pour the liquor into the glass that had been brought along with it. At Slade's approach, he glanced up, swaying slightly in his chair as he squinted his bleary eyes into focus. Spying the gunslinger, he scowled darkly.

"Well, damn, if it ain't my notorioush brother—hic—in-law!" he droned, slurring his words. "What happened to

you? Black eye, split lip. You look like you've been—hic
—run over by a freight wagon or sumpin'. Whatsa matter?
Rachel get mad 'n' take her—hic—rollin' pin to you?''

"No," Slade said tersely, disgusted. "I had a mild dis-
agreement with Gus Oxenberg over a chair—not that it's any
of your business. Mind if I sit down, Beecham?''

"It'sh a free country, isn't it? Shuit yourshelf. Jush don't
tell me it'sh mornin' already! I jush got here, 'n' it wasn't
—hic—even sundown when I came in. I haven't been here
—hic—that long, have I? Or have I? Come to drown me in
a water trough, as usual, Maverick?''

"No. In case you haven't noticed, Beecham, I've given
up trying to reform you. This is the first time I've sought you
out in days.''

"Oh. Well, whaddaya want, then, if it isn't to—hic—
force me into sweatin' like a goddamned darky out there on
that friggin' farm?''

"I want you to sign a paper, Beecham, duly appointing
me as the legal guardian of my nieces and nephews, and
giving me sole custody of them.''

"Whaaat?'' Jonathan exclaimed, straightening up some in
his chair, in an obvious but a vain attempt to appear more
sober. His eyes narrowed warily with suspicion. "Whaddaya
want me to do that for?'' he asked sharply. "*I'm* their father,
aren't I? 'N' I'm not dead yet—least, not so far as I know
—hic.''

"No, but at the rate you're going, you soon will be,''
Slade stated grimly, "and you're unfit to rear them, besides.
You don't give a damn about those poor kids, and you know
it! So, before you wind up pushing up daisies, I want this
matter settled legally, to my satisfaction. I don't want to have
any trouble with a court trying to take those youngsters away
from me after you're dead and buried.''

"Whatsa matter? 'Fraid the law mightn't find a gunslinger
a shuitable guardian?''

"That's right.'' Slade nodded, reaching into his pocket to
withdraw one of the documents he had had prepared at At-

wood and Little. After motioning over one of the saloon girls, he instructed her to bring a pen and an inkstand. Once she had plunked both down before him, he pushed them and the paper across the table toward his brother-in-law. "Go on, Beecham. Sign it," he demanded.

"'N' jush what makes you think I'm gonna do that, huh?" Jonathan sneered, snickering as at some joke, before taking another long draft from his whiskey bottle, then wiping his mouth off with his sleeve.

"Because if you don't, I'm going to kill you, Beecham," Slade threatened quietly, his eyes glinting like blue steel.

Jonathan snorted, then laughed outright.

"I mush be drunker than I—hic—thought!" he declared, slapping the table. "'Cause I damned sure don't see any gun belt slung around your hips, Maverick! Was you aimin' to cut my throat with one of those Mexican cartwheels you seem to favor as spurs—or jush batter me to death with your hat?" He chortled at the latter idea.

"Neither. Don't let my unarmed appearance fool you, Beecham, because you know what? I've got the sweetest little hideout gun you ever did see, a two-shot Derringer I carry in my right boot, just for occasions like this," Slade lied smoothly, his face inscrutable. "And right at this very moment, I'm holding it under the table, trained square at your belly—and at this close range, I don't hardly see how I can miss."

Jonathan's eyes widened with alarm at that, and his supercilious smirk disappeared as though it had been abruptly slapped off his face. He glanced around the barroom wildly, as though expecting somebody to observe what was happening and come to his aid. Then, recognizing that the saloon was so boisterous that probably no one would even notice if he suddenly keeled over dead at the table, he licked his lips nervously and smiled sickly.

"You're bluffin', Maverick," he insisted, trying to muster a brave front. "I know you're bluffin', tryin' to make a fool outta me, you sorry son of a bitch!"

"You want to bet your life on that?" Slade queried. He paused. Then he ordered, "Pick up the pen, Beecham—before I blow a hole right through you."

At last, after a long, tense moment, Jonathan cursed angrily under his breath, then snatched up the pen and, without even bothering to read it, scrawled his name on the document the gunslinger had shoved in front of him. He did not want to lose his life—miserable as it was—especially over a parcel of what he considered thankless, troublesome whelps who he now heartily wished had never been born. Despite his being their father, he would be well rid of his children, he told himself heatedly. The mealymouthed brats didn't care about him anyway, he thought, conveniently forgetting that he himself was to blame for their lack of affection.

"There!" Jonathan churlishly threw down the pen and flung the paper at his brother-in-law. "The ungrateful little bastards are all yours, Maverick! Take 'em, 'n' be damned! Now, g'wan. Lemme alone, why don'tcha? Jush lemme alone."

"Not so fast, Beecham. Not so fast. There's still the matter of my expenditures on your property to settle." Once more, Slade delved into his pocket. "Here are the receipts. I'd like to be reimbursed for them—now . . . and in cash."

Jonathan's eyes popped, and his face blanched as he gazed at the sheaf of bills in the gunslinger's outstretched hand and thought again of the pistol concealed under the table, pointing right at his belly—or so he believed.

"You—you can't possibly expect me to—to pay you for all them friggin' chits!" he sputtered, indignant. "I—I don't have that—that kind of money—not anymore, not since the war. 'Sides, I didn't authorize you to make any improvementsh on my property anyhow!"

"Too bad," Slade growled. "I did, and now, you're going to reimburse me for them. I'm warning you, Beecham: I've got a real itchy trigger tonight, and you know what? It's so goddamned rowdy in here that I'll wager nobody will even hear my Derringer go off. It's not like my Peacemakers. It doesn't have much of a kick at all, just sort of a soft . . . *pop*!''

At the startling sound, fearing, in his alcoholic stupor, that he had been shot, Jonathan jumped a mile. Losing his balance, he fell heavily to the floor, knocking over his chair in the process. He lay there groaning, while Slade, watching him coolly, struck a match, lit a cigarillo, and puffed on it slowly, a wolfish smile curving his lips. After a moment, realizing he had not, after all, been drilled by a bullet, Beecham struggled to his hands and knees, righted his chair, and crawled into it. The scare had humiliated and enraged him, and sobered him up some, too. This time when he spoke, he didn't slur his words.

"That wasn't funny, Maverick!" he spat, feeling like a fool.

"It wasn't meant to be. Now, where's my money, Beecham?"

"I told you . . . I—I don't have any to give you!" Jonathan paused, thinking hard, for there did not seem to be any way out of his dilemma. Then, his eyes shifting, he suggested slyly, "Why don't I play you for it? Five-card draw. One hand. Winner takes all."

"You just said you don't have any money," Slade pointed out, dragging on his thin black cigar. "So just what were you planning to put up as stakes?"

"My farm," Jonathan announced, reaching for the whiskey bottle again, and then drawing back, evidently thinking better of it. "It's mortgaged, but even so, I reckon it oughta be worth those goddamned receipts you're holdin'. If I win, you just hand 'em over 'n' forget about ever collectin' for 'em. If I lose, I'll deed the farm over to you, in lieu of payin' you for the bills."

"Sounds fair to me," Slade agreed, hardly daring to believe his luck, that his brother-in-law had actually proposed the poker game he himself had meant all along to bring about.

They called for a deck of cards, and the saloon girl who had delivered the pen and inkwell earlier brought a fresh pack to the table, broke the seal, and opened the deck. At the gunslinger's direction, she shuffled and cut the cards, then dealt five facedown to each man. Slowly, Slade and Jonathan looked at their hands. As the stakes of the poker game had been predetermined, there was no additional betting by either man.

"Cards, gentlemen?" the girl inquired laconically, her dull eyes flickering briefly with interest as she glanced at the gunslinger.

"Three," Beecham grunted.

"One," Slade said, smiling inwardly as he picked up the card the girl had laid before him and saw that it was the queen of hearts. It seemed an auspicious omen. "Well, Beecham, play or pay. What's it to be?"

"Three of a kind," Jonathan crowed as he spread his hand faceup on the table, certain he had won. "Aces. Read 'em 'n' weep, Maverick!"

"Not tonight," Slade jeered softly, smiling in a way that made his brother-in-law's skin crawl. "First rule of farming, Beecham: Never count your chickens before they hatch." With a dexterity born of years of gambling, he fanned his cards across the table. "Queen-high flush—and so far as I know, that still beats three aces any day of the week. Tough luck, Beecham."

From his pocket, the gunslinger withdrew the second document he had had drawn up at Atwood and Little, and deliberately tossed it at Jonathan.

"I believe that's one farm you owe me, Beecham," he uttered triumphantly. "Just sign on the dotted line, and I'll have the change of ownership recorded first thing tomorrow morning."

"You bastard!" Jonathan hissed furiously as he stared at the paper. "You arrogant, double-dealin' son of a bitch! You planned to take my farm even before you got here, didn'tcha? You planned to take my farm, 'n' you tracked me down like a bloodhound tonight, just so you could get it! How else could you have had that paper all ready 'n' waitin' in your pocket, huh? You thievin' bastard! Takin' my kids wasn't good enough for you, was it? You had to get my farm, too! Well, I'm not signin'! You hear me? I'm not signin' that goddamned paper, you friggin' son of a bitch!''

"You welshing on our bet, Beecham?" Slade asked, his silky tone deceiving. "Not smart. Not smart at all. I guess you must be forgetting about that deadly little Derringer I'm still holding under the table. Why, once the law learns you were a cowardly cur who refused to pay his gambling debt, I doubt very much if I'll even be fined for killing you." He paused, then went on. "I'm waiting, Beecham, and my trigger finger's getting itchier all the time. Think real hard, and while you're thinking, remember this: If you decide wrong, it'll be the last decision you ever make! Now, make up your mind, Beecham, one way or the other."

Jonathan longed frantically to peek beneath the table to see if his hateful brother-in-law really did have a hideout gun under there or if he was actually bluffing, as Beecham had wondered all along. He ought to have looked when he had fallen out of his chair, he thought, ill with fright and disgusted at his lack of perception. He felt just as he always had before a battle during the war, as though he were going to throw up or pee his pants. His stomach alternately roiled and cramped, and the urge to relieve his bladder was tremendous. Sweat broke out on his forehead and beaded his upper lip, and his hands felt cold and clammy.

That stinking, lousy farm wasn't worth dying for, Jonathan told himself; and despite his halfhearted suspicion that his brother-in-law was cozening him by claiming to have a two-shot Derringer aimed straight at him beneath the table, that the gunslinger was telling the truth was a much more likely possibility, he was reluctantly forced to admit. Slade Maverick was certainly bold and daring enough to risk getting caught in Wichita, with a pistol in his boot; and a man in his dangerous profession no doubt had any number of other dirty tricks up his sleeve, besides. Finally, deciding, as before, that he dared not take the chance that his brother-in-law had nothing under the table but his hand, after all, Jonathan swore and signed the paper transferring ownership of his property to the gunslinger.

"Wise move, Beecham," Slade stated, his taut, sinewy body slowly relaxing as the uneasy moment when he had been uncertain whether Jonathan would call his bluff passed. Gathering up both the documents on the table, the gunslinger had the saloon girl and one of her friends, neither of who could read or write, make their marks as witnesses on each paper. Then he carefully wrote the girl's names below their X's and gave each of them two dollars for their trouble. "Much obliged, Beecham," he said as he carefully folded the documents and put them into his pocket.

"What about the receipts?" Jonathan asked curtly.

Slade's glance slid to the sheaf of bills on the table.

"Why, you can keep those, Beecham," he replied. "That was the deal, and unlike you, I'm a man of my word. Take 'em. Do whatever you want with 'em. Pitch 'em, burn 'em, or use 'em in the outhouse. Frankly, I don't much care." He pushed his chair back from the table and rose.

"Answer one more thing before you go, Maverick." Jonathan spoke dully, like a man who knows he has been wiped out. "I need to know: Do you or do you not carry a Derringer in your boot?"

For a moment, Slade puffed on his cigarillo, blowing a cloud of smoke into the air. Then, slowly, he shook his head, grinning.

"Why, no, Beecham," he drawled insolently. "I don't stick anything in there but my foot."

"You black-hearted bastard!" Jonathan snarled.

"That's funny, Beecham. That's real funny. You know why?" Abruptly, the smile faded from Slade's dark visage, and his midnight-blue eyes turned hard as flint. "Because I'll bet that's what India thought about you just before she died."

Then, spurs jingling, the gunslinger strode out of the Summer Garden into the darkness, the saloon's jalousies swinging shut behind him, muting some of the clamor that echoed up and down the street. He was so angry, Slade realized, that he was actually trembling; so for a moment, he just stood outside, inhaling the cool night air deeply in an attempt to still the rage that boiled within him.

It was the sound of shots that finally stirred him to action, since, for a wild, nerve-racking instant, he thought Jonathan, crazed with ire and drink, had somehow managed to get hold of a weapon and come after him. Swiftly, Slade pivoted so his back was flat against the outside wall of the saloon, his hands simultaneously reaching for his Peacemakers, only to discover that his gun belt was missing. He cursed shortly, feeling naked and defenseless, then began laughing sheepishly to himself a few minutes later, when he realized the gunfire was coming from the region of a mule tied up at a nearby hitching rail.

Curious now, Slade strolled over to find out what was happening, just as local policemen arrived on the scene. From what the gunslinger could discern, it appeared, much to his amusement, that one of the numerous Texans in town, not wishing to exchange his pistol for a metal token, had draped his gun belt over his saddle horn instead; and every time his fractious mule twitched or stamped, the revolver was discharging. After a hot but, to Slade, vastly entertaining debate with the mule's fast-talking owner, the policemen finally left, reluctantly conceding the Texan's point that there was no law in Wichita against a mule shooting a gun inside the city limits.

Chuckling to himself, his terrible wrath at Jonathan now abated, his burning desire to avenge India's death now gratified, Slade retrieved his horse and galloped out of town, heading toward the farm where he knew that Rachel would be waiting.

Chapter Eighteen

The March wind gentled, and Slade at last completed his work on the Beechams' new log cabin and took the children there to live. Though the youngsters were no longer underfoot every minute, Rachel was not as devastated by this as she had once thought she would be; for every morning, when he drove the five oldest Beechams into town to attend school, the gunslinger dropped Andrew, Naomi, and Tobias off at her farm for the day. Then, in the evenings, when he came to pick up the three youngest Beechams, the two families ate supper together.

To the meals Rachel cooked with Eve and Susannah's help, Slade, for his part, diligently contributed wild game—buffalo, venison, antelope, rabbits, wild turkeys, prairie chickens, quail, and the like—as well as fish from the big and little rivers, black catfish and white bass, mostly. Since first taking in the Beecham children, Rachel had not been able to hunt or fish much. As a result, her stores were now running low, as was what little hard cash she had on hand; for previously, the meat and poultry, at least, that she, Fremont, and Poke had not needed, she had peddled in Wichita to William "Buffalo Bill" Mathewson's store on Douglas Avenue, which, in addition to feed, bought and sold wild game.

Still, Rachel felt that the loss of her time to hunt and fish, as well as the small but additional income the former had provided, was a small price to pay for keeping the Beecham youngsters; and it was easier for both families to take supper as one, besides, since then there was food enough for all and neither she nor Eve and Susannah, both in school now, were solely burdened with preparing the evening meal.

Often, Slade and the children stayed until well after sunset. By the soft glow of the oil lamps, the five oldest youngsters studied their lessons, while the battles over the checkerboard raged and Rachel cut and sewed her new dress from the fine blue silk she had bought at the New York Store. Afterward, Fremont smoked his pipe, Poke chewed his tobacco, and Slade played his harmonica. So, despite Rachel's earlier fears, it was, to her profound happiness and relief, almost as though nothing had changed, except that Gus came only now and then, and then only as a friend, as he had promised.

Gus was much more animated these days, talking excitedly of the Old Country, of growing up in Sweden, and of his family's good friends, the Svensons, soon to arrive in America. Most often, he spoke of Livie Svenson; and Rachel realized, with a strange mixture of joy and sadness, that she had already lost her place in his heart to the unknown Swedish girl. For he no longer hinted in his reticent fashion at marrying Rachel, nor did he woo her anymore.

Since she could not love Gus other than as a friend, Rachel was glad for his sake that it should be so. But she could not help grieving over losing him, too, for it seemed as though he had always been there before, a bulwark against her becoming an old maid, if she had decided she wanted him, after all. It had been unfair to Gus, she knew, and yet she had held on to him. Now, she must let him go, and for the first time in many a long day, Rachel felt herself truly alone, irrevocably destined to wind up a spinster. For if a man such as Gus could change his heart's allegiance so easily, how could she expect a man like Slade Maverick to give his heart at all?

Yet she was uncomfortably aware that he had somehow taken Gus's place in her life, that even Gus himself behaved as though the gunslinger were courting her. Slade no longer treated the Swede as a rival, either. Instead, as though he and Rachel were already engaged or married, the gunslinger greeted Gus as an old friend they both welcomed at the farm.

Rachel was puzzled by this; she could make neither heads nor tails of it. Slade had not made his intentions known to her; nor did he act any differently toward her than he had previously. Yet she sensed a proprietary air in his manner, as though he had in some way marked her as his and everyone knew it but she. She did not know that, having made up his mind to wed her, Slade considered the matter settled; and despite her falling in love with him, if Rachel *had* known this, she would have been furious at his arrogance in not even bothering to consult her about her feelings one way or the other. But this, the gunslinger did not do. Ignorant of her love for him, he believed she might reject him, and he was both unwilling and determined not to accept no as his answer.

Often, she would find him watching her speculatively in the evenings, his eyes hot and hungry as they raked her possessively, making her blush and glance away, unable to meet his gaze. Even more confusing was that he made no attempt to press his attentions on her anymore, though Rachel had to admit she took care to give him no opportunity to do so. Not only could she not trust him when he was alone with her, but she could no longer trust herself, either. She knew that if Slade took her in his arms again, she might be unable or, worse, unwilling to stop him from having his way with her. Even more unsettling was the thought that even if he did not marry her afterward, she would at least have the memory of his making love to her—and perhaps even have his child—to sustain her through the years of loneliness and longing to come; and right or wrong, deep down inside, some wild, passionate part of her wanted that.

So Rachel kept her distance from the gunslinger and tried to guard her heart so it would not be too badly bruised and battered by him, never dreaming that, in his mind, she already belonged to him, body and soul.

* * *

Now that the Beecham farm was legally his, Slade worked harder than ever on it. In addition to Gus, he had got Fremont and Poke to agree to help him with his plowing and planting, in exchange for his assistance in getting their own fields tilled and their crops sown; and with four men laboring at it, the chore went quickly. Once the plowing was finished, they planted winter wheat, a hard-stemmed variety of grain that was Turkish in origin and that had been brought to America by Russian Mennonites. Having learned through years of experience the foolhardiness of relying on just one crop in Kansas, the other three men encouraged Slade to sow corn, rye, barley, oats, and sorghum, also, which he did. He even decided to plant one field with cotton, for last year, William "Dutch Bill" Greiffenstein had opened the Wichita Cotton Ginning and Pressing Company, and the crop was at least one with which Slade was familiar from his youth in Louisiana—though he deemed it a waste of time to attempt to grow rice, since Kansas lacked the bayous to support the necessary paddies. After laying out a large orchard, he cultivated apple, peach, plum, pear, and cherry trees, too, as further insurance against the erratic Kansas weather and invasions of pests. In a smaller garden near the house, he planted vegetables and berries.

Slade could not afford to have his crops fail. Jonathan, he had discovered after registering the change of ownership of the farm, had not only mortgaged the place, but had been two months behind on his payments, as well, and the bank had been threatening to foreclose on the property. Slade had used the last of his hard cash to bring the mortgage current. Now, unless he took up gunslinging, bounty hunting, or gambling again, his livelihood was dependent solely upon the farm.

So, with the same drive and determination that had led him to acquire his skill with his pistols, he now threw himself into his new life as a farmer. Each night, after he had brought the children home from Rachel's log cabin and put them to bed, he read every book on domestication and agriculture he

could find to broaden his knowledge. With the information
he gleaned, Slade instigated improvements on his own farm
and helped Fremont and Poke, and also Gus, to do the same
on theirs.

By the time the April showers came, the fields at all three
places were tilled and sown, and each sported an innovative
system of irrigation. This, the gunslinger had devised from
iron cisterns and long pipes drilled with sievelike holes, hoping that it would aid them in getting their crops through the
long, hot, and dry Kansas summer, which would soon be
upon them.

Because she was not needed in the fields, Rachel was, for
the first time since the deaths of her parents, able to devote
herself to spring cleaning, and with a vengeance, she set about
the task. There were shelves and cupboards to be emptied of
their meager contents, scrubbed with strong lye soap and
water, and restocked. The cast-iron stove must be scoured of
spatters and grease. Winter garments and bedding had to be
washed, dried, and carefully folded away, nestled with sweet-
smelling sachets inside cedar-lined trunks, which would keep
moths at bay. Summer clothes and linens must be unpacked
and aired. Shutters were gaily flung open wide to let in the
sun, and windows were polished until the panes sparkled.
Ashes had to be shoveled from fireplaces, and hearths brushed
of traces of soot. Furniture needed to be dusted, rugs taken
outside and beaten, and floors thoroughly swept of dried grass
and mud tracked in during the cold months.

Outside, the root cellar must be opened up and cleared of
vegetables and other foodstuffs that had inevitably rotted,
despite the cold, or that had fallen prey to insects, mice, and
other scavengers during the winter. Old hay and manure had
to be mucked out of the barn, the pig sty raked, and the
chicken coop scraped of residue. Rachel's small garden must
be hoed and sown with vegetables and berries that would
feed her, Fremont, and Poke, as well as any visitors, through
the long summer and even longer winter.

Andrew and Naomi helped with as many of these jobs as

they could, while, from the packing crate that served as his cradle, Tobias watched curiously the hustle and bustle that went on around him, as though a dust devil had invaded the house.

In addition to her spring cleaning, Rachel had her usual chores to do, also. Besides tending her livestock, she cooked, mended, sewed, and did laundry, most of it for the industrious, and therefore hungry, men laboring in the fields and the five oldest Beecham youngsters who, since they now attended school, could not go about looking like ragamuffins, she insisted staunchly. Yet she did not mind all the hard work. She enjoyed loading the younger children, who stayed with her all day, into the wagon and driving out with the dinner basket to whichever field the men toiled in. It was a chance to see Slade, and despite her resolve to have nothing further to do with him, Rachel was drawn to him like steel to a magnet.

Surreptitiously, her eyes riveted to his tall, handsome figure as he strode behind the plow or dragged heavy stones from the furrows the men tilled. His dark skin was slowly turning to bronze beneath the mellow spring sun, making his midnight-blue eyes and even white teeth stand out startlingly in his face, she observed. Nor could she help but notice how his chambray work shirt and denim breeches, drenched with sweat, clung to his hard, lean body, outlining plainly the muscles that bulged and rippled in his strong arms and legs as he labored. Sometimes, if the day were unusually warm, he dispensed with his shirt entirely, and his smooth, naked flesh glistened beneath the yellow sun, slick and sheeny with perspiration.

Then Rachel would remember the feel of him lying atop her in her bed, the way the muscles in his back had bunched and quivered beneath her palms as she had clutched him to her, and the fierce, burning ache she had felt then would rise hotly once more within her. Sometimes, the feeling was so intense that she longed violently to press her lips to Slade's skin, to lick away the sweat that beaded his chest, as he had licked his way down the valley between her breasts before his moist mouth had enveloped her nipple and his tongue had stabbed her with its heat. The unbidden image and the memory it evoked were so tantalizing that, sometimes, she was forced to close her eyes and bite her lip to fight the tumultuous emotions that swept through her then, so strong that she often feared she would cry out or swoon.

But if Slade were aware of this, or of her at all, he gave little sign of it, Rachel thought, anguished.

She did not know how the gunslinger yearned, when she appeared in the fields at dinnertime, to rip off her sunbonnet and snatch the hairpins from her hair, to watch her long blond tresses tumble free and billow about her young, lithe body in the whispering spring wind. She did not know how he wanted to press her down upon the tall, greening grass and undo the buttons of her bodice one by one, to see her full, round breasts gleaming bare and golden beneath the sun, their roseate nipples like ripe cherries bursting to be tasted.

The rest of her would be golden, too, Slade reflected, her legs long and graceful as a filly's. He pictured them entwined with his or wrapped around his back as he made love to her, and sometimes, it was all he could do to refrain from flinging her down then and there, and taking her. Frequently, he considered riding into Wichita to slake his lust on one of the local whores. But he never did. Even in his memories of them loitering upon the city's streets, their painted mouths smiling enticingly as they beckoned to passing men, they seemed coarse and frowsy when compared to Rachel's gentility and cleanliness.

Slade loved the smell of her, the subtle fragrances of soap and lilacs that always wafted from her skin, the fresh scent of starch that emanated from the plain, homespun gowns she brightened with a bit of ribbon or lace. She ought to be dressed in silk or satin, he thought, regretting that he could not buy her such; and for a moment, he hated the new life that, with the advent of India's letter, had been thrust upon him, for as a gunslinger, he had always had hard cash in his pocket. Now, he had none, and until he did, his pride would not permit him to ask Rachel to marry him, no matter how much he wanted her.

So, still, he said naught to her of wishing to wed her, and Rachel returned home from the fields, an ache in her heart.

In the evenings, she sat before the fire that burned in the hearth to take the chill from the still-cool spring nights, and she mended rips in Slade's shirts and sewed loose buttons on more firmly. Sometimes, tears blurred her eyes as she bent her head over the wifely task and realized she would never know what it meant to do such small, loving things for him as her husband.

The feeling was worsened when she took Toby in her arms to feed him and rock him to sleep, for he grew to resemble his uncle Slade more and more each day. She loved Toby with all her heart, his soft black hair, his curious blue eyes, his sweet smile, and his gentle gurgle. Maternal emotions stirred deeply inside Rachel as she gazed at the baby and held him. He might have been her child—and Slade's. They were, after all, the only real parents he had ever known.

She did not know that the same thoughts crossed the gunslinger's mind as he watched her with the baby, observed how lovingly she cooed to Toby, how tenderly she cradled him. Sometimes, as the lamplight cast a halo on her golden hair, Slade found himself thinking how much she resembled a madonna with her child; and the feelings he had long believed sealed in Thérèse's crypt came to life once more within him and began to grow and flourish.

These days, he discovered that it was difficult even to recall Thérèse's face clearly. It was gradually fading to reveal Rachel's countenance in its place, like the pentimento sometimes found beneath old paintings. Now, it seemed somehow as though Rachel had always been there, Slade thought; and to his surprise, he realized he could no longer imagine his life without her.

And so the days passed, one much like another, while the hopes and dreams in Rachel's heart, and Slade's, budded quietly and began slowly but surely to unfurl, each secret from the other.

Chapter Nineteen

April gave way to May, and the rain that had poured down following the plowing and planting of the fields ceased, leaving in its wake a prairie whose rich black earth was moist and burgeoning with life. The mixed grasses of the plains grew, all of varying lengths and ranging in color from deep blue-green to light golden-green. Tall, spiky bluestem, sometimes called "gumbo grass," pushed its way to the surface of the land, along with blue grama, short buffalo grass, plumelike Indian grass, and western wheatgrass. Wildflowers bloomed. Slender stalks of white evening primroses, woody plains larkspur, podded blue wild indigo (which was really amethyst in color), spiny small soapweed, poisonous silverleaf nightshade, and leathery green antelope horn towered gracefully above smaller blossoms of delicate prairie violets, pinkish pale poppy mallow, trailing wild strawberries, woolly white field pussytoes, radiant carolina anemones, and branches of scarlet globe mallow. Such a profusion of color strewed the prairie that it resembled a patchwork quilt and was at the peak of its beauty, Rachel thought, for she loved the plains in the springtime, when they teemed with life.

The tiny brown sparrows indigenous to the prairie had remained through the winter. Now, they were joined by the brighter-hued birds that had flocked south last autumn. Fat, red-breasted robins, scolding blue-and-white jays, and elegant scarlet cardinals darted among the green-leafed cottonwood trees that lined the riverbanks and rustled in the gentle wind. Yellow-breasted meadowlarks warbled their songs amid the swaying tall grass, and lone hawks soared in the blue, blue sky. Ground squirrels and prairie dogs crept from their burrows, and herds of graceful deer and antelope raced across the plains.

In the mornings, as now, dew sparkled like prisms or diamonds scattered upon the earth, reflecting a rainbow of colors, and fairy rings filled with clumps of beige toadstools sprouted upon the grass, so thick and luxurious that Rachel could almost believe that the fanciful winged creatures had danced there. From the door of her log cabin, she could see for miles in every direction. The vast, imperceptibly rolling prairie seemed to sweep infinitely across the earth, far beyond the horizon, and for a moment, she imagined it stretching to the very ends of the world. She inhaled deeply the fresh, invigorating morning air. Then, smiling with sheer joy at just being alive, she continued her chores.

Today was washday. Hoisting a basket of heavy laundry upon her hip, she walked toward the clothesline to start pegging the clean garments out to dry in the warming sun. Nearby, Andrew and Naomi, with a small stick, investigated a small hole in the earth down which some spider had crawled, while Toby, lying upon a blanket Rachel had spread on the ground, cooed and gurgled and, with wide-eyed wonder and interest, surveyed his surroundings.

"Look, Andy!" Naomi cried suddenly with excitement, pointing at the ground. "Here's another hole. It must be the spider's back door. Get some water, and we'll fill it up 'n' see if he comes out the other end!"

"Andrew," Rachel called warningly as, from the corners of her eyes, she observed the boy start to lug a bucket of water over to the newly discovered hole. "If that's a fiddleback down there and it bites you, you'll be numb for a week."

"We'll be careful, Aunt Rachel," he promised solemnly, then began carefully but enthusiastically to pour the water into the tiny tunnel.

Shaking her head and smiling ruefully, Rachel gave up her attempt to dissuade the youngsters from their endeavor. In her childhood, she herself had whiled away many an hour, flushing an insect from its burrow, and she was not so old that she had forgotten her glee when it had come scurrying out the other exit. Sighing at the remembrance, she turned back to her laundry, wondering what prompted children to take delight in such peculiar pastimes. Bugs certainly didn't fascinate her now—especially after the grasshopper invasion last year. The fields this spring had been riddled with eggs laid by the insects, and even now, the hideous locusts were still hatching, devouring the new green shoots that had surfaced on the land. Some of the fields had already had to be replanted. Rachel could only hope the returning flocks of birds would eat most of the young grasshoppers before the crops were destroyed again.

She picked up her empty basket and started back toward the washtub to wring out another clean batch of clothes. Then, her attention caught by a rider on the distant horizon, she dropped the basket where she stood, scooped up Toby, and ran toward the house, shouting at Andrew and Naomi to follow. Once they were all inside, she slammed shut the door and latched it. Then she grabbed her shotgun and peered warily out the window. There was no reason to believe that the approaching figure intended her any harm. But Rachel was alone with three small youngsters at the log cabin, and she wasn't taking any chances. Bands of wild Indians occasionally still attacked the farms of isolated settlers, and evil white men—unconscionable drifters and hardened outlaws—were known to commit robbery, mayhem, rape, and murder, too.

As the rider drew near, however, she saw with relief that it was only a young man, probably seventeen or eighteen years of age, she judged, certainly not much younger than she; and she had just turned nineteen in March. He was mounted on a big bay gelding, and the only weapon he carried was an old Sharps carbine. Still, prudently, Rachel did not yet go outside. Even young men could be dangerous. Witness Henry McCarty, alias William Bonney and known far and wide as "Billy the Kid," whose mother, Catherine McCarty, had run the City Laundry on North Main Street in Wichita before she had moved to New Mexico a few years back.

Slowly, the young man drew his horse to a halt in front of the house and glanced about curiously, as though expecting someone to appear. When no one did, he called, "Hello. Miss Wilder? Hello. Anybody home?"

It was then that Rachel spoke through the half-open window, making it plain she held a shotgun at the ready.

"Who are you, and what do you want?" she asked.

"I'm Adam Keife, ma'am," he responded politely, "and I'm lookin' for Miss Rachel Wilder. My family just bought some land a few miles over yonder." He jerked his thumb toward the east. "We're plannin' on farmin' it, and we need to dig a well. Somebody in town told my folks that, next to an old half-breed Indian by the name of Seeks, whose whereabouts are unknown to us, Miss Wilder was the best dowser in these here parts. Have I come to the right place, ma'am? Are you Miss Wilder?"

"Yes to both questions. Just a minute, and I'll come outside."

Still gripping her shotgun, though she no longer had it leveled at the young man, Rachel stepped out onto the stoop. Without any apparent concern, Adam Keife eyed her trusty weapon appreciatively for an instant. Then, whistling nonchalantly, he dismounted and tied his horse up at the hitching post, making no move at all toward the old Sharps carbine jammed into the leather scabbard on his saddle. Doffing his battered felt hat, he walked toward Rachel and extended his hand, obviously taking it for granted that she wouldn't refuse it. His lean young body, the way he swaggered toward her, and his bold effrontery in offering his hand to her reminded her so much of Slade in that moment that she couldn't help but smile.

"How do, ma'am," he greeted her, grinning, as he pushed a shock of dark brown hair back from his face. His startling green eyes sparkled as they met hers clearly. "I'm mighty pleased to make your acquaintance."

"Hello," Rachel said, shaking his hand. His grip was firm but friendly, his brazen manner engaging. A dimple peeped at the left corner of his mouth as he continued to grin at her winningly, and she decided she liked him and had nothing, after all, to fear from him. "Excuse me just a moment while I fetch the baby." At his nod, she went back briefly into the log cabin, reappearing with Toby in her arms and Andrew and Naomi peeping from behind her skirts. "Say hello to Adam Keife," she instructed the two older children.

"Hello, Adam Keife," they chorused as one.

"Well, hello there." The young man hunkered down to their level. "Who are you?"

"I'm Naomi," the little girl piped up, "'n' this here's my brother Andy, 'n' that's my brother Toby over there. We *were* chasin' a big old spider outta his hidey-hole till *you* came," she announced somewhat crossly. "Andy was just pourin' the water down inside to skeer him out the other end when we had to go into the house, 'case you were a bad man. I'll bet he's 'scaped now 'n' runned away." Her dejection at the thought was plain.

Adam laughed.

"Well, maybe he hasn't," he told her, his eyes twinkling. "Spiders like cool, dark places. He might still be in there."

"Really? Do you think so?" Naomi queried, brightening. She turned to her brother, grabbing him by the hand. "Come on, Andy! Let's go see!"

The youngsters scampered off to resume their investigation and flooding of the spider's tunnel, while Rachel laid the baby on his blanket and handed him a gourd rattle to play with. Adam got to his feet.

"Cute kids," he observed, dusting off his breeches.

"Yes, they are," Rachel answered. "Do you mind if I go on with my work while we talk?" She indicated the half-finished laundry. "I need to get these clothes wrung out and hung up before dinnertime."

"Not at all, ma'am. Excuse me, Miss Wilder, but if you don't mind me sayin' so, you seem awful young. I mean . . . well, you bein' an experienced dowser and all, I was expectin' somebody a lot older, and I guess you must be, what with havin' three kids, when I thought—Well, to be frank, ma'am, I just don't hardly know what my pa's goin' to say when he sees you, what with you bein' just a mere slip of a girl and all."

"You were expecting a wizened old witch, perhaps?" Rachel questioned, amused, as she fished a clothespin from the pocket of her apron and pegged one sleeve of a shirt to the clothesline. "Well, I can't say I'm sorry to disappoint you, Mr. Keife. As you can see, I'm neither wizened nor old—and the children aren't mine, either. They belong to a dear friend who died. I take care of them while their uncle's away in the fields.

"But despite your thinking me 'just a mere slip of a girl,' I'm a woman full grown, and I *am* experienced at what I do. I've been divining since I was fourteen, and if your family needs a well, I can tell you where to dig it. I don't come cheap, however. I charge ten dollars, though I'm willing to barter. But except for Seeks, who taught me, I'm the best there is hereabouts. If you'd rather wait for Seeks, however, he generally shows up sometime around the first of June, to sell his winter furs to the Hays and Brothers store in town. You might can catch him then."

"No, ma'am." Adam shook his head. "We've got to get our well dug first thing. Pa said there was no use buildin' the house when the well might wind up havin' to be located half a mile away."

"He sounds like a smart man, your father," Rachel noted.

"Yes, ma'am. So, when could you come out to our place, Miss Wilder? I mean . . . I don't want to press you, but Pa said the sooner, the better."

"How about tomorrow afternoon, then?" she inquired, smiling.

"Why, that'd be fine, just fine."

It was as Adam was giving her directions to his family's parcel of land that Slade galloped into the yard, foam flying up from his black stallion's lathered chest and his visage grave with worry. At the sight of Rachel standing there in front of the log cabin, laughing and chatting gaily with a strange young man, the gunslinger hauled his horse up short, scowling darkly and cursing under his breath.

"Slade! What's wrong?" Rachel cried, gathering up her skirts and running toward him, her face ashen at the thought that there might have been some sort of accident in the fields.

"Nothing at all, evidently!" he snapped as he swung down from his saddle, his spurs jingling. "Damn it, Rachel! Do you know what time it is? Do you see where the sun is in the sky? When you didn't come with the dinner basket, we all thought something had happened to you and the kids! I rode back here hell-bent for leather, and what do I find? You passing the time of day just as sweet as you please, flirting with a total stranger!" Slade's eyes were murderous as he glanced at the young man. "Who is he?"

"Adam Keife—and I was *not* flirting with him!" Rachel retorted hotly, stung by the reproach and stricken to have forgotten the men's dinner.

"Well, what in the hell is he doing here?" the gunslinger asked, his gaze raking her sharply, possessively, then shifting back to the young man, who, thumbs hooked in his belt, returned Slade's stare coolly—as though issuing a challenge, the gunslinger thought, enraged. "The cocky bastard! *He* doesn't look like the sort to wait for an invitation, I'll tell you that, Rachel! By God! If he's come here thinking to take Gus's place—If he's laid a hand on you—even so much as his little finger—I'll kill him!"

"Don't be ridiculous! It's nothing like that!" she exclaimed. "Why, how could you even think such a thing? I don't even know him. I just met him this morning. He came here to ask me about locating a well for his family. Oh, for heaven's sake, Slade! He's only a boy, scarcely any older than Eve."

"He looks eighteen, at least, and that's damned well old enough—and nearer your age than Eve's!" the gunslinger shot back furiously. "He's got some nerve, I'll say that for him—standing there, making eyes at you when you've only just met!"

"Well!" Rachel huffed, not only affronted, but angry herself now, also. "As I seem to recall, *you* not only 'made eyes' at me, but kissed me, too, just shortly after we met!''

Slade was taken aback by the reminder, but only for a moment, after which he recovered masterfully.

''That was different!'' he ground out, a muscle throbbing in his set jaw, because he didn't really know *how* it had been any different, just that it had been. Not wanting to give Rachel any time to ponder the dubious distinction, however, he pressed on persuasively, ''You sorely provoked me, and you know it, Rachel! And I was India's brother, besides—not just some smart-assed saddle tramp who rode in from nowhere! You don't know the first thing about him, and I don't want him hanging around here, especially with your being alone here all day! Now, since I know how much good manners mean to you, be polite, and make the proper introductions. Then send that young man packing—and don't encourage him to come back!''

Sensing there was something wrong with Slade's reasoning, although she didn't quite know what, and mortified in any case, lest he somehow be right, Rachel uneasily introduced him to Adam. She did not like at all the wicked gleam in either man's eyes as each surveyed the other warily, then shook hands, Adam scrutinizing the gunslinger's Peacemakers keenly, enviously. It was therefore much to her relief that, shortly afterward, all too aware of the tension in the air, the young man declared he must be on his way and mounted his big bay. The gelding danced fractiously for a moment before Adam reined it in. Then, pausing momentarily in the act of setting his spurs to the horse's sides, he touched the brim of his hat, glancing down intently at Rachel.

''I'll see you tomorrow afternoon, Miss Wilder,'' he drawled. Then, nodding curtly in Slade's direction, he cantered off.

''Why, that damned impertinent young son of a bitch!'' the gunslinger burst out softly, his eyes narrowed and hard as he stared after Adam Keife's retreating figure.

''Rather like you at that age, I should imagine,'' Rachel

remarked dryly. "In fact, I'll wager you haven't changed much at all over the years, Slade. I can't think why you took such a strong dislike to that young man. But then, one so often despises one's faults when one sees them in others, don't you agree?" she needled, her voice sugary sweet.

Fortunately, Slade was spared the indignity of a reply, as, just then, Naomi shrieked, "Aunt Rachel! I ax'dent'ly drowneded that spider, and now, Andy's mad, and he's trying to put it down the back of my dress!"

After Adam Keife had gone, Rachel fixed a cold dinner as quickly as she could, uncomfortably aware of Slade's barely suppressed ire the whole time. Once she had finished jamming everything into the wicker hamper, she slammed shut the lid and silently handed the basket to the gunslinger, thinking he would ride back with it to the fields. To her surprise, however, he insisted on loading her, the children, and the hamper into the wagon; and tying his horse to the tailgate, he drove them all out to the fields to eat dinner with Fremont, Poke, and Gus. After that, Slade took Rachel and the youngsters into town with him to buy a new hoe and rake, as though he suspected that if he left her alone at the log cabin, Adam Keife would return in his absence to make further attempts at charming her.

Rachel could not understand it. Slade was acting as though he were jealous of the young man, she mused. Then, suddenly, it dawned on her that he actually *was* jealous! What else could account for his surly mood and his churlish behavior? Her cheeks flushed rosily, and her heart beat fast at the realization, for it could only mean he cared for her in some fashion, something she had not dared to believe until now. Covertly, she glanced at him sitting beside her on the wagon seat, and she saw that his ill temper had not improved. A frown still creased his brow, and his mouth was turned down sourly at the corners, as though he had just bitten into a tart persimmon. It was all Rachel could do not to laugh aloud at the sight. Despite herself, hope soared wildly in her breast, and closing her eyes, she smiled softly, as though a glimmer of light had just illuminated the darkness in her heart.

"What's so funny?" the gunslinger inquired acidly, eyeing her witheringly as he sensed the subtle change in her mood.

"Why, nothing, Slade. Nothing at all," Rachel answered.

"Then why are you smiling?" he prodded, glowering at the notion that her good humor was born of the call the handsome young Adam Keife had paid her that morning.

"Oh." She shrugged noncommittally. "No particular reason. Just because it's a beautiful day, and I'm glad to be alive, that's all."

It would not hurt to spur his jealousy a little, she decided. It might even goad him into taking action where she was concerned, although she was not at all sure that the action he took would be the one she wanted.

At her vague reply, Slade glanced at her sharply, but as her long, thick lashes were demurely lowered, he could not read her thoughts. Swearing under his breath, he slapped the reins down hard on the backs of the draft horses that pulled the wagon, not liking at all the even wider smile that curved Rachel's generous lips at that, as though she knew a secret he did not.

One thing was certain, the gunslinger assured himself grimly: She wasn't going out to the Keife place all by herself tomorrow afternoon—not if he had to rope and hog-tie her to prevent her from doing so! When Slade Maverick wanted a woman, he did not lightly step aside for a rival—as young Adam Keife was going to learn to his sorrow if he got any bright ideas about sniffing around Rachel's skirts!

The impudent pup! I'll not only send him home with a flea in his ear, but his tail between his legs, too! Slade thought vehemently, nearly biting off the tip of the thin black cigar he had clenched between his teeth.

As his scowl waxed even more ominous, Rachel bit her lip so hard that she drew blood in an effort to smother her growing mirth. She was not, by nature, coquettish or deceitful. But now, she was beginning to wonder if there wasn't something to be said, after all, for the tricks with which women beguiled men. She hadn't seen Slade so angry since the morning she had deliberately ruined his breakfast. If just a perfectly innocent conversation with Adam Keife had caused such a fierce reaction, she wondered what effect an intentional flirtation with the young man would have upon the gunslinger. If Slade truly *did* care for her, as she now hoped, it would no doubt be like setting a lighted match to a keg of gunpowder, she surmised, shivering at the thought; for he was a dangerous man to cross, as none knew better than she. Still, her curiosity was such that she resolved to test her theory at the first opportunity.

This came even sooner than Rachel had supposed; for after completing Slade's errands, picking up the five oldest Beecham children from school, and starting for home, who should they chance to meet on the outskirts of town but the audacious Adam Keife? He had ridden into Wichita to transact some further business for his father and was now headed back to his family's parcel of land. Much to Slade's annoyance and Rachel's delight, as the young man was traveling in the same direction they were, it was only natural that he accompany them. Ignoring the gunslinger, Adam reined his horse in along Rachel's side of the wagon and proceeded to strike up a lively conversation with her. She was soon laughing like a giddy schoolgirl—or so Slade thought sourly.

As they rode along, Rachel introduced Adam to the Beecham youngsters he did not yet know, totally unprepared for what happened when his gaze fell upon young Eve. In that moment, he looked, Rachel reflected, exactly like a poleaxed steer just before it collapsed and died. He stared so hard at the girl that Rachel wondered if his eyes were going to pop clean out of his head, and if he had sidled his big bay up any closer to the wagon, he would undoubtedly have been run over. The notion evidently occurred also to Adam, for appearing suddenly to gather his wits, he reined the gelding over slightly, seeming to fall back quite naturally a few paces in the process, which placed him squarely between Rachel and Eve, who was sitting directly behind her in the wagon bed. After that, redoubling his efforts to please, Adam glanced boldly at Eve, deriving a great deal of satisfaction from the fact that she had obviously noticed him and was shyly attracted by his handsome looks and sassy manner.

But she's only a child! Rachel thought, startled and dismayed.

Despite herself, somewhat piqued, as well, she turned sideways a little on the wagon seat, ostensibly out of politeness to Adam, who now trotted slightly behind her, but really to get a better view of Eve. Studying the girl now from a whole new perspective, Rachel saw then what had so dazzled Adam Keife: Somewhere along the way, Eve had left her childhood behind and blossomed into a beautiful young lady poised breathlessly, expectantly, on the brink of womanhood.

Eve was her mother made over, Rachel now slowly realized, with long, silky blue-black hair, sapphire-blue eyes that stood out strikingly in her white, oval face, and a finely chiseled nose set above a perfect rosebud mouth. Her body was slender and graceful as a swan's, as India's had been, with budding, round breasts that strained with innocent allure against the tight bodice of her too-small gown. Beneath Adam's frankly appraising glance, Eve's thick, sooty lashes were modestly downcast, though she peeped up at him surreptitiously now and then. And as he grinned at her engagingly, her cheeks stained a dusky-rose hue, and her breath came quickly and shallowly, as though she scarcely breathed at all, aware as she was for the first time of a man's interest in her.

India, oh, India, Rachel cried silently, sudden tears blurring her eyes, *how I wish you were alive to see her! How lovely she has grown! You would have been so proud of her. . . .*

Adam was right to have perceived her as a woman. It was indeed time now for Eve to put up her hair and let down her skirts, Rachel recognized, stricken and ashamed that she had not observed this before, for she felt she had failed Eve in this regard. The girl badly needed some new clothes, and some motherly words of wisdom about men, too, from the looks of things. But Rachel felt she was hardly in a position to offer this latter, for how could she provide Eve with any guidance in this direction when she couldn't seem even to keep her own wanton emotions and wayward impulses in check? Why, until she had grasped how smitten Adam was with Eve, she had been planning to flirt with the young man herself—and not because she was the least bit interested in him, either, but because she had hoped to make Slade Maverick jealous and rile him into admitting he cared for her! That surely was not the scheme of a woman qualified to give advice to another about affairs of the heart.

Rachel sighed with despair at the realization. Really, she could not for the life of her imagine what had made her ever believe that such an ill-conceived plot would succeed. Surely, it had been nothing more than wishful thinking on her part; for it was now clear to her that Slade didn't care a snap about her anyway, that she had been mistaken in concluding that his earlier wrath stemmed from jealousy. He certainly did not seem the least bit irate now at Adam's presence, she thought. Somewhere along the way, his frown had vanished, and he was now actually discussing almost affably with the young man the merits and drawbacks of various guns with which they were both familiar.

Rachel did not know that, inwardly, Slade was seething at the appreciative glances and splitting grins Adam kept casting in her direction, and the way (or so the gunslinger believed) that she herself sat contemplating the young man raptly, as though lost in a daydream about him. It was all Slade could do to refrain from giving her a rough shake, and the urge he had to thrash Adam soundly for his presumptuousness was almost overwhelming. But the gunslinger was not about to make a fool out of himself again in front of Rachel by letting her see how the young man irritated him. Instead, he planned to get Adam alone and issue him an explicit warning. Then, if the strutting peacock didn't lay off, Slade would take sterner measures against him.

As for Rachel—who had so blatantly disregarded his earlier

strictures about encouraging the young man—well, the gunslinger was resolved that, this time, she would get the message loud and clear!

Despite his desire to set Rachel straight immediately, Slade forced himself to wait until Adam had reluctantly taken his leave of them and they had arrived at Rachel's log cabin. There, he pulled up in front of the house, set the wagon brake, then jumped out and went around to the tailgate to let the children out. Then, coolly ignoring the fact that Rachel was waiting expectantly on the wagon seat for him to assist her down from the vehicle, Slade scrambled back up beside her and drove on toward the barn.

"Just—just what do you think you're doing, Slade?" she inquired a trifle nervously, uncertain what he intended, for he had never done such a thing before.

"Relax, Rachel," Slade reassured her, his tone smooth and falsely pleasant as he shot her a covert, sidelong glance. "I just want to talk to you alone for a minute, that's all, and we won't have any privacy inside the house."

"Oh," she said, curious now as to what he wanted to discuss.

She chewed her lower lip, thinking hard. She had done nothing she knew of to displease him, and he did not appear mad, besides. Nothing untoward had happened in town, and his attitude toward Adam on the way home had been almost amiable. The only thing that occurred to her then was that Slade, too, had marked the young man's attentions to Eve and realized as suddenly as Rachel had that the girl was no longer a child. No doubt, he was going to suggest that Rachel take Eve into town soon and buy her some material for garments that would fit her properly. Rachel went crimson at the thought, for Slade was certainly indelicate enough to mention to her the topic of the girl's abrupt blossoming, and Rachel already felt guilty enough about not noticing Eve's unsuitable clothes until today.

Spying Rachel's pink cheeks, the gunslinger scowled darkly, wondering at the cause of her embarrassment. Doubtless, she was recalling some suggestive remark made to her by that insolent young fool, Adam Keife, he thought heatedly, as he unharnessed the team from the wagon and led each draft horse into its large stall. He latched both stall doors, then turned to help Rachel alight from the wagon, his hands hard and strong about her waist as he swung her down to the floor. Instead of releasing her, however, Slade slowly backed her up against the wagon and placed his arms on either side of her to prevent her from escaping, paying no heed to her stammered questions and squeaks of alarm at his unexpected but inexorable action.

"Rachel," he drawled, his face now black and lowering as a thundercloud again, his voice holding a subtle note of menace that made her shudder with sudden trepidation, "I thought that I told you this morning not to encourage Adam Keife, that I didn't want him hanging around here . . . around you."

"Wh-Wh-What?" she stuttered, stunned, for this was absolutely the last thing she had anticipated.

"You heard me," Slade asserted, his eyes glinting as they roamed over her assessingly for a moment, then returned to her face. "Jesus! He flirted with you nearly all the way home! And you . . . you sat there mooning over him like a silly, starry-eyed schoolgirl—urging him on as shamelessly as any hussy on any street in Delano, I might add! Christ! I thought the brazen young dolt was going to fling himself on you right there in the wagon!"

Rachel was so shocked and outraged by this unfair accusation that, for an instant, she was speechless. The blood drained from her face, as though Slade had struck her a violent blow, and her body trembled uncontrollably with the ferocity of her emotions. Then, at last, infuriated, she found her tongue, and the hot words that bubbled up in her throat came heedlessly spitting out.

"How dare you talk to me like that!" she snapped, so incensed that she didn't even bother trying to explain that Adam had been admiring and smiling at *Eve*—not her! "Why, you—you—you—O-O-Oh! I can't even think of anything bad enough to call you! Just who do you think you are—telling me what I can and cannot do? Huh? You're nobody, that's who!'' she declared, her voice rising the more wrought-up she got. ''So, let *me* tell *you* something, Slade Maverick: I'll flirt with Adam Keife any time I durned well please!'' she shouted perversely, for she knew she would do no such thing. ''Do you hear? He happens to be the—the . . . *nicest* young man I've seen in many a long day, and you're just jealous because you're nothing but a—but a low-down, gunslinging sidewinder! So just where do you get off—sticking your two cents' worth in where it's not wanted? Huh? What gives you the right, Slade Maverick? *What gives you the right*?'' she yelled, then paused to take a deep breath, gathering more steam.

''*This*!'' he hissed in the sudden silence, significantly laying one hand upon his gun belt, reminding her that he had killed before and could kill again. His eyes glittered like shards of dark blue glass in his swarthy visage, seeming to impale her as they raked her body hotly, possessively, then once more riveted on her face. ''*And this*'' . . . he muttered fiercely, as he swept her ruthlessly into his arms and crushed his mouth savagely down on hers.

His teeth grazed her lower lip, drawing blood, but she did not care. At his kiss, a wild, fearsome thrill, as though the earth had suddenly dropped from beneath her feet and she were tumbling into an endless black void, rushed through her like a roaring wind, both frightening and exciting her so, that all thoughts save those of Slade were driven from her mind. And then, after a breathless moment, it seemed she had no mind at all, was just a mass of sensation, vibrantly alive and quivering all over in response to his brutal kiss. His mouth was hard, demanding against hers, bruising her tremulous lips as his tongue forced them to open, and then pillaged the softness inside, compelling it to yield to him.

Rachel tried to resist him, but he was too strong for her, his embrace like a band of steel, his mouth setting her aflame. Of their own eager volition, her hands crept up to fasten about his neck. Her supple body molded itself sinuously to his. She felt liquid as quicksilver, boneless, spineless, as, violently

aroused by her acquiescence, Slade bent her backward, his
powerful arms all that prevented her from falling as her knees
buckled from the pressure he exerted upon her. The blood
rushed to her head, pounded in her ears, causing her to feel
dizzy and faint. Tiny pricks of light, like stars, exploded in
her brain as, again and again, his tongue shot, hot as a sizzling
bolt of heat lightning, deep into the dark, moist chasm of her
mouth, sending a charge, like foxfire, surging through her
body, making even her fingertips tingle. Soon, her lips parted
for him of their own accord, and then she was kissing him
back, her tongue entwining fervidly with his, her fingers
wrapped in his black mane of hair to draw him close.

This was what she wanted of him, what she yearned for,
this nameless thing that had snatched her in its grip. Rachel
could no longer deceive herself about that. Yet she was terrified by its intensity, its intimacy. She had never in her life
felt so utterly bewildered and lost as she did now, as though
she were caught in the eye of a tornado, spinning blindly
toward some unknown destination that would suck her down
into its treacherous depths and never release her. Her heart
thudded erratically in her breast, and she clung to Slade desperately, as though she would be whirled away if she did not
hold on tight to him.

Groaning, he dragged his mouth from hers and clutched
her to him, burying his face against her shoulder and kissing
that sensitive place at the curve of her nape. He pressed his
lips to her throat, scorching her with the fire of his kisses.
He trailed his mouth down the hollow between her breasts.
Feverishly, he nuzzled her, his lips gliding across her nipples
through the fabric of her bodice, making them ache with
passion and grow rigid with delight. Slade wanted more of
her—much more. His loins were taut with desire, and he
longed urgently to slake his lust for her. But this was not the
time or the place. Anyone might walk in on them, as he was
well aware. Still, he could not resist covering her mouth with
his own once more; and as, relentlessly, he plundered her
lips, his craving for her was such that he gradually slid one

hand down her back to cup her firm, round buttocks, forcibly arching her beneath him.

Rachel gasped and cried out sharply, acutely cognizant now of how his corded legs straddled her body, of how his muscular thighs hugged hers tightly, and of how, through her skirts, his potent masculinity sensuously rubbed her womanhood as, slowly, tantalizingly, he began to rock her against him. As the hard heat of him stroked some vital, throbbing spot between her thighs, a burning ache seized her there, at her secret heart, agonizing in its torment; and when his mouth again blazed its way down her throat to the valley between her breasts, his tongue laving her nipples through the material of her bodice, she moaned low in her throat, an animalistic sound of need and wanting.

"Slade . . . Slade . . ."

It seemed that her whimpering his name brokenly brought him suddenly to his senses, for without warning, the gunslinger yanked her up roughly and loosed her so swiftly that Rachel nearly stumbled and fell. Startled, confused, and hurt, she stared at him, a shaking hand pressed to her lips to hold back the sob that rose in her throat. His breath coming in hard, quick rasps, Slade stared back, a muscle working tensely in his jaw as he fought visibly to regain control of himself.

"Tell me that Adam Keife can give you that, Rachel!" he grated harshly. "Tell me that any man but I can give you that, and I'll never touch you again, I swear!"

Rachel tried to glance away, but his eyes held her captive, as though she were a butterfly pinned to a board; and although she did not want to answer, it seemed that her response was somehow constrained, wrenched from her by some unknown entity.

"I can't, Slade," she whispered, knowing that her words spoke volumes but unable to stop herself from saying them. "I can't tell you that, because it isn't true. Only you have ever made me feel this way."

"Then you know what gives me any rights at all where

you're concerned," he stated, walking toward her slowly, boldly, like some predatory cat stalking its prey, and pulling her, helpless and unresisting, once more into his arms. With one hand, he caught her jaw and tilted her face up to his, his eyes piercing hers, seeming to ferret out the innermost secrets of her heart and soul. "I want you, Rachel—I've staked my claim on you, whether you like it or not—and in my own sweet time, I'll take you. You know that, don't you?"

"No," she breathed, quaking at his words, a strange, electric mixture of exultation and apprehension jolting her, making the pulse at the hollow of her throat flutter wildly. "No."

Deliberately, his hand slid down her throat, tightening there briefly before his thumb began to trace a tiny circle about her jerking pulse.

"Then you know it now," he uttered softly, his mouth brushing hers, once, twice, as though to hammer home his point. "I want you—more than I've ever wanted any other woman in my life—and I intend to have you, Rachel. Be very sure of that . . . and of this: I'll kill any man who dares to try to take you away from me! So, do that young, hotheaded, hot-blooded Adam Keife a favor, for his sake, and yours, hmh? Don't encourage him anymore. It wouldn't be . . . wise."

"No, I can see that now," she conceded, realizing with a shiver that the gunslinger had meant what he'd said. "But —but it—it wasn't me he was smiling at, Slade. It—it was Eve. He could hardly keep his eyes off her."

"Eve? But . . . she's only a child!"

"No, Slade, she's not," Rachel asserted earnestly, her face beseeching as she thought of his rage unleashed on the young girl. "Have you looked at her lately? *Really* looked at her, I mean? She turned fourteen in February, and out here on the prairie, that's old enough. Besides, she's had enough hardship and suffering in her life that she's had to grow up fast. Having your mother die young does something to you inside, too. It makes you older than your years. I ought to know that as well as anyone, I reckon."

"Yeah, I know. Sometimes, I forget you're barely more

than a girl yourself, still half child, half woman—and both halves mine, Rachel. Mine!"

"You're so sure of that, Slade! So sure of me!" she protested, angry and afraid, despite her love for him. For he had not spoken of loving her, only of wanting her—more than he ever wanted any other woman in his life, it was true. But still, he had not spoken of marrying her, only of taking her. Uncertainly, she went on. "Maybe you're right to be so sure of me, because of how I've—how I've let you—let you kiss me and—and—" Finding the going difficult, she broke off abruptly, biting her lip. Then, after a moment, she said quietly, "I'm not a whore, Slade. I won't come easy or cheap. I won't!"

"I never thought you were, Rachel. Or would."

She was silent for a time, digesting this, wondering what he meant by it but too reluctant to ask, too fearful his reply might not be the one she wished so fervently to hear. So, instead, she changed the subject.

"About . . . Adam and Eve, Slade . . ." she began hesitantly, her voice trailing away as the gunslinger lifted one satanic black brow, his mouth turning down sardonically at the corners.

"Yeah, what about them?" he prompted dryly. "Didn't they beget Cain and Abel?" He paused expectantly, then chuckled at her frown. "Not funny, huh? Well, I'll bet poor Abel didn't think so, either, when he saw older brother Cain coming after him with a club! You see, much as you may disagree, Rachel, my sweet—and you *are* my sweet, you know—it wasn't really the almighty God who equalized men, but the almighty Samuel Colt, and unfortunately, he hadn't yet come along back then. Why, you're wincing, Rachel. What's the matter? Did I accidentally step on your foot? No? What, then? Shall I guess? You weren't speaking of the biblical Adam and Eve, is that it?"

"Gee. You catch on real fast, Slade."

"I'm very smart. Shall I go on?"

"Please do," Rachel urged.

"Is that an invitation?" Slade's arms tightened around her,

his gaze lingering on her mouth, making her blush and veil her eyes with her lashes.

"It certainly is not!" she retorted primly.

"For shame, you irreligious woman!" he chided, an insolent grin slowly curving his lips. "If you'd read your Bible, you'd know that things are supposed to go together in twos."

"That was Noah's ark, and we were speaking of paradise."

"Ah, yes. I know it well. A rapturous place. Hot. Exciting. I could take you there. I *will* take you there," he vowed, his voice thick. "Soon."

"You are more likely to cause me to be cast out instead! You are a devil, in truth! You should not talk so to me . . . take such . . . liberties with me. I—I do not know what is wrong with me that I permit it! I should put you off my land, never speak to you again—"

"Then why don't you?"

"I don't know! I don't know! Because I—Oh, let me go, Slade, please! It's getting late. The sun has nearly set. Grandpa and Poke will be home soon, and I need to get supper started. The children are probably hungry, and no doubt wondering where we are, besides—"

"Let them wonder! Answer the question, damn you! Why don't you send me packing, Rachel?" he demanded, his voice low, his face suddenly very still, his eyes flickering with an odd, eager light. "I confess I have wondered before why you did not."

She looked away, unable to meet his penetrating gaze any longer.

"What—what reason could I give to Grandpa and Poke for doing so?" she asked. "The truth? If they learned it, one or the other would feel honor bound to call you out, and you would kill him. You have just threatened to do as much to any man who might dare to try to court me! And you would take the children away from me, too. I—I couldn't bear any of that!"

"I see." Slade spoke, his eyes shuttered now, so she could not read his thoughts. "It is fear, then, that makes you suffer my advances, is that it?"

"Yes."

"That's a lie, Rachel, for though that may be a part of it, there is more to it than that—and we both know it." His index finger traced slowly the outline of her mouth, tugging at her lower lip, before he suddenly ceased the erotic motion. "However, I will let the matter slide for now," he declared, not unpleased with her response. Then, abruptly, he changed the topic. "What was it you wanted to say to me about Adam and Eve?"

"Only this: Don't tear them apart before they even have a chance to know each other, Slade. Please. I know that they're young, but . . . falling in love can be a . . . painful and difficult thing, especially—especially when it's—when it's the first time."

"I know," Slade told her gently, wondering how she knew such a thing. Had she loved some boy in school? He didn't know, and he found suddenly that he wanted to know everything about her, though he felt he had pressed her hard enough for now. "I wasn't much older than Adam when I lost my heart to a girl in New Orleans," he confessed, the words slipping out before he thought.

"What—what happened?"

"She . . . died."

"I'm—I'm sorry," Rachel stammered, stricken. "I—I didn't mean to pry. I—I didn't realize. I'm so sorry."

"So was I," Slade admitted reluctantly, though, to his surprise, the pain and grief he normally felt at remembering Thérèse were dull, faint, as though they were almost healed, now nothing more than a scar. More hurtful, in fact, was the anguish etched upon Rachel's piquant face that she had unknowingly reopened an old wound. "Look, Rachel, it was a long time ago, and it's over and done with now," he insisted, though he knew that it was not, that it never would be until he was sure that Digger was dead, that he had killed him. . . . With an effort, Slade shook himself from his reverie, abruptly recalling the present. "About Adam and Eve, Rachel—because you ask it of me, my sweet, and so long as they don't appear to be . . . tempted by any forbidden fruit, I won't be the serpent in their Garden of Eden, I promise."

"Thank you."

"And now, I suspect we had better go inside, hmh?" he suggested.

"Yes, I guess so," Rachel agreed.

Slade stared at her searchingly for a moment, one hand caressing her face lightly, marveling, as though he were blind and seeing her for the first time with his fingers. Then, sighing, he smoothed back a loose strand of hair from her brow and reluctantly released her.

"Pity," he said, smiling ruefully. "I wanted so badly to offer you an apple."

Chapter Twenty

The following afternoon, while Fremont and Poke watched the three youngest Beecham children, Slade drove Rachel over to the Keife family's parcel of land.

For the most part, the two of them made the trip in silence, each intensely aware of the other, and of what had passed between them yesterday in the barn. It had caused a subtle change in their relationship—and they knew it.

Now, Rachel had a half thrilling, half uneasy sense of belonging to Slade that she had not had before, as though, despite her fears about his possessing her completely, they had reached an understanding between them and it was, as he had claimed, just a matter of time before she would be his. They were not exactly engaged, she realized. But after a great deal of reflection, she simply did not know what else to make of their relationship. She felt that even Slade was not so callous as to run off any would-be rivals for her hand if he did not intend to marry her himself. Such an act would not only be deeply hurtful to her, but hideously unconscionable on his part; and somehow, Rachel just could not reconcile this image of him with that of the gunslinger who, despite his notorious reputation, had, upon learning his guardianship was required for eight nieces and nephews he had never even laid eyes on, dutifully forsaken his way of life forthwith to care for them. Such a man could not possibly be so cruel as to set out deliberately to deprive her of any hope of a husband, take her virginity, and then abandon her. He *must* mean to wed her, even if he had not said so.

But still, how could she marry a man who did not love her, even if he *did* want her? Rachel asked herself, torn. She had hoped that Slade cared about her, that he did not desire her just out of amusement or pity; and after yesterday, it seemed clear to her that his feelings for her ran much stronger and deeper than that. But still, he had not spoken of loving her, and Rachel felt sure in her heart that it was because he did not. To her sorrow and despair, she could not forget the tortured look on his face when he had told her of losing his heart to a girl in New Orleans, a girl who had died.

He still loves her, Rachel thought, aggrieved. *He still loves her, and he has no room in his heart for another. That's why he only wants me in that—that physical way. If she were alive, he wouldn't look twice at me, I'll wager. But she's dead, and India's dead; and he's alive, a virile man with a virile man's needs, and eight motherless nieces and nephews to rear, besides. And since I'm unmarried, and he wants me, and the children already know and love me, I'm the obvious solution to all his problems. Oh, it's all so very simple. Why didn't I see it before?*

Maybe Slade believed that she had seen it, Rachel mused. Maybe that was why he had held off asking her to wed him. After all, he knew she hadn't leaped at the chance to marry Gus, despite her being a spinster and Gus's having been a good, kind man who had genuinely loved her, and who had had a farm of his own to offer her, besides.

Not only did Slade not love her, but so far as Rachel was aware, he didn't own anything in the world but his horse, saddle, and Peacemakers. Both the Beecham place and the youngsters belonged legally to Jonathan, she thought, and despite her considering it highly unlikely, since, these days, he appeared to be permanently ensconced as the town drunk, she supposed he could show up at any time to reclaim them. Not that she believed for a second that Slade would permit this. Indeed, Rachel felt almost certain that were Jonathan to make such a foolish attempt, Slade would shoot him on sight. But the fact remained that the law would be on Jonathan's side in the matter, if he chose to pursue it.

How, then, could the gunslinger possibly think she would marry him just because he wanted to bed her, and because she was the ideal remedy for all that ailed him, barring Jonathan's interference? Well, surely, he couldn't, Rachel reasoned, with what seemed to her perfect logic. He wasn't dumb. He surely had to know that her pride, if nothing else, would be stung by his all-too-practical and unemotional grounds for wanting to wed her and that she would refuse him. So, if he were smart, he would bide his time and make her fall in love with him. And he was, and he had, and she had. Only Slade didn't know she loved him, Rachel realized. She hadn't told him. Well, thank God, she had not! He would surely use the knowledge against her, as he used her unwitting desire for him against her, and she could not bear that.

Yet what else could she do? He had got rid of Gus—yes, he *had*; Rachel saw that now, for if the gunslinger had not meddled in their relationship, Gus would still be hers—and with the unexpected advent in her life of Adam Keife, whom he had also viewed as a threat, he had made it plain to her that he would get rid of any other man who stood in his way, as well. Even if she wished to, Rachel had no way of stopping him. Her love for her grandfather, Poke, and the children effectively prevented her from taking any action against Slade, as he well knew and was obviously counting on. Now, he need only wait for her to grow weary of the chase, for her to decide that marrying him was preferable to winding up an old maid—and, in the meanwhile, give her a taste of what she would no longer be missing as his wife.

In that moment, Rachel nearly hated him. Yet she could not deny that she was neatly trapped and that, despite her anger at the gunslinger's arrogance and audacity, her heart cried out to her to take him on whatever terms he dictated, that having him however she could get him was better than not having him at all.

That Slade honestly had not meant to place her in such an uncomfortable and untenable position, Rachel did not know and would not have believed if she had. Nevertheless, it was true. He had intended to woo her just as any other man would have done. But the sight of her smiling and blushing like an enamored schoolgirl in the face of Adam Keife's admiration had caused him such anger and anxiety that he had just snapped, rashly acting instead of carefully thinking the matter through. Now, however, the gunslinger decided that perhaps it was not such a bad thing, after all, that he had inadvertently landed her in such a predicament, because now, despite her pique and however ambivalent her feelings toward him, Rachel would *have* to wed him—whether she wished to or not.

Slade was a man of his word, and if, after his having made her choice clear to her (however cavalierly or wrongly he had done so), she henceforth attempted to thwart him, he was grimly determined to ensure she remained a spinster the rest of her days—or at least until she relented. Since he couldn't imagine any woman choosing to be an old maid when she could be his wife instead, he felt smugly that he could now safely assume that the subject was settled.

Oh, Rachel's prickly pride and tart temper would make her hold out for a while, he expected, just to find out whether he really was serious about running off any potential suitors. But in the end, when she learned he was, she would be forced to give in to him, and they would all be better off, the gunslinger loftily postulated. After all, it wasn't as though he didn't want her, or she him, or that he had nothing to offer her, either, now that he owned the Beecham farm and was the legal guardian of his nieces and nephews.

Further, he didn't know what Rachel could find to complain about at the prospect of his being her husband, anyway. Between his guns and the farm, he was well able to provide for her, one way or another. He would not beat her or otherwise abuse her, as so many men did their wives. Nor did he smoke, drink, or gamble to excess; and of course, once they had tied the knot, he would give up whoring altogether, as it was his view from years of observation that this caused more trouble in a marriage than it was worth.

All Rachel would have to do in return as his wife was cook, clean, care for the kids, and be ready and willing in his bed whenever he desired her. Since she already did three of the four, and since she was not nearly as averse to his kisses as she tried to pretend, it should not prove too difficult for her to resign herself to the latter and just move right into his house and his bed, Slade imperiously concluded.

In fact, the more he dwelled on it, the more he thought Rachel should consider herself lucky to be getting such a good deal. After all, although he found her mighty appealing physically, most men would have labeled her plain, and while in and of themselves not particularly objectionable perhaps, her looks were compounded by the fact that neither her tongue nor her temper was especially sweet when she was riled. Indeed, until Slade had come along, "old Ox" was the best she had managed to do for herself, and while the gunslinger both liked and respected the Swede, he could not think Gus was nearly so desirable a catch as himself. Truly, now that he had contemplated the entire affair at some length, Slade was actually convinced it was Rachel who ought to go down on bended knee for *him*!

Had she known the gunslinger's thoughts, Rachel would have been so outraged by his vanity and gall that she would have boxed his ears furiously. She did not know, however, and so she sat beside him silently on the wagon seat, all too aware of his strong, muscular thigh pressed against hers through her skirts, and of what he would expect of her if he really *did* mean to wed her and she consented to become his wife—something it seemed, from his attitude, that he already took for granted, the self-assured rogue! He looked so complacent that Rachel could hardly bring herself to glance at him, and when she did, his eyes appraised her so boldly and covetously that it was clear he already regarded her as his. Hadn't he told her as much yesterday? Her cheeks stained with crimson at the memory. But then, why should he think any differently? she asked herself. Nobody—man or woman—wanted to end up old and lonely and alone, and if Slade persisted in cutting any man but himself out of the running for her hand, she felt that, in the end, she would be compelled to marry him.

He would be free then to do exactly as he pleased with her, and Rachel knew that it would not stop at his just kissing her. The gunslinger would demand his husbandly rights of her whenever and however he wished, and she would be helpless to deny him. The realization both frightened and excited her. She would give herself up to him eagerly, willingly, she admitted, if he loved her. But he did not, and that knowledge brought her full circle in her musings. How, then, could she wed him?

Oh, if only she had a bundle of beaux from whom to choose! If only Slade was not an infamous gunslinger, so certain of his ability to vanquish any other man who might want her. If only she did not love him. If only *he* loved her . . .

She could refuse to marry him, Rachel thought. If and when he ever asked her, she could simply refuse. But in her heart, she did not know if she could bring herself to be so brave in the face of her love for him and the empty years that would then lie ahead of her without him.

And so she sat beside him on the wagon seat and felt herself ensnared, and she did not know whether to scream or to laugh or to cry.

* * *

In the absence of a house, the Keife family had pitched
two large tents on their land, and it was these in which they
were living—Adam, his two younger brothers, and his father
in one; his three younger sisters and his mother in the other.
They were just finishing their dinner, and at the wagon's
approach, they slowly rose from the picnic blanket they had
spread on the ground beneath the shade cast by the tents, and
moved as one to greet Rachel and Slade. Pulling the vehicle
to a halt just before reaching the tents, the gunslinger set the
brake, jumped out, then turned to lift Rachel down, casually
but deliberately ensuring that Adam, who had stepped up to
the wagon, had no chance to assist her. Then they met Adam's
family, the young man making the introductions.

"Pa, Ma, this here's Miss Rachel Wilder, the dowser, and
that there's Slade Maverick, a friend of Miss Wilder's
family."

"Actually, more than just a friend," the gunslinger cor-
rected smoothly as he shook the elder Mr. Keife's outstretched hand. "I'm Miss Wilder's fiancé," he announced,
never batting an eyelid and staring coolly, with some amusement, at Adam, whose jaw had just dropped open.

Rachel felt certain her own expression was equally stupe-
fied. How dare Slade presume such a thing and state it publicly
without bothering even to ask her feelings about it one way
or the other? Why, the very idea! The nerve of the man!
Really, it was not to be borne! She would have voiced an
indignant protest. But before she could manage to get the
words out, Slade shot her a warning glance and slid his arm
proprietarily around her waist, his embrace like a steel band,
nearly shutting off her breath. Rachel knew then that there
was no telling what he might do next; and realizing that any
objection she raised might not only worsen matters, but make
her look foolish, as well, she abruptly closed her mouth and
forced herself to smile up at him, as though he were indeed
her beloved betrothed. After that, they said hello to Adam's

two impish brothers and three shyly giggling sisters, and politely refused the Keifes' kind offer of dinner, having eaten before leaving the farm. Then, once the amenities were out of the way, the gunslinger directed the conversation to the business at hand.

"Rachel honey," he drawled, gazing down at her from beneath lazy lids and grinning impudently as her mint-green eyes sparked up at him, "why don't you fetch your divining rod from the wagon, so these nice folks can get started digging their well. Then I'll unharness the team and let them graze a while until we're ready to go."

"Of course, Slade," she assented, her voice so sweet that he—who now knew her well—was certain she was absolutely seething inside, and he made a mental note to himself to partake of supper that night at one of the restaurants in Wichita rather than risk dining at her table.

Rachel retrieved her witching stick, which, in keeping with folkloric tradition, was a small, forked branch from a hazel tree and slightly larger in diameter than her thumb. Other woods could be used, rowan or ash, and some diviners employed a long wire of copper or bronze bent at right angles, or a silk thread with a pendulum attached to its end. But she preferred her hazel branch, for the old half-breed Indian Seeks had taught her to use this in the art of dowsing, and it was of the utmost importance that she feel familiar and comfortable with the implement.

She knew that Adam's father was skeptical of her skill, though he had not voiced his doubts as stringently as Adam's comments yesterday had led her to believe he might. She felt that perhaps the elder Mr. Keife's reticence stemmed from the fact that he had taken Slade's measure and decided that it would be unwise to press his complaints, and she thought dryly that there was something to be said, after all, for having the gunslinger at her side.

Nevertheless, Rachel was long accustomed, because of both her gender and youth, to suspicion and criticism, despite how many people, for lack of any other means of finding water, called upon her ability at the art. So she paid no heed to Mr. Keife's pessimistic expression as she grasped her divining rod at both ends and began her preparations for the ritual.

Taking a deep breath, she closed her eyes and ears tightly to shut out her surroundings, and started to gather her strength, to summon her power. This was like nothing else she had ever known, a strange force that coursed through her entire body, like the jolting reverberation one feels upon striking a stout club hard against some immovable object. Consciously, Rachel emptied her mind of all thoughts save that of water, and upon this, she concentrated with all her being. In brilliant colors and detail, she imagined a clear spring bubbling far beneath the earth's surface, longing to break free of its confines, to gush forth to the sky; and at last, slowly, she began to walk forward blindly, eyes closed, for she no longer needed to see. She was one with the land, and it steered her, the sun lighting the dark path of her mind, the wind whispering in her ear the direction she should take.

Mesmerized, Slade watched her. This was a Rachel he had never glimpsed before, though, deep down inside, he had sensed her fey qualities, her earthy passions, her spiritual oneness with the land, and been instinctively drawn to them. A man did not live as he had lived and stay alive without developing a similar intuitiveness, an atavistic knowledge of where the sun would cast one's shadow, of the sounds and scents that soared upon the wind and spoke their warnings, and of the spoor that marked the earth and told its own tale, if one knew how to look and listen.

In this respect, Rachel was wise beyond her years, the gunslinger realized, as he himself was; and he felt closer to her in that moment than he had ever felt before, as though they were alike, the same, yet different, two sides of a coin that fitted together utterly to make a perfect whole. He could almost see through her eyes, hear through her ears, smell through her nostrils, feel through her hands the elements that guided her in her quest as she moved in an ever-widening radius across the grassy ground. Her blond hair was haloed by the spring sun, her face rapt in its trance, so she appeared like some unworldly being, illuminated by a light that was not of this earth, but of some primal place where angels trod and envisioned the shape of things to come for lesser mortals.

Slade knew now why some muttered that she was a witch; in his past, he, too, had been cursed as a devil by those who feared what they could not understand. But suddenly, to him, Rachel seemed as a breath of life, vital, necessary as food or drink, as though God had, from the very beginning of time and creation, always meant her for him, and he for her. In that moment, a door somewhere in the darkness of the gun-slinger's heart unlocked and, on creaking hinges, swung open a crack, and the ghost of Thérèse stood upon the threshold, as though she had yearned for some time now to be free of the walls that had confined her, to slip away to the shadowed land where she belonged.

In that instant, too, the hazel branch in Rachel's hands began suddenly to twitch, and then to flutter so wildly, so uncontrollably that it seemed she would be struck violently in the face by it or would lose her hold on it entirely. A smile exploded upon her countenance, so joyous, so exultant that Slade sensed that the emotion behind it was almost sexual in its nature and intensity, and he knew instinctively that that was the way she would look if he ever made love to her, brought her to the peak of rapture—like a pagan goddess, golden and glorious. His loins tightened at the image, and her exhilarated cry rang in his ears like a cry of ecstasy and surrender. Then, just as though she were gliding down from the pinnacle of some splendorous height, she slowly opened her eyes to meet his.

Slade's gaze locked with hers, and Rachel saw in his eyes his hunger and need, and something more she could not name—though in another, she would have called it love. Her eyelashes swept down, a blush rose to her cheeks, and her heart beat fast with the sudden hope that burgeoned within her breast. Then, after a minute, she turned away, recovering, and spoke.

"There is your water, Mr. Keife," she uttered triumphantly, pointing at the ground. "Fetch your shovel and dig and see if it is not so."

For a short while, the Keifes stood motionless, as though in awe of her, and terrified by the treasured gift she had set before them, though they had asked that it be bestowed upon them. Then, gathering their wits, Mr. Keife and his sons ran to get their shovels and started excitedly to dig. Catching their enthusiasm, Slade stripped off his shirt and gun belt, and joined in. Soon, he, too, was knee-deep in the moist, dark reddish brown clay that lay beneath the rich black topsoil of the prairie, while Rachel studied him surreptitiously and, despite herself, wondered how it would feel to have his lean, hard, naked body cover hers intimately, completely, and take what he desired of her, what she, deep down inside, longed so fervently to give to him.

The afternoon wore on, and still, the men dug, erecting a makeshift wooden structure with rope and bucket to haul up the dirt as they shoveled deeper and deeper into the earth. As they worked, Mrs. Keife served cold plates of the chicken and potato salad left over from dinner to fuel their energy and strength, and poured lemonade to quench their thirst. Rachel sat on the picnic blanket and watched, as fascinated as the three young Keife girls, who skipped about impatiently with eager anticipation and peered nosily now and then into the hole as it gradually took shape, its clay walls smooth and packed hard.

The men were fortunate that they did not hit rock, as was sometimes the case on the plains, and that they did not need to dig so far as some. Shortly after sundown, in the silver-grey half light of the gloaming that foretold of summer's approach, Rachel heard Adam give a jubilant whoop and knew that the fears of the elder Mr. Keife were now laid to rest.

"Pa!" Adam yelled from below the earth's surface. "I'm standin' ankle-deep in water! Do you hear, Pa? Miss Wilder was right! There's water down here, plenty of it—and sweet as Christmas mornin'! Yahoo!"

Shouting a warning, the young man tossed his shovel up out of the hole. Then, grabbing the rope, he scrambled up himself, his face beaming, his high spirits bubbling over. Spying Rachel, he impulsively caught hold of her hands and pulled her from the picnic blanket, laughing and dancing her about wildly for a moment. She flushed, embarrassed. But she laughed, too, despite herself, and her skirts swayed and flew like those of a schoolgirl, showing a flash of shapely ankles in the twilight as Adam swung her around and around dizzyingly.

Despite his quick stab of jealousy at the sight, Slade, as he climbed more slowly from the hole they'd dug and, picking up his crumpled shirt, wiped mud from his cheek, took pleasure in Rachel's carefree happiness, also. She had so little of it in her life, he thought, that he could not grudge her this moment. So he stood by, looking on in silence until at last Adam became aware of the impropriety of his actions and released Rachel abruptly, sheepishly apologizing to both her and Slade for his zeal.

"I'm sorry. I—I guess I just got a little carried away, what with the water bein' right where Miss Wilder said and all. I had my own doubts about it, I'll admit, just like Pa. I—I didn't mean any harm or offense," Adam declared.

"None taken," the gunslinger droned laconically, acutely conscious of Rachel's breathlessness, of the high color in her cheeks, and of the way her eyes refused to meet his. He paused. Then he continued. "Well, it's getting late. We'd best be going so you people can turn in. I reckon you'll want to get up bright and early tomorrow morning to finish digging that well. Rachel honey, why don't you settle up with Mr. Keife, while I harness the team to the wagon."

"Yes, Slade," she said.

Rachel took five dollars hard cash from Mr. Keife and accepted the rest of her payment in precious foodstuffs, of which, being newly arrived from back east, the family had in abundance compared to what prairie folk possessed. She was especially looking forward to the jar of grape jelly she had picked out. She could almost taste it even now, good and sweet, spread on hot, freshly baked bread. Carrying carefully, as though it were gold, the basket in which Mrs. Keife had packed the foodstuffs, Rachel said her good-byes to the Keife family, then glanced around expectantly for Slade. He was sitting in the wagon, talking to Adam, who stood nearby. Her heart lurched a little in her breast at the sight, for the two men spoke so softly that she could not hear what they were saying, and she hoped that the gunslinger was not threatening the young man in some manner. Adam's face seemed very earnest and serious in the dusk.

"Mr. Maverick," he said to Slade, "I really do hope you're not angry at me for dancin' with Miss Wilder—and not just because of your—of your notorious reputation as a hired gun and a bounty hunter, either, of which I am not, as you see, unaware."

"Oh?" Slade lifted one eyebrow demonically.

"No, sir. Guns interest me," Adam explained, "so I try to keep up with who uses 'em well. That's why I know you're one of the best and why I wouldn't want to slight you. But there's more to it than that. You see I—I also know you're Miss Eve's uncle, and . . . well, I'd—I'd like to have your permission to—to call on her, sir, if you don't mind."

"So it *was* young Eve who caught your fancy, was it?" Slade prodded, now faintly amused by the brash young man. The gunslinger had to admit that Adam had grit. Not many men, young or old, would have dared to dance with a man's fiancée without his consent—and then had nerve enough to ask him for a date with his niece. "Funny. I could have sworn that it was Rachel."

"Miss Wilder? Oh, she's friendly and nice, and I like her and all. But she's older than me, I gather; and besides, although I didn't realize until today that she was your betrothed, it was clear to me yesterday in which direction the wind blew there. I hope that you don't think I'd be so foolish as to tread on your toes, Mr. Maverick. I may be a lot of things, but stupid ain't one of 'em. No, it was Miss Eve who took my eye, and I'd like to see more of her."

"She's only fourteen." Slade's voice was curt.

"So was my ma when my pa first courted her," Adam insisted. "It's old enough—and you know it . . . sir."

"Yeah," the gunslinger agreed, his amusement gone, a subtle note of warning now creeping into his tone, "just like I also know this: I know *you*, Adam Keife—what you think, what you want out of life—just as well as I know myself, and I'm older and a hell of a lot more experienced than you, besides. I've already been where you are, and where you're going, as well. So, don't go getting any bright ideas, because no matter what, I'll always be one step ahead of you—and don't you forget it! That understood, you can call on Eve if you please. But you had damned well better treat her right, or before you even know what hit you, you'll find yourself standing in church and repeating your vows to her just as sweet as you please, her hand in yours and my guns at your back, if need be! Do I make myself clear?"

"Yes, sir. Quite clear."

"Good. Then there's just one thing more, and then this conversation is finished: Keep your distance from Rachel, Adam Keife. I won't have her trifled with—not by you, not by anyone. So if you do decide to call on Eve, make sure it's *Eve* you're calling on! Do you get my drift?"

"Strong as a blizzard in December, Mr. Maverick."

"Then I expect we'll get along real fine. Good night, Adam Keife."

"Good night, sir."

Slade slapped the reins down on the backs of the draft horses, and the team leaped forward, the wagon wheels churning behind them. He circled around to pull up slowly in front of Rachel, and Mr. Keife assisted her into the vehicle. Once the gunslinger was certain Rachel was securely settled beside him on the wagon seat, he tipped his hat politely to Mrs. Keife and her three daughters, then drove away into the coming darkness.

On the horizon, the evening star that heralded all the rest had risen, an omnipotent orb bright and gleaming in the silver-grey sky fading slowly to black; and just ahead, as though wielded by some vast invisible hand, the moon hung like a sickle at its nadir, poised to cut the tall grass on the plains down to size. A breath of breeze sighed, and the prairie murmured, rippling faintly as a quiet sea, and shiplike, the wagon rode its waves, the draft horses turned headlong into the wind, like the figurehead upon a bow. Other than these sounds, the air was hushed, peaceful, for the night creatures had yet to bestir themselves, and those of the day had already made fast their snug nests and burrows, were still as the mouse when the hawk flies over.

Only Rachel was in a turmoil, rent inwardly by the day's events, stricken by Slade's so casually claiming her as his intended bride, startled and confused by the soulful expression she had glimpsed in his eyes when the witching stick had quivered in her hands. Still, it was not until she and the gunslinger were out of earshot of the Keife family that she spoke, confronting head-on the issue about which she had been compelled to remain silent all afternoon and which, as a result, was now uppermost in her mind.

"Slade Maverick," she began, suddenly rounding on him fiercely, shattering the tranquil silence, "whatever possessed you to tell the Keifes you were my fiancé—when you know durned good and well you're not?"

"Because, Rachel honey, I am," he drawled matter-of-factly, his words sending a tiny thrill of fear and some other indefinable emotion down her spine. Sensing her shiver, he grinned at her insolently in the darkness that now enfolded them like a cloak, his even teeth flashing white beneath his mustache. "I don't know what you're so inordinately riled up about, my sweet. You aren't by any chance suffering from a belated attack of virginal qualms or something, are you? After all, we talked about all this in the barn last night, and you didn't raise any demurrals then, maidenly or otherwise. So, naturally, I assumed that the topic was settled."

"Why, you—you never said one word about—about *marrying* me!" Rachel burst out hotly.

"Maybe not. But even so, Rachel honey, what else did you think I had in mind?" Slade's eyes roamed over her purposefully, lewdly, his meaning plain. Her gaze fell before his, and her cheeks flamed. He laughed softly, wickedly, at that. "Dishonorable intentions?" he accused, his voice low, mocking. He shook his head, *tsk*ing. "For shame, Rachel—and you a lady born and bred! My sweet, if all I wanted was to bed you—and I *do* so badly want to bed you—I'd do so and have done with it. Further, I suspect that, deep down inside, you know I would. I wouldn't care how many beaux you had, so long·as I came first with you—and I damned sure wouldn't bother running any of 'em off at gunpoint."

"Then why didn't you tell—tell me that last night? Why didn't you just—just ask me straight out to wed you?" she asked.

"Because you'd have said no, just like you're fixing to right now, and I don't want to hear it, because I'm not aiming to accept that as my answer. So I figured I'd give you some time to think on the subject, to consider all the . . . ramifications of your decision, before you rendered your verdict."

"Well, I *have* thought," Rachel insisted, her mouth dry, her palms sweating, and her heart pounding, "and I've made up my mind."

"And?"

"And my answer is still no, Slade."

There. She'd got it out . . . somehow, some way. But to her dismay, the gunslinger didn't seem the least bit perturbed by her refusal, though, unbeknown to her, his hands tightened suddenly on the reins and a muscle twitched in his cheek.

"Well, unfortunately, I can't say as how I'm too surprised," he asserted, his tone deliberately casual. "I mean . . . after all, you *did* say that the *only* man you're going to marry is the one who brings you five hundred head of cattle for your south forty—and I sure as hell don't have five hundred head of cattle! But what if I did, Rachel honey?" he inquired lightly, his eyes hooded so she couldn't read his thoughts. "What, then?"

"Hmph!" she sniffed disdainfully, though her heart was now thrumming so hard and so loud that she thought he surely must hear it. "That'll be the day—and I *still* wouldn't wed you, Slade Maverick!" she lied.

"Oh, but you would, my sweet," he countered coolly, hard stung now by her continued rejection. "You *will*. Like I told you last night in the barn, it's just a matter of time, and then you'll be mine." He shot her a smug, significant smile at the thought, his eyes surveying her again slowly, intently, lingering on her mouth.

"Why, you—you conceited, cocksure, insufferable swine!" Rachel hissed, humiliated, her body trembling all over with the violence of her emotions, with the knowledge of her love for him, and his all-too-apparent lack of love for her. "What makes you so certain of that? Huh? Oh, yes, you might can drive off my suitors, leave me a spinster, threaten me all you want, or even beat me, I reckon, if you've a mind to, since you're bigger and stronger than I. I know that! But the fact remains: Regardless of what you do, you can't make me marry you, Slade! And I won't! I won't, do you hear? You only want me because—because you'd like to—to . . . well, you know, and because you need someone to cook and clean and care for the kids permanent. I guess you think I'd suit you just fine for all that, and maybe I would. But you never even cared enough about me to ask if that was enough to suit me, did you? Well, it isn't, and I won't wed you on those terms, do you hear? I just won't! And what's more, you can't make me, Slade Maverick!" she wailed once more, anguished.

"Oh, but I can, Rachel honey," the gunslinger rejoined softly, menacingly, enraged now by her insults, her heedlessly throwing his proposal, such as it was, up in his face as though it were nothing, less than nothing.

Gripped now, as well, by a dreadful fear of losing her before she was ever really his, he abruptly jerked the team to a halt and spun on the wagon seat to face her, his eyes smoldering as he loomed over her, his dark visage satanic in the moonlight, she thought, biting her lip. He didn't touch her, but still, Rachel cringed, scared and thinking she had pushed him too hard and too far, hoping he would admit there was some spark of caring in him for her, after all.

"I *can* make you marry me, Rachel!" he ground out savagely again. "I could do so this very moment, if I chose! I could fling you down in that wagon bed back there and ruck up your skirts and brutally force myself on you, and you'd be powerless to stop me! Oh, yes, you would, Rachel, because as you so correctly pointed out earlier, I'm bigger and stronger than you, and we're all alone out here, miles in the middle of nowhere, with nobody close enough even to hear you scream." He allowed her to digest the full import of this. Then he jeered, "But then, you wouldn't scream for long, would you, my sweet? Because in the end, you'd want me —I'd *make* you want me—and what's more, you and I both know it! Then, afterward, you'd damned well *have* to marry me, wouldn't you? Lessen you'd be disgraced, and maybe even with child, to boot! You'd be glad enough then to wed me, I'll wager. Wouldn't you, Rachel? *Wouldn't you*?" he demanded, giving her a small, rough shake.

"Yes," she whispered brokenly, terrified. "Yes."

"Then don't sit there and tell me what I can and cannot do—because you don't know the first thing about what a man such as I am is capable of doing!" he grated harshly, struggling to master his emotions. Then he swore. "For Christ's sake, Rachel! Do you think my notorious reputation is based on lies? Well, it isn't! Until I came here, I was a hired gun and a bounty hunter—one of the best. I *killed* men, Rachel! That's how I made my living. The fact that those men were animals who deserved to die is beside the point. I killed them, and I got paid damned well to do it." He was silent for a moment, remembering. Then, his wrath dissipating a little, he went on more evenly.

"Now, I'm just a farmer—not that I'm complaining, mind you, because the farm's mine, Rachel, free and clear of Beecham. I won it from him at cards, and I persuaded him to sign over legal custody of the kids to me, too. You didn't know that, did you? Well, it's true. So, yes, I want you to cook and clean and care for the kids permanent and do all those other things a good wife does. And yes, I want you the way a man wants a woman—lying naked in my bed at night, warm and willing beneath me. So shoot me for that, damn it, why don't you? For being a man who finds you extremely desirable and doesn't bother to hide it!'' His nostrils flaring, he paused once more, then continued.

"But whatever you may believe to the contrary, I wasn't thinking of taking without giving, Rachel.'' He spoke, his voice gentler now. "Because in return for all I expect from you as my wife, I'll treat you right as your husband, I swear! Come hell or high water, I'll always take care of you, because I'm smart, and I'm strong, and I'm not afraid to turn either my brain or my back to a bit of hard work—and I've got a gun hand like greased lightning, besides. That's more than your dear friend Gus or that whelp Adam Keife or any other man could offer you! So, what more do you want, Rachel? Huh? Jesus!'' Slade cursed when she didn't respond, and gave her another little shake. "Answer me, damn you! What more could you possibly want?''

"Well, if you don't know, you arrogant fool, there's no point in my telling you!'' Rachel cried.

Then, without warning, she burst into tears.

Stricken as understanding suddenly dawned—too late— Slade swore softly and yanked her into his arms, cradling her against his broad chest, stroking her hair soothingly, and kissing the top of her head lightly. He felt terrible, eaten up with guilt and shame. He had never before seen her weep, and her sobs were devastating to him, small, pitiable, ragged gulps, like those of a wounded child.

"Shhhhh,'' he crooned. "Shhhhh . . . oh, hell, Rachel honey, don't cry! Don't cry! Please, sweetheart. Don't cry anymore. I'm sorry. I didn't mean to hurt your feelings. Shhhhh. I'm so goddamned sorry—'' He broke off abruptly. Then, after a moment, he declared ruefully, "You were right, you know. Lord, were you right! I *am* an arrogant fool! I reckon I've consorted with whores for so long that I've forgotten what a woman like you expects. I should have known you'd want more than what I offered you. I should have known what it was.

"You want me to hold your hand and gaze deep into your eyes, take you for long walks and murmur sweet nothings in your ear, don't you? You want candy and flowers, bad poetry and tender kisses in the moonlight." Rachel didn't reply, but since she sobbed all the harder, her shoulders shaking, Slade figured he was on the right track. "Oh, Rachel honey! I know a thousand pretty, practiced phrases and tried-and-true tricks with which to flatter you into falling in love with me, and to make you believe I love you. Don't you know that? But— but—" Again, the gunslinger paused, groping for the words to explain. "But a man like me doesn't really mean those things when he says and does them. They're like rot-gut whiskey: You buy it because it's cheap and comes easy, and you swill it down without hardly even tasting it, because even though it's raw and awful, it's all you know, and since it's like fire burning down your throat, setting your belly ablaze, you reckon it'll make you just as drunk as the expensive bottle of fine old French cognac that, bleary-eyed, you spy sitting just out of reach on the glass shelf above the bar, tempting you because you can't afford it and mocking you because you tell yourself you don't give a damn that you can't.

"Then one day, when you least expect it, you walk into a saloon somewhere, and you start to order that same old rot-gut whiskey, as usual. But before you can get the words out of your mouth, you see clearly—because you're stone-cold sober now—that expensive bottle of fine old French cognac sitting just out of reach on that glass shelf above the bar, tempting you, mocking you, like always; and you want it so badly that you can almost taste it. And this time—this one, single, once-in-a-lifetime moment—somehow, some way, you've got enough money for it in your pocket. So the barkeep pours it into a glass, and then you *do* taste it, and you realize that, no matter what you told yourself before, it's not the same at all. It's mellow and sweet and goes smooth as velvet down your throat, so you want to sip it and savor it and make it last forever and ever instead of guzzling it. And the heat seeping down in your belly is so slow and so sensual that it's a whole 'nother kind of drunk, a better kind of drunk than you've ever known before. . . .

"Do you know what I'm saying to you, Rachel honey?" the gunslinger queried softly as, she lay still and silent now against his chest, her breath caught in her throat. "You're like that expensive bottle of fine old French cognac. You aren't made for swilling, but for sipping and savoring. And words and deeds—the kind that would mean something to a woman like you, anyway—come hard for a man like me. A man doesn't stay alive in my profession as long as I have by letting his feelings get the best of him, so he learns to keep 'em bottled up inside, and after a while, he gets to where he doesn't know how to let 'em out anymore. Sometimes, they're buried so goddamned deep that he doesn't even know what they are. Do you understand what I'm trying to tell you, Rachel?"

"Yes, yes, I think so, Slade," she breathed, tears welling up in her eyes again. "You're—you're trying to tell me that I'm—I'm . . . different from any other woman you've ever known, and that while you . . . want me enough to—to marry me, you don't know if you—if you . . . love me, or ever will, and that you won't pretend otherwise, because I—I deserve better than a lie. Is—is that it, Slade?"

"Yes. Yes, that's it. Is that enough for you, Rachel?" he asked, his voice low and rough now as he tilted her face up to his, his eyes searching hers deeply, his thumbs slowly wiping away her tears. "Because if it isn't, you'll just have to live with it, no matter what. For I won't let you go. Not now. Not ever. I want you too much for that."

Then his mouth claimed hers possessively, his fierce kiss speaking for him all the words he could not bring himself to say.

Chapter Twenty-one

On a hot summer day in June, the old half-breed Indian Seeks came to the farm. In a pale blue sky almost seared of all color the brilliant, burning yellow ball the sun had become with spring's exodus blazed directly overhead, beating down ruthlessly upon Rachel and the vast, sweeping plains, as though it meant to scorch the very life from the prairie, or at least to weed out those unworthy of survival. For the heartland, despite its name, was not kind during summer, and only the strongest could withstand the temperature that, on the worst days, the dog days, rose high as a 115 degrees in the shade—where any was to be found. It was enough to make a person think longingly of a winter blizzard.

Rachel sweated profusely as she bent her back to her hoe, hacking savagely at the abundant scraggly weeds that threatened to overrun her small vegetable garden. A dull, dizzying sensation throbbed in her skull as she worked, and she felt sick at her stomach, too. Her shoulders and back ached, and despite her worn gloves, her callused palms were blistered afresh from chafing against the wooden handle of the tool. At last, gasping for breath, she straightened up, leaning her hoe against her shoulder as, with the back of one hand, she pushed back the loose strands of her hair and wiped her grimy brow and upper lip, both beaded with perspiration. Then, clenching her fist, she rubbed the small of her back tiredly, easing out the knots and kinks. After that, one cupped palm traveling to her forehead to shade her eyes against the glare of the sun, she glanced toward the house.

Near the log cabin, which, on one side, cast some sort of

a shadow, however meager, and at least gave the impression of coolness, Andrew and Naomi squatted on the ground. Without much enthusiasm, they played a game of marbles, and now and then swatted the biting flies away from baby Tobias, who lay naked upon his blanket, listless and cranky in the heat that had caused an ugly red rash to spread over his bottom and the backs of his thighs. It was for this reason that Rachel had left off his diaper and powdered him with cornstarch, though it hadn't helped much, she thought.

Sighing, she walked toward the well, drawing a pail of water, and then scooping some of it up in the tin dipper that hung to one side. She sipped it slowly, knowing from the past that those who swigged down water in the summer heat either vomited or peed it out again in a matter of minutes. The fiery sun would sweat it out of a person soon enough without that. Seeing what she was about, Andrew and Naomi left their pouches and marbles scattered in the dust and ran forward eagerly for a drink. Then Rachel filled the baby's bottle.

After that, she just stood for a moment, leaning against the fieldstone wall that encompassed the well, too hot and exhausted to take another step. She gazed out over the plains of bluestem, blue grama, buffalo grass, Indian grass, and western wheatgrass, all of its lush spring greenness already beginning to fade here and there, tinged with the first of the strawlike gold that, by August, if not sooner, would cover the entire prairie. The wildflowers of April and May were already withered, dry husks among the grass. Now, tall, spicy western yarrow, aromatic pink mintleaf bee balm, thorny wavyleaf and yellow-spine thistle, graceful purple prairie clover, hard-nutted western marble seed, and whitish grey whorled milkweed stood watch over thick, trailing vines of buffalo gourd and bushes of wild Arkansas roses, clumps of violet wood sorrel, yellow-floreted ironplant, tufted crazyweed, and prickly-pear cactus. An odd tumbleweed or two lay brown and lifeless where the waning prairie wind had scattered them earlier that spring.

Heat rose in visible shimmering waves from the land, blurring the distant horizon, where Rachel now spied a lone rider leading two heavily laden pack mules and coming toward her at an unhurried pace. The heads of the brown-and-white pinto and the pack mules were hanging, but the old man astride the horse sat tall and stoically upon the blanket tossed across the animal's bare back. In one hand, he carried a large, battered straw parasol to protect him from the sun, and from the back of his head, two long, bedraggled feathers poked up like the horns of an antelope. Rachel would have known him anywhere.

"Seeks!" she cried, running to greet him as he slowly approached. "Seeks!"

She did not know how old he was—he had been old even when she was young—but though he moved with the stiffness of his age, as well as the toil taken on him by the hard winter just past, there was an overwhelming dignity about him as he solemnly folded his parasol and lumbered awkwardly from the pinto. He did not speak at first, but stood surveying Rachel wordlessly, his steady brown eyes staring deeply into her heart and mind and soul as he searched her face intently.

She supposed that many would have thought him a comical figure, standing there wrapped in his eloquent silence and a tattered plaid blanket. But none who knew Seeks would have found him so, for despite his rough, unkempt appearance and strange, incongruous mixture of Indian and white-man's clothes, his innate bearing and stateliness defied laughter.

Around his head was tied a bright red bandanna, in whose knot were stuck the twin eagle feathers of his youth. His long hair, dark grey and sprinkled with white, hung loose except for two slender braids in the front, bound with strips of hide and fur, and ornamented with beads and tiny feathers. His copper skin was weathered from years of exposure to the elements. His proud face, with its hawkish nose and high cheekbones, was leathery and lined as a map. He was neither large nor small, but of medium build, his body thickset and sinewy with a strength born of a life both primitive and harsh. A loose white chambray shirt, long-sleeved and resembling a man's undergarment, was buttoned up to his throat. About his neck were a gaily patterned handkerchief, its ends woven through an ornate brass belt buckle; many strings of colored beads threaded on leather thongs; and an old fur piece fashioned of two soft, bushy racoon tails. Fringed buckskin breeches encased his legs, and a pair of scuffed moccasins covered his feet. He looked just as Rachel always remembered him looking, as though only the seasons, not he, changed.

She had been just thirteen when she'd found him her first bleak, bitter winter upon the prairie. Set upon by a group of unscrupulous and drunken white traders, Seeks had been brutally beaten, robbed, and left for dead. But somehow, he had managed to struggle across the plains, toward the light that had glowed like a beacon from the one window of the dank, dark soddy they had lived in then; and when she had gone outside for snow to melt upon the hearth, because the water in the well was solid ice, she had discovered him lying half frozen upon the cold ground. Fremont, Poke, and her father, Ulysses, had dragged him inside to thaw by the fire, while she and her mother, Victoria, had scurried about fetching steaming tea laced with brandy; hot, nourishing soup; and soft, thick blankets with which to warm him.

Gradually, as the days had passed, Seeks had recovered, and upon learning that it was Rachel who had first spied him, he had felt he owed his life to her. In recompense, he had taught her, over the years, all the lore he knew, both the Indian's and the white man's, finding in her an eager and a willing pupil.

Rachel loved him as she loved her grandfather and Poke, with all her heart and her deepest respect. But it was Seeks with whom she shared a special bond born of their oneness with the land. She felt joy at his coming, for with his arrival, it always seemed somehow as though some of her heavy burdens slipped from her shoulders, thanks to Seeks's sage counsel. She felt that she could confide in him even more than she could her grandfather and Poke, who were more apt to tease her and pass judgment. Seeks judged no man or woman, good or bad. He only listened and pondered long and deep before he spoke his words of advice. As she gazed at him now, Rachel longed more than anything to hug the Indian tightly and pour out her heart and soul about Slade to him. But she refrained, for this was not Seeks's way, and he would have rebuffed her kindly but firmly.

Still, as though sensing her need, he slowly stretched out one hand and laid it lightly, marveling, upon her head. Though he loved her as though she were his own grand-daughter, this was the only physical gesture of affection Seeks ever showed her. Her blond hair fascinated him. It was like corn silk, and he liked to feel its softness and texture, as though he might in this way discover the secret of its golden color. Now, it was nearly flaxen, bleached and streaked by the summer sun that had also darkened Rachel's skin to honey and dusted her nose and cheekbones with further freckles. At his touch, she closed her eyes, feeling his inner peace and love for her flow through her as surely as though he were a priest blessing her. Then, after a moment, he dropped his hand to his side and spoke.

"You are well, Wildflower-Woman," he uttered in his slow, deep, rich voice, calling her, as he always did, by the Indian name he had bestowed upon her in her youth. "But in your eyes, there are shadows that were not there many moons ago, and your heart sings and weeps as one."

"Yes," Rachel replied, knowing that this was the truth. "Much has happened in your months away from us, Seeks, which I will relate to you by and by, the worst of which, much to my deep sorrow, was the death this past winter of my dear friend India, she whom you called 'Raven-Woman.' "

"I am sorry to hear such sad news, Wildflower-Woman, and my heart grieves at her passing. It is hard to lose a friend. She was a fine woman, a true and faithful sister to you, and I know that you must miss her."

"Yes, it has been a dreadful loss to me, Seeks, though her eight children, for whom I have been caring ever since, have proved a great comfort. Together, we have managed some-how; and India's brother, who arrived shortly after she died, has been a big help." Rachel paused, remembering her friend.

Then, determinedly shaking off her heartache, she urged, "But come, Seeks. Tell me of yourself and of your travels. You look well, and the winter hunting was good for you, as usual, I see." She indicated the two heavily laden pack mules.

The Indian nodded.

"Yes, the winter moons were cold but generous," he agreed, "as a last burst of dying sun before the snows sweep across the land, though I took only what I needed, no more—and sorrowed even at this. Since the coming of the white-eyes, the mighty buffalo are fallen, and now, soon, I think they will not rise again. Already, their bleached bones are scattered like the wind across the land, and speak their story. But the white-eyes shut their eyes and ears, and do not see or listen. In my heart, there is a terrible heaviness at this, Wildflower-Woman, for when the last of the buffalo are gone, so, too, will the old ways be gone forever." Heaving a deep sigh, Seeks stared off into the distance, as though envisioning the winds of change whose coming he foretold.

Then, recalling himself to the present, he continued. "But that time is beyond my own, and for this, my heart rejoices. Come, Wildflower-Woman. You must choose a pelt for yourself, as always, and I have some trinkets for the little ones, too."

Moving to his pack mules, Seeks untied the large bundle of skins heaped upon each animal's back and spread the furs upon the ground. Rachel saw that it was as he had told her: The buffalo hides were few, though they would fetch a good price for him in town. Knowing this, she chose instead a black wolf pelt, having some notion of making from it a vest or gloves, perhaps, for Slade, which he could wear next winter. She thanked Seeks gravely for the gift, then invited him inside the log cabin.

Hearing this, Andrew, who, mindful of his manners, had been waiting politely, though scarcely patiently, to one side, now ran forward excitedly to greet the Indian. Naomi, however, who was too small to remember him from his last visit, hung back warily, awed and a little scared. But Seeks soon won her over, and after stabling his pinto and pack mules, he followed the children into the house, where Rachel was now trying to comfort the fractious baby.

Spying her difficulty, Seeks studied the child carefully, his keen old eyes taking in all Toby's symptoms. Then the Indian suddenly reached forward and, poking his index finger into the whining baby's mouth, ran it experimentally over Toby's gums. At that, a wide grin split Seeks's face.

"Small one has first tooth coming, Wildflower-Woman," he declared with satisfaction. "Needs licorice. No one needs to be skilled medicine woman to see that!"

As Rachel grasped what ailed Toby, she smiled sheepishly at Seeks's gentle rebuke, realizing she ought to have thought of the problem sooner. She hurried to the kitchen, where she had a large basket of fresh herbs and wildflowers she had gathered just that morning. Licorice was in bloom now, and picking up one of the reddish brown plants, she quickly sliced off and cleaned the sweet root. Soon, Toby was gnawing the raw tuber contentedly, his teething pains eased.

The afternoon slipped away, and toward sundown, Slade, Fremont, Poke, and the rest of the youngsters returned to the log cabin. Much was made of Seeks, who was warmly welcomed by "Man-Who-Walks-On-Tree-Branch" and "Buffalo-Man," as he had named Fremont and Poke years ago. Then the Indian turned to Slade and, after scrutinizing him for several long, silent minutes, announced soberly, "And you I will call 'Dog-Soldier,' because I sense that you are a brave warrior who has counted many coups."

That evening, and for many evenings afterward, the gunslinger and the children stayed until well after dark, enthralled by the tales Seeks told them as he sat cross-legged on the puncheon floor of the log cabin and smoked his long, bead-and-feather-bedecked calumet. During the day, he rode his pinto into town, searched the plains for herbs and wildflowers to replenish his stores, or meditated in the tipi he had erected near the house, so Rachel had little opportunity to speak privately with him.

But at last, there came a night when Seeks paused on the log cabin's stoop, where she stood, having accompanied him outside, and he spoke of that which troubled her, his voice low and vibrant as it echoed on the humid evening wind. And the words that sprang from his lips and from the universal fountain of wisdom and age, the words he dropped like precious jewels into her lap in the still of that summer night, Rachel was to remember and to treasure the rest of her life.

"Despite your silence, Wildflower-Woman," the Indian began slowly, "I have heard the unspoken words that lie on your tongue like melting snow on distant mountain peaks, yearning to rush forth in a babbling stream. But like that of the stream, the path you must follow is steep and rocky, and so you are afraid, unsure of your way, and you have hesitated to speak to me of what is in your eyes and in your heart. You would tell me of your hopes and fears. This, I know. But I say to you that there is no need for words between us, Wildflower-Woman. I am an old man, wise in the ways of the world. I have seen how you look at Dog-Soldier in the evenings, when you think no one is watching, and I have seen your heart in your eyes. In this manner, you have already spoken, and I have listened and thought. Now, I will speak, and you must be silent and listen and learn. Hear my counsel, then, if this you would have." Seeks paused for a moment, as though carefully weighing and measuring his words, deciding how much to tell, how much to hold back. Then, finally, he went on.

"Though you are a woman grown, Wildflower-Woman, you have been as a selfish child in this matter, thinking only of yourself, of your own tears, of your own pain. And so I ask you: What of Dog-Soldier's tears, Wildflower-Woman? What of *his* pain? Do you think that it is easy for a man such as he to search deep in the darkness of his heart, to open doors that have been long closed, not knowing what he will find? I tell you that it is not. But like a stubborn child, you have refused to see this, Wildflower-Woman. You have thought only that it is enough for a woman who loves a man to have her heart in her eyes. But I say to you this night that it is not. For a woman who loves a man truly will also have her eyes in her heart.

"Open yours now, and see this: To each thing belongs its own season and its own way; and as the wild wind comes to the land, so does love come to the heart—in its own time and at its own will, as each man must learn for himself. Would you harness the wild wind? No, you would not, for it is a power that must not be harnessed, lest the very essence you would tame will be lost forever. No more must you try to command love, Wildflower-Woman, for it, too, is a spirit that must soar freely—or die. And this, I think you know in your heart, you, who are one with the elements, and with the land.

"So I tell you: Heed the voice of your heart, Wildflower-Woman. Be patient, as all who are wise are patient, and weep if you must—because a cupful of tears shed out of love is sweeter than the sweetest wine—and know that to those who wait, all things come in the end, and they are only stronger for the proving. For truth is omnipotent; and as the tall grass does not dance unless touched by the wild wind, the heart does not sing unless touched by love, as he who listens to his own heart will discover in time."

Seeks fell silent then and, after a moment, turned away and soundlessly disappeared into his tipi. Lost in reverie, Rachel was hardly even aware of his leaving as she slowly sank down on the stoop, where she sat for a very long while afterward, mulling over the old Indian's sage counsel. She *had* been as selfish and stubborn as a thoughtless child, she recognized now, stricken. Oh, she *had*! How clearly she saw this now, and sorely lamented it.

She had always been so secure in the love of those who surrounded her—Fremont, Poke, Seeks, and before they had died, her parents and India—that she had expected Slade to love her, too, just because she loved him and, worse, despite the fact that she had never told him of her love. In her aloneness, she had been crying for the moon, never grasping that perhaps the moon cried, also, because it, too, was alone, far more alone than she had ever been.

Slade had no one.

The realization struck Rachel like a blow, bringing hot

tears to her eyes. He had been cast out of his home and cut off without a cent by his autocratic father; even his very name had been blotted from the family Bible as though he had never existed. His mother had died young—

Having your mother die young does something to you inside. . . . It makes you older than your years. I ought to know that as well as anyone, I reckon.

The tears of anguish in Rachel's eyes now slipped down her cheeks as she recalled her earnest words to him. *Yeah, I know*, Slade had replied, and he *did* know, only she hadn't regarded it, had callously brushed aside the admission, too concerned with her own feelings to pay it any heed. And in her deep sorrow over India's death, hadn't she also ignored Slade's own grief and torment? India had been his half sister, after all, and he had loved her. But he had not even had a chance to tell her how much, as Rachel had. Now, it was too late. India was dead, as everyone Slade had ever loved was dead, even the unknown girl in New Orleans. . . . Oh, cruel, *cruel*, not to have considered these things before! Rachel scourged herself.

How *could* Slade speak of love to her? He had known so little of it in his life, and what he had known had been so fleeting, so brutally taken away from him. Might he be afraid, then, to love her or, if he did love her, to put his emotions into words, lest somehow she, too, would be snatched away? Might he not instead bury his feelings deep inside him, so deep that even he didn't know what they were anymore? Rachel's heart broke with understanding, for had Slade not tried to tell her these very things himself? Oh, yes, yes, he *had*! In his own way, because he *did* care for her somehow, somewhere deep inside, he *had* tried, though the words had not come easily to him.

Indeed, now that she looked not with her heart in her eyes, but with her eyes in her heart, could she not see beneath his hard, arrogant, mocking exterior the lost, lonely little boy hiding deep inside him, crying out—in the only way he knew how—to be heard?

*What of Dog-Soldier's tears, Wildflower-Woman? What of
his pain?*

Rachel buried her face in her hands and wept, bitterly
ashamed. She had thought she loved Slade so much. Now,
she knew she had loved him too little. Her heart sang, yes,
but it was a keening song; and blinded by her tears, she did
not see the tall grass dancing in the sultry night wind.

Chapter Twenty-two

There was a bright full moon hanging low in the inky night
sky, a circumstance Rye Crippen felt boded ill for a man in
his dubious line of work. He preferred rustling cattle at the
dark of the moon, or at least when there was no more than
a sliver of one winking in the firmament. But he had had
quite a bit to drink at the Silver Slipper this evening, and he
had, for a change, won quite a bit of money at keno, as well;
and now, astride his swaybacked nag standing just beyond
Rachel Wilder's cow pasture, he was flushed with both the
saloon's potent forty-rod lightning and his own unexpected
but auspicious luck at the gaming tables. What could possibly
go wrong now after that? Determinedly, he shrugged off his
apprehension about the full moon's being a harbinger of bad
tidings.

The pitifully disgusting sight of Jonathan Beecham seated
at the Silver Slipper's battered old piano had first turned Rye's
muddled thoughts to Rachel Wilder, a mean-mouthed, nasty-
tempered bitch if he had ever seen one. Only witness poor
Beecham, the whining slob! He was a prime example of how
her sharp tongue and surly disposition could destroy a man.

Once, Beecham had owned a halfway decent farm outside of town. Now, thanks to Rachel Wilder, he was doing his damnedest to coax some semblance of music out of a dented-up instrument that couldn't have emitted an on-key note if it had had one—and this in exchange for nothing more than a handful of meager tips, a couple of bottles of watered-down booze, and a fifteen-minute go once a night at the fat, blowsy, painted-up whore Emmalou upstairs. Pathetic!

Rye sure as hell didn't intend to wind up like that—although he would, he knew, if he had to keep listening day in and day out to his shrill-voiced, sour-faced wife, Prudence. Although he prayed fervidly to God every night for the withered-up stick of a witch to croak, so far, God hadn't answered his prayers; and Crippen hadn't as yet sunk so low as to commit murder, though he wished he *could* work up the nerve to strangle the old bat! She never let him forget that it was the hard-earned money of her thrifty father, who owned a dry-goods store, which enabled them to live; nor was she any too eager to let Rye spend a nickel of it. Often, he felt as though he would be forced to take his crowbar to her to pry open her purse—much less anything else.

Prudence just didn't understand how hard it was for him to hold down a job, and she punished him for it in myriad manners. What was so wrong, Rye had asked her countless times, with a man liking his whiskey and a little flutter at the gaming tables now and then? Every man did, after all. Was it his fault that, as a result of his own overindulging, he was so sick the next day that he could hardly drag himself out of bed and so generally failed to report for work? It was only menial labor anyway—not fit for a man of his aesthetic, cultured nature.

Crippen had wanted all his life to be an artist, but people had simply been too bourgeois and stupid, his sainted mother had indignantly declared, to appreciate the genius of his skill and method. That was why none of the charcoal drawings he had ever attempted had sold. But he could scarcely be blamed for that, could he? After all, it was not his fault if people were ignorant and didn't have good taste.

In the end, however, Rye had been compelled to give up sketching, and he had then set his heart on becoming an attorney. But could he help it if he had failed to pass his law exams? Certainly, his cherished mother hadn't thought so. She had known how hard he had tried and how much his jealous and resentful teachers had hated him, assigning him so many books to read and papers to write that his studies had taxed even his intellectual gifts, and had almost ruined his health, in addition.

Rye had a delicate constitution, or so Mother had always claimed; and after his return home from the school that had proved so difficult and undeserving of his aptitude, she had tried to shelter him from life's unpleasantnesses—the main one of which was being forced to toil with his hands for a living. But Prudence only snorted insensitively at this, insisting that he was hale as the next man and that a little honest hard work might even "beef up his puny muscles some."

It just wasn't right of her to talk like that. If his adored mother were alive, she would agree that it just wasn't right, Crippen knew. Mother would have asserted stoutly that Prudence ought to get out and try to hold down a job herself, as he himself had told her a hundred times if he had told her once. But no, she was too good for that, the snobby bitch! So why should he be any different? Rye asked himself resentfully. And so he bumbled along as best he could, missing his mother and thinking how different things would have been if she had lived, because then Prudence would have learned to toe the mark or else; and he drank and gambled a little more each month to perk up his low spirits.

One evening when he and his pals Harlow Filbert and Dooley Tuttle had dropped by the Silver Slipper to have a go at bucking the tiger, Rye's life had taken a turn for the better. There, they had all three got nicely liquored up; and as the night had worn on, one of them (they had later concluded that it must have been Dooley, who, it was agreed between them, had nothing between his ears but his unmanageable red cowlick and his sadly spotted face) had somehow taken into his head the notion of rustling a few cattle for a lark. After cogitating on the idea for several more rounds of drinks, they had finally pronounced it a splendid suggestion; and thus decided, they had promptly fetched their horses and ridden out to Old Man Jessup's place, where, after a great deal of bungling, they had eventually succeeded in rounding up his prize milch cow and two sad-eyed heifers.

It had indeed proved vastly entertaining sport until, unfortunately, one of the lumpish heifers had got scared enough to start bawling its head off, at which point Old Man Jessup had come roaring out of his house, with his double-barreled shotgun loaded for bear. He had cursed and yelled and fired at them like a madman, damned near pitting their backsides with buckshot, while they had skedaddled fast as they were able, unwittingly chousing the terrified cattle before them.

What they considered a near brush with death had sobered the three men up in a hurry. There they had been, out on the lonesome prairie, each of them with a mournful cow on his hands and no means of effectively ridding themselves of the dumb creature, unless Old Man Jessup had gone back to bed, which hadn't seemed likely. They had all been so angry by then at his having dared to shoot at them that none of them had wanted to return his old cattle anyway. Dooley had proposed that they just ride off and leave them, but Rye and Harlow had voted this down as being not only poor-spirited, but the height of foolishness. After all, they had gone to a lot of trouble to acquire the cattle to begin with—though both Rye and Harlow had started to wonder what they had ever intended to do with them in the first place.

Thus having actually made off with the vexatious cows, the three men had found themselves at a loss, since cattle rustling was a hanging offense and the prospect of a rope had loomed uncomfortably large in their minds. So Rye (who, it was agreed, had all the brains between them) had scratched his hind end and chewed over both a weed and the subject of their calamitous predicament at some length. Then, finally, he had allowed as how, since it was too late now to undo all the damage they had done, they might as well be hanged for sheep as for lambs. That being the case, it was plain to him they ought to change both the earmarks and the brands on the cows and sell all three of them as quickly and slickly as they could to some tinhorn dolt who wouldn't know to look closely or ask hard questions. That way, they would at least get *something* worthwhile out of the deal, and Old Man Jessup would get his just deserts for having had the gall to draw a bead on them when they had just been having a spree.

Matters thus decided, Dooley had built a fire, while Rye and Harlow had roped and hog-tied the cattle. Then Rye, with his sharp Arkansas toothpick, and Harlow, with his curved Green River knife, had carved each cow's under-bit earmark into an under-slope. After that, seeing that the fire was now blazing high, Rye had hitched up his right pants leg and pulled out the crowbar he always carried in his boot for protection, it being illegal, of course, to tote a gun in town. He had heated up one end of the crowbar until it had glowed red-hot, after which he had set about applying his unappreciated talent at charcoal drawing to turning Old Man Jessup's Rafter J's into Swinging W's. The brands had looked so damned good when Rye had finished with them that nobody had ever spotted that they'd been altered.

So pleased had Crippen been with his success that he had deemed it a sign from heaven that he should continue his new line of work, in which he could not only employ all his considerable artistic ability, but could also thumb his nose at the law that had once rejected him as unqualified to practice. After that, it had been just a short step to getting his own running iron, with which he had promptly and imaginatively proceeded to transform, blot, or otherwise mutilate brands from one end of Kansas to the other.

It was just his rotten luck that, one otherwise fine day on the prairie, that bitch Rachel Wilder had spied, accidentally sticking out of his boot, the primary tool of his God-chosen trade and that she had not only haughtily disparaged him, and then snootily threatened him, but had also dutifully reported her finding to Marshal Mike Meagher. Though Rye had made sure there had not been any hard evidence of wrongdoing on his person, Rachel's importune meddling had compelled him to forgo his nocturnal activities for several long weeks while the marshal suspiciously kept him under sharp observation.

Crippen had from that day forward held a deep-rooted grudge against Rachel, and sensing with a coyote's cunning how much her piddling herd of cattle meant to her, he had been picking them off one by one ever since. They were worth neither the risk nor the bother, but then, it was the principle of the thing that counted, after all. He might have to take whatever his shrewish wife, Prudence, dished out. But he damned sure didn't have to take crap off Rachel Wilder; and every time he stole one of her measly old cows, Rye felt he struck a blow for men everywhere against the tyranny of all vituperative and vindictive women.

So, tonight, his mind made up, he had suddenly clapped on his hat and jumped up from his table at the Silver Slipper. Shaking his head at the sorry sight of Jonathan Beecham hunched in an alcoholic stupor over the saloon's pitiful piano, Crippen had then ridden posthaste to Rachel's farm, where, despite the full moon, he now intended to rustle another one of her cows—and to teach her a well-deserved lesson.

It was on this same night in late June that Seeks entered the log cabin to announce soberly that someone was disturbing Rachel's herd of cattle.

"I heard rapid hoofbeats, one horse, one rider," he stated firmly. "This was followed by the lowing of cows, Wildflower-Woman. Someone tries to steal them—a white-eyes, not an Indian, who would not be so foolish as to make such a din."

Rachel thought instantly of Rye Crippen, as did Slade; and together, along with Adam Keife, who had arrived to call on young Eve, they hastily retrieved their horses from the barn and set out at a gallop for the pasture the gunslinger had so recently fenced in to protect Rachel's precious herd of cattle.

It was this barrier, in fact, that prevented Rye from escaping them, for it had not been there the last time he had stealthily invaded Rachel's fields, and it slowed him down considerably. Initially, as he prided himself on being a man who kept up with the changing times, he was not particularly disconcerted at finding the barbed wire strung around the pasture. It was at best a minor nuisance he could handle. But he cursed even so as he dismounted to approach the barrier, for cutting it took time, and the cattle were already nervous. Nevertheless, it was easier to snip the fence than to search for the gate, which might be some distance away; and still buoyed up with the inordinate amount of bad whiskey he had drunk earlier, as well as with his good luck at keno that evening, Crippen reached into his back pocket for the wire cutters he always carried with him.

Perversely glad now of the moon that enabled him to see what he was doing, he started impatiently to work on the top strand of the fence. After a moment, it snapped in two and sprang apart, and he stepped back a pace to avoid being raked by the barbs as each half of the wire twined around itself loosely. Grabbing the end of one side, Rye wrapped it about the nearest wooden post to get it out of his way, then did the same to the other. Then he awkwardly cut through the middle strand, and then finally the bottom. He was so intent on this task, and the cattle were now twitching and stamping and occasionally mooing so anxiously, that he failed to notice the sound of the nearing riders.

Having got through the fence at last, Crippen remounted his horse and spurred the animal through the now open space between two of the wooden posts. Then he set about to chop one of the cows out of the herd, swearing as they all suddenly fled, dispersing in every direction. It was a real bitch to drive one of them off, as Rye knew from experience, for Rachel's cattle were accustomed to running wild. They were seldom checked on and herded, as they were *supposed* to be, Crippen thought to himself irritably. Trust a fool woman to do just the opposite of what she ought! The Texas drovers who had so carelessly sloughed off their unwanted calves on Rachel Wilder must have been out of their minds, thinking a female knew the first thing about cattle! Much to Rye's exasperation, the dense creatures would run this way and that, always circling back toward the rest of the herd, refusing to be chopped; and there was one, a chongo—a steer with a dropped horn—that was also wicked as it looked, being a hooking cow, besides. More than once, it had charged Crippen and, with its askew horns, tried viciously to gouge him. But undeterred, he had persisted in his endeavors, as he did now; and finally, just when he was about to give up and go home after all, he managed to cut a gangling heifer loose from the herd.

"Well, it's about time!" he snapped to himself, highly annoyed.

He was in the process of driving the unhappy cow toward the downed fence when, their horses lathered and blowing, Rachel, Slade, and Adam arrived at the field, taking in at a glance the provoking scene.

"It's Black-Eyed Pea!" Rachel cried with concern for her heifer, causing Rye's head abruptly to swivel like a puppet's in their direction. "He's trying to make off with Black-Eyed Pea! Rye Crippen, you poisonous, yellow-bellied snake! I recognize you! I'd know you anywhere with the moon shining on that oily old black hat of yours that looks worse than a puddle of grease! Don't you ever wash your hair? Get away from my cow! Get away from my cow, you durned thieving cross-brander, before I shoot you!"

Rye didn't need to be told twice. Rachel herself didn't frighten him, but the tall, dark, menacing man who rode at her left side did; for like everybody else in town, Crippen was aware that the infamous gunslinger Slade Maverick had come to Wichita and that he had not only assumed responsibility for the care of his nieces and nephews, the Beechams, but was purportedly courting uppity Rachel Wilder, too. Rye's beady eyes bugged out of his head, and his prominent Adam's apple bobbled in his throat as the gunslinger, his bronze visage murderous in the moonlight, started toward him purposefully, looking like Satan himself on his bold black stallion. Letting out a squeak of alarm, Crippen hastily reined his poor scrub mare about and, roweling and lashing it for all it was worth, took out at a dead run across the pasture, dodging with difficulty the cattle that bawled and scattered like a child's jacks before him, impeding his headlong flight.

Slade was so enraged at the wiry little weasel's trying to steal Rachel's heifer that his first thought was simply to shoot Rye right out of the saddle. But then he had an even better idea. Grinning maliciously to himself, the gunslinger reached for the rope coiled around his saddle horn. Swiftly, he played out the lasso, and after giving it a few hard twirls to work up some speed, as well as to judge the timing and propulsion he would need, he sent it spinning powerfully through the air. With a sharp *whoosh*, the lariat dropped squarely over Rye's cringing head and stooped shoulders.

Immediately, Slade dallied the rope around his saddle horn, a dangerous technique, since his thumb could accidentally be sawed off in the process, but it was either that or lose Crippen. As the loop began to tighten around his saddle horn, Slade yanked his stallion up short and tugged smartly on the rope. Rye was jerked violently backward, and as his horse kept on going, he sailed clean out of his saddle, flying through the air like an artillery shell fired from a cannon. With a bone-jarring thud, he hit the earth baked hard by the summer sun and rolled like a marble struck by a taw before at last coming to a stop.

Dazed, bruised, and gasping for breath, he staggered to his feet, his fear propelling him onward. Lurching from side to side on the uneven ground, he raced across the field. He didn't get far, for the rope was cinched tight as a noose around his arms and torso, restraining him like a leash and snatching him back unmercifully. Somehow, Crippen wriggled his arms free, but before he could get the rope from around his waist, Slade slowly hauled him in, as though reeling in a fish struggling to slip off the hook.

"Well, well"—the gunslinger spoke unpleasantly when finally Rye stood cowering and sniveling before him, his thin, pasty face ashen and terrified in the moonlight—"what do we have here? Looks like a refugee waddy from a greasy-sack outfit—or else something slimy that crawled out from under a rock!''

"It's Rye Crippen!" Rachel spat as she pulled up at Slade's side, while Adam loped on to chase down Crippen's horse. "I *told* you it was! You rotten, stinking skunk!" she shrieked at Rye. "Just what do you mean by sneaking around here, trying to make off with my cattle? Tarnation! I *knew* that you didn't tote a running iron in your boot just so you could pick your teeth! And now that I've finally caught you red-handed, I'm going to personally escort you into town and turn you over for cattle rustling to Marshal Meagher. And then after your trial, I'm going to stand at the gallows and watch you hang!''

"Why, Rachel honey, I'm surprised at your even suggesting such a thing,'' Slade declared mockingly, a derisive smile curving his lips as he stared hard at Crippen. "There's no call at all to waste the marshal's valuable time with this no-account vermin, nor the court's, either. Hell. We'll just string him up ourselves and save the law and the taxpayers the trouble. Adam''—he turned to the young man who had just ridden up, leading Rye's crowbait mare—"get down off your horse there and draw that rope up tight around that scurvy scum's throat. He's just volunteered to serve as the guest of honor at a small, impromptu necktie sociable I'm fixing to hold this evening.''

"Gee, Slade,'' Adam drawled, tipping back his hat and, as he joined in the harassment, grinning wickedly at the gunslinger, "I'd surely like to oblige you, seein' as how I'm courtin' your niece and all. But there ain't hide nor hair of a tree in sight—nary even a tall bush, more's the pity—and I just don't know how you're figurin' on stretchin' any hemp without one.''

"Now, that's a fact, Adam,'' Slade observed. Cocking his head thoughtfully, he continued to gaze contemptuously at Crippen, as though seriously examining their lack of a hanging tree and pondering how to overcome it. "That purely is a fact, and we all know there's no disputing a fact. Still, it seems a real shame to have to cancel our little party. I was so looking forward to it.''

"Even so, we haven't got any tree, and it just ain't polite to hang a man in front of a lady, besides," Adam insisted, his green eyes gleaming devilishly as he, too, scrutinized Crippen. "One of 'em turns blue, and the other one turns white, and before you know it, the blue one's keeled over dead, and the white one's keeled over in a dead faint."

"I reckon you have got a point at that," Slade conceded dryly. "So I'll tell you what we'll do instead: You ride on back to the house, Adam—quick as you can—and fetch us some tar and feathers, while I show this lousy highbinder how to eat drag-dust."

"No! Please, no!" Rye croaked at that, horrified, though nobody was sure which particular prospect had frightened him more. Seeing that neither Slade nor Adam was moved by his entreaties, he glanced wildly at Rachel, whimpering, "Please, Miz Wilder, save me! I'm sorry I took yore cattle. I'll never touch another 'un agin as long as I live, so help me, God, I swear! Please, save me! I didn't mean no harm. I got a wife, 'n' I ain't so fit, neither. It's tough fer me ta hold down a job, 'n' I gotta have some way of makin' ends meet. I—I—'' He broke off abruptly, his eyes popping and his Adam's apple sliding like a rubber ball down his gullet as he swallowed convulsively, then emitted a gurgling, choking sound from his throat.

For a minute, Rachel thought he might pass out, for briefly, he swayed on his feet, as though his knees were buckling, and sweat erupted all over his pale, ferretlike face. Then, suddenly, trying as he moved to tear free of the rope that imprisoned him, he broke into a run. Ruthlessly, Slade wrenched him back, and Crippen stumbled and fell, sprawling facedown in the dirt, where he groveled and blubbered for mercy.

"Just take him on into town, Slade," Rachel told the gunslinger, having no stomach for this pathetic, disgusting display.

"Do you really want to make his poor, unfortunate wife a widow, Rachel?" Slade probed. "I'll admit we might be doing her a real favor. But if we turn him over to the marshal, they *will* hang him, you know." He permitted this to sink in. Then he said softly, "No, my sweet, I didn't think you truly wanted to be responsible for that. Then allow me and Adam to handle this in our own fashion, hmh? Go and gather some dried cow chips and build us a fire, Rachel. We're going to roast us a chicken! Adam, what're you shilly-shallying around for? Go on! Get your tail in gear! Hie yourself back to the log cabin and get the stuff we need. Hurry!"

"Yes, sir!"

Whooping and hollering with glee, the young man cantered away. Then, before Rachel realized what Slade himself intended, he gave what she surmised was the notorious Rebel yell, dug his spurs sharply into his stallion's sides, and took off at a gallop, dragging the hapless Rye behind him. She found it hard to feel especially sorry for Crippen, knowing that he was a criminal and that the two men might well have lynched him with impunity. He squealed like a skewered pig as he was relentlessly towed along the rough ground, and he clutched the taut rope desperately with both hands, attempting feebly to hold his face down between his outstretched arms, so it would not be slashed too badly by the tall grass. Nevertheless, he was soon scratched and scraped over both his face and his stringy body, and Rachel knew that his palms must be burned raw by the rope, too. Indeed, she saw he had now loosened his grip on it and was bouncing and rolling along like a child's top erratically winding down.

By the time the gunslinger had decided Crippen had eaten enough dust as punishment for his crime and had slowly lugged him back to where Rachel waited, Adam had returned with a bucket of tar and an old feather pillow. His handsome young face looked so demonically triumphant at his having obtained this booty that she knew for certain then that he was indeed cut from the same cloth as Slade.

When the gunslinger drew his stallion to a halt before her, he was annoyed to see that she had made no move to start a fire as he had directed. Frowning at her lollygagging, Slade dismounted. Then, together, he and Adam collected some dried cow chips, tossed them into a heap, and ignited them, after which they placed the bucket of tar on top of the pile to heat.

"Surely, you're not—not *really* going to tar and feather Rye, are you?" Rachel asked the two men, appalled, while, a few feet away, Crippen lay on the ground, writhing and groaning and wishing he had never thought of rustling her cattle—tonight or any other night.

"You're damned right, we are!" Slade growled. "He's lucky we don't do worse! Because when a man steals another man's—or woman's—cattle, he's not just robbing them of their cows, he's robbing them of their livelihood, maybe even of their hopes for the future, too!" The gunslinger paused, eyeing her so intently that Rachel knew that she had misjudged him before, that he had never laughed at her when she had told him of her dreams. Then, more quietly but just as fiercely, he added, "And nobody's going to destroy your hard work, Rachel honey—not ever, not if I can help it!"

She thrilled to hear his words and, in that moment, longed to be enfolded in his strong, protective arms, where she would be safe and secure; for had he not promised her that? At the expression on her face, Slade's eyes flickered with that hot, hungry flame she had come to know so well, and Rachel knew that if they had been alone, he would have pressed her down into the tall grass and furthered her education in lovemaking. But as so often seemed to be the case, now was neither the time nor the place; and at last, he turned back reluctantly but determinedly to the business at hand.

With the rope that had been used to capture and drag Crippen, Slade and Adam trussed him up like a Thanksgiving turkey, binding his hands tightly behind his back, while he bitterly denounced them and decried his sore fate. Then, despite his wailing and begging them to desist, they doused him from head to toe with the warm, gooey tar, after which they zealously ripped open the feather pillow and unabashedly strewed its contents all over him. Hoisting him up, they flung him backward into his saddle, secured his feet to his stirrups, and tied his running iron to another, shorter rope, which they twisted prominently around his neck, so all who might happen to see him would get a good view of the stampless brand and know why he was in such a miserable state. Then, lest his skinny horse be inclined to poke and graze along the way, Slade and Adam shoved several fat, prickly cockleburs under Rye's saddle and fastened to the mare's tail a string of rusty tin cans, which Adam had on impulse grabbed earlier, when he had brought the tar from Rachel's barn. After that, enthusiastically hurrahing and wildly waving their hats, they spooked Crippen's now frantic mount into bolting pell-mell toward town, tin cans rattling in its wake. Rye, his eyes and nose smarting from the tar, did his best to stay aboard as he sneezed furiously and trailed a cloud of white goose feathers behind him.

"You ever come back, and I'll kill you, you brand-blotting bastard!" Slade shouted after Crippen's ignominiously retreating figure, though the gunslinger didn't really believe that the threat was necessary.

He felt sure that Rye had got the message loud and clear, and that he would not bother Rachel's small herd of cattle ever again. Her dreams were intact now, and as it was somehow very important to Slade that they were, he smiled with satisfaction as, in high spirits, they all three rode back to the log cabin, the full moon lighting their path.

Chapter Twenty-three

As Eve Beecham turned slowly to gaze at herself in her "aunt" Rachel's dressing-table mirror, her heart seemed to skip a beat, and she closed her eyes tightly, then opened them again, just to make sure it really was her own reflection that peeped back at her, smiling with wonder and delight.

"Oh, Aunt Rachel!" she breathed, her cheeks stained the color of dusky roses. "Can it truly be me? Can it?"

"Only you, Eve, and none other," Rachel replied, smiling gently at the girl's obvious pleasure and at the lovely picture she presented as she stood there poised on the threshold of womanhood and love.

With Adam's calling on her, Eve had blossomed radiantly as a flower after the April rains. Now, she looked so beautiful in the pristine white cotton lace dress that she and Rachel had made that Rachel's breath momentarily caught in her throat, and her eyes filled with tears. It was like seeing India alive again, young and vibrant as Slade must have known her before hardship and heartache had aged and killed her.

Eve's long, thick, glossy hair was blue-black as the midnight sky over the prairie, her soft skin white as a white evening primrose and touched with the blush of dawn on her high cheekbones. Her jet brows arched like raven's wings above wide, dark blue eyes with stars of flame at their centers, like the sapphires they so resembled. Beneath her straight, classical nose, her perfect, cupid's-bow mouth—short of upper lip, full of lower—was rose-red and sensual.

This Fourth of July morning, the graceful curve of Eve's nape was prettily enhanced by her partially upswept hair, from which curls interwoven with white ribbons cascaded. The tight, ruffled basque of her gown emphasized her young round breasts and slender waist; and for the first time in her life, her hem brushed the floor when she danced a few steps across the room, her long skirts swaying and floating about her, revealing a flash of her shapely ankles. She laughed, but when she once more glimpsed herself in the mirror, she sobered, and her eyes were shadowed with pain as she spoke.

"Oh, Aunt Rachel! How I wish Mama were here to see me!" she exclaimed wistfully. "Do you—do you think she would have been proud of me?"

"Yes, oh, Eve, yes! How could you even doubt it?" Rachel

blinked back the tears that now threatened to spill at the girl's poignant question. "Eve honey, your mother was my dearest friend, closer than a sister to me; and so I know that if she were standing here right this moment, looking at you, she'd be so proud that she'd think the sight of you now made up for every unhappiness she ever suffered in her life."

"Do you—do you really think so, Aunt Rachel? Really?"

"I know so. In fact, she's probably up there somewhere in heaven right now, smiling down at you and wishing more than anything that she could tell you how much she loves you."

"Oh, Aunt Rachel"—tears sparkled on Eve's own lashes now, and a pensive smile trembled on her lips—"I think that's the nicest thing anybody's said to me since—since Mama died! Thank you. Thank you for being so kind to me and the others. I—I just don't know what we would have done without you and Uncle Slade!"

"And I don't know what I would have done without you, either," Rachel told the girl quietly. "We've helped one another, and that's the way life ought to be. Now, hurry on down, so I can finish dressing myself—and don't you dare let yourself get mussed before Adam sees you! Why, I reckon he'll be so smitten by the sight of you that he won't know three ways from Sunday!"

Stammering and flushing with happiness and anticipation at the notion, Eve descended the ladder from the loft, while, lost in her memories of India, Rachel moved slowly to complete her own toilet. After a moment, she determinedly shook off her sad thoughts, as thrilled and excited today in her own way as Eve. They were all going into town for the Fourth of July buffalo barbecue that was held every year on the east bank of the Big Arkansas river, and Rachel could hardly wait for all the festivities.

As she surveyed her reflection critically in her dressing-table mirror, she could not help but be pleased with her own appearance. She had parted her long blond hair in the middle, divided it, and braided each half, intertwining it with pale blue satin ribbons. Then she had wound the two thick plaits about her head to form a coronet and pulled a few tendrils loose on either side to frame her face softly. Her sun-streaked hair combined with her gold-dust skin to make her sparkling, mint-green eyes stand out brilliantly in her face, and her cheeks and lips were the delicate pink of moth mullein in bloom.

But it was her pale blue silk gown of which Rachel was proudest. It was lovely, she knew. She had worked hard on it, fitting and pinning it carefully on her dressmaker's dummy to be certain she got it just right, then sewing it with small, neat stitches. Its ivory-lace-trimmed sleeves were puffed and fancily caught up at the wide shoulders with bows of ribbon, in pretty contrast to the plain, widely curved edge of the bodice, cut modestly low to reveal just a hint of her full, ripe breasts. The back was more daring, falling in a deep vee from her shoulders down almost to her willowy waist, which the gown showed off to perfection. From there, the full skirt swept like a bell over the small bustle to the floor. The hem was bordered with a deep flounce, beneath which peeked the toes of her high-button shoes.

Rachel had had just enough fabric and ribbon left over to make a long, fringed shawl and a drawstring reticule to match. Now, she draped the shawl around her shoulders to hide her back until evening, when it would be proper to permit it to show, and tied the wrap's ends together, arranging them so they rested at the vee of her bosom. After pinning her wide-brimmed straw hat firmly to her hair and knotting its trailing blue ribbons in a bow under her chin, she gathered up her parasol, reticule, white kid gloves, and feathered turkey-wing fan. Then she climbed down the ladder of her bedroom loft to the log cabin below, where she joined Eve in finishing the last-minute preparations for the holiday.

A few moments later, Slade came inside. Rachel inhaled sharply when she saw him, for she had never seen him look more handsome. He had exchanged his usual shirt and breeches for an impressive suit of black broadcloth. Its well-tailored jacket clung snugly to his broad shoulders and muscular arms. His shirt was of crisp white cambric, with a frothy lace jabot and cuffs, and at his throat was a black satin cravat, held in place by a pearl stickpin. His firm, flat belly was encased in a black-and-pearl-grey paisley waistcoat adorned with solid silver buttons and the sterling-silver chain of his pocket watch, which bore a single fob. His tight pants hugged thickly corded thighs and calves. The only familiar items of apparel he wore were his black sombrero, boots, and silver spurs—and his gun belt and pistols.

The gunslinger took one look at the two women in the kitchen, then drew up short, his face whitening with shock under his tan.

"India," he breathed, his eyes stricken and incredulous, and then suddenly lighting with joy. "India!" Then, after a moment, he recognized that it was Eve he was staring at, and he shook his head, as though trying to clear it, and laughed regretfully. "Eve honey, what a turn you gave me!" he declared. "I've never seen you all fixed up before, and for a minute, I thought that it was your mama standing there. I didn't realize until just now how much you favor her."

"Do I, Uncle Slade?" the girl asked, her face brightening.

"Why, you're as like her as a twin, and so pretty! Adam had best watch his step, or he'll be falling head over heels!"

Pleased but embarrassed, Eve blushed shyly, while Rachel gave Slade a warm, grateful smile for overcoming, for the girl's sake, his initial prejudice against Adam. More than she could say, Rachel also appreciated Slade's being so understanding of this painfully awkward and sensitive time in the motherless Eve's life—especially since it must be difficult for him to be so vividly reminded of his beloved half sister.

"Grandpa," Rachel called loudly, not wanting Slade to dwell on his hurtful memories, any more than she had wanted to dwell on her own. "Are you ready? Everybody's waiting!"

"I'm coming, I'm coming," Fremont muttered grumpily from his bedroom. "No need to get in one of your dithers, Rachel! Mind your tongue, and I'll be out in a minute."

Shortly after that, he appeared, looking so fine in his Sunday-go-to-meeting clothes, with his whiskers neatly trimmed and smelling pleasantly of bay rum, that Rachel felt a rush of pride and affection when she saw him, and she beamed with approval at him. Her grandfather only scowled at her fiercely, grousing under his breath about "durned females and their fool notions about making a poor old man get all duded up for no good reason." Then he broke off abruptly, gaping at Slade, and began to chuckle.

"Damned if we ain't a pair!" Fremont exclaimed, his keen old eyes twinkling merrily. "Slade, tell me we don't look like two tinhorn dolts just off the stage from back east."

"You don't!" Rachel spoke tartly before the gunslinger could reply. "You look very handsome—both of you," she added shyly.

Slade grinned.

"Why, thank you, Rachel," he said. "And may I say that I can't remember when you've ever looked more beautiful yourself." His gaze was frankly admiring, causing her to flush and glance away, her heart beating fast. Chivalrously, he offered her his arm. "If you're ready, ma'am, your carriage awaits."

From the table, Rachel fetched the picnic basket she and Eve had prepared earlier, in case the children got hungry after sunset. Handing the basket to Slade to carry, she tucked her arm in the crook of his elbow, feeling fine as a newly minted gold eagle as they stepped outside into the morning sun. There, she saw that Poke had driven their wagon around front and was now settling half the Beecham youngsters in it so they wouldn't be so crowded in their own vehicle. In addition, the Keifes, who were accompanying the party, had just pulled up, also. With a gallantry to rival Slade's, Adam jumped down from his family's wagon to assist Eve into the wagon bed, so dazzled by her appearance that his younger brother Hosea asked him teasingly if one mule of their team had accidentally kicked him in the head. Adam cuffed his brother soundly, and with much talk and laughter, the small caravan began to rumble slowly toward Wichita.

* * *

The thin grey mist that earlier had drifted in from the rivers
to veil the city had faded under the onslaught of the bright,
hot July sun. Now, both rivers, which were too muddy to
reflect the blue of the sky, gleamed like topaz in the morning
light as they coursed their ways across the prairie. Ducks and
geese paddled contentedly in the water, and in the breeze
wafting off the rivers, the stands of cottonwood trees along
their banks stirred ever so faintly, looking like splotches of
green paint spattered by a careless artist against the canvas
of the horizon. Above the peaceful scene, the air reverberated
with the noise of the Fourth of July celebration already in
progress. Hearing the sounds of the festivities, Rachel leaned
forward eagerly on the wagon seat as Slade guided the vehicle
into town and turned onto Douglas Avenue, the hub of the
city.

Here, numerous brass bands were booming lively music,
and a platform for dancing, already in use by several couples,
had been erected outdoors. Not far from this was another
stage, where balloon ascensions were being conducted. All
along the main street and the side streets, brass bands called
attention to the amusements to be found in the saloons and
gaming hells, as well as to the freak shows that lined the
boardwalk. Hucksters and merchants hawked their goods;
some of the vendors, with cardboard signs hung front and
back over their shoulders, paraded up and down before their
establishments to advertise their services and wares.
"Smoothest shaves in town! Also, hot or cold baths, 50¢,"
read one such billboard. "We sell genuine Bull Durham
smoking tobacco! Fine Havana seegars, too (5¢ apiece),"
proclaimed another.

The townspeople strolled through the city, pushing and
elbowing their ways to the gaily colored tents and booths that
had been erected in every free space on the boardwalks and
streets, from the west end of Douglas Avenue to the east
bank of the Big Arkansas river. Texas drovers eager to spend

their thirty dollars-per-month wages filled the saloons and gaming hells to capacity, while businessmen and farmers escorted their womenfolk to stands that offered lemonade and apple pie, among other temptations.

From the big river wafted the appetizing aroma of buffalo roasting over deep pits where fires had been burning since late last evening and were now long troughs of glowing red embers. The hot, spicy barbecue sauce, which mingled with the rich fat and savory juices of the sweet, tender buffalo slowly turning on the spits, trickled down with a hiss onto the fiery coals, sending little puffs of acrid, tangy-smelling smoke swirling upward into the aquamarine sky. Roasting venison, wild turkey, quail, and prairie chickens, and bass and catfish frying in iron skillets gave off their own tantalizing odors.

There was an abundance of entertainment, from shooting matches to trotting races to a group of laughing young men and women gamely trying to drive croquet balls through hoops lost amid the tall prairie grass. A troop of traveling players was enacting a melodrama, from a show wagon. The audience hissed and booed their disapproval of the villain and pelted him with peanuts every time he appeared. A Punch-and-Judy puppet theater had children howling with merriment, and medicine wagons peddling such concoctions as liver pills, heart and kidney remedies, snake-oil potions, and restorative tonics were doing a brisk trade among the city's elder citizens.

At last, Poke, Slade, and Mr. Keife managed to find space enough to wedge their wagons in among the rest of the horses and vehicles that littered the streets and east banks of the rivers, and everyone piled out to join in the festivities. Despite herself, Rachel was as agog as the round-eyed youngsters as they traipsed from stall to stall, gawking with astonishment at oddities and gazing with longing at enticements. There were so many exciting things to see and do that the day seemed to fly by in a whirlwind of activity.

Everybody ate so much at the barbecue that all the children got sick, and Slade was compelled to buy them peppermint sticks to settle their upset stomachs. Sucking slowly on the candy to make it last, for it was not an everyday treat, his nieces and nephews then prevailed upon their uncle to sign up for one of the shooting matches, during which Rachel was finally able to see for herself that the gunslinger's skill with his pistols was, indeed, considerable. Although several other professionals vied against him in the contest, Slade succeeded in shattering a hundred bottles, with no misses, to take the fifty-dollar first prize, much to the envy and admiration of Adam, who had also entered the competition but who was eliminated on the third round of firing—due chiefly to his unfortunate propensity for showily "fanning" the old Navy Colt revolver he had borrowed from his father.

"Adam, you've been reading far too many of those ex- aggerated dime novels," Slade reprimanded him lightly but sternly as they walked off. The gunslinger shook his head at the young man's reckless handling of his pistol. "That's no way to shoot a gun. Holding the trigger in and knocking back the hammer like that with your free hand might *look* stylish; but unless you're very deft—which you aren't, I might add —it sure as hell doesn't do you much good if you're aiming to hit something! Besides, a technique like that's only good at close range, anyhow. You come on over to the house some afternoon, and I'll teach you how to shoot proper."

"Gee, Slade, really? Thanks!" Adam replied, so delighted with the offer that he found it easy to swallow the criticism.

It was nearly sundown when the gunslinger finally managed to arrange for him and Rachel to slip away alone together. Ignoring her halfhearted protests at leaving the others, he determinedly whisked her off to supper at the famous Oc- cidental Hotel at Second and Main streets, perhaps the most beautiful building in Wichita and certainly the largest and most luxurious hotel in Kansas. It had been contracted in 1873, at a cost of $29,985, to the firm of Millis and Stem, who had done a magnificent job in its construction. The local company of Hartell and Longbottom alone had laid 600,000 bricks for the edifice, to say nothing of the four thousand feet of stone and 140,000 feet of lumber also used in its formation.

Painted white, the hotel was three stories high, contained seventy-six suites and rooms, and housed five shops on the ground floor. The public dining room was so elegant that it took Rachel's breath away when she saw it. Surely, Slade did not intend for them to eat here. She feared that the cost of their meal would prove more than he could afford, despite the prize money in his pocket. But when she voiced her anxieties, Slade disregarded them and propelled her through the doorway.

"This is my treat, Rachel," he stated firmly, "and you're not spoiling it with any foolish objections. After all the good meals you've cooked for me, you deserve a special one in return. Now, stifle that unruly tongue of yours and get moving!"

The large, oval tables of the public dining room were covered with spotless white linen cloths and laden with an array of fine china and silver. The supper plates, as was the custom of the times, were overturned, with the silverware crisscrossed and balanced on top, and in each crystal wineglass towered a rolled-up, starched white linen napkin. A revolving server with cruets of vinegar and oil, and other stoppered bottles of condiments sat in the center of every table, along with a sugar bowl and creamer, and a saucer heaped high with pats of butter laid upon slivers of ice from the local icehouse.

As Slade pulled out one of the wooden Windsor chairs for her, Rachel sat down gingerly and spread her skirts carefully around her, half afraid of committing some dreadful faux pas. This was where the elite of Wichita dined, and she had never expected to find herself among them. The waiter handed her a menu, and wide-eyed, she studied the list of sumptuous soups, meat, game, vegetables, cold dishes, cakes, pastries, puddings, creams, and ices. Sixteen hot relishes were served with one multicourse supper alone. Never having heard of even half of what was offered and so having no idea what most of the fancily named and priced food was, she allowed Slade to order for her.

Then, after they had consumed what was surely the most

wonderful meal she had ever eaten, they waltzed to the music of the orchestra. As Slade whirled her around the floor, Rachel was intensely aware of his gloved hand pressed against her bare back (for gentlemen were not permitted to touch with their naked hand a lady's back when dancing), and that he held her more closely than was strictly proper. But she did not care. She was young, and in love, and he waltzed with the assurance of a man schooled in the art. Giddy with the champagne they had drunk at supper, she felt as though she could have danced forever, held fast in his arms.

But at last, warm and out of breath, they left the Occidental Hotel and walked west toward the cool evening breeze that drifted in from the rivers. There, beneath the slowly darkening twilight sky, Rachel and Slade spied a large, brightly striped tent that had not been on the riverbank earlier that day. Curious as to why it was so crowded that it bulged at its frayed seams, they decided to step inside to find out. That was how they came to be present when all hell broke loose at Preacher Proffitt's revival meeting.

Seeing that it was nothing more than a religious gathering, Slade would have left. But the tent was, by now, so full that when he and Rachel tried to push their way back outside, the crowd had no room to budge and, moreover, gave them such nasty looks for disrupting the service that, in the end, they were forced to stay put. Shaking his head, Slade smiled wryly at Rachel and shrugged.

"This is definitely *not* what I had in mind to round off our nice evening together," he told her ruefully, "but I guess we're stuck now. I just hope this thing doesn't drag on all night!"

"I don't know if it will or not. I've never attended a revival meeting before. I don't know anything about them," Rachel confessed.

"Shhhhh! Shhhhh!" people behind them began hissing loudly, interrupting their murmured conversation. "Be quiet! Be quiet! We want to hear what Preacher Proffitt's saying!"

Grimacing at each other, regretful that the remainder of their evening should be spent in such a fashion, when each of them had had in mind a moonlit stroll along the riverbank and a few lingering kisses exchanged beneath the starry night sky, Rachel and Slade politely fell silent and dutifully fixed their eyes toward the front of the pavilion, where, like a locomotive, Preacher Proffitt was churning along with his sermon, slowly building up to full steam.

Phineas F. Proffitt was not, let it be said, an ordained minister. He was the bastard son of an itinerant flimflam man, "Doctor" Proffitt; and until Phineas had embarked on his godly career, his knowledge of the Bible had been limited to such distorted admonitions mouthed to him by his father as "The love of money is all," and "It is more blessed to receive than to give."

Toward this end, then, young Phineas had learned at his father's knee the tricks of the trade from which Dr. Proffitt had earned his living: rolling dabs of flour or cornstarch in sorghum to manufacture pills (the pills might not do people any good, but they wouldn't do them any harm, either, his father had pointed out); mixing brandy and laudanum with molasses to produce a soothing sleeping aid (if that wouldn't put a body to sleep, he didn't know what would, Dr. Proffitt had declared); lacing various berry juices with pure grain alcohol to peddle as health remedies (at least the potent concoctions would make people *think* they felt better, even if they really didn't, his father had explained); and the whipping up of other assorted phony pastilles, powders, and potions, all designed with one goal in mind: to separate the ignorant and the gullible from their wallets and purses (which they were too stupid to have charge of in the first place).

In the end, his father had been chased down and lynched by a mob of righteously enraged men, one of whom had, some days previous, lost his wife. She had been poisoned by taking, for a toothache, two heaping spoonfuls of Dr. Proffitt's Prodigious Pain Reliever, which was supposed to alleviate pain by effecting bodily numbness but which did so, unfortunately, by means of a small but significant quantity of rattlesnake venom. Luckily for Phineas, however, after a heated argument between the murderous men, he himself had been judged too young to hang, and he had been let go with a stringent warning not to show his face in those parts again. That was how he had inherited his father's dubious title and medicine wagon.

Despite Dr. Proffitt's untimely bad end, Phineas had continued his father's "practice" until the day he had barely escaped with his own life from a handful of angry, partially or totally bald men whose shiny scalps had broken out in a hideous red rash following the application of Dr. Proffitt's Fabulous Hair Tonic.

After that incident, Phineas had felt that it might be provident to seek a new line of work. Being a keen observer of human nature, he had noticed during his travels that many people were moved to action when God's name was invoked; and now, he shrewdly decided to capitalize on this fact by taking up evangelism as his profession. At this, he was a natural, for he loved an audience, and he was a vigorous and an impressive orator, besides—a talent that had served him well during his years as a "doctor," and of which he now made equally excellent use as a "preacher."

To assist him in this new endeavor, Phineas returned home to round up the slatternly woman he vaguely remembered marrying during a drunken spree some years back, and the two sluttish daughters she claimed were his offspring. Then, with the cash gained from selling his unsavory nostrums, he purchased some conservative paint to tone down the garish colors of his medicine wagon, a big old circus tent that could be folded up and transported strapped on top of the medicine wagon, and some clothes more suitable for the sober roles he and his family were to play. After that, he ruthlessly scrubbed his wife and two daughters in a washtub, combed and dressed them, and skillfully applied a light dusting of rouge and powder to their faces to enhance the natural beauty he had fortuitously discovered beneath all their caked-on paint and layers of dirt. Then he set off to hold his first revival meeting.

Fueled by his own zealous rhetoric and the enthusiastic response of his impromptu congregation, Phineas thundered and threatened; he exhorted and extorted; and he chastised and collected. He collected so much, in fact, that when the rousing redemption service was over, he had heard the word—and the word was money. From that day forward, Phineas was a devout disciple not only of the almighty dollar, but of the almighty religion that had caused it to be so gladly and generously poured into his collection plates.

Now, as he stared out over the crowd packed in his tent along the east bank of the Big Arkansas river, he was carried away by his own fervent speechifying. His head, with its long white woolly hair, shook like that of a charging buffalo as he bellowed his words from his portable wooden pulpit, his penetrating blue eyes glazed and bloodshot from a lifetime of overindulgence. He was sweating so profusely in the muggy pavilion that the long, curling ends of his waxed white mustache now drooped haphazardly; and his face was such a blistering shade of red that Rachel, eyeing him askance, wondered nervously if his collar was too tight and was somehow forcing the blood to rush to his head. She had never in her life seen anybody so worked up; and if Preacher Proffitt had not been a man of the cloth, she would have suspected him of drinking. He swayed on his feet, as though he were in a trance or might collapse at any moment, and he slurred his impassioned words in a syrupy drawl that a Texan would have envied. An ugly blue vein throbbed so hard in his forehead as he strode like a madman up and down the tent's temporary dais that Rachel half feared that he would have a stroke then and there. But as she glanced around covertly, she realized that she was the only person present who seemed to harbor such disturbing thoughts about Preacher Proffitt's apoplectic appearance. Everybody else was staring at him as though hypnotized, hanging on his every word, cheering and applauding him so wildly that half of them looked maniacal themselves.

Now and then, as though overcome by emotion, Preacher Proffitt paused and turned his back on the gathering, ostensibly to wipe the perspiration from his brow and upper lip, but in reality to sneak a quick sip from the flask concealed in his overly large handkerchief, which he pulled dexterously from his breast pocket—having also, as a boy, learned the value of sleight of hand from his father. Thus restored, Preacher Proffitt abruptly pivoted back around to face the audience and continued his ardent sermon.

"Brothers and sisters," he roared, spittle flying from his lips as he held up his Bible and pounded it vehemently, "I tell you that the Good Book does not lie when it says—as it does in Galatians—that a man who curries the favor of other men is no servant of Christ. Therefore, I seek no favors here tonight. I seek only to spread the word of the Lord, who has called upon me to be His true and faithful servant and to save poor sinners of this world. So, hear me! You who are slothful and sinful, who would grow as the lilies of the field, which neither toil nor spin, or, worse, you who would indulge in strong drink, lewd women, and the evil like, be warned: There is nothing to be gained by idleness and wickedness! Make no mistake about this: You shall each of you reap what you sow. So never tire of doing good, for if you do not slacken your efforts, you shall in due time reap your harvest, as I shall reap mine, also!" He paused, then indicated his wife and two daughters, who stood nearby him on the platform. "Sister Jemima and Sister Oralie shall now pass the collection plates," he announced, "while Sister Tansy Mae leads us in making a joyful noise unto the Lord. I ask you to join her, brothers and sisters, in singing 'What a Friend We Have in Jesus,' because we do, indeed, have a friend in Him!" He pointed skyward dramatically as he made this pronouncement.

As Tansy Mae (who quite mistakenly believed herself to have the voice of a nightingale) started to sing, those in the tent chimed in eagerly, while Preacher Proffitt shouted to be heard above the din, admonishing all present to dig deep into their pockets and tithe unstintingly. Evidently, the congregation was taking his urgings to heart, for Rachel heard much tinkling of coins being dropped into the two tin gold-mining pans that served as the collection plates.

Despite her thinking that Preacher Proffitt was not at all a likely sort of man to be spreading the gospel, she dutifully reached into her own reticule for an offering, only to have Slade stay her hand.

"Keep your money, my sweet," he whispered in her ear, "for you need it far worse than that sodden old hypocrite up there. Why, if he gives even so much as one-tenth of what he takes in here tonight to any church, mission, orphanage, or the like anywhere, I'll eat my hat!"

"You mean—you mean he's a—a *fake*?" Rachel exclaimed softly, horrified.

"Oh, no, I wouldn't precisely call him that. After all, he preaches the word right enough, if that's what you're asking, Rachel honey. Still, he ought to be horsewhipped for persuading all these honest, hardworking people to believe that the donations they can ill afford to give in the first place go to some worthy cause, because I'm willing to wager my last dollar that the only charity Preacher Proffitt is funding is that of himself and those three women. Why, if that healthy glow on their cheeks didn't come out of a rouge pot, I'll eat my boots, too!"

Shocked, Rachel peered suspiciously at Sisters Jemima and Oralie as they passed the collection plates down the rows formed by the assembly. Now that she stared hard at the two women, it certainly did appear as though they owed their wholesome good looks to more than just Mother Nature; and further, Rachel observed that the bodices of the sisters' dull grey gowns were cleverly cut to gape when either woman leaned forward slightly, seeming to expose innocently, at the crucial moment when each extended her collection plate to a man, the deep cleavage of her ample bosom. One elderly farmer so favored by Sister Oralie prolonged his view by reaching slowly into his pocket for three successive contributions.

Once the hymn was finished, Preacher Proffitt surreptitiously examined his hoard of newfound riches. Then he redoubled his efforts at expounding on his chosen text, spouting such a smoothly interwoven mixture of biblical verses and his own words that even Rachel, who knew her Bible well, was uncertain where it left off and he began. Yet the gathering did not seem to notice these small but perturbing discrepancies. In fact, as they had been all along, people were madly clapping, stomping the ground, and whistling as they egged Preacher Proffitt on.

"Brothers and sisters," he cried, pointing accusingly at the half-filled collection plates, "is that miserly pittance the best you can do? For shame! For shame! I can see I have not arrived in your fair city a moment too soon! Truly, rumor does not lie, and this is indeed a town of such vice and corruption as to rival Sodom and Gomorrah!

"But, what reward has a man for all his labor, his scheming, and his toil here under the sun? you may ask of me, as the question is posed in Ecclesiastes. Is it not better to eat, drink, and be merry? No, I tell you, for where is the profit in that? Money answereth all things, and to spend it foolishly is to defraud the Lord, for did He not tell you, through His servant Malachi, that you had defrauded Him of His tithes and contributions? And did He not say there was a curse on you all, the whole nation of you, because you had defrauded Him? And did He not demand for you to bring the tithes into the treasury, all of them . . . as we shall do now! Sisters Jemima and Oralie, pass the collection plates again, while Sister Tansy Mae leads us in singing 'Bringing in the Sheaves,' as we rejoice that the curse laid down by God on these miserable and unworthy sinners may be lifted by their benevolence and generosity!"

It was during the second passing of the collection plates that Rachel became aware of a rumbling sound outside, like thunder. At first, she thought anxiously that a storm was breaking, and then she realized that the noise was, in reality, the explosions caused by the fireworks that traditionally ended the Fourth of July. Now that the stars had appeared in the night sky, the revelers outside the tent were igniting their rockets, catherine wheels, sparklers, and firecrackers. Rachel wanted more than anything to see the brilliant displays, but the pavilion was now so jammed with those who had come to hear Preacher Proffitt speak that there was scarcely room even to move, much less to escape from its confines.

She was not the only one to stir restlessly, however. A few people in the audience, fanning themselves rapidly in the heat and humidity, now began to cough and shuffle their feet as Sister Tansy Mae wailed yet another chorus of "Bringing in the Sheaves." One young woman even went so far as to push away impatiently the collection plate proffered to her by Sister Jemima, snapping some remark at her—evidently a rude one, Rachel surmised from the stout sister's affronted glare and disdainful sniff. As Sister Jemima huffily moved on, Rachel was able to get a better view of the discourteous young woman, and she saw with a small start that she was hanging like a leech on Gustave Oxenberg's arm.

Why, she must be Livie Svenson, the Swedish girl Gus is planning to wed, if she'll have him, Rachel thought, and she bent forward slightly, peeking down the rows of people to study more closely the young woman, who was not at all what she had imagined.

Rachel had expected a tall blond Viking. Livie Svenson (for it *was* she) was instead a short, plump dumpling, with brown hair coiled into a bulky bun at her thick nape and one of those pudgy, full-moon faces that, in a child, is generally described as being cute as a button but that too often makes an adult resemble an absurdly fat, overgrown pixie. She had wide brown eyes round as O's and spiked with black lashes, which she batted at Gus flirtatiously whenever she looked at him; prominent, applelike red cheeks; and an excessive smattering of brown freckles that, along with her pert, snub nose, gave her such a bouncy, speckled puppyish appearance that Rachel would not have been surprised to see her sit up and beg, pink tongue lolling out of her small, pursed mouth, which was, however, more inclined toward pouting than panting. Right now, Livie had her gaze fastened piously upon Preacher Proffitt, a benign, saintly smile on her countenance. But despite their childlike raptness, the young Swedish woman's eyes were hard and cold, Rachel thought, and there was a decidedly mulish set to her chin. Instinctively, Rachel did not envy Gus his prize. She sensed he was going to have a difficult row to hoe in his marriage if he wound up wedding Livie Svenson, as he doubtless would.

"Brothers and sisters," Preacher Proffitt bellowed hoarsely, interrupting Rachel's reverie and drawing her back to the present, "I am fair to bursting with happiness that you have heard the word and seen the light, as your kind offerings have now so plainly shown me! When that terrible but inevitable Judgment Day comes, those of you who have given so unsparingly of yourselves here tonight shall surely cross that wide River Jordan to find a place in the Lord's heavenly mansion; and so to each of us his own reward!"

This statement was received with several loud, boisterous calls of "Amen, Preacher" from the congregation, whose feverish excitement had now reached a delirious pitch. Rachel wondered uneasily if soon people would be rolling rabidly on the earth and speaking in tongues. The revival meeting was like nothing she had ever before seen in her own church, whose rites were hushed, solemn, and dignified. Even the Negroes' religious ceremonies she had witnessed in Pennsylvania, while joyful and exuberant, had been orderly and respectful. But this unbridled raucousness resembled the fierce, uncontrollable furor of a riotous mob. It was dangerous, she thought, like a keg of gunpowder, its fuse exposed and susceptible to sudden ignition. Yet Preacher Proffitt did nothing to quiet those in the tent. In fact, he lashed them to an even greater frenzy; and at the back of the pavilion, unbeknown to Rachel, Jonathan Beecham stood unsteadily, held up by those squeezed close around him, as intently enthralled and violently stimulated as the rest.

Fortified with a good deal of the Silver Slipper's forty-rod lightning, Beecham did not recall how he had come to be upon the riverbank, much less in attendance at the revival meeting. But now, it seemed to him in his alcoholic stupor as though the Lord must have directed his steps; for surely, God spoke through Preacher Proffitt's mouth, and Sister Tansy Mae was an angel from heaven, with her crimson hair and sloe green eyes, her scarlet mouth and milk-white skin. Her voice echoed like the harp of a seraph, and her bountiful breasts were softer than clouds, Jonathan fancied in his befuddled mind, yearning to bury his face prayerfully between the celestial globes that strained against her bodice with each breath, to kiss them worshipfully and to fondle them reverently.

Sister Tansy Mae would save him, rotten sinner that he was. She must! He was not going to wind up like that poor, dumb bastard Rye Crippen—tarred and feathered, and made a laughingstock before the entire town when his bony old nag had lurched like a drunk into Delano one night, whinnying shrilly, a string of tin cans banging behind it. The commotion had caused everyone up and down the street to run from the saloons and gaming hells to see what was the matter, and there Rye had been, looking silly and stupid as a jackass, courtesy of Slade Maverick and Rachel Wilder. If the two of them would do such a thing to Rye Crippen, who had tried only to drive off one of Rachel's trifling cattle—and that just as a joke, Rye had claimed—Jonathan couldn't imagine what they had planned for him, who had never been in their good graces. He only knew he didn't want any part of it. Somehow, he just *had* to find a way to save himself from them—before it was too late!

"Brothers and sisters! Brothers and sisters, despite your beneficence," Preacher Proffitt declared, "I fear that there are still sinners among you, and those, I beseech with all my heart: Repent! Repent! Repent now, I say, and be saved! Be saved—before it is too late! Has that old demon whiskey got you in his grip?" he asked, even as he took a long draft from the flask hidden in the breast pocket of his white jacket. "Turn your back on that devil, I say! Have no truck with him or with his handmaidens, those painted whores of Babylon! For if you do, you shall surely be damned and shall burn, burn, burn in hell for all eternity, utterly consumed by its flames—"

It was at that very moment that, by one of those supremely ironic twists of fate, a rocket lighted outside by one of the rowdy merrymakers whistled through the air like an artillery shell shot from a cannon to explode without warning directly above the tent. As fragments of the rocket spun away, they, too, erupted into flame, landing on the peaked roof of the pavilion and setting it ablaze. Initially, all inside just stood there, stunned and stricken, not knowing what had occurred and momentarily deafened by the horrendous bang. Then, as the tongues of fire began to lick their way across the striped canvas, someone pointed at the flames and yelled, "Lord, save us! It's Satan's own fire! God's judgment is upon us!"

At that, the assembly panicked and screamed and bolted instinctively en masse toward the tent flaps, pummeling and trampling one another in their haste to escape. Seeing that the opening was now blocked by the horde of people rushing through it, others swarmed onto the dais, where Preacher Proffitt and his wife and two daughters stood, ashen-faced, petrified, as though fearing that God had indeed smote them all with His wrath. Several persons dropped to the ground and crawled under the edges of the canvas walls, causing the pavilion to shift and sway precariously, as though it would cave in, while others, crying out, fell to their knees and prayed as though they were immune to the fire, as though their prayers would save them. Showers of sparks flew, and blazing strips of the canvas started to curl away from the tent itself, floating to the earth to kindle the dry summer grass. Acrid smoke filled the air, blinding and gagging everyone.

Instantly, Slade whipped his handkerchief from his pocket and pressed it to Rachel's face. Then, one strong arm around her shoulders to hold on to her securely and protect her from the fire, he shoved her roughly through the crazed crowd, powerfully forcing a path to open for them as he shouted at her to keep her head down and to try not to breathe the smoke. He was terrified that he might not get her out alive, and he was like a savage beast as he propelled her through the berserk throng, snarling and barking at people to stay calm, and nearly dislocating an elderly woman's arm as he snatched her up to prevent her from being crushed underfoot. Then the impetus of the mindless drove surging forward jerked the old woman away, and he could only hope she escaped.

Though more frightened than she had ever been in her life, Rachel had not panicked like the rest, for deep down inside, she trusted Slade to see her through if it were humanly possible; he would not let her die here in this inferno. She believed that with all her heart, and she repeated it to herself like a litany as they stumbled on, coughing and choking from the pungent smoke.

Seconds later, a man staggered hard into Rachel, nearly knocking her down. She tripped, and as Slade caught and steadied her, she glanced up, realizing dazedly that the man who had bumped into her was none other than Jonathan Beecham, his eyes glassy and glittering with a peculiar, fervid light. Before she could stop him, he raced on toward the platform and the flames, shrieking, "I repent! I repent! Save me! Save me!" When last she saw him as she squinted back over her shoulder, he was on his knees upon the dais, groaning pathetically and clutching Sister Tansy Mae desperately, his face mashed between her pendulous breasts as she struggled furiously to wrench herself free of him and flee from the burning pavilion.

A few moments after that, Rachel spied Gus hauling Livie Svenson through the frantic mob. She was crying and sobbing hysterically, "Hoourry, Goourry, Gooustave, yoou ox! Hoourry and get me out of here! Hoourry, Gooustave!" and at last, grunting at the effort, he heaved her over his shoulder and brutally plowed his way out of the tent, tearing up one side of the canvas and snapping several of its ropes from their stakes in the ground. Immediately, as the wind gusted in from the rivers, the pavilion billowed up with a great roar, like a strange, ascending kite, straining at, and finally tearing loose from, its remaining singed and rapidly unraveling tethers. The canvas flapped, belching fire and smoke into the night sky amid the fireworks still bursting like bombs all around it. Then, slowly, the huge tent began to sail back down. A herd of people stampeded from beneath it before, inevitably, the entire pavilion collapsed like a punctured balloon, engulfed in crackling flames.

Slade managed to pull Rachel out just in the nick of time.

But even before he could heave a sigh of relief, he realized to his utter horror that the hem of her gown was ablaze, flames shooting up her back. Rachel did not even know she was on fire until, like a lunatic, the gunslinger tackled her, sending her sprawling upon the ground, knocking the wind from her as he rolled her over and over, beating at her skirts wildly until he was sure beyond a doubt that every single spark was extinguished. Then, muttering fiercely, "Oh, my darling, my darling!" he yanked her up and clasped her tightly in his arms, holding her as though he would never let her go. She trembled against him, in shock at their narrow escape, at the dim comprehension that her dress had actually been aflame, that Slade had saved her life.

The tent was now blazing like a bonfire, the high-pitched screams of those still trapped inside ringing horribly in the ears of those who had managed to get out safely and who now stood numbly some distance away, watching what might have been their own funeral pyre. Rachel wondered sickly if Jonathan Beecham was one of those whose hideous shrieks slowly faded to moans, then finally died altogether as the pavilion was consumed by the flames. She didn't know.

The calamity had happened so fast that, at first, those who had witnessed it had mistaken the burning tent for some giant fireworks display. But now, as understanding dawned, men, women, and even children came running from every direction toward the riverbank, hastily scooped up pails in hand. Wichita had only a small volunteer fire department, so, expecting no further help, the townspeople organized themselves into a bucket brigade from the big river to the pavilion, to put out the blaze before it could spread. There was not a person in the city who did not know and dread the damage that could be done by a prairie fire, one of the most fearsome perils of the plains. Rachel and Slade pitched in with the rest to help douse the flames, and soon, all that was left of Preacher Proffitt's revival meeting was a sodden heap of charred canvas and several blackened bodies.

A number of newspaper reporters and local policemen arrived on the scene, most of them, having viewed the aftermath of many such catastrophes, inured to the horror that gripped everyone else. So some time was spent by both reporters and police questioning those gathered around the somber sight of the smoldering ashes that were now all that remained of the blaze. How had the terrible tragedy begun? Had some villain torched the tent? the sensationalistic reporters pressed excitedly, eager as bloodhounds to sniff out the story. One dogged reporter, spying Rachel's scorched gown, begged shamelessly and persistently, despite her pale, tearstained face and whimpered objections, to take her photograph, from which an artist could work to produce a sketch for publication in the newspaper. Slade got so angry at this that he not only grabbed the man by the collar and, with a well-placed boot to his rear, speeded him on his way, but also smashed his camera as extra insurance against his bothering Rachel again. The police were kinder but no less determined to get their answers. Who had been in the pavilion when it had caught fire, and, worse, who was now missing? the officers wanted to know. In this manner, the horrific tale was drawn from the survivors, and identification of the corpses was made. Preacher Proffitt and his entire family were among those who had perished, as was Jonathan Beecham.

This last discovery was the crowning blow of the cruel end to the Fourth of July holiday. Streaked with smoke and soot, Rachel and Slade walked in silence back to their own two wagons and that of the Keifes, wondering painfully how they could most gently break the news to the Beecham youngsters that their father was dead.

The next day, all the newspapers in the city distributed extra copies emblazoned with huge, bold black headlines set in what was commonly referred to as "the Second Coming of Christ" type and that reduced the dreadful disaster to such sordid and lurid proclamations as "HELLISH FIRE ROASTS REVIVAL TENT" and "SINNERS BURNED ALIVE IN DEVILISH INFERNO." At five cents apiece, every copy of every newspaper in Wichita was sold out before the morning was half over. Local police released the badly blackened bodies to the bereaved families of the dead, and eventually, the town moved on to other things. The identity of the culprit who had lit the misguided rocket that had started the awful fire and killed so many people was never learned.

Chapter Twenty-four

Because of the summer heat, they buried Jonathan's body as quickly as possible the following day, after the police had given them leave to take away his corpse. They laid him in a grave beside India's, which was not very far from those of Rachel's parents. As Rachel stood by silently, solemn-faced and dry-eyed, Slade, Fremont, Poke, Seeks, and Gus shoveled the dirt back in to fill up the six-feet-deep hole in which Jonathan now rested for all time. Gazing at the four graves on the patch of border ground that separated her land from Slade's, Rachel thought sadly that, someday, her grandfather and Poke would lie here, too, as would Seeks, if he wished it, and she herself, though she did not want to contemplate any of these deaths—or even death itself—on this hot summer day, brilliant with yellow sunshine, a slight breeze stirring, and the honeybees and the bluebottle flies buzzing among the wildflowers scattered across the prairie. Still, it was a peaceful place, a good place to be buried, Rachel thought. There were the sweeping plains, a hillock, a lone tree she had planted when her parents had died, and the ceaseless wind. That was all, since Slade had built his log cabin some distance away and had torn down India's old soddy and barn, which had stood within sight of the graves.

Poor Jonathan, Rachel mused, sighing, as the funeral service drew at last to a close. His life had been such a useless waste, such a needless mess. He had been just thirty-six. It was a hard land, the heartland. It was a hard life. The meek inherited not the earth, but dirt, and only the strong survived.

She glanced at the children. They were crying, as she had expected they would be. They had not totally hardened their hearts against their father, and his dying had no doubt brought back memories of the death of the mother they had loved. Slowly, Rachel moved to round them up and take them back to the house, while Slade thanked the reverend for coming, shook his hand, and paid him his fee. Rachel could not help but remember taking care of this at India's funeral because Jonathan had been too drunk to do so.

A lot of her previous burdens, Rachel knew, had somehow been shifted quietly onto the gunslinger's strong, broad shoulders. But even she had not realized until yesterday and today just how much she had come to depend on him. It was Slade who last night had identified Jonathan's remains, Slade who early this morning had picked out Jonathan's coffin and made all the funeral arrangements. It was Slade who had sent Adam to apprise the neighbors of Jonathan's death so the youngsters would not be hurt and embarrassed that no one had come to their father's funeral. It was Slade who had seen that the children were properly dressed and shepherded to the grave-side, and it was he who had greeted the mourners and accepted their murmured condolences on the family's bereavement.

All Rachel had done was to cook the meal that would be served now that the funeral was ended. Despite there being eight youngsters in the log cabin, the gunslinger kept his house immaculate. Rachel had not even had to clean; and she could not help but recall how, just seven months before, she had worked so hard to try to make India's dank, dark soddy presentable for mourners. If only India had written Slade earlier about the true state of her marriage and of her life, she might be alive today.

I won't think about it now, Rachel told herself sternly. *I won't think about it ever again. She's dead, and there's nothing I can do to bring her back or to make her life any easier than it was. Easy or hard, we all die in the end. Papa and Mama are dead, and now, Jonathan's dead, too; and*

Grandpa, Poke, and Seeks won't live forever. Then there'll be only the kids and Slade—and me, if I want him. And I do want him. I love him. I love him with all my heart, and even if he doesn't love me, he cares for me after a fashion. I just know he does! A man wouldn't do all the things he does for me if he didn't care—at least a little. Isn't that enough for me?

Yes, Rachel realized slowly, it was. It had not been before. But now, it was. Life was too precious, too short to waste, as Jonathan had wasted it. No matter how young you were, death could come for you at any moment, as it had come for her parents, and for India and Jonathan—as it would have come for her, too, had not Slade determinedly beat back its flames and saved her life. Her beautiful pale blue gown was ruined, and she would never wear it again, though she had kept the silk scraps and satin ribbons to remind her of how she and Slade had danced at the Occidental Hotel that evening before the tragedy had struck. It had been the most wonderful night of her life until then. No, she didn't want to die without having made the most of whatever time they might have together. If part of the gunslinger were all she would ever have, it would mean more to her than having all of any other man in the world; Rachel knew that for certain now. She had not left it too late.

The first chance she got, she intended to tell Slade that she loved him and that she would marry him if he still wanted her as his wife.

It was a few days after they had buried Jonathan that the baby, Tobias, took sick.

The first inkling Rachel had that something was amiss was when Slade did not bring the children to her log cabin in the morning. Then Gideon, Caleb, and Philip arrived in their wagon to tell her that Tobias was ill and that she was needed at their house. She immediately fetched her wicker basket, filled it with a wide assortment of herbs and wildflowers, and, joining the three boys in the wagon, set off at once for Slade's log cabin, praying there was nothing seriously wrong with the baby, who held such a special place in her heart.

Much to Rachel's relief, Toby seemed only to have caught a small cold in town, or perhaps at his father's funeral. He was not feverish, merely sniffling, sneezing, and coughing a little. After inspecting him closely, she dosed him with an infusion of licorice to clear up the inflammation of his nose and throat, as well as any earache he might be suffering; and she also gave him a spoonful of molasses laced with a thimbleful of brandy to help him sleep. Then, not having any in her basket, she gathered some roots of the purple poppy mallow, which was now in bloom, and instructed Slade to burn them in the hearth, under a pot of boiling water, so Toby could inhale both the medicinal smoke and steam.

This, the gunslinger religiously did, and for several hours afterward, the baby appeared to improve. Early the following morning, however, Toby was worse than before, and anxiously, Slade sent again for Rachel. This time, when she examined the child, her face was somber, for he was slightly feverish, and she did not like at all the small wheezing in his chest. She feared, now, that this was more than just a cold and that the infection was working its way down into his tiny lungs. She stayed all day at the gunslinger's house, treating Toby not only with the licorice infusion and the brandy-and-molasses mixture, but also with a stronger decoction she made from several dried leaves of mintleaf bee balm. She continued the burning of the purple-poppy-mallow roots in the hearth, as well as the boiling of a pot of water to produce steam, and in addition, she fixed a warm, soothing poultice for Toby's chest.

By late afternoon, he breathed more easily, and his forehead seemed cooler to Rachel, so she returned home to cook supper for her grandfather and Poke. After that, she sought out Seeks in his tipi, to tell him about the baby's symptoms and to ask his advice in the matter.

"Do not fear. You have followed the right path, Wildflower-Woman," the Indian assured her. "Now, if small one

worsens again this night, give him great mullein. Burn stalks
in fire for good smoke, and make hot tea from leaves. If he
is not better after that, you must use strong medicine of
milkweed from which butterflies drink. Tomorrow morning,
I come and see for myself what ails small one. This is no
insult to you, Wildflower-Woman, for you have learned well
what I have taught, and you are fine medicine woman. But
I have seen many summers and winters, and many times, old
eyes see more clearly and wisely than young ones. Your love
for small one may have blinded you to his needs. Tomorrow,
I come. Together, we see."

Before going back to Slade's log cabin that evening, Rachel
made certain she had in her basket a sufficient supply of
flannel mullein, the plant Seeks called "great" mullein, because it was used to treat so many different ailments. Then,
once at the gunslinger's house, seeing that Toby's fever
climbed and his breathing grew more stertorous as darkness
fell, she did as the Indian had bidden her and replaced with
tall stalks of the mullein the purple-poppy-mallow roots burning in the hearth. After that, she made a hot tea from the
mullein leaves and, when the liquid had cooled slightly,
spooned it little by little down Toby's raw throat. Then she
gave him some more of the licorice infusion and the brandy-
and-molasses mixture, and changed for a fresh one the warm
poultice on his chest.

Late into the night, Rachel sat beside the child's cradle,
tossing more mullein stalks onto the hearth and brewing more
hot tea. Every window in the log cabin was flung open wide,
but the house was stifling from the fire blazing in the sultry
July heat. Rachel was perspiring profusely, but although Toby
sweated, his fever did not break, and at last, despite her
protests, Slade ordered Rachel to go to bed, saying that he
would watch over the baby and call her if she was needed.

"You'll do Toby no good at all, sweetheart, if you fall ill
yourself," he told her. "Go on. Get some rest. I won't let
anything happen to him, I promise."

Seeing the sense in his words, Rachel crawled, bleary-eyed
and tired, into Slade's empty bed and slept. It was a restless

slumber, however, for she kept one ear cocked at all times for the sound of Toby's ragged breathing and fretful whimpering. Several times, she heard Slade speaking softly to the child and walking the floor with him, and she was thankful Toby was in the gunslinger's strong, sure hands. Yet how odd it was that she should take comfort in that fact. Stranger still that Slade's hands, so quick and deadly with a gun, should be so kind and tender with the baby.

He had been so wrong about himself not being an ideal guardian for the children, Rachel thought drowsily, as though in a dream; he was more of a father to them than Jonathan ever had been. She found it difficult now to believe that there had once been a time when she had not wanted Slade to care for the youngsters, when she had considered him totally incapable of doing so. She had been wrong, too, so very wrong. She knew that now. As Rachel drifted more deeply into slumber, Slade played softly an old French lullaby on his harmonica, and studied her face—so careworn but so beautiful to him in the firelight—and gently rocked the baby to sleep.

In the morning, Seeks arrived, and after stiffly dismounting from his pinto and calling out politely, as was the Indian way, he entered the log cabin to examine Toby. By this time, however, Rachel did not need Seeks to tell her that the child was so desperately ill that he might not recover. Despite all she and Slade had done for him during the night, Toby had taken a turn for the worse. They seemed only to have postponed the inevitable and lethal effects of his illness.

Toby's big blue eyes watered and were rimmed with red, and beneath them were two huge, half-moon smudges of purplish blue, as though someone had given him twin black eyes. His nose ran constantly with cloudy mucus, and every time he coughed—hoarse, hacking whoops—he choked up thick, yellowish green sputum. He literally gasped for air, unable to fill his tiny lungs, and his sides sank in and out so deeply with each hard breath that his ribs showed plainly, as though he were wasting away before their very eyes. He was burning up with fever, and the wheezing in his chest was now such a pronounced rattle that Rachel no longer had to press her head to his little body to hear it. His cries of pain were mere croaks. She was terrified, sick with fear.

All day long, despite the heat, she, Slade, and Seeks kept the hearth blazing, feeding it continuously with the tall stalks of flannel mullein to make the medicinal smoke, and filling and refilling the boiling pot of water hanging over the fire to produce steam. They brewed one kettle after another of the hot mullein tea and forced both it and a butterfly-milkweed decoction into Toby's mouth, stroking his raw throat to make him swallow when he attempted to refuse the bitter tonics. They changed the warm poultice on his chest again and again. But none of these things helped, and finally, Rachel and Seeks knew nothing more to try. They had exhausted their store of knowledge. In despair, Rachel told Slade he must ride into Wichita for a doctor.

"They're not all quacks. There are some good ones in town," she insisted. "Go to Dr. Andrew Fabrique's office, Slade, and ask him to come. If he's not there, fetch Dr. Henry Owens or Dr. E. B. Allen." She did not add that this last had served as one of the first county coroners. She did not want to face the fact that Toby might die.

Mounting his black stallion, Slade took off at a gallop. There was nothing to do after that but to attempt to keep Toby comfortable and wait and pray for the gunslinger to return with one of the city's physicians.

In the end, Dr. Fabrique came, and as he had delivered many of Wichita's babies, he was familiar with infant illnesses. He examined Toby thoroughly, listening especially closely to his chest and his heartbeat, which was very weak. Afterward, the physician sighed heavily and shook his head gravely, announcing that Toby had bronchitis. Dr. Fabrique did everything that was within his power to do for the child. But he informed Rachel and Slade that, even so, he did not hold out much hope for Toby's survival.

"The baby is very small and frail, not nearly so large and heavy as we would expect a seven-month-old child should be," the physician explained. "This is why the bronchitis is so severe. The baby is simply not strong enough to fight it off. Please, don't blame yourselves. You have done all you can, as have I. The rest is up to God now. I'm sorry. If the baby lives—" He broke off abruptly. Then he said, "I will come back again tomorrow if you need me."

Shortly after sunset, declining their offer of supper, the kindly doctor departed. After he had gone, taking his black bag and Rachel's hope away with him, she sat down by Toby's cradle, rocking him gently and fighting back her tears as she pleaded and bargained silently with God to let the baby live. Her heart lurched in her breast with Toby's every painful breath, and she was filled with a terrible anger and agony to know she was powerless to save him. That was the worst of all—her impotence when she loved him so much and he needed her so desperately.

As the long night wore on, the baby's mouth and fingernails began to turn a faint, bluish color. Then, suddenly, just after midnight, Toby gave a sharp gasp, as though he were suffocating, and died.

The abrupt silence told Rachel the child was dead, but she refused to accept the fact and kept right on praying. Finally, she knelt over his cradle, slowly laid her head upon his chest, and heard and felt that he no longer breathed.

"Toby!" she cried softly, still disbelieving, despite the evidence. *"Toby!"* Thinking in some dim, wild corner of her mind that she must have been mistaken about his not breathing, Rachel put her palm up frantically to his mouth. But no air came out. Then, in desperation, she shook him roughly, as though she could somehow jar him awake. But still, Toby didn't respond. "No! Oh, please, God, no!" she moaned, turning away, her trembling hand pressed to her lips to stifle her wrenching sobs. *"No!"*

She sank back on her haunches, burying her face in her hands, weeping, her heart breaking inside her. Her body felt cold as ice. She thought dumbly that she must somehow be slowly freezing clear through to the very marrow of her bones. Her stomach heaved, as though the earth had fallen away without warning from beneath her feet, making her feel so sick and dizzy that she feared she would swoon. Her mind went blank, and a queer daze took hold of her, so she couldn't seem to think rationally anymore.

No! No! He's not dead! He's not! she thought, anguished. *He can't be! He just can't be! Oh, Toby! Toby!*

This was her baby, her child. In her heart, he had been hers, and now, he was dead, and nothing was ever going to bring him back to her. It just didn't seem possible that he had been there one minute and was gone the next. She remembered holding him, feeding him, rocking him, marveling at his small hands, his tiny fingers, playing "This Little Piggy Went to Market" with his toes, recalling how he would coo and gurgle and laugh as she did so. She remembered his eyes round with wonder, the sweet, milky, powdery scent of him, the clutch of his little fist around her finger, his first genuine smile, the first time he had ever sat up by himself, and his first tooth. All that was gone now, too swiftly, too soon, and forever—just as her mother had gone. Rachel had been motherless, and now, she was childless, too. It ought not to have happened like that. Toby should have lived. She should have been able to watch him grow up, become a man, and have children of his own. Now, that would never be, and she felt empty and old inside—and alone, so alone.

No, not alone, she realized slowly, for after a moment, she felt a pair of hands upon her shoulders, not her mother's loving hands that had once soothed away her many sorrows, but Slade's. He was there for Rachel now, as he had always been there for her since his coming. Quietly, he raised her to her feet and led her from the log cabin so she would not waken with her tears the poor baby's sleeping siblings. They had suffered enough already, without this, too, coming hard on the heels of their father's death. They had *all* of them borne enough without this, Slade thought, as within him rose a deep, murderous rage at God for letting Toby die.

Slade guided Rachel toward the barn, where she could cry in privacy over her loss and attempt to recover her brave front—even if she was aching with torment and sadness deep down inside. She would want to compose herself, somehow, some way, he thought. She would not wish for the rest of the children to see her like this, he knew. She would want to be strong for their sake, because that was the selfless sort of woman she was.

From the shadows where he sat beside the house, Seeks spied the two of them crossing the yard, the gunslinger's arm around Rachel's shaking shoulders and her head bent blindly into his chest. Knowing from this that the child had died, Seeks rose slowly from the ground and walked into the darkness. A short distance away, upon the prairie, he lifted his palms to the starry night sky and began to chant melodiously his Indian prayer for the dead.

Inside the barn, Rachel wept against Slade's chest, while he held her close and stroked her hair soothingly, not knowing how else to comfort her.

"Why, Slade? Why?" she asked him, as though, hurt and bewildered, she thought he would somehow know the answer to her question. But he did not. "Why did Toby have to die? *Why?*"

"I don't know, Rachel. I don't know why these things happen. I don't know why God *lets* them happen! I wish I did, but I don't. It's not right, and it's not fair. But that's the way life is, sweetheart, and there's nothing we can do to change it. We just have to live it the best way we know how."

"But Toby—Toby was only a—a baby! He never even had a chance to live! He never even had a chance! And now, he's—he's dead, and he was so—so little and so young . . too young to die!"

"We're all dying, Rachel," Slade told her softly. "From the day we're born, we are all of us dying. Some just die sooner than others, that's all. Maybe Toby was one of the lucky ones. I don't know. Life's hard, Rachel, and in the end, we don't any of us get out of it alive. The strong just fight harder and take longer to die, that's all."

"Then, what's the point, Slade?" she queried bitterly, dashing away her tears. "If it's all for nothing, then what's the point in us even being born?"

"I don't know, sweetheart. Only God knows the answer to that."

They were each silent then, alone with their thoughts. As the sound of the Indian's chanting upon the plains reached them, a thousand memories rushed without warning to engulf Slade: memories of the Negroes on Sundays, singing their spirituals in the slave quarters on his father's plantation, Cypress Hill, and of Baptiste Robillard, his mother, dancing in the big ballroom whose French doors had opened out onto the Mississippi River; of Thérèse Duvalier running in a white dress across the moonlit grass, gardenias in her hair; and of his beloved half sister, India, her blue eyes laughing, her black hair flying. . . . All of them were dead now, except the woman he held in his arms—Rachel, quick and warm, a world of strength in her seemingly fragile young body, a wealth of courage in her gallant heart. But even she was bowed by Toby's death.

"He was ours, Slade," she whispered fiercely, lifting her tearstained face to his, and he knew she meant the dead child. "He was ours! Oh, I know we weren't his real parents, but he never knew India or Jonathan. Toby was *ours*! As surely as though we made him together, you and I—Oh, Slade, make love to me!" The words burst from her suddenly, feverishly. "Make love to me! Here. Now. I don't want to think about death anymore. I'll go crazy if I do! I know I will. Make love to me! Take me, teach me. Please, I want you to. I—"

She had her arms around his neck by then, her body pressed close to his, and she was raining hot, urgent kisses on his face, his mouth. He would had to have been a monk not to be aroused—and Slade was no monk. Inflamed by her unexpected assault, he crushed her to him, deep longing and exigency crying out violently in them both as his lips captured hers and his tongue stabbed her with its heat. Fiercely, he kissed her, his mouth hard and demanding upon hers, as though, with her onslaught upon his senses, she had loosed some dark, savage thing within him. But Rachel did not fear it, for it matched the hot, brutal passion igniting and exploding inside her own self. Wildly, she kissed him back, as though she were an empty ewer craving to be filled and his kisses were but a trickle of the sweet summer wine she ached to contain. Her tongue darted forth to wreathe his, twisting, turning, tasting in quick little laps and licks that made his loins tighten sharply with desire. Eagerly, her moist mouth swallowed his breath. Her teeth nibbled his lips. Her tense hands moved on his muscular body desperately, tearing like claws at his shirt. She raked his bare chest with her fingernails, bloodying him in her frenzy.

It was this that brought Slade abruptly to his senses. Without warning, he pushed her away roughly, his fingers curled so tightly around her arms that Rachel knew she would have bruises on them in the morning. He was a gunslinger, so he knew what she was feeling, the driving, instinctive need within her now to create life in the face of death. He had felt it himself a hundred times before in the past. She wanted him to fill up her emptiness, to make her forget that life was hard and that Toby was dead, to take away her pain and mend her broken heart. And Slade wanted to do all those things for her. He wanted to do them so badly, just as he wanted her. But this wasn't the time or the place or the way. Rachel wasn't the type of woman to give herself like this, right now, without regretting it and despising herself afterward; nor was he the type of man to take advantage of her in her moment of weakness and grief. He couldn't do that to her. He *wouldn't* do that to her. He must have been mad to let things go as far as they had.

"No. No!" he denied her flatly, his voice a rasp, his breath coming hard. "We will not do this! I tell you, we will not! I want you, Rachel. You know I do. But not now! Not like this! Listen to me! You'd hate yourself for it afterward— making love with me, with that baby lying there dead in the house—and you'd hate me, too. And I couldn't bear that. I—'' He broke off abruptly, a muscle twitching in his cheek. Then, more kindly, he said, "Go on back into the house

Rachel honey. Please. We've a child in there who needs burying, and what there is between us must wait, and will be sweeter for the keeping, I swear.''

Stricken, horrified that she had lost her head and flung herself at him so shamelessly in her sorrow, Rachel turned and stumbled blindly from the barn, thinking she must be out of her mind. At the door of the log cabin, she paused, sobbing, to catch her breath and to steel herself as best she could for what awaited her inside.

Then, slowly, she lifted the latch and went in to the baby who lay so still and silent in his cradle.

Chapter Twenty-five

Life went on as before, except that, now, there was no baby in the house and, beneath the lone tree Rachel had planted on the distant prairie hillock, there were five graves instead of four.

She went there, sometimes, of an early summer morning or a long twilight evening, to think her quiet thoughts and to scatter wildflowers upon the mounds of earth that lay beneath the wide, grassy plains. Jonathan's grave, she tended as carefully as the rest, forgiving him in death what she had not forgiven him in life.

Seeks was gone—he had already lingered far longer than usual—and sadly, Rachel did not know if she would ever see him again. She had realized suddenly that, despite her thinking he never changed, he was an old man, his heart heavy with his vision of a future that held no place for him or for his kind. His way of life, so in harmony with nature, was vanishing with the vast buffalo herds, as he had told her.

Each winter, death nipped a little more closely at his heels, and now, she knew in her heart that he welcomed its coming.

She was kneeling beside the graves on the prairie, the morning sun turning her hair to gold, when he came to bid her good-bye. Slowly, mounted upon his pinto and leading his two pack mules, he approached her; and even before he drew to a halt and, with the stiffness of age, eased himself from his horse's bare back to stand beside her as she rose respectfully to her feet, Rachel knew he was leaving. Her heart ached at the thought, at the painful knowledge that this loss, too, she must somehow endure; and she wondered how it could possibly be true that God never gave a burden too heavy to bear to the one He had chosen to carry it.

For a moment, Seeks was still, staring at the lone tree that stood upon the hillock, that, despite the long, hot summers, the bitterly cold winters, and the constant soughing of the wild wind, bravely lifted its branches to the sky, as though in prayer—or reaching for the sun, the stars.

Then he observed, "It is good place to be buried, Wild-flower-Woman."

"Yes," she uttered quietly, knowing then that he, who had no family but hers, wished to lie here, also, when his time came.

"You will see to it." It was a statement, not a question.

"Yes," she told him.

He nodded, having expected no less. Then, as his dark eyes surveyed and memorized her face, he stretched out one hand and, in his dear, familiar gesture, laid it lightly upon her hair.

"Is like sunshine, I always think," he said.

"Oh, Seeks! Seeks!" Rachel cried softly.

Blinking back tears, she impulsively flung her arms around her friend and hugged him tightly. For a long minute, he held her close, and his gnarled old fingers stroked her hair lovingly. Then, shaking his head and harrumphing his disapproval of this display, he gently but firmly thrust her away, turning aside so she would not see the emotion on his face. After a moment, deliberately stoic, he removed his battered old straw parasol from the pack on one of his mules and climbed onto his pinto. Then he glanced again at Rachel, who stood by mutely, watching him and now weeping unashamedly.

"Next summer, I come," he promised her, pretending not to notice her tears, "and will expect then to dandle on knee small one of Dog-Soldier and Wildflower-Woman. Dog-Soldier is wise man, like Seeks, and though wise man never tries to command love, he always hears heart sing when it comes."

Then, with a little click, the Indian raised his parasol and rode away, a proud, incongruous figure against the horizon. Rachel gazed after him until he was out of sight, her tears glistening on her sun-kissed cheeks, her heart filled to over-flowing with emotion. For in his own way, Seeks had just told her that he loved her—and that Slade loved her, too.

July faded, August bloomed, and the plains were rich with the scent of newly harvested fields, as the men worked from before sunup until long after sundown, reaping what they had sown in the spring. Every hand was needed with the harvest, so all the boys, even Andrew, helped, while all the girls, including small Naomi, assisted Rachel in the kitchen, cook-ing for the hungry men. All around the surrounding country-side, the men went from farm to farm to share in the chore of harvesting, as the women went, also, to share in the feeding of them. At Gus's farm, a dual celebration was held, for with true midwestern practicality, he took advantage of the pres-ence of those gathered to reap his crops to marry Livie Sven-son and hold their wedding reception, as well.

Rachel wished the couple every happiness. But she knew she was not, after all, mistaken about Livie, who like the pagan god Janus, Rachel thought, was two-faced. Outwardly, she was warm, bubbly, and friendly, but this was merely a facade for the bitterly unpleasant person underneath. Livie was extremely jealous that Gus had once been Rachel's beau, even though Rachel had never wanted him; and more than once when she thought Rachel wasn't watching, she gave her such needlelike stares that Rachel went home feeling like a pincushion, bewildered by the Swedish girl's hatred and hostility. Livie was very clever at hiding her ugly inner nature, however, and had fooled everyone at the reception, except Rachel, into believing she was a sweet, caring woman who would make Gus a wonderful wife.

And she probably would, Rachel reflected dryly. Livie would undoubtedly work hard at attempting to ensure that every neighbor within ten miles envied her competence as a farmer's wife—not grasping that they were all so busy making their own farms prosper that her success, or lack of it, would prove meaningless to them. Though Rachel could not like her, she pitied in her heart the Swedish girl, for she did not think that Livie would ever know true happiness, but would be forced to make do merely with its hollow trappings—and, what was somehow even sadder, would never know the difference. Rachel felt even sorrier for Gus, for being so taken in. But perhaps his love would, with time, enable Livie to grow less unsure and afraid, kinder and more loving. Perhaps he would never see the poisonous person Rachel had seen in Livie. She didn't know.

She had her own problems to worry about; and as, good or ill, human nature is such that the pain a person feels upon stubbing his big toe is of more concern to him than the loss of his neighbor's foot, she did not for long dwell on Gus and Livie's marriage. Indeed, she forgot them altogether the evening Adam arrived bearing what she ever after thought of as the fateful message for Slade.

Rachel was to remember it so long as she lived, for she had never before seen, nor did she ever again see, such an expression come over his face. He looked so terrifying when Adam handed him the innocuous-looking playing card that, despite her deep love for him, Rachel was chilled to the very marrow of her bones; and she thought suddenly, fearfully, intuitively: *Something has happened, something so dreadful that all is changed between us and perhaps will never be the same again.*

"I got into a faro game at a saloon in Delano last night,"

Adam began, by way of explaining how he had acquired the card. He flushed at the admission, not daring to glance at Eve, who had inhaled sharply upon hearing this piece of news and was now staring, with quiet accusation in her eyes, at him. "At any rate, that's neither here nor there," the young man continued hurriedly. "What's important is that there was this fellow at the table—not the usual sort you see in Delano, but an expensively dressed gentleman. I thought at first that he was only some greenhorn dude just in off the stage from back east, a dandified Frenchie—no offense, Slade. But he wasn't.

"He drank quite a bit—good stuff, too—but he held his liquor as well as you, Slade, though he must have been drunk, even so; for I don't know what else could account for his behavior. For as the evenin' wore on, he began to suspect that the faro dealer was somehow cheatin' him, and maybe it *was* true, I don't know. I didn't see how it could be, but anythin' is possible, I suppose. Anyway, they got into an argument over it, and the dealer slid a knife out of his sleeve, and before anybody else at the table knew what was happenin', the Frenchie quick yanked a Derringer from his pocket and, just as cool as you please, plugged the dealer right square between the eyes. I've never before seen anything like it, Slade, blood sprayin' all over the place—" Adam cut himself off hastily when he saw Eve blanch. He paused. Then he continued.

"The thing of it is, after it was all over and done with and they'd carted away the dealer and the Frenchie had bribed the barkeep into forgettin' about sendin' for the marshal—I kind of got the impression he's wanted by the law—he calmly sat back down at the table, just as though the whole thing had never taken place.

"Well, you know how I am about guns and such, Slade, so I got to talkin' to him, and durin' the course of our conversation, I just naturally happened to mention to him that we had a gunslinger right here in Wichita. And the Frenchie said, 'Oh, who's that?' And I said, 'Slade Maverick.' And then a real peculiar look came over his face, and he sat there for a minute, like I'd clubbed him over the head or somethin'. Then he reached for the dealer's shoe and, almost like he was in a frenzy, started to snatch all the cards out one by one until he came to the one you're holdin'. After that, he stared at it for a real long time, like it meant somethin' special to him. Then he slowly handed it to me and asked me if I'd be so kind as to deliver it to you, seein' as how I knew you and all; and then he told me to ask you if you still remembered how to buck the tiger. What's it all mean, Slade?'' Adam inquired curiously. ''Do you know what it means?''

The gunslinger was silent for such a long time afterward that Rachel thought he didn't intend to answer the young man's question. Finally, he grunted, ''Yeah, I know.'' Then he abruptly stood and strode from the log cabin, startling them all and leaving them just as much in the dark as they had been before. Nobody spoke a word until at last Rachel rose and said she had best go see if Slade was all right. Quietly, she opened the door and slipped out into the night, her eyes searching the darkness for him. He was standing, stock still in the moonlight, a short distance away on the prairie. Slowly, not knowing what to expect, Rachel walked toward him, her heart in her throat.

The gunslinger was unaware of her approach, for he was staring, as though in shock, at the playing card he held in his hand. It was the three of hearts—the last losing card Digger Thibeaux had bet on at the faro table the night Slade had taken Digger's mistress, Thérèse Duvalier, away from him. The three of hearts, the card that represented the deadly triangle of passion and jealousy they had formed between them more than ten years ago now. The three of hearts, the card on which Digger had scrawled the insulting challenge that had brought the three of them to the infamous elms where duels in New Orleans had been fought. The three of hearts. Thérèse dead, and Digger still alive. *Still alive!* Slade's gorge rose, and he fought to keep his hold on reality.

He was so engrossed in memories as he gazed at the card that he did not hear the sound of Rachel's crossing the dry prairie grass until she was nearly upon him. His gunslinger's instincts in full force, Slade pivoted, dropped the card, and drew his pistols.

"Jesus, Rachel!" he swore when he saw her, and then shoved his revolvers back down into their holsters. "Don't ever sneak up on me like that again!"

"I wasn't sneaking." Deliberately, she bent and retrieved the fallen card. "What does it mean, Slade?" she questioned, holding it out to him, her fingers pale and trembling. "What does it mean?"

"Don't ask, Rachel," he ordered curtly, "because you don't want to know."

"Yes, yes, I do," she insisted. "I have a *right* to know, Slade!"

"No, you don't."

"Yes, I do! You gave me the right, Slade—running Gus off and telling the Keifes I was your fiancée. You ought not to have done those things if you didn't want me to have any claim on you, if you didn't intend to make me a part of your life. So, now, I'm asking you: What does this card mean?"

"All right, then," he agreed after a moment. "I'll tell you. But you won't like it. So, don't say I didn't warn you, because I did—and still, you asked for it." He paused. Then he asserted grimly, "It's a tasteless mockery, a deliberate insult, a challenge I can't refuse. It means that if I have any pride and guts at all—and I've got more than my fair share of both, Rachel—I have to ride into town and kill someone."

Ever since Adam had handed Slade the card, Rachel had feared something like this, yet she whitened as though he had struck her.

"But . . . why? *Why?*"

Slade's answer was slow in coming. Then, finally, breaking open reluctantly the sealed doors of his dark past, he spoke, revealing to her the story of his wild youth, of his scandalous duel in New Orleans, and of the unknown girl he had loved. Rachel listened quietly, not daring to interrupt, sensing he was telling her things he had never told anyone else in his life.

"Do you remember that girl I told you about, the one I

lost my heart to in New Orleans, the one who . . . died?"
he asked. Rachel nodded, and he went on. "Well, her name
was Thérèse Duvalier, and she was a faro dealer in a gaming
hell in the French Quarter. She was also an octoroon and a
whore, because in those days, being one generally meant
becoming the other if you wanted anything out of life at all."
Slade paused for a moment, recalling how it had been back
then for a woman like Thérèse Duvalier. Then he continued,
the words pouring out of him now, as though they had too
long been bottled up inside him. "Oh, Rachel honey, she
was dark as you are fair, with long, jet-black hair and skin
so pale that it was almost white. She was so beautiful, and
I loved her so much," he confessed, his words like a knife
twisting slowly in Rachel's heart. "I loved her, even though
I knew, because she was an octoroon, that I could never
marry her. That would have been the crowning blow to my
father. It would have killed him, and though I despised him,
I didn't want to be the cause of his death.

"But I had a friend—at least, he started out that way—
Digger Thibeaux, and he loved Thérèse, too; and in the beginning, she chose him over me. He was five years older than
I, and more experienced and sophisticated, I suppose—and
he certainly had more money, since my father had cast me
out of Cypress Hill and cut me off without a cent. But Digger
was wild, Rachel, even wilder than I; and the Thibeauxes all
had a streak of cruelty running through them, besides. They
had intermarried so much with their cousins over the years
that their entire family was half crazy, and Digger was one
of the worst. Even so, he was a great favorite among all us
young planters' sons.

" 'Digger' wasn't his real name, of course. It was Dominique. We only called him Digger because of the nasty habit
he had of dispatching his dueling opponents to their graves.
The nickname was a macabre joke, because they don't bury
dead bodies in New Orleans; they entomb them above ground.
Otherwise, the corpses would be uprooted and would float
away on the floods when the river rises. We all used to get
drunk and say Digger's victims got so nervous facing him

that they wound up floating away on their own blood when their shivers rose. As I said, a macabre joke.

"At any rate, he abused poor Thérèse terribly, whipping her, as he had his slaves before the war, and making her suffer in countless other ways too cruel to describe. I tried several times to talk her into leaving him. But she was terrified of him, of what he might do to her, although we had fallen in love and were meeting secretly by then, every chance we got. I told her I would protect her, but still, she was afraid.

"Then, one night, while we were playing faro at the gaming hell where Thérèse worked,. Digger accused her of somehow stacking the cards in the shoe in my favor, causing him to lose and me to win. He got up from the table, and he shook her and slapped her brutally; and that was when Thérèse finally snapped. She started screaming at him, and it all came pouring out then: how she hated him, how she and I were lovers behind his back, how she was going away with me and never wanted to see him again. She was hysterical by then, so I took her home, and while we were there, a message arrived from Digger—a challenge he had scribbled on the back of the three of hearts, the last losing card he had bet on that night at faro. He'd been drinking and didn't want to wait for the duel to be conducted properly. He wanted to meet right away; and as I'd been drinking, too, and was too proud and angry to refuse, I agreed to meet him.

"Despite my objections, Thérèse insisted on accompanying me. She waited in the carriage under the elms, while Digger and I stood back to back and started to count off the paces, Digger's dueling pistols in hand. I don't know what was in Thérèse's mind then. But at the last moment, as we each turned to fire, she scrambled out of the carriage and came running toward me from the trees. Maybe Digger had cheated and turned early and she was trying to warn me. Or maybe he played fair, after all, and she was just afraid I couldn't best him—he'd killed so many others—and she had some misguided notion of trying to save my life. As I said, I don't know; and I'll never know now, because instead of firing at me, that goddamned bastard Digger shot Thérèse.

He shot her down in cold blood. He *murdered* her, Rachel, right in front of my very eyes, knowing how much I loved her. Sometimes—sometimes, I think I'll never get it out of my mind—'' Slade broke off abruptly, a muscle working tensely in his set jaw as he fought to regain control of his emotions. Then he went on quietly.

"I'll never forget how he stood there and laughed afterward, like a madman, how he went on laughing even as I fired at him and he fell. I didn't wait to see if he was dead. I swept Thérèse up into my arms and laid her in the carriage and drove like hell to the nearest doctor. But it was too late. She was dead by the time I got there.'' The gunslinger paused again, remembering. Then he said dully, "I've been ridding the world of vermin like Digger Thibeaux ever since—and now that I know he's still alive, I've got to finish what I started that night in New Orleans. I owe it to Thérèse. I owe it to myself.''

Tears, like tiny prisms in the moonlight, penciling her cheeks at his tale, Rachel started to speak, to protest—loving him, afraid of losing him, as Thérèse Duvalier had been afraid, also. But with an upraised hand, Slade stopped her.

"No, don't say a word, Rachel. You'd just be wasting your time, trying to persuade me not to go, because you can't. I already know all the many good reasons why I shouldn't meet Digger again, and only one compelling reason why I should—but that one's enough. It outweighs all the rest. So, please. Just go on back into the house. Please, Rachel. I need to be alone for a while to think things through, to get things clear in my mind.''

With her hand pressed to her mouth in a vain attempt to repress her sobs, Rachel turned and ran back to the log cabin. Slade watched her go, his throat tight with the emotion that threatened to overwhelm him. After a while, purposefully, he headed for the barn to hitch the team to the wagon so he could take the children home.

It was there Poke found him. The gunslinger glanced up at him silently in the flickering lanternlight, then deliberately returned to buckling the harness onto the draft horses. Seeing this, Poke sighed, knowing that the task he had set for himself was not going to be easy. Still, he plunged on determinedly.

"Slade, Ah wants ter talk ter yo fo' a minute," he announced.

"Come to meddle in my affairs, too, Poke? Goddamn it! Can't a man get any peace or privacy around here?" the gunslinger barked, making his annoyance plain. Then he inquired suspiciously, "Did Rachel send you?"

"Nawsuh, she din—an' Ah would advise yo ter keep a civil tongue in yore haid when yo talks ter me, Slade Maverick! De war is ober, an' Ah is a free puhson o' color," Poke reminded him, "not one o' yore daddy's slave niggahs! An' yo would do well ter 'member dat, 'cuz Ah ain' so ole yet dat Ah cain' whoop yore hide if'n Ah teks a notion ter! Somebuddy's got ter speak up fo' Miz Rachel, an' right now, Fremont's so gawdblamed mad at yo fo' huhtin' dat gal dat he's fixin' ter give yo de bizness end o' his shotgun!" Poke allowed this to sink in. Then he said softly, "Yo knows Miz Rachel loves yo, Slade."

The Negro had the keen satisfaction of seeing the gunslinger go very still. Then, after a time, Slade forced himself to continue with his work.

"You're dreaming, Poke," he growled.

"Nawsuh, Ah ain'. Why, de day ole Ox done up an' conked yo on de haid wi' dat chair, Ah thought de chile would pass out when she seed yo lyin' der so still on de ground, lookin' lahke yo had gone ter meet yore Maker. Why, she wuz so upset dat she picked up one o' de busted chair laigs an' lahked ter kilt ole Ox wi' it! Beat him all 'round de haid an' de shoulders sumpin' fierce, she done. Yassuh, Ah've knowed Miz Rachel since de day she wuz born, an' Ah'm heah ter tell yo dat Ah ain' neber seed her in sech a tekin' as she wuz when she thought yo wuz daid. An' now, yo wants ter up an' run off an' meet dis heah Frenchie on de field o' honah someplace an' mebbe git yoreseff kilt in de process!"

"Rachel tell you that?" Slade asked sharply.

"Nawsuh. Ah din need nobuddy ter tell me dat, 'cuz if'n

eber Ah seed a man starin' at a ghost, it wuz yo lookin' at dat cahd, dat trey, ternight. Ah wuz raised in de South. Ah knows 'bout gempmum's duels an' sech. An' heahin' Adam's story an' knowin' yo wuz a gunslinger 'fo' yo come heah, it jes' natch'ly stands ter reason dat dis heah Frenchie is somebuddy from out o' yore past an' dat dat cahd is a challenge. But Ah'm heah ter tell yo dat de days o' duelin' are ober an' dat de past is daid an' burried, Slade; an' yo cain' change it—not now, not eber. Ain' nobuddy whut kin do dat, an' dat's a fac'!''

"Maybe so, but a man with any kind of honor and courage at all just doesn't walk away from a challenge," Slade insisted.

"Ah thought so, too, once," Poke admitted, "a long time ago, 'fo' Ulysses taught me dif'rent. Yo neber knowed Ulysses, Miz Rachel's daddy. But he an' Miz Victoria, Miz Rachel's mama, dey wuz fine folks, de finest. Dey took me in years ago, 'fo' de war come, 'fo' Miz Rachel wuz eben born. Ah wuz a fugitive slave from down South, an' Ah had managed ter mek mah way ter de Nawth somehow. Ah wuz stealin' food an' sleepin' in a alley, skeered out o' mah mind dat de slave catchers wuz gwine ter git me, when Ulysses found me an' took me home. Ah wuz 'shamed o' runnin' away. Ah felt lahke Ah wuz a coward. But Ulysses tole me dat, sometimes, it teks a heap mo' gumption ter run away from somethin' dan it do ter stand an' fight.

"I din have no fambly. Mah chilluns wuz all sold down de riber; an' mah woman . . . well, de white man—if a puhson could call him a man—whut owned us, he got drunk one night, an' he beat an' raped her, 'cuz she din want ter pleasure him an' some o' his friends. Den dey all took turns on her. She wuz daid when dey finished. Ah kilt him aftahwards. Dat's how come Ah had ter run away an' why Ah wuz so skeered de slave catchers wuz gwine ter git me. Ah knowed dey wuzn't gwine ter give up, an' dey'd have hung me fo' sho'—a niggah killin' a white man. But Fremont, Ulysses, an' Miz Victoria, dey hid me an' perteck'd me, an' aftah dat, dey wuz mah fambly.

"Dat's why Ah come ter talk ter yo, Slade, 'cuz Ah cain' bear ter see Ulysses an' Miz Victoria's chile huht, an' Ah knows dat dat li'l gal in der's gwine ter have her haht broke ober dis heah thing if'n sumpin' hap'ns ter yo an' yo doan come back. Now, is yore intentions toward dat chile hon'r- able, or ain' dey? Ah mean . . . seein' as how yo been hangin' 'round heah fo' months, actin' yo is a paht o' dis heah fambly, well, Ah reckoned dat yo an' Miz Rachel had reached a undahstandin' between yo an' dat yo wuz plannin' on mah'ryin' her. Am Ah wrong 'bout dat?"

"No," Slade responded curtly.

"Den how come yo wants ter tek a chance on mekkin' Miz Rachel a widder 'fo' she's eben a wife? Doan hahdly seem right ter me, runnin' off ole Ox lahke yo done an' now runnin' off yoreseff, leavin' dat gal high an' dry. She din care nothin' 'bout ole Ox. But she loves yo, Slade, an' Miz Rachel is de kind o' woman whut gives her whole haht ter a puhson. Ah'm tellin' yo right heah an' now dat if'n sumpin' hap'ns ter yo, dat chile woan neber git ober it, not so long as she lives. Seems ter me lahke a man who loved a woman wouldn't want ter tek a chance on doin' sumpin' lahke dat ter her!"

"No, Poke, he wouldn't," Slade agreed, as he climbed into the wagon seat. "But like it or not, a man's got to do what a man's got to do. But don't you worry about me—or Rachel, either—you hear? She's a strong woman, and if she loves me, as you say, she knows in her heart that I've got to put the past behind me and wipe the slate clean if we're to have the sort of life together that she wants—and that I want, too, I reckon. Otherwise, I wouldn't be so torn up about what this thing might do to her. But never you fear. I can take care of myself, and I'll be back. You can count on that."

Chapter Twenty-six

Long after Slade, Adam, and the children had gone that evening, and Fremont and Poke had retired, Rachel sat outside on the stoop of the log cabin, and she thought, and she prayed. She knew that she couldn't prevent Slade from meeting Digger Thibeaux, that the gunslinger would feel less than a man if he backed down from this challenge; and in a strange way, she did not even want to stop the forthcoming duel. The unexpected reappearance of Thibeaux in Slade's life had reopened all his old wounds, and reawakened all his old feelings for Thérèse Duvalier. Before, both wounds and feelings had been only dying memories, Rachel sensed, almost forgotten. But now, it was as though Digger had breathed new life into them, imbuing them with all the pain and passion they had possessed over ten years ago. In her heart, Rachel knew that, now, if Slade were ever to be free to love her and to build a life with her, he must in some way write "paid in full" on his past and close the book on it.

She tried to quell her fear by reminding herself that Slade was a professional, that he was good at what he did, that he had to be, else he could not have survived as long as he had. But rationalizing didn't help. There was something about his story tonight that now filled her with terror, though she could not quite put her finger on what it was. She knew only that it was something more than that Digger Thibeaux was a cold-blooded murderer. Again and again, Rachel mulled Slade's tragic tale over in her mind. But always, the terrifying something eluded her. She knew only that Slade might die and that she had never even told him she loved him. Between her deep grief at the baby Toby's death and the long, hard hours she and Slade had worked during the harvest, the time had never seemed quite right, somehow.

Had she now left it too late, after all? Rachel couldn't live with that. The thought gnawed at her so, that she almost saddled her mare right then to ride to Slade's farm. Then she realized that he was probably asleep and that the youngsters certainly were, and she didn't want to wake everybody up and have an audience present when she told the gunslinger what was in her heart. She would tell him tomorrow, Rachel decided, first thing. God owed her that chance, didn't He? Surely, He couldn't be so cruel as to take Toby away from her, and then take Slade, too, before she had even told him she loved him. No, she couldn't believe that. She wouldn't accept it. She would find a way, somehow.

Off in the distance, heat lightning flashed like a wondrous display of fireworks in the black night sky. But neither thunder boomed nor rain fell, and Rachel shivered at the realization. Something ominous was building up in the atmosphere, she thought. All her earlier terror returning, she went into the house to bed. Still, it was a long time before she slept that night, and when she finally did, it was an uneasy slumber, one troubled by dreams of Slade standing on the prairie beneath a roiling black sky, while a shadowy figure laughed and his revolver shot flames.

In the morning, the sky was leaden, a darkness slowly massing in the distance, as of rain clouds; and the air was thick and muggy, the wind sluggish and oppressive, almost still, the unnatural calm that presages a summer storm. From atop her horse, Sunflower, Rachel scanned the horizon anxiously, fearing that a horrendous cloudburst, or worse, was in the offing. Still, she pressed on determinedly, undeterred from her mission. It would not be the first time she had been soaked by a thunderstorm. Doubtless, it would not be the last.

Eve had told Rachel that Slade had ridden out earlier that morning—not toward town, but toward the distant fields. He had been carrying two large sacks of bottles and tins cans with him. So Eve had felt he must be going to do some practice shooting to warm up before meeting Digger Thibeaux. That was how Rachel found the gunslinger, firing at the bottles and tin cans he had lined up on a jagged fieldstone outcrop on a small rise on the prairie.

He glanced at her sharply as she approached and dismounted. Then, his face closed, unreadable, he studiously looked down at the pistol he held and began deliberately to eject its spent cartridges and reload its chambers.

"You have wasted your time coming here, Rachel," he told her curtly. "I will not be dissuaded from my purpose."

"I know that."

At that, he was silent for a moment. Then he spun the revolver's cylinder experimentally and, satisfied, dropped the gun back into his holster. Arms folded, he turned to face her.

"Then, why *have* you come?" he asked, staring at her coolly.

Rachel had not seen this hard side of him for many a long day now, and it made her feel awkward and uncomfortable. She found that in the face of his implacable distance, she could not simply blurt out her love for him. She did not know what to say, what to do. Almost, she wished she had not come. Yet she could not bring herself just to get back on her mare and ride away. She swallowed hard. Then she spoke.

"I—I came to—to tell you good-bye, in case—in case—" Rachel broke off, biting her lip, tears stinging her eyes. Then, her voice tremulous, she cried, "Oh, Slade! Why must you be so hard now, when you must know how I—how I— I don't deserve that! I know I don't—"

"No, you don't," he muttered as he moved swiftly to enfold her in his arms, clasping her to his chest, his lips against her hair. "I'm sorry, sweetheart. I'm sorry. If I'm hard, it's because I fear that, otherwise, I'll break, that I won't be strong enough to ride off and leave you, and I must—Rachel, you do understand that I have to go, don't you? And why?"

"Yes. Yes. I understand, and I hate it, because I don't want you to go—Oh, Slade, I'm so afraid. So afraid—You will be careful, won't you?"

"Yes, I'll be careful, I promise." He was silent for a time, holding her trembling body against his tightly, as though he could not bear to part from her. His face was buried in her hair, his eyes were closed, and his hand stroked her tresses lightly. Then, at last, his attention caught by the nervous nicker of his stallion, Slade glanced up. He swore softly, dumbfounded at the incredible, fearsome sight that met his eyes. "Jesus Christ," he breathed. "What in the hell is that?"

Rachel turned, her face blanching, her heart leaping to her throat as she gazed at the scene behind her. The sky as far as she could see looked like a massive bruise. It had turned a pale, sickly green shot through with thin veins of yellowish grey, and on the horizon was an unbelievably gargantuan purplish black darkness, like Tyrian dye boiling over, swelling, spreading, seeping, staining the whole of the endless firmament. The torpid wind that had slogged its way earlier across the plains had died, and that in itself was chilling, for the prairie was never still. Yet now, frighteningly, there was not the slightest sound or movement anywhere. The plains were still with a silence that was deafening, terrifying, for it was as though the very earth itself, in its entirety, had somehow been suddenly smothered.

Breathless, Rachel and Slade stared at the behemoth blotting out the sky, awed and totally diminished by its sheer magnitude and power as it swept toward them, gobbling up the celadon firmament, like a dense fog rolling in from a sea. Yet this was not the lowering of maddened thunderheads preparing to split open and disgorge their contents. No erratic forks of lightning shattered this colossal cloud; nor did the air echo with the rumble and crash of thunder. On cat's paws, it seemed, the titanic thing came, creeping quickly and stealthy as a cougar pouncing upon its prey. Slade had never in his life seen anything like it. But Rachel had.

"It's a tornado." She spoke grimly, her ears popping from the sudden pressure against them. "We've got to get back to the house, to the root cellar, where we'll be safe."

As one, they raced for their horses, which were now glassily white-eyed and whinnying shrilly with instinctive fear, dancing and prancing so skittishly that both Rachel and Slade had difficulty mounting and controlling the animals. Fortune reared, and Sunflower bucked. Then both took off at a dead run across the prairie. Yet even so, looking back apprehensively over her shoulder, Rachel knew in her heart that it was too late. Even now, the amorphous mass was upon them, roiling and shuddering as it spasmed and strained to reveal its true self to them—a swirling, satanic spawn of demonic might and hellish rage, a giant saucer spinning in the sky, lurching and twirling like a dervish, expanding, stretching, lengthening into a funnel that spiraled ferociously downward to drill the earth.

And then the sound came.

It was the droning of a zillion locusts, the buzzing of ten times as many bees or bluebottle flies. Impossibly, it grew louder, and louder still—until it was the clamor of a thousand prairie winds, all whining and snarling and howling in unison, a terrible, rasping chorus, a tremendous, horrible wailing of countless devilish voices raised in one furious, all-powerful shriek that exploded across the plains as the earth and sky were fiendishly, unnaturally, connected.

Immediately, the hungry hound of hell feasted, sucking into its hollow gullet all that lay in its path, devouring dirt and debris, fattening its ghostly body until it darkened and materialized into the mammoth, coiling snake of a cyclone that it was, slithering and undulating, its deadly, diabolical tongue striking helter-skelter at whatever took its capricious fancy as it lunged and gyrated across the plains, its body thickening and bloating grossly as it stuffed itself.

"Ride, Rachel, ride!" Slade shouted above its dreadful rattle, its hissing roar, as he glanced back and saw the hideous freak of nature that had descended from the sky to the ground and that now pursued them relentlessly. "Ride for your life!"

"No! No! We can't outrun it, Slade!" she screamed, the words ripped from her mouth by the ungodly twister. "That's what killed my parents! They tried to outrun one! They waited until it was too late to find shelter! Get down off your horse! Get down, Slade!"

Even as she spoke, Rachel was jerking her mare to a halt, winding her reins quickly around the saddle horn, and dismounting. Her feet hardly skimmed the ground before Sunflower bolted, leaving her behind. Slade cursed, thinking that she was crazy, clean out of her mind, and that, now, Fortune would have to carry them both. He yanked the horse around, galloping back to retrieve her. But she refused to be lifted onto the stallion.

"Get down, Slade!" she screamed again. "Get down, or you'll be killed!"

The gunslinger knew he could not abandon her to save himself, and finally, thinking that at least they would perish together, he swung from the saddle, wrapped his reins about the saddle horn, and turned Fortune loose. Rachel's long hair had been torn from its pins by the wind and now billowed and eddied about her wildly, making her appear like the madwoman Slade thought her to be. She had her back to the tornado, and her skirts stood out stiffly before her, like a flag whipping in the wind. She staggered forward uncontrollably, fighting to stay upright, as, with both hands, she pushed her streaming hair back from her face, squinting her eyes against the dust that whirled about them both, nearly blinding them, stinging their bodies, like a spray of buckshot blasted from a shotgun.

"There!" she cried, pointing. "The buffalo wallow."

Compelled into a crouch now, she stumbled toward it, Slade's arms around her, helping her, trying to shield her from some of the dirt and wind. But even he was not strong enough to stand against the monumental force that at last knocked them to their knees. They crawled the last few yards into the shallow depression, then flattened themselves against its very bottom, Slade's body half covering Rachel's.

The cyclone was now dark as a night sky, made so by the

tons of rich black topsoil it had sucked up its enormous, gaping maw from the plains, so that, despite the dust, Rachel and Slade could see clearly that it was headed straight toward them. Yet they could do nothing but hope and pray. They were impotent, as all are impotent, in the face of God's power and wrath; and they thought themselves surely doomed as they waited for the twister to smite them. Their hearts pounded as one against each other, racing with fear, and with a strange, wild, reckless excitement, also, as though if they must die, it would take something with the might of a tornado to kill them.

It was fast closing in on them, they knew. The noise of it was deafening now, as though a leviathan locomotive were bearing down on them, its whistle blaring, the ground thrumming beneath the hundreds of wheels churning along its track. And then, suddenly, it was upon them, a huge black monster barreling up over the crest of the buffalo wallow. Such a stupendous pressure crushed them then that their eardrums nearly burst and their breath was violently expelled from their bodies as they were mashed flat against the earth. Grit blinded and scoured them unmercifully, and they clung to each other tightly as each tried futilely to protect the other. In that moment, they knew nothing but the awesome, inconceivable power of the brutal, ungovernable entity beneath which they paled into absolute insignificance. They waited to die, to be snatched up and hurled into infinite oblivion by the force that assailed them. In that fleeting eternity, sweet, shared memories engulfed them. Each ached with love for the other, and bitterly regretted not speaking of what their hearts held. Now, it was too late.

But then, hard on the heels of this understanding came the knowledge that death had chosen not to take them, that they were to be spared, after all; for instead of augering its way down the hillock to the bottom of the buffalo wallow, the cyclone arbitrarily skipped over them to the knoll upon the other side. It poised there for a moment, as though surveying its surroundings. Then, without warning, it veered sharply away, embarking upon a new course of destruction. It would be miles away before it finally lost its momentum and, ripping free of both the ground and the sky, collapsed like a squashed spring, revolving ever more slowly until at last it broke apart completely and dissipated into nothingness.

A hush fell, as though the earth now breathed again, though not loudly. The dark firmament lightened as the sun struggled to pierce the few remaining clouds and the thin veil of dust that floated in the air.

For a long while after the twister had wended its way across the prairie, Rachel and Slade lay still and silent, not quite believing that it had passed them by, that they had survived its tumultuous, unbridled fury. Yet to her astonishment, Rachel could still hear her heart throbbing, and Slade's, and feel his breath warm against her skin, so she supposed they must be alive, after all.

A tide of emotion such as she had never before known rushed through her then, as fierce and invigorating as the tornado itself. She felt almost a goddess to have lived through it—unscathed. *Unscathed!* The blood roared in her ears at the realization, rushed vitally through her body as though vesting her with some great, mystical power; and as she slowly turned and looked into Slade's gleaming eyes, she saw he felt it, too, and understood. He must have felt it many times as a gunslinger, this staring into the face of death and triumphing over it. But for Rachel, it was an exhilarating first and she wanted to share it with him. With all her heart and soul, she wanted *him*.

The cyclone had brought home to her again how swiftly and mercilessly death could come—for her, for those she loved. Now, Rachel knew without a doubt that if Slade were killed today in the forthcoming duel with Digger Thibeaux, she wanted the memory of his pressing her down into the sweet summer grass and making love to her. She wanted it tucked away in her mind for all time. She wanted to know that, if only for a little while, he had been hers, all hers, only hers—no matter what.

"I want you, Slade," she breathed. "Take me. Make love to me. Please."

For a timeless moment, he stared down at her, his gaze searching her joyous countenance intently, taking in the dishevelment of the long golden hair tangled about her like stalks of ripe wheat, making him long to bury his face in it, to burrow his fingers through it and wrap it about his throat. He could drown in the green, shimmering depths of her eyes, Slade thought. The nostrils of her finely chiseled retroussé nose were flared with the elation of survival, and, now, too, with anticipation, as though something else were slowly wakening inside her, something that quickened her breath and made her heart beat fast. . . .

Desire. It was as Rachel had said. She wanted him. Slade could feel it in the way she trembled beneath him. She was one with the land, and she vibrated so with life that it threatened to burst from her, to spill out of her in a torrent; and she instinctively sought release. This, the gunslinger understood as well as he had understood her reaction the night Toby had died. But in her response today, there was no grief, no weakness, no shame. This expression of passion, she would not regret.

His eyes darkened, and in that moment, Rachel knew he would not deny her. A wild, atavistic thrill shot through her at the recognition. Her lips parted in breathless expectation as, with a low growl, Slade fell upon her blindly, his mouth claiming savage possession of hers. With every fiber of her being, she met and gloried in his assault, opening herself to him, receiving him with eager lips and welcome arms as she molded her body to his, thinking how well they fit together, as though they were made for each other.

Kissing, clutching, they rolled and tumbled, each tearing frantically at the other's clothes until both lay naked and unashamed upon the prairie. Slade's breath caught in his throat at the sight of Rachel, for she was golden as the plains, more beautiful even than he had ever imagined. Urgently, he reached for her, and just as urgently, she came into his arms, not knowing then where she ended and Slade began. Flesh to flesh, they melded—tasting, touching, taking, giving.

The violence of her longing, her passion, her need overwhelmed Rachel. She had not known that it would be like this, a wildness, a madness consuming her, overwhelming all her defenses, leaving her exposed and vulnerable—and uncaring that she was so. Her heart beat frenziedly in her breast; her pulse raced crazily, hammering in her ears and in her throat, making her feel faint and light-headed, as though she had run a long distance and could not catch her breath. Feverishly, she strained against Slade's ardent mouth and tongue and hands, seeking more.

His fingers tunneled through her unbound hair, raising her face to his. Boldly, his tongue teased her lips, outlining their shape, taunting their corners before urging her mouth to open so he might explore the softness that quivered and yielded beneath his demanding lips. His tongue darted greedily in and out of her mouth, ravaging the dark, moist cavern expertly until Rachel moaned low in her throat and kissed him back fervidly, her tongue wreathing his until they both gasped for breath.

Sensuously, his lips sucked hers, his mustache tickling her. His teeth nibbled her mouth, as though he would devour her—and perhaps he would, Slade thought in some dim corner of his mind, for his hunger for her was a driving need that had long badly wanted sating. Again and again, he kissed her, savoring the honeyed taste of her as his tongue delved between her soft, pliant lips, rough, insistent, dizzying her, arousing within her all those exquisite emotions and yearnings only he knew how to evoke.

Rachel's fingers crept up to enmesh themselves in his shaggy mane of black hair, pulling him closer as his mouth seared its way across her cheek to her temple. He buried his face in her hair, inhaling deeply the lilac scent of her mingled with the sweat that set her body glistening in the sultry air.

"Rachel honey," Slade murmured hoarsely against her ear, his warm breath sending a thrill through her, making her shudder. *"Ma chérie, mon amoureuse!"*

He groaned and whispered to her in French, as though English could not possibly express his emotions. She did not understand any of the words. She did not care. The sweet, lilting sound of them was music to her ears as he kissed her, caressed her, increasing her desire for him with every passing moment.

His lips lit a trail of fire down the slender column of her throat to the pulse fluttering like a moth at its hollow. The heat of his tongue burned her there, while his hands roamed tantalizingly over her body, gliding over her breasts. She inhaled sharply as the wind swept across her bare skin, brushing her nipples, as Slade brushed them with his palms, lightly, lingeringly, before he cupped her firm, full breasts, his thumbs flicking their tiny buds. Brazenly, his mouth traveled down the valley between her breasts to one rosy crest. He took it between his lips, grazing it with his teeth as he drew it into the warm, wet cavity of his mouth. His tongue traced a languid circle about her areola before scorching its center, setting Rachel aflame. Waves of fiery pleasure radiated through her body. She could feel her nipple stiffening, growing hard as a sweet chickasaw plum ripe to the point of bursting as, on and on, he sucked it, laving it with his tongue until she thought she could bear no more and writhed beneath him wantonly, her fingers entangling his hair. Like wildfire, his lips scorched their way across her chest, enveloping her other nipple, igniting it as he had its twin. Tightly, he embraced her.

The dark hair that matted his chest was like silk beneath her palms and against the sensitive tips of her breasts as her hands slid around his smooth, bare back. Rachel could feel his muscles bunching and rippling beneath her fingers, and she raked his back lightly with her nails, whimpering as Slade sank his teeth into the sensitive curve where her nape met her shoulder. His bite turned into a kiss as he nuzzled her neck. Then he captured her mouth with his again, his tongue shooting deep between her lips, while his hands once more fastened on her breasts. His fingers fondled their rigid peaks enticingly. As his thumbnails skimmed them, the tips contracted sharply with delight, and Slade's loins tightened with matching passion. His palms lifted Rachel's breasts covetously, pushed them up, positioning them for his mouth as he lowered his head and sucked her nipples avidly once more.

Time passed. She scarcely knew how much as she lay in his arms and let him do as he wished with her. She knew nothing but the sensations that coursed through her as he set his brand upon her. He was like a fine elderberry wine, intoxicating her. She was breathless in his wake, discovering him, as he did her. She was like the prairie grasses twining about the wind, her long hair a web of wildflowers, ensnaring him, drawing him to her, wrapping them both in a gossamer cocoon. Her lips and tongue and hands flitted like a butterfly's wings over Slade's body, tasting and touching him everywhere she could reach, he and her instincts guiding her. She relished the feel of him, his skin smooth as fine leather in places, hard as buffalo horn in others where old scars were white against his darkness, testament to his will to survive. She marveled at the strength, the power of him, and how she tamed it, if only for this moment, as he tamed her.

Yet even so, there was in their mating the wildness of the wind, the savagery of the plains. Each had been too long denied, and now, like the tornado, they took fiercely, hungrily, all that lay bare for the taking. Never had they felt like this before, known what they knew in each other. Bigger than them both, passion consumed them utterly as they turned and twisted and tangled, each leaving no plane, no angle, no curve of the other unknown, unmapped.

"God, how I want you, Rachel honey," Slade muttered thickly. "Touch me, sweetheart. See how I desire you? Ah, yes, Rachel, yes!"

Deep within the secret heart of her, a burning desire was kindled and took flame. As though sensing her desperate need, he covered her body with his. One knee nudged her thighs apart, opening her to the onslaught of his fingers as he sought the swollen folds beneath the velvet curls that nested between her legs. Gently, he cupped her womanhood, brushed her with his palm. A low, primitive moan issued from Rachel's throat at this intimate invasion before Slade silenced her mouth with his own as he began tenderly, rhythmically, to stroke her, his thumb rotating over the tiny nub that was the key to her pleasure. Unable to prevent herself, she whimpered and undulated beneath him, her head thrashing from side to side as he tormented her sweetly.

Then, at last, his tongue cleaved her lips as, simultaneously, he probed her deeply, finding her hot and wet with wanting. Rachel gasped as, with his encroaching fingers, he mimicked the movements of his tongue, swirling, fluttering, readying her to receive him. And all the while, his thumb flicked the small button that sharpened her desire for him, honed it to a keen edge.

His free hand wrapped in her hair, he kissed her, ravishing her with his tongue. His knee compelled her thighs farther apart. His thumb continued its teasing of her sensitive mound, and his fingers caused the agonizing throbbing at her core to heighten with unbearable intensity. On and on, he taunted her, until Rachel could no longer even think, could only feel, engulfed by the torrid emotion now ruthlessly sweeping her along in its wake, as though she were being buffeted once more by the tornado. She felt as though she were on fire; sparks showered within her, embers of desire that grew hotter and hotter, lighting some fuse within her, which she felt would soon cause her to explode.

She cried out her surrender, and with primal male instinct, Slade sensed she was nearing her peak. Trembling with passion and the effort it had taken to control himself until this moment, he poised himself above her. The tip of his maleness found her, piercing her so suddenly and violently that Rachel felt as though she were being impaled by him, then split asunder. But she did not care. Her breath caught in her throat as white-hot pain and pleasure burst within her. She bucked uncontrollably against him, aiding unwittingly his penetration of her. Swiftly, he withdrew, then drove hard and deep again into her.

"Now, it's done, Rachel," Slade whispered triumphantly against her throat, "and you're mine, only mine, forever mine."

He lay still atop her a while then, accustoming her to the feel of him inside her, while his mouth pillaged hers, nuzzled her nape and breasts, and sucked her nipples until she felt as though she were a boneless mass, fluid as quicksilver, tingling all over, her body screaming for release. Then, after a time, he began to thrust in and out of her again, powerfully, the muscles flexing sinuously in his back and arms. Intuitively, she arched her hips against him, seeking and then finding the rhythm as he rocked her, plummeted down into her over and over, faster and faster, until the world spun away and she reached blindly for some nameless thing she felt she must attain or die. Then, suddenly, she stiffened beneath him, a thousand splendorous fireworks bursting inside the black void of her, taking her breath away.

From someplace far beyond the prairie, it seemed, she felt Slade's fingers tighten on her painfully, bruising her, magnifying the fervor of what they shared between them. He groaned, and an uncontrollable shudder racked the entire length of his body as he spilled himself within her, then finally was still.

It was ended. Beneath him, Rachel lay drained and exhausted, her heart still thrumming erratically in her breast, her pulse still racing. She could feel Slade's chest pounding hard against her own until he slowly withdrew from her and pulled her into his sheltering embrace, cradling her head against his shoulder. Her arms tightened around him, as though she would never let him go. For all too soon, reality intruded as Rachel thought of losing Slade now, after what they had shared, and she cursed his past and his pride, though they were what had made him the man she loved.

"I love you, Slade," she murmured fiercely. "I love you, and I don't want to lose you!"

"Oh, Rachel honey." The gunslinger spoke gently. "Before today, I would have given anything to hear you say those words. But not now. I'd rather you hated me now, because I don't want you to grieve for me if I'm killed—"

"No, don't say that! Don't say that! You won't be killed! You won't! You told me you had a gun hand like greased lightning, Slade! And I saw you! I saw you shoot on the Fourth of July in town! You hit your mark every time, and you were the fastest one there!"

"Yeah, I'm fast all right," he agreed slowly, a muscle working in his jaw. "But Digger was always faster."

Now, suddenly, Rachel knew what it was that had so terrified her about the story of Slade's past. If Slade had shot first, Thibeaux wouldn't have lived to murder Thérèse Duvalier. Digger had been faster off the mark than Slade.

"But—but when you faced Digger the first time, Slade, you used standard dueling pistols, didn't you? You didn't draw from holsters, did you?"

Slade glanced down, smiling, and kissed her on the tip of her nose.

"Sweetheart, you are the smartest woman I know. You're absolutely right, and that's what I'm counting on—that Digger can't outdraw me."

But between them lay the unspoken question: What if he could?

Rachel's heart lurched in her breast at the thought. In her mind was a picture of Slade falling, blood staining the ground beneath him, while Digger Thibeaux laughed and his revolver shot flames. Her dream. Her nightmare. Now, Rachel knew, beyond a shadow of a doubt, what Thérèse Duvalier had felt that night beneath the elms in New Orleans: fear that Slade, the man she loved, would be killed, taken from her for all time. At the last, she had not thought. She had not reasoned. She had only acted—blindly, out of fear—and been killed herself for it, murdered by Digger Thibeaux. Rachel shivered, as though a goose had just walked over her grave, and Slade's arms tightened about her.

He kissed her deeply. Then, wordlessly, he took her again, more gently; and this time, there was no pain, only a bittersweet poignancy that it might be the last time he ever kissed her, held her, pressed her down into the summer grass, and took her to the stars and back again. When it was done, they rose and dressed, and he spoke.

"Rachel," he said quietly, "I never told you before, because somehow, I never could find the words. But now, I want you to know that I love you. I've loved you for a long time and just didn't want to let go of Thérèse because of what I felt I owed her. But today, one way or another, my debt will be paid." He paused for a moment. Then he continued.

"It's funny, because I've felt for quite a while that she was here in my heart, trying to tell me something, and now, I understand what she's been saying to me: It's that she's dead and that I can't ever bring her back again, no matter what I do, and so I should forget the past and make a new life for myself with someone else. Because if you love someone, you want him to be happy, not to spend the rest of his life, grieving over you. Do you know what I'm trying to say to you, Rachel? If I don't come back, remember me, yes. But don't cut yourself off from other men. Don't make me a shrine. Find someone and build a life together with him. Be happy. Will you promise me that, sweetheart?"

"Oh, Slade, no! How can I?"

"You can. You will. Because you're strong, and I love you, and that's what I want for you if I don't come back. So promise me. Please."

"All right, Slade," Rachel choked out softly. "I promise."

He smiled tenderly, his eyes filled to the brim with his deep, abiding love for her. Gently, he kissed away the tears that streamed down her cheeks.

"Thérèse would have liked you, Rachel," he observed, his voice husky with emotion. "She would have liked you very much, indeed."

Then, lest he break down, Slade turned and walked rapidly away, leaving her standing there, weeping, on the prairie.

It was the hardest thing he ever did.

Chapter Twenty-seven

Digger Thibeaux had not changed, except to grow older and more dissipated. He had been handsome in his youth, a tall man, broad of shoulder, narrow of hip, with jet-black hair and eyes, and pale, fair skin. But though he had not lived a hard life, he now looked as though he had. Anyone seeing him would have guessed him to be forty-five years of age, not the thirty-five he really was. Webs of fine wrinkles splayed from his malicious black eyes, which were bloodshot, rimmed with red, and puffy with bags from too many late nights of carousing. He was pasty-faced, and the deep, hard grooves that bracketed his mouth gave him a severe expression. Indeed, Digger rarely smiled unless he thought he was about to get the best of someone. Then his grin was chilling. His physique was still trim. He burned up too much energy with his vices to grow fat. But there was a waxy, ghostlike quality to him now; he seemed, some said, like a walking cadaver.

Though his body might be wasting away, his inherited insanity was growing, twisting his mind into convolutions of hatred. He was a product of his haughty French family's efforts to keep their bloodlines blue by intermarrying with their cousins, the Lamartines. Unbelievably, he was saner than most of his relatives, the most lunatic of whom were now either dead or locked away in prisons or asylums, where they quite rightly belonged. Digger, however, possessed a certain shrewd, ingenious cunning that often enabled him to pass as merely eccentric. This had shielded him from his relatives' appropriate fates—though he had certainly committed more than a few crimes for which he would be imprisoned or hanged were he ever to be caught, and he surely ought to be in an asylum.

The great love of his life, he had convinced himself, had been Thérèse Duvalier; and it was true that the night she had died, some vital link between his brain and reality had snapped, leaving him even more deranged than he had previously been. In his more lucid moments, Digger realized he had murdered her, had shot her down in cold blood, and this certain knowledge drove him into fits of black depression for days following the remembrance. The remainder of the time, he ascribed her untimely death to Slade Maverick, and it was during one of these increasingly more frequent periods of delusion that he had run into Adam Keife at a local faro table and had issued the challenge to Slade.

Even on his maddest days, Digger never mistook what the three-of-hearts playing card meant to him, for the trey had initiated the first challenge and, as a result, Slade had fired the bullet that had shattered a goodly portion of Digger's right hip. Afterward, Digger was able to walk only with the aid of a cane, and though he found it amusing that, with his malacca sword stick, he was able to dispatch so many unsuspecting fools to their Maker, he never quite forgot that the three of hearts was the cause of his now having three legs.

This deep, festering wound had prompted him to issue the second challenge to Slade. But now, on this late August afternoon, as Digger stood on the prairie, preparing to face down the gunslinger, he had a niggling suspicion that perhaps he ought to have let well enough alone. Slade did not look at all like the rash hothead he had been in his youth, and gazing at him, Digger was surprised to feel a faint, unfamiliar shiver of apprehension chase down his spine.

Each man was positioned so the sun was not in his eyes, and each stood, legs spread, waiting. But there, the similarities between them ended. Slade was cool, implacable, his thumbs hooked in his belt, while he waited for Digger to draw. Thibeaux himself shifted and fidgeted as though he were an opium smoker in need of a pipe, and anyone watching would have thought him too tense to shoot straight. But as Slade had known Digger all his life, he did not make so foolish a mistake, for this very error had put several others before him in their graves. Digger's nervous energy just never allowed him to be still.

No wonder Adam had initially scorned Thibeaux as a dude, Slade thought; his fancy taste in clothes had not changed. He was even wearing a silk bowler hat. But there was nothing amusing about the Smith & Wesson American revolver that rode high on his belly and slightly to the left, butt end facing out of his holster. It was an unusual way to carry a gun, but Slade had seen the technique before and knew that a man who employed it could be dangerous. He never took his eyes off Digger for an instant.

The bright August sun that had appeared following the tornado beat down upon the plains relentlessly now, sheening the skin of both men with sweat. Heat rose in shimmering waves from the land, blurring the images of the two who stood upon the prairie. Each man's figure wavered before the other's eyes, and in that moment, in the minds of both, the years fell away, as though the ceaselessly turning wheel of time had somehow reversed itself, flying back ten years.

Moonlight streamed through the branches of the elms, dappling the infamous grassy meadow with pieces of silver, and wisps of Spanish moss danced on the wind. Two men stood in the clearing. A woman in a white gown waited in a carriage under the trees. All was still, save for the rustling of the leaves and the soft lap of the Mississippi River against a shore somewhere in the distance. The air was fraught with tension. Suddenly, the woman could stand it no longer. She screamed and leaped from the carriage to race across the glade. A dueling pistol shot flames. The woman stumbled and fell, blood staining her white gown with crimson, flying up to fleck with scarlet the spray of gardenias she had pinned in her long black hair. Thérèse! Thérèse! The man who had fired the gun laughed, his teeth flashing white in the moonlight, the horrible mocking sound ringing across the meadow. . . .

The maniacal laughter echoed across the prairie, clamoring in Slade's ears like a death knell as Digger jeered at him and began suddenly to shout insults to rile him and make him edgy. Thibeaux yelled dreadful affronts, many of them denigrating Thérèse Duvalier, others boasting of heinous crimes, all described in grisly, gory detail. They turned Slade's stomach, making him feel as sick as he had been that night under the elms.

His hands trembled, his belly roiled, his knees shook. If only he hadn't drunk so much at the gaming hell. He felt as though he were going to vomit. Digger's dark visage blurred before his eyes, then cleared as he wiped away the sweat that blinded him. Beyond, in the shadows, Thérèse's face was ashen with fear for him. She believed that he was about to die, that Digger would kill him. His stomach heaved at the notion. He had seen men die, in the war, torn apart by bullets, their blood running red upon the ground. He was young. He was afraid. He did not want to die. He waited for Digger to fire. . . .

Thibeaux went on laughing, flinging abuse at him, like a madman. Digger was, Slade realized, quite mad, scarcely responsible for his actions—though it did not make him any less dangerous; indeed, it made him more. He was wanted, dead or alive, for murder, armed robbery, and several other assorted crimes in at least five states and territories. There was a price on his head of a thousand dollars—or so the poster tacked up in Marshal Meagher's office had proclaimed. A thousand dollars would buy a lot of cattle, Slade thought —then hated himself for thinking it. Digger was insane. He needed to be locked away in an asylum, where he would receive medical treatment. Slade ought to pity him and see that he got the care he needed. They had been friends—once. But what was Digger remembering as a sneer crossed his face?

He would kill Thérèse. He decided it spontaneously as he

spied her running across the glade, her white gown fluttering like a moth's wings as it edged too close to a flame. She deserved to die, and Slade, who had once been his friend, deserved to live and suffer her loss, as he, Digger, had suffered it. He aimed his dueling pistol, cocked the hammer, and fired. Thérèse went down in a pool of blood. It flowed from her like a river as her life ebbed away. Soon, she would lie in her grave. Well, wasn't that why they called him "Digger"? A macabre joke. He laughed.

Still laughing, Thibeaux opened his mouth and gibed, "I hear you got yourself a new *petite chérie*, Slade. Why don't we do it like we did in the old days, *mon ami*, and take turns—only this time, I'll cuckold you instead. Sounds like a real good idea, don't it? I just know you'll agree, because it sure would be a shame if your new lady friend was to wind up like Thérèse now, wouldn't it?"

Thérèse falling into a puddle of seeping vermilion, gardenias dripping, himself kneeling, turning her over, only to see that her face was Rachel's face—Slade recoiled, horrified, from the image. Fear and fury such as he had never before felt consumed him. *He's too dangerous to live, my love. Too dangerous to live*—Thérèse's last words before dying. *Forgive me, Thérèse, for being so young and afraid then. I will make it up to you now.* . . .

"You never did know when to keep your mouth shut, Digger," Slade said softly—and then he reached for his guns.

At the log cabin, Rachel waited for Slade, pacing to the wide-open door every two or three minutes to glance outside. Still, there was no rider in sight, and anxiety gnawed at her, pressing her to the edge of hysteria. Hours had passed, a hideous eternity in which she imagined Slade alive but grievously wounded or lying cold and dead. Now, she knew why Thérèse had insisted upon accompanying him on that fatal night to the duel beneath the elms. Anything was better than this endless waiting.

Watching her torment, Fremont sighed and shook his head. Then he knocked the dottle from his pipe, rose from his chair, and crossed the room to lay his hands comfortingly upon her shoulders.

"He'll come, Rachel," he assured her gruffly, his heart aching for her. "Give him time. He'll come."

She blinked back tears.

"And what if he doesn't, Grandpa?" she asked. "What if he doesn't?"

"Then you must face his loss, and accept it—as Slade would have wanted."

"But I love him, Grandpa! I love him so much—"

"I know, Rachel. I know."

They spoke no more, but stood silently, looking out over the prairie, where, on the distant horizon, a cloud of dust now swirled almost like a dust devil. As she shielded her eyes against the glare of the sun, trying to discern the cause of the dust, her heart leaped hopefully for a moment, then sank as she realized the cloud was too large to be accounted for by a single rider. In bitter disappointment, she turned and went back to the kitchen to busy herself with her chores, in a futile attempt to concentrate on anything but Slade.

Suddenly, there was a terrible commotion outside. An awful hammering shook the front of the house, as though someone were trying to knock down the wall. And then Rachel heard the shouting of men and the mooing of cattle. It sounded as though the Wichita stockyards had been transported to her front yard. She rushed to the door of the log cabin and opened her mouth in amazement at what she saw.

Her entire yard was filled with cowpokes hooting and hollering, and cattle milling and mooing—and chomping and trampling what remained of her vegetable patch, too! Rachel's astonishment turned to rage, and she marched outside. Whoever was in charge of this misplaced roundup would get a piece of her mind!

Before she could get any words out, however, the hammering started again as two men nailed to the front of the house a big, painted sign that read: *Heartland Ranch*. It was then that understanding dawned. Whirling about, her heart beginning to soar wildly in her breast, she searched the dusty, cacophonic confusion for the man who must be the cause of all this.

"Slade!" she cried, her eyes lighting with fierce joy when she spotted him calmly hunched in his saddle, that dear, familiar, and positively insolent grin on his handsome face. "Slade!"

She tried frantically to reach him, but the cattle in her path would not move. Finally, Slade scattered them with his stallion and swept her up onto his saddle, where she clung to him unashamedly, sobbing his name over and over, tears of happiness raining down her cheeks. Even Slade's eyes were moist as he embraced her tightly. The cowboys cheered, and Fremont, Poke, and all the children, now gathered outside, clapped their hands.

After a time, Rachel managed to speak.

"Slade Maverick! Just what is this, may I ask?" she inquired tartly, though it was all she could do to repress her smile.

"Well, Rachel Wilder," he drawled, tipping back his hat and leering at her possessively, "just what in the hell does it look like? It's five hundred head of cattle, that's what! And I reckon that makes me the 'only man you're going to marry'!"

"Well!" Rachel sniffed, her eyes dancing. "If that isn't the durnedest proposal I ever heard in my life—"

"Is that a yes, sweetheart?" Slade asked teasingly.

"I guess . . . maybe . . . oh, you fool, you know it is!"

"Then shut up and pucker up, Rachel honey. You're about to be kissed!"

And she did, and she was—and she knew in that moment that there, in the heartland, all her dreams had come true.

EPILOGUE

Heartland

Chapter Twenty-eight

The Prairie, Kansas, 1915

From an open window of her upper-story bedroom in the old white farmhouse she had lived in for the last thirty-five years, Rachel Wilder Maverick gazed down at the front yard below. Touched and pleased, she smiled to herself at the welcome sight that greeted her eyes. Out on the wide, sunny lawn was gathered her huge family—all of them shouting, talking, and laughing boisterously while they cooked the beef barbecue, set up the picnic tables and benches, and played games. They were all together for once, despite the great war going on in Europe and so many of the country's young men joining America's allies far across the Atlantic Ocean.

How wonderful it is to have the entire family assembled here today to help Slade and me celebrate our fortieth wedding anniversary, Rachel thought, her heart replete with happiness. *How nice it is that they all came, every single one of them.*

She could see Adam and Eve, themselves married thirty-seven years now, with their three grown boys (thank heavens, they were *not* named Cain, Abel, and Seth!), the boys' wives, and all their offspring. There were the other six Beechams, each with their spouses and all their offspring; and her own five children—three sons and two daughters—each with their spouses and all their offspring. Rachel and Slade had thirty-eight grandchildren and, so far, fourteen great-grandchildren Slowly, she shook her head with disbelief at the realization It just didn't seem possible.

Where had all the time gone? she wondered. The years just seemed to have flown by somehow, each more swiftly than the last—as though she had looked into her mirror and seen a girl fresh as spring, and then, a few moments later, had turned around, looked again, and seen a woman in the autumn of her life. Yet even so, she found it hard to grasp that she was now fifty-nine years old. *Fifty-nine*! Although Rachel had to admit she *was* starting to feel her age slightly, deep down in her heart, she felt as though she were still just nineteen, still that young, springtime girl Slade Maverick had wooed and won so long ago in 1875.

Dropping the Victorian lace curtain she had pulled back a little to get a clearer view out the window, she moved away to study herself in the tall oak cheval mirror that stood in one corner of the bedroom she had shared with Slade for so many years now. Her long blond hair, swept up into a knot on top of her head, was streaked with more than a few strands whiter than flax now, and there were fine lines around her mint-green eyes. Her gold-dust freckles were these days more brown than gold, as well. But she had aged well, she thought. She was fortunate to have possessed the high cheekbones and the firm jaw that, even now, made her look years younger than she really was. She was still slender and strong, too, from working in the house, and in her flower and vegetable gardens. Today, in honor of this very special occasion, she had donned her ivory wedding gown, yellowed now with age to the color of rich buttermilk. It had a high lace collar, yoke, and cuffs; long, flowing sleeves; and a full, deeply flounced skirt that fell to the floor and that, from the waist down, was gathered at the back in a cascade of bows, ruffles, and silk roses that swept to a short train, all of which had used to emphasize gracefully the small bustle she had once worn with the dress. It was not at all fashionable anymore, with ladies' skirts being so tight and narrow these days and hemlines slowly (and scandalously, in Rachel's opinion) beginning to inch up. But after all these years, the dress still fit.

Staring now at her reflection, she would have lost herself in memories of her wedding day. But suddenly, she heard a sound like gunshots, and then a horn blasting maniacally in the front yard. Someone was yelling for her! Bewildered, she hurried back to the window to see what was causing all the commotion below.

"What in tarnation— Oh, for land's sake!" she exclaimed to herself, as, with one hand, she drew aside the curtain, her other hand going in dismay to her breast. "That durned old man's going to kill himself yet!"

For there was Slade Maverick, her husband of forty years, having the time of his life as he pulled up in a brand spanking new automobile, weaving like a drunk all over the lawn, because they had never owned one of the machines and he didn't know how to drive. He looked as thrilled and delighted as a child on Christmas morning, she thought, his pale grey hair and mustache gleaming like quicksilver in the brilliant afternoon sun, a wide grin plastered on his bronze, weathered face, as he jubilantly blared the car's horn to beat the band —*toot! toot! toot!*—and called at the top of his lungs for Rachel to come outside and see.

Everybody was shouting and laughing as they ran forward to get a better look at the vehicle, then dashed away, shrieking, as it veered this way and that toward them, lurching, grinding, sputtering, and backfiring. The poor chickens that usually strutted all over the yard squawked and flapped their wings, their feathers flying as they fled in fear for their lives; and Rachel saw that a row of one of her neat flower beds was in dire peril of being mowed down like the front line of an army.

"Lord save us!" she muttered to herself, aghast despite her amusement, for at seventy years of age, Slade—not a young man anymore—was as bold and daring as ever. "I guess it's true, and there's no fool like an old fool! I hope to heck he's only borrowed that dreadful contraption!" But still, knowing her husband, she had a rueful, sneaking suspicion that this was not at all the case.

Just then, Rachel's youngest great-grandchild, three-year-old Tobias, came barging through the bedroom door, banging it so hard against the wall as he flung it open that it nearly vibrated off its brass hinges. Wound up, he bounded like a startled jackrabbit around the room and stumbled so over his words in his excitement and glee that he could hardly get them out.

"Grandma! Grandma! Come see! Come see!" He leaped up onto her bed and started jumping up and down exuberantly on the feather mattress, making the springs squeak ominously. "Grandpa's boughten an aut'mobul for you for your an'vers'ry!" He unwittingly confirmed what she had already guessed. Then he hopped off the bed, landing on all fours and skidding slightly on the cheerful braided rag rug upon the floor. "Whooa!" he blurted, squealing and chuckling, as, agilely, he recovered and sprang to his feet. Then, grabbing her hand, he began to haul Rachel impatiently toward the door. "Come on, Grandma! Hurry up! Quick! Quick! Grandpa wants you to come see!"

"I'm too old to move quick," she retorted, as, his high spirits undampened, the boy skipped away and vaulted back onto the bed, "and quit bouncing on my bed like that before you bust the durned slats clean in two! I'm *not* too old to tan your hide good with a willow switch! You see if I'm not, Tobias Maverick!" she threatened, wagging her finger at him reprovingly, though it was all she could do to maintain her severe frown in the face of his giggles.

Of all her grandchildren and great-grandchildren, this bright, energetic little boy with his impish grin and impertinent manner was Rachel's favorite. He had a cap of unruly black curls on his handsome head and a devilish gleam in his big, thickly lashed blue eyes, and he reminded her so much of the baby, Toby, as he might have been had he lived that she never could quite put her whole heart into reprimanding the boy. This, her great-grandchild knew and took shameless advantage of, sweet-talking her and winding her around his little finger as smoothly and charmingly as Slade ever had.

"If you're not too old to whip me with a switch, you're not too old to hurry up, Grandma," Tobias insisted sassily, scrambling off the bed and tugging on her hand again.

"Hmph! You're too smart for your own britches, I'd say! You go on now," she ordered. "Phew! Just watching you's enough to tucker me out. Go on now, I said. Get! I'll be along in a minute." Then, as the boy scampered off, Rachel marched back to the open window, stuck her head out, and shouted, "Quit honking that durned fool horn, Slade Maverick, lessen you want every neighbor within ten miles of here to be deaf by sunset! I'm coming! I'm coming!" After that, she started downstairs, grumbling to herself every step of the way. "Durned old man," she groused under her breath. "Bought *me* a new automobile for our anniversary, did he? Hmph! Bought *himself* one is more like it! I don't like those infernal machines, and I won't have one! A strong team and a stout wagon's good enough for me. Always has been. Always will be. Durned old man. He'll probably kill us both in that crazy contraption!"

The car was gorgeous, a glistening, pale lemon-yellow Packard convertible, with black leather upholstery front and back, brightly polished headlamps, and white rubber tires. Slade had finally managed to bring it to a halt; and now, as Rachel slowly approached, he leaped out of the automobile, came around the other side, and chivalrously opened the door for her, unabashed by the martial glint in her eye.

"Well, what do you think of your anniversary present, sweetheart?" he inquired, beaming with pride and delight. "Isn't she a beauty? I ordered her especially to match the color of your hair. Get in. I'll take you for a spin."

"No, thanks, Slade," Rachel rejected his offer firmly. "I've already seen how you drive, or, rather, how you *can't* drive!"

"Aw, Rachel honey, come on," he drawled, grinning at her insolently, his midnight-blue eyes dancing. "I was just getting warmed up. I've got the hang of it now. Get in, and I'll show you.''

At last, reluctantly and much against her better judgment —because she didn't trust anything not pulled by a horse or a mule and had never thought to live to see the day when vehicles ran of their own accord—Rachel allowed herself to be persuaded into the long, shiny Packard; and Slade took off with a jolt and a bang.

In some respects, things weren't so bad once they eventually got going, because at least they didn't jerk around as much anymore. But Rachel held on tightly to the edge of the car door, lest she somehow fly out, because she had never before gone so fast. She glanced over at the speedometer and saw they were racing along at forty miles per hour, and she nearly shrieked with fright. Then she really did scream, because at about that time, Slade flattened a whole row of poplar saplings planted just that spring, not far from the house; and this calamity sent the automobile into a skid that propelled them straight toward her clothesline.

Rachel didn't even have time to duck before Slade hit the clean laundry wafting on the line and the vehicle was blanketed with fresh white linen. Two sheets tore free of their clothespins, billowing behind the Packard like the trailing tail of a kite for a moment before blowing away as the car plunged on without slowing. Part of the third sheet caught on the brass edging around the windshield. Unfortunately, Rachel, lacking one clothespin when hanging the wash out to dry, had simply tied one corner of the sheet to the wire. She had not expected her demon husband to come plowing along in a Packard, and now, the impetus was such that, before the cotton sheet finally ripped in two, the clothesline was forcibly dragged forward, causing the wooden poles at either end to tilt alarmingly. Rachel heard a sharp *twaaang* and, daring to risk a quick peek over her shoulder, saw that the wire had snapped abruptly in half and that exactly one-third of her clean laundry was now lying in the dirt, while what remained on the other two sagging lines dragged the ground.

"Slade Maverick!" she shrilled, incensed and distressed.

"Slade Maverick! Look what you did, you reckless lunatic! You stop this noisy, good-for-nothing contraption right now, do you hear? It's dangerous! Why, you durned near killed us—"

But after forty years of enduring Rachel's tongue, Slade was immune to its rough edges. Favoring her with a clearly unrepentent glance, he threw back his head, roared with laughter, and then impudently floored the accelerator, causing her to bounce back against the seat and clutch the edge of the car door again to keep from plummeting to the floor.

"I'll tell you what it is, Rachel," he yelled at her over the loud revving of the engine. "We're too confined. This yard is like a damned obstacle course—kids, animals, and plants everywhere you—" He broke off in midsentence, spinning the steering wheel sharply to avoid colliding with a roqueted croquet ball that (in what Rachel was sure was a highly illegal shot) had been smacked arrantly hard away by one of their grandchildren from its advantageous position near a hoop and was now sailing across the lawn at them.

With a thud, the ball struck one of their rear tires. Rachel had a brief glimpse of their grandson Blaze Beecham's half-mirthful, half-stricken face at having inadvertently scored a direct hit, before the automobile charged on. Slade now wisely headed it toward the open prairie, lest it fall victim to a worse disaster.

"Which one of the brazen young hellhounds was that?" he barked, scowling at the injury to the Packard. "Blaze, wasn't it? Damned whippersnapper! I tell you what, Rachel: I don't know what the world's coming to. This new generation is a disgrace! They've got no manners, no respect a-tall for a man's property. Why, Blaze might have dented one of the fenders of my brand new car—and I swear he was chortling about it, the rascal!"

"I thought you said that it was *my* car," Rachel pointed out, turning away so her husband wouldn't see the knowing smile of amusement that curved her own mouth.

"What? Oh, yes. So I did. And it is. It is," Slade hastened to assure her. "But—but . . . well, what I mean is . . . you don't really want to *drive* it . . . do you?'' He peered over at her anxiously, as though half afraid she might actually seize possession of his new toy.

Rachel bit her lip so hard that she drew blood in an attempt to stifle the laughter that threatened to bubble from her throat.

''*Drive* it!'' she cried, eyeing him askance. ''Why, I didn't even want to come along for the ride!''

Still, it wasn't as bad as she had originally feared, she was forced to admit. Indeed, despite the fact that the speedometer had now climbed to the horrendous speed of fifty miles per hour, tooling along in the Packard was actually proving to be quite a pleasure, now that Slade was truly beginning to get the knack of it.

The hot August sun beating down from the pale blue sky, and the wind whipping over the vehicle felt good against Rachel's skin as they sped across the plains. All around them, tall branches of hemp dogbane and white prickly poppy blossomed, mingling with fruited Illinois bundleflower, splendrous snow-on-the-mountain, delicate sprays of elderberry, and fluffy field snake cotton. Tiny azure pitcher sage and devil's-claw, with its long, hooked horns, sprouted amid beautiful rosy Indian blanket, purplish pink dotted gayfeather, and florets of ironweed. Now, too, were all the varieties of the sunflowers in bloom—the common, the Maximillian, and, prettiest of all, Rachel thought, the prairie sunflower, like a golden sunburst. In the distance, she could see squares of brown that were newly harvested fields, devoid now of their amber grain, and the pungent scent of freshly cut alfalfa was carried to her nostrils by the wind.

As the car swept on, she spied an old log building just ahead of them on the plains. Half tumbled down, it was all that remained of what had once been her barn when Fremont, Poke, and Seeks were alive. They lay now, all three, under the grassy earth that covered a certain prairie hillock, beneath the lone tree that had grown tall over the years and that still stood strong, despite being twice struck by lightning. Her old log cabin was gone, too. She didn't know why Slade hadn't sent some of their hired hands out here to tear down the barn, also. It was no doubt in such sad shape that it constituted a hazard.

Even as the thought crossed her mind, Rachel saw a large, ponderous animal suddenly come plodding out from behind the barn, directly into the path of the onrushing automobile.

"Chili Pepper!" she screeched, startled and upset. "Good Lord, Slade, it's Chili Pepper!"

She didn't know what her feisty old prize bull was doing way out here in the middle of nowhere. All that flashed through her brain after that was the knowledge that he must have somehow escaped from his pasture and the sudden, horrifying realization that Slade could not possibly halt the vehicle in time to avoid hitting the beast. She screamed as her husband stamped on the brake, his powerful arm shooting out to slam her against the seat, preventing her from being thrown through the windshield as the car lurched violently, swerving, then sheering into a spin. Terrified, the bull let out a deep, angry bellow and took off running, while the automobile careened around and around, Slade wrestling with the steering wheel for control. It seemed like forever, but in reality, just seconds later, the Packard managed to straighten itself out. But to Rachel's horror, it kept right on rolling uncontrollably forward, and before Slade could bring the vehicle to a stop, it barreled directly through the closed wooden doors of the old barn, shattering them.

Inside the building, there was nothing but a massive, forgotten haystack, which the car rammed, sending a flock of startled pigeons twittering up from the rafters to wing their way toward the wide, jagged gaps in the decaying roof. As it burrowed into the haystack, the automobile halted abruptly, hay cascading down over its windshield and long yellow hood, nearly burying Rachel and Slade in the avalanche.

After a moment, they realized shakily that they were still alive and sat up, coughing and sneezing as they worked their way from beneath the pile of hay to stare at each other silently, each so relieved that the other was unhurt that there were not words for the love and emotion that overwhelmed them.

Then, finally, cringing guiltily at the look on Rachel's

ashen face, Slade murmured dryly but contritely, "Well, that was sure one hell of a ride, wasn't it, sweetheart?"

"You durned old man!" she shrieked, enraged and frightened. Tears streamed down her face as she suddenly began to beat wildly with her fists upon his chest. "You durned old man! You purt near killed me—and, worse, my best prize bull, too!"

And then, somehow, she was enfolded in her husband's arms, trembling and sobbing quietly against his chest, while he stroked her hair soothingly and crooned sweet words of love and apology to her. And all was right with her world again. After a time, recovered and placated, she drew away and sniffed.

"Well, so much for my anniversary present!" she averred, gazing at the wrecked Packard.

"Yes, well"—Slade squirmed on the seat uncomfortably—"I'm afraid I have a small confession to make about that, Rachel honey," he announced in his best wheedling tone. "You see, I really bought the car for myself, because I knew how much you'd want me to have it for an anniversary present, sweetheart, but that, despite our having money to burn, you just wouldn't quite be able to bring yourself to open up your purse wide enough for the moths to flutter out, lessen there might not be enough left over to stash in the tin box on the shelf in the kitchen so you'd always feel safe. I, on the other hand, can't reasonably see us sitting with forty thousand acres and damned near a half a million bucks in our bank account and not enjoying some of it while we're still alive to do so! So I got myself the Packard, from you; and I got this for you, from me." He reached into his breast pocket and withdrew a small package, which he handed to her appeasingly. "Happy anniversary, Rachel honey."

Despite herself, her fingers shook eagerly with excitement as she ripped away the fancy ribbons and gay paper (the box was store-wrapped, she knew; Slade couldn't wrap a gift so prettily and neatly to save his life, but that was all right). Then she lifted the lid and folded back the tissue paper inside to reveal a solid-gold, heart-shaped brooch studded with rubies all the way around its border. In its center was engraved a single word: *Heartland*.

"My, oh, my!" Rachel gasped as she saw the brooch, a lump forming in her throat as her emotions threatened to overcome her.

Then, as she slowly picked the brooch up, she observed the little, pastel-flowered notecard lying underneath. This, she could hardly read for the tears that suddenly blurred her eyes as she opened it up, for inside, written in her husband's bold black scrawl, was this message: *My dearest Rachel, despite all the forty thousand acres, and through each and every one of all these forty years, wherever you were has always been the land my heart called home. Then, now, and forever, I love you with all my heart, honey. Slade.*

"Oh, Slade. Slade! I love you, too!" she whispered fervently, weeping and smiling tremulously at the same time. She flung her arms around his neck and hugged him tightly for a long, poignant moment. Then she reached for the brooch and asked, "Will you—will you pin it on for me, please? My hands are still shaking so badly that I don't think I can manage it."

"Of course. Do you like it, sweetheart?" he queried as he fastened the brooch to the high lace collar of her wedding gown.

"Like it? I *love* it! It's just beautiful, Slade—the most beautiful thing I've ever owned."

"Then I guess you won't mind too much if I keep the car, hmh?"

Rachel laughed through her tears and shook her head wryly.

"Poor Chili Pepper," she sighed. "I'll bet he's halfway to Oklahoma right now, wondering what almost hit him. It'll probably take him a month to recover his usual feisty self. Thank heavens for that haystack! We might be pushing up daisies right now if it weren't for that. It sure smells musty, though. I wonder how long it's been in here, moldering away? You really ought to have some of the hired hands tear this old barn down, Slade—"

"Why, I most certainly will not!" he burst out indignantly, glowering at her for even suggesting such a thing to him. "And I don't want to hear another word about it—and that's final!"

"Well, I don't know why not. It's not safe and—"

"It's the place where I first kissed the woman I love," he stated stoutly, "and it's not coming down until I do!"

"Why, you *did* kiss me here for the very first time, didn't you?" Rachel rejoined softly, pleased and touched that he should feel so sentimental about that day long ago.

"Yes—and what's more, I think I'll kiss you here again this very minute!"

Deciding that this sounded like a really inspired idea, Rachel settled herself expectantly on the seat. But much to her surprise, confusion, and disappointment, despite his proclaimed intention, Slade made no move in her direction; and at last, peeping at his still figure and wondering at his rather bristly silence, she inquired hesitantly, "Well?"

"Well, what?" he grunted grouchily, stiffening like buckram beside her on the seat, his eyebrows drawing together severely.

"Well, are you going to kiss me or not?" she prodded tartly, more puzzled than ever by his strange behavior, and now beginning to feel highly piqued, too.

"I'm waiting," he ground out through gritted teeth.

"Waiting?" she parroted lamely. "Good Lord, Slade! Waiting for what?"

"An invitation," he growled, glancing at her fiercely, as though daring her to laugh. "I figured that since it was our fortieth anniversary, after all, I'd be polite for once."

"An invitation!" Understanding dawned at last. Immensely tickled as she got the joke, Rachel slapped her knee, her laughter ringing out like the joyful pealing of a bell in the quiet, sun-streaked barn. "Mercy! I don't believe it! Slade Maverick, do you mean to sit there and tell me that after forty years, I've finally succeeded in teaching you some manners?"

"I reckon so, because I'm sure waiting—and getting mighty damned impatient about it, too, I might add!"

"My goodness gracious!" Rachel smiled, shaking her head gently. "How times have changed!"

She sat there upon the black leather seat of the Packard, lost in reverie, remembering the years that had come and gone since Slade had first kissed her one winter's day so long ago in this old barn. Through the chinks in the roof, the yellow August sun streamed in radiantly, enveloping them in a halolike cloud of gold as the hay wisps and dust motes swirled in the air, stirred by the slight breeze soughing through the barn doors splintered open by the automobile. Forty years. Was it really possible so much time had passed? she wondered, as she had earlier this day. Yes, it had passed surely enough—in the blink of an eye, the shadow of a smile. Yet so many memories were pressed like a treasured flower into the pages of her mind that they now filled it to overflowing. As she counted her husband and all her family, her Heartland Ranch (now one of the biggest in Kansas), the money in the tin box upon the kitchen shelf (and, more prudently, in the bank, as well), and all her other blessings, Rachel knew that, truly, her cup had run over, that she could have asked nothing more of life than what it had given her.

"Well?" Slade snapped, exasperated, interrupting her musings.

"Well, what?" she queried absently, her mind still on the past.

"What do you mean . . . well, what?" Slade demanded. "Are you going bats on me in your old age? Because if you are, well, I just won't have it, that's all! For forty years, I've put up with your barbed tongue, Rachel, and I've put up with your bad temper—and I've loved every single moment of it, too, since I always got the best of you in the end," he asserted arrogantly, giving her a wicked grin. His eyes roamed over her admiringly. "And your best was always very good indeed," he avowed appreciatively. "But I'll be damned if I'll put up with your going bats on me! Now . . . er . . . where was I? Oh, yes. I'm still waiting. Are you going to issue me an invitation to kiss you or not, old woman?"

"Why, yes," Rachel said slowly, her eyes twinkling as

she looked at him, her heart filled to bursting with forty years of love for him and all the joy it had brought her. "Yes, I believe I am." She paused. Then she declared positively, "Consider yourself invited, old man!"

And his heart singing loud and clear, Slade did.

Author's Note

Dear Reader:

I want to take this opportunity to thank you so very much for buying and reading this novel, *Heartland*, which, more than any other book I have ever written, has been a labor of love for me.

Although I was born in Knoxville, Tennessee, I have for most of my life called the Great Plains home, and no matter how far away from them I have traveled, I have always been glad to return. We have no vast oceans, no towering mountains, no mighty forests, and no painted deserts, it's true. But to those of us who know and love them, the sweeping Great Plains, like England's windswept moors, have a stark, haunting beauty all their own. Vividly, I remember standing, on a blustery January day in 1984, on England's Salisbury Plain and being reminded of Kansas.

The wild, ceaseless wind of the heartland is not fictional, and during the time in which this novel is set, it was so fierce and relentless due to the lack of any windbreaks that it often did drive people to madness or suicide. Only with the advent of trees and buildings has it mellowed, though it is not tamed, as anyone nowadays who has heard it howling on a bitterly cold winter's eve across the prairie can attest. Indeed, the name "Kansas," taken from the Kansa Indians, means "People of the South Wind."

For every novel I write, I utilize numerous reference books and resources for historical and background material, though seldom does any particular one stand out among the rest. In this case, however, I would be terribly remiss if I did not give enormous credit for assistance to a nonfiction work that was constantly at my side during my writing of this novel.

That work was *Wichita: The Early Years, 1865–80*, by H. Craig Miner, Ph.D. (published by the University of Nebraska Press, 1982). Dr. Miner's book is an excellent examination of this turbulent time period in Wichita's history and proved invaluable to me, saving me months of difficult research; and for that, Craig, I thank you and am indebted. Much of the background and many of the anecdotes I have related about Wichita in this novel are from Dr. Miner's book, although the few liberties I have taken, for plot purposes, with a small portion of the material, or any errors I may have inadvertently made, are my own. For anyone interested in learning more about early Wichita, I highly recommend Dr. Miner's fine, informative book.

The town of Dry Gulch, Texas, is fictional. But I have portrayed the city of Wichita as it was in 1875 as accurately as possible, down even to the street names, some of which are now changed. All buildings described in this novel as being part of the town actually existed in 1875, with the sole exception of the Silver Slipper saloon, which is my own invention—though one in keeping with the saloons and the spirit (no pun intended) of the rollicking times.

It is often a source of humor to America and a real annoyance to many Kansans that the righteous attitudes resulting from, and the now many archaic but then truly necessary laws governing, this tumultuous time period of the state have frequently through the years impeded its modern progress (my husband always jokingly reminds me upon our return home from a trip to set my watch back a quarter of a century!). But in light of its wild history, it is perhaps understandable that Kansas has so determinedly sought to avoid a return to the "good old days." The uninhibited and many times violent, even murderous, behavior promoted by the rowdy saloons of yesteryear, for example, as well as the literal barroom hatchet-jobs to which they subsequently inspired infamous Kansas resident Carry Nation (who, alas, came too late for this novel), caused open saloons to be outlawed in Kansas for over half a century afterward, and a state bill allowing restricted liquor by the drink on a county by county basis was only recently passed. On a more positive note, however, its modern-day restraint has prevented Kansas from suffering many of the wholly undesirable side-effects that too often accompany progress; and as a result, the state has only recently been forced to deal with many of the current issues and problems that have plagued its more liberal fellows for decades.

The dreadful red-lamp district of Delano no longer exists. But the Occidental Hotel, where, in my imagination, Slade and Rachel dined one hot summer's Fourth of July evening, still stands, recently restored to all its former glory, though it now houses an office plaza instead of hotel suites. A few of the other buildings have been preserved and moved, and may be seen today at Wichita's Old Cowtown Museum, a historic depiction of the town and Sedgwick county during the years 1865–1880. Sadly, most of all the other buildings are now much altered or have gone by the wayside entirely, including the lovely little St. John's church Rachel attended, though the one that stands now in its stead is just as beautiful —as I should know, since, in November 1983, my husband, Gary D. Brock, and I were married in it.

I should also point out that although there was indeed a fire in the city in 1875 (which destroyed much of Douglas Avenue and Main Street), I have instead, for plot purposes, permitted my totally fictional account of the revival tent's more limited burning to serve in place of the real blaze. (The shooting of fireworks, by the way, due directly to the number of prairie fires they ignited in the past, is now prohibited in Wichita, with the exception of supervised public displays.) Preacher Proffitt and the three "sisters" lived and died only in my imagination, though many other of the town's characters were real, the most well known of which is, of course, Wyatt Earp.

Contrary to popular legend and belief, Wyatt Earp was never a marshal, or even a deputy marshal, of Wichita. He was only an officer of the local police force, and his notorious exploits as one have been grossly exaggerated, besides. In reality, he spent most of his time inspecting chimneys (stray sparks flying up from chimneys could cause prairie fires), sweeping boardwalks, chasing down the truly numerous and bothersome dogs of the city (which "purps" the police threatened to cremate if unlicensed), and removing animal carcasses from the streets. Further, in 1876, after attacking and beating William Smith, Marshal Mike Meagher's opposing candidate during a close election for the marshal's job, Earp was ignominiously fired by Meagher for conduct unbecoming to an officer.

Truth is indeed stranger than fiction, for this novel owes at least a part of its existence to the fact that, over a hundred years ago, Colonel Marshall Murdock was induced into coming to Wichita to begin publishing his newspaper. His *Wichita Eagle* (which now also incorporates the *Wichita Beacon*) still serves as the city's newspaper and continued, until sold to the Knight-Ridder chain some years ago, to be owned for many years by his descendants. One of these, Victor Murdock, in 1974 established at The Wichita State University a scholarship to be awarded to deserving students of journalism. Thanks to Victor Murdock's generosity and to the recommendations on my behalf of Dr. Loyal N. Gould, then chairman of the Department of Journalism at The WSU, I was twice privileged to receive this scholarship, without which it would not have been financially possible for me to complete my B.A. in journalism, which began my writing career. So, to Marshall and Victor Murdock, wherever you may be, and to Dr. Gould, now chairman of the Department of Journalism at Baylor University in Waco, Texas, go my heartfelt gratitude and deepest appreciation. I hope that with the writing of this novel, I have in some way honored this irrecompensable debt.

Today, the dream of Wichita's founding fathers over a century ago has come true: An attractive, prosperous (the thriftiness of the town's businessmen remains unchanged!) city now wends its way along the banks of the Big and the Little Arkansas rivers, and is still known—and rightly, many would argue—as "the Peerless Princess of the Plains."

At its very heart, at the confluence of the two rivers where the scattered lodges of the Wichita Indians once stood, now stands appropriately what I personally think is one of the most beautiful sculptures anywhere and certainly, in my opinion, the most beautiful in Wichita, bar none. This is "The Keeper of the Plains," created, before he died, by the city's own well-known Indian artist Blackbear Bosin. This huge, rust-colored metal statue is of a marvelously wrought Indian in full head- and ceremonial dress, his palms cupped and uplifted to the heavens, as though reaching for the stars. In my mind, Blackbear Bosin has, with his poignant sculpture, captured not only the undaunted essence of the native Indians who first roamed the Great Plains, but also the shining courage of the frontier pioneers who came after, both of which peoples so truly typified the Kansas state motto: *Ad astra per aspera*— To the stars through difficulties.

If I have succeeded in these pages in bringing to life for you, the reader, even a small portion of these peoples' gallant, indomitable spirit, then I am richly rewarded.

Rebecca Brandewyne
Wichita, Kansas
November, 1989

Love, Cherish Me
Rebecca Brandewyne

The man in black shows his hand: five black spades. Storm Lesconflair knows what this means—she now belongs to him. The close heat of the saloon flushes her skin as she feels the half-breed's eyes travel over her body. Her father's plantation house in New Orleans suddenly seems but a dream, while the handsome stranger before her is all too real. Dawn is breaking outside as the man who won her rises and walks through the swinging doors. She follows him out into the growing light, only vaguely aware that she has become his forever, never guessing that he has also become hers.

___52302-7 $5.99 US/$6.99 CAN

Dorchester Publishing Co., Inc.
P.O. Box 6640
Wayne, PA 19087-8640

Please add $1.75 for shipping and handling for the first book and $.50 for each book thereafter. NY, NYC, and PA residents, please add appropriate sales tax. No cash, stamps, or C.O.D.s. All orders shipped within 6 weeks via postal service book rate. Canadian orders require $2.00 extra postage and must be paid in U.S. dollars through a U.S. banking facility.

Name_____
Address_____
City_____ State_____ Zip_____
I have enclosed $_____ in payment for the checked book(s).
Payment <u>must</u> accompany all orders. ❏ Please send a free catalog.
CHECK OUT OUR WEBSITE! www.dorchesterpub.com

And Gold Was Ours

Rebecca Brandewyne

In Spain the young Aurora's future is foretold—a long arduous journey, a dark, wild jungle, and a fierce, protective man. Now in the New World, on a plantation haunted by a tale of lost love and hidden gold, the dark-haired beauty wonders if the swordsman and warrior who haunts her dreams truly lived and if he can rescue her from the enemies who seek to destroy her. Together, will they be able to overcome the past and conquer the present to find the greatest treasure on this earth, a treasure that is even more precious than gold. . . .

___52314-0 $5.99 US/$6.99 CAN

Dorchester Publishing Co., Inc.
P.O. Box 6640
Wayne, PA 19087-8640

Please add $1.75 for shipping and handling for the first book and $.50 for each book thereafter. NY, NYC, and PA residents, please add appropriate sales tax. No cash, stamps, or C.O.D.s. All orders shipped within 6 weeks via postal service book rate. Canadian orders require $2.00 extra postage and must be paid in U.S. dollars through a U.S. banking facility.

Name_____
Address_____
City_____State_____Zip_____
I have enclosed $_____ in payment for the checked book(s).
Payment <u>must</u> accompany all orders. ❑ Please send a free catalog.
       CHECK OUT OUR WEBSITE! www.dorchesterpub.com